BOOKS BY MARTYN W[...]

THE TOM KILLGANNON SERIES
The Old Religion
The Sinner
The Gravedigger's Song

THE JOE DONOVAN SERIES
The Mercy Seat
Bone Machine
White Riot
Speak No Evil

THE STEPHEN LARKIN SERIES
Mary's Prayer
Little Triggers
Candleland
Born Under Punches

STANDALONE NOVELS
The Woman in Black: Angel of Death
The White Room

NONFICTION AS A CONTRIBUTOR
Great Lost Albums

AS TANIA CARVER

THE BRENNAN & ESPOSITO SERIES
The Surrogate
The Creeper
Cage of Bones
Choked (US title: The Black Road)
The Doll's House
Truth or Dare
Heartbreaker
The Lost Girl

THE
GRAVEDIGGER'S
SONG

THE GRAVEDIGGER'S SONG

MARTYN WAITES

BLACK STONE PUBLISHING

Copyright © 2022 by Martyn Waites
Published in 2022 by Blackstone Publishing
Series and book design by K. Jones
Cover design by Luis Alejandro Cruz Castillo

Printed in the United States of America

First paperback edition: 2022
ISBN 979-8-200-72237-2
Fiction / Mystery & Detective / General

Version 1

CIP data for this book is available
from the Library of Congress

Blackstone Publishing
31 Mistletoe Rd.
Ashland, OR 97520

www.BlackstonePublishing.com

PART ONE
THE RITUAL

1

ALONG THE LANE THEY CAME. Punch and Judy at the front, Turnip Head leading the Horse by the reins. None spoke. None needed to.

The night was clear and bone cold, black winter ascendant. No stars, the moon distant, cloud-imprisoned. The trees and bushes on either side were deep, unyielding. Their shadows and hollows black doorways into underworlds of uncertain mud, moss, stone, and spiked branches.

The four knew the route. Every turn, hidden sinkhole, bog of no return. Every wayward meandering trail. Light or dark didn't matter. This was their home. Their land.

The bell on Mr. Punch's pointed jester's cap jangled in time with his step. He carried a heavy fire iron. His face was painted with two bright red circles on his cheeks, his eyes circled with black and blue, his scarlet lips an upturned razor's slash.

The man beside him was dressed as Judy and carried a besom, his other hand held up a trailing skirt. Long black lines beamed outward from his eyes, mimicking eyelashes. The same rosy cheeks as Punch, his thick black beard turned the painted red lips into a sucking wound.

Turnip Head's face couldn't be seen beneath his mask. The skin of a dried, hollowed-out Halloween turnip lantern—wizened, lumpen, and lichened—stretched around his head, tied at the back with baling twine. His features were the stuff of nightmares. A living, long-dead bog mummy. Long, coarse black hair spilled out through the twine. His eyes were empty black pits. Coal dust and charcoal covered his bare arms and shoulders. He wore an old sack over his upper body with slits for arms and led the Horse.

This fearsome beast's skull gleamed white, its gemstone eyes glittering in the weak moonlight. Its necklace was of dried flowers. The bottom of Horse's sackcloth shroud was filthy from road dirt and showed two booted feet underneath.

They rounded a corner. The light ahead brightened as they approached a high brick wall and a set of double gates. Beyond that was the outline of a large old-stone house with a sweeping gravel drive in front, the surrounding wildness tamed into manicured lawns and neat flower beds. The residence radiated wealth, ease, exclusivity, and superiority. A warm interior glow spilled out from its windows and shutters. Its occupants had settled in for the night, the winter. Hibernating.

The four paused before the gates, sharing a look. Again, no words needed. They nodded. The Horse threw back its skull-head and neighed. Petals from its dead flower necklace fluttered in the air like loose flakes of dead skin. Turnip Head pulled on the reins, calmed the Horse down.

Mr. Punch pushed open a gate.

They walked up the drive.

Ready to gain admission. Sing their blood harmonies.

SIMON WEST HATED ALL OF THEM. *All. Of. Them.*

Sitting downstairs playing happy families, all of them complicit in their lies—to him and to each other. Talking like nothing had happened, like their new lives were perfectly normal. Pretending so hard to enjoy it that it became enjoyment. Simon couldn't join in. Didn't want to be part of them ever again.

His bedroom door was closed, but the muffled TV noise still found its way upstairs. *His* bedroom. *His* door. Pathetic. It wasn't his and never would be. Wasn't theirs either; this house, any of it, despite their playacting.

He had brought very little from home. Hadn't been allowed to. Just the basics, they'd said. Whatever you can fit into two suitcases. Simon had balked: his life, his memories, were all in his stuff. Make new memories then, he was told, they'll go with your new life. Simon didn't need that; he already had memories that meant something to him. Friends that mattered. Accomplishments that he was proud of. Mementos were how he marked his life. He had tried to put up photos, but his dad had quickly taken them down, reminding him why they were there and how any ties to the past could cost them.

"You know the rules, Simon. Can't have anything that might provide a link, draw attention. Sorry, son, but that's the way it is. For all of us." Dad had looked sad when he said it, but Simon wasn't fooled. By that point, he'd already heard enough of his father's previous shit to not believe him.

So he lay on the bed—more like a cell than a teenager's bedroom—staring at the wall. He toyed with the brand-new top-of-the-range iPhone his father had bought him out of guilt. It was pointless because there was no one Simon could call or text or even go on social media to chat with.

And then there was his slag of a stepmother. Ludmilla. Always telling him to turn his music down, in that East

European accent of hers that sounded like a dog being sick. Parroting his father's line about attracting attention. Simon didn't like using his earbuds because the sound up that close just got into his head, emphasizing to him how alone he really was. He told his stepmother that they were in the middle of nowhere, for fuck's sake, it was just her being miserable and asked his dad to back him up. His dad took her side, of course, even though Simon could see he didn't agree with her and was scared of going against her. Simon would say she had his dad wrapped around her little finger except he didn't think that was what Ludmilla was using to control him. His stepmother. His *slightly older than his sister and looking just like her* stepmother.

EastEnders, that venerable soap opera, drifted through the gap under the door. At least Simon assumed it was that show from the Cockney accents, gearing up for the usual Christmas carnage. "This is gonna be the best Christmas in Walford ever!" God, how stupid were they to say that? And how stupid were the people watching to believe it? Or maybe the viewers weren't stupid. Maybe that's why they watched it: to see it all go wrong. Relishing the buildup to disaster. People were fucking horrible. They'd feel differently if they had to live through it themselves.

Before they'd stopped communicating earlier that evening, when all of them were in the living room pretending to play happy families, his dad had said something stupid along those lines after Simon had—once again—pointed out just how hideous his life had become and how much he hated Dad because of it.

"Look, mate." His father's smile was as fragile as the expensive vases his stepmother bought with his money. His eyes were dark and tired. "I know you think like that at the moment, but it'll pass." Dad had nodded, like he was convincing himself more than Simon. "We're here now and we've got to stay, so we may as well make the most of it. Enjoy ourselves." And then he'd smiled.

But mainly, Simon noticed, Dad was smiling at Ludmilla, the wicked stepmother whore. When his dad backed up the bitch stepmother instead of him, something broke inside of Simon. That's when he knew he'd lost the father he'd once adored. The man before him was just a sad, fat, middle-aged loser.

He stared at his dad, the hatred behind his eyes bursting out faster than blood from an elevator in an old horror movie. He looked away, tried to catch the eye of his sister for backup. But Angelica just sat in an armchair, studiously examining her new iPhone, eyes screen-lit and unreadable. No support from her. She had always acted the perfect Daddy's girl, played up to him, even with Ludmilla in place—in fact, more so now because Angelica could play on Dad's guilt to get whatever she wanted. And as long as she did, she wouldn't speak out. And the wicked bitch stepmother was right at his father's side, claws at the ready, like a Barbie attack dog.

"What?" He stared at Ludmilla. "It's not enough you got him to ditch our mother for you, you have to pretend you're loyal to him as well, do you?"

"He did not ditch your mother, you know that. And I am loyal to him."

"Yeah. Loyal to his money. I know what you are. We all know what you are."

Ludmilla's eyes flared. "Your son is not going to speak to me like that, Nick. Nick. Tell him."

"Simon, take that back." His father, red-faced, stumbling over his words. "Simon. Did you hear me? Simon."

He didn't take it back. Instead, Simon told Ludmilla exactly what he thought of her, using the harshest, most hurtful language he could dredge up. It had the desired effect.

And then that final, devastating line. Oh, yes. Knowing how to hurt was the only bit of power Simon had left.

He ran upstairs, slamming the door behind him as hard as he could.

AND THOSE WERE THE LAST WORDS he exchanged with them.

Now Simon lay on the bed, listening to them arguing down below, stumbling through the debris after his verbal hand grenade had detonated. Ludmilla shouted for his father to defend her honor. To go upstairs and show his ungrateful, disrespectful son what he thought of him. *Honor.* Simon smiled at the word. How could his father protect something that wasn't there? Ludmilla kept screaming, his father halfheartedly trying to placate her. He imagined Angelica staring even more intently at her phone, biding her time till this storm blew over.

His father used to laugh about East Europeans. Say how thick they were, how they'd work all hours doing shit jobs no Englishman would, and for barely any money. Simon, not knowing any better, laughed along with him. Yeah, those stupid East Europeans. And then his mother became ill and quickly, unexpectedly, died. And his father suddenly had an East European girlfriend. And this one didn't seem so stupid. She knew exactly what she was doing. Dad had said Ludmilla had comforted him after Simon's mother's death. But Simon knew his father had money, even now, after everything that had happened. But he sure wouldn't have it much longer with Ludmilla around. None of them would. But his dad was too sex-blind to see that. Simon hated to think of him like that.

He felt tears prick the corners of his eyes. Wouldn't let them fall, wouldn't let them downstairs have the satisfaction. Instead, Simon would lock it away. He sighed. Took out his phone, the twin of the one his father had bribed Angelica with, and idly played with it.

Even Christmas in *EastEnders* would be better than this.

And then he heard the doorbell.

NICK WEST STARED AT THE TV SCREEN, pretending to watch whatever was on. He didn't see it, didn't hear it. Just shapes and colors dancing in front of his eyes. He might have been staring at concrete for all the difference it made to him.

Simon. Nick's ungrateful bastard of a son had alluded to things before, talked around them, insinuated. But never said any of it outright, to his face, to Ludmilla's face. The entitled, privileged little prick. Standing there, whining about not being able to see his mates again. But the fact was, the little brat couldn't go out until he could be trusted not to tell anyone who he was and why he was there.

Nick had replied with his *hey, I'm your dad; everything's going to be OK* voice. Come on, mate, that's a bit harsh. You know why we're here, why we have to keep quiet for a while, then start again. Look, Angelica's managing, why couldn't Simon? And his son's reply? *Because when she starts moaning on, you buy her something to shut her up.* When Simon said that, Angelica had almost glanced up from her iPhone that Nick had bought her. Almost. It had taken his all, but Nick remained calm. Look, mate, we all have to make sacrifices. We pull together, like families do. Simon's reply?

Tell that to Mum.

Nick had reddened at the words, hitting him with the force of a slap to the face.

Tell that to Mum.

Ludmilla had stepped forward, started to tell Nick and

Simon what she thought of them both. Simon didn't give her the chance. He started straight in on her, calling her all sorts of horrible names he'd clearly been saving up. Eventually, with no words left, he'd stomped upstairs, Nick shouting after him. Ludmilla had tried to vent her anger on Nick, but for once he wouldn't let her. After his halfhearted defense of his son, he retreated to the lounge, fell into the armchair, and stared at the TV.

That ungrateful little shit. After everything Nick had done for him. OK, yes, maybe there had been a little bit of overlap between starting to see Ludmilla and ending it with Claire. But Claire was in a hospice; the cancer wasn't getting any better and she wasn't going be around for much longer, so what was he supposed to do? No one could blame him. Not really. Nick had desperately needed someone to hold, to look after him. Someone who showed him love. Ludmilla had done that, all right. So, yes, maybe their coming together had been a bit unconventional, but one way of looking at it was that Nick had rescued Ludmilla from a horrible future. He was her knight in shining armor. Surely, that counted for something?

Yes, Ludmilla would have preferred his kids not to live with them, but what could Nick do? They had to go somewhere, and it wouldn't be forever, he'd assured her. Boarding schools, and that. Then this happened and they had to make the big move. The four of them ended up stuck with each other, whether they liked it or not.

But that didn't excuse Simon's awful behavior. Nick should not have to put up with that, and he wasn't prepared to. Even in this house, under these conditions.

Just let him say something more. Just let him try again and see what he gets. He'll—

The doorbell rang.

"What the fuck is this now?"

Nick carried over his anger, yanked open the door.

He jumped. There were four of them.

The big bloke looked like he had some advanced and terminal skin disease, but Nick quickly realized it was just a mask. His bare arms were muscled, hairy, and seemingly impervious to the cold. He wore an old sack, and he held a decorated horse skull on a rope. The horse costume had someone beneath it, wrapped in a sheet and operating the jaw. Like a ghost horse in a cheap pantomime.

And the other two were, if anything, even odder. Two men dressed like Punch and Judy, their faces garishly made-up. Judy had a beard. Punch held a large metal poker, Judy a witch's broom constructed with a wooden tree-limb handle and bristles of twigs. Punch, Judy, and the big one with the rotting face and the wild hair were all in soot, like they'd just emerged from down a pit.

"We have to sing to be allowed entrance," said Punch, his voice as bizarre as his puppet show counterpart.

"You're not coming in here."

Punch grinned. It split his bright red lips like a knife across a throat. "Yes, we are. We sing, you battle us in song and rhyme. You admit defeat. Then we enter and entertain you."

Before Nick could reply, Judy, in a high, strained voice at odds with the bearded face, started singing:

"*Bright sun, dark death, lord of the winds, lord of the dance—*"

"Right, just shut up and leave now." Nick tried to close the door, but the big masked guy wedged his booted foot in the doorway. Punch slowly shook his head. Judy continued the song.

"*Sun child and winter-born king, hanged one, untamed,*

*untamed, stag and stallion, goat and bull, sailor of the last sea,
guardian of the gate, brother and lover—"*

"Stop it!" shouted Nick. "Stop it!"

His cries brought Ludmilla to the door. "What is this?"

Nick turned to her helplessly while the song continued. "They just . . . they won't go away."

"Seed sower, grain reborn, come horned one . . ."

Ludmilla yanked the door wide open. "Leave here. Now."

"Our song has ended," said Punch. "Now it's your turn."

"Leave," said Ludmilla once more, in a voice that usually had others cowering. "Now."

The four looked at each other and quickly arrived at a decision. Punch said, "We win."

He pushed his way inside the open door. The others followed. "You can't, just, please . . ."

Nick flapped impotently around them as the four strode into the grand house like they owned the place. Ludmilla looked between her ineffectual husband and the intruders, following them into the living room. *EastEnders* still played in the background. Angelica looked up from her phone, eyes widening. She didn't move.

Punch moved over to the fireplace. "Let the battle of poetry and song commence . . ."

Nick ran up to him. "Look, just who are you? What d'you want?"

Punch squared up to him, staring him in the face. Something unpleasant danced behind his eyes. "It's tradition. You of all people should know that. You've even got a traditional name. Nicholas. Nick. Saint Nick," he said, his voice singsong. He leaned in closer. An unpleasant odor that Nick couldn't identify emanated from him. "But you're no saint, are you, Nick?" He stretched the name out slowly.

"What—? How do you know my name?" Nick looked around, his anger giving way to fear. "Who are you?"

"Just locals, welcoming the incomers. Traditional, this time of year."

Before anyone else could speak or move, the Horse started whinnying and neighing. Rearing its head up, shaking the desiccated decorations around its neck, ringing its bells. In its eye sockets were what looked like two green-glass bottle bottoms. Reflecting light made jewels of them. The Horse snapped its skeletal jaws, ducking and diving as the person underneath maneuvered. The masked man holding the rein made a faint pretense of trying to tame the wayward creature.

"*Whoa* there," he said as uninterestedly as possible—an actor chosen for his physique, not his ability.

The Horse, as seemed to be the plan, ignored his handler. He dropped the rein, and the Horse cavorted around the living room, weaving its way between pieces of furniture, stopping to stare and snap at Angelica, putting its boney snout right in her face.

She screamed, screwed her eyes tight shut, tried to curl up inside herself. Even Ludmilla, famous for her fearsome temper, cowered in the corner.

"What are you doing?" shouted Nick. "Why are you doing this? Please leave. Now."

They ignored him. Judy began sweeping the rug with the witch's broom. Punch opened the wood burner and poked at the fire inside. The Horse kept galloping. The one with the rotted face just watched.

"You shouldn't let us do this," said Punch, hitting burning logs with his poker, sounding even more like the seaside puppet he was trying to be. "You shouldn't let me rake out the fire. When it's gone, it's gone."

Nick didn't know what that meant, but it didn't sound good.

"I'm phoning the police." He grabbed Angelica's mobile, but the masked man suddenly came to life. He was surprisingly quick, grabbing the phone from Nick's hand, crushing his fingers in the process. He threw the device into the wood burner where Punch hit it with the poker.

"Naughty phone! Naughty phone! Can't have that, can we?" Punch smashed it into hot little pieces. "Can't have our festive fun spoiled."

Angelica curled into a fetal ball, arms covering her head. Whimpering.

"What do you want?" Nick screamed as hard as he could, terrified.

Punch straightened up. Stared at him.

"Don't you know?"

"No."

"Guess."

A realization dawned on Nick's face.

"No . . ."

Punch smiled before addressing his comrades: "Search the house."

SIMON HEARD THEM COMING. He had been listening at the top of the stairs, catching glimpses of the inexplicable visitors. Now, upon hearing that ominous command, he ran back into his bedroom and closed the door.

Thankfully, the noise the intruders were making masked the sound of his movements. The Horse was screeching, and Punch and Judy were in full character, loudly screaming, "That's the way to do it!" The burly masked one grunted and growled as the four of them enthusiastically wrecked the house. Furniture tipped and ripped, ornaments smashed on the parquet floors and against the walls. Bellowing, cackling, and giggling as they went. Simon heard the kitchen being turned upside down, drawers pulled out and upended, crockery taken from cupboards and smashed. Pots and pans were thrown, smacked off walls, windows.

Now they were coming upstairs.

Simon frantically tried to think. Phone someone? The police? No time. A scan round the bedroom, desperate for somewhere to hide. Under the bed. No. That'd be the first place they'd look. The wardrobe. That would be the second. The window was an old-fashioned sash window, big enough for him to climb out of. But where would he go? On the second floor, he had a hell of a drop to the ground.

Something crashed on the landing right outside his door.

He turned back to the window.

Began to raise it.

Then stopped.

A thudding on his door. Once. Twice. Three times.

The door gave way.

Simon stood and stared, unable to move.

A pantomime horse stood there, its bottle-green eyes gazing blankly back at him.

Neither moved.

The Horse's jaw opened, and it threw its head back, whinnied shrilly. Ready to charge at Simon.

That broke the spell. Simon reached for the window and jumped.

NICK PUT HIS ARMS around both Angelica and Ludmilla, making themselves as small and insignificant as possible, cowering behind the sofa as the mayhem rolled on. The living room was systematically reduced to worthlessness around them. The sofa presented no real barrier. The three were terrified of what would happen next.

They watched as their Christmas tree—huge and real, with what Nick considered expensively meager but Ludmilla described as tastefully minimal decorations—was pulled to the floor and trampled into pine needles and shattered glass.

Punch swung his poker with glee, sparks from the fire arcing from it.

And all the while the Horse whinnied and neighed. The person beneath, draped in that filthy white shroud, remained completely hidden, even their gender a mystery. Just a pair of heavy boots poked out below. And even among the deranged behavior displayed by the four intruders, there was something particularly unhinged about the Horse's, as if the costume allowed its wearer to luxuriate in psychosis.

Having destroyed the living room, they began working their way through the rest of the house. Left alone, Ludmilla turned to Nick, her face streaked by tears, more angry than fearful.

"Nick, do something."

"Like what?"

"You are the man of the house. Stop them. Reason with them."

"I . . . I . . ." said Angelica

They both turned toward her as she struggled to speak.

"I . . ."

"What is it, sweetheart?" Nick tried to be consoling, even in this situation. Still a great dad, he thought.

"I want to go home."

Ludmilla sighed, dismissing the girl. "What do we do?" she asked, looking around. "They've gone. Run for the door."

"What?" Nick sounded even more terrified.

"The door. Run. Quick. Outside. Get help."

Nick paused to take everything in. Noise came only from other parts of the house. And it was a big house. If he could get to the front door and away, her plan made sense. If . . .

"Nick. You are a man. Do it."

He looked at his weeping daughter, his angry wife, and wished he had never done the thing that had necessitated their move to this remote part of the world. He had been blinded by love, wanting to do what was right, to be worthy in Ludmilla's eyes. No, that was a self-aggrandizing lie. Nick had been greedy. Stupid. Trying to impress her, if anything. It was too late now. He had to make a decision.

"Nick. You be man. Or I will do it."

He sighed, stood, and still stooped, as if afraid to pull himself up to his full height, looked around. None of the invaders were in sight. Aware of Ludmilla's eyes on him, Nick made for the door.

There was no one in the hallway. He crept along, the front door ahead, eyes darting this way and that. He reached the door. Opened it, ready to run.

"Boo."

Mr. Punch stood just outside on the porch, blocking the way.

"Going somewhere?" he asked. Punch entered, slammed the door behind him. Turned the lock. "Can't be too careful, can we?" He put his face close to Nick's. Eye to eye. Breath to horrible breath. "Naughty, naughty, naughty . . ."

"Just . . . just leave . . . please."

Punch drew back, smiled. "Come on, Nick. Don't be like that. You've got a wife and daughter we could have fun with while you watch. Really want that to happen?"

Before Nick could answer, Judy, still using that ridiculous high voice, shouted from upstairs, "There's a room up here with an open window."

Punch turned back to Nick. He was no longer smiling. "Where's the boy?"

"I . . . Out. He's out." Nick could only hope his quick thinking would allow one of them to get away. Despite everything, Simon was still his son, and Nick loved him.

The sound of splintering wood came from upstairs.

"*Nah*," called Judy. "Horse says he was here. Gone now."

"Well, well, well," said Punch. "So the boy wasn't out at all, Nick. You lied. Want us to go look for him?"

Nick found a surge of resistance. "Good. I hope he's gone. I hope he—"

Nick never felt the blow from behind. But he felt the hard wooden floor as he hit it face-first. He opened his eyes, tried to clear the sudden pain in his head. His face felt different. He couldn't breathe through his nose. He looked up.

The masked man stood over him. His face looked like he had been dead, buried, and resurrected. An instrument of death from the earth itself. He smelled like it, too.

Punch looked between Turnip Head and Nick, back to Turnip Head again.

"Women first," he said. "This thing later."

Turnip Head grunted in what could have been pleasure and stomped off.

Nick lay where he was.

"Not long now, Nick, not long. And it'll all be over for you."

Nick closed his eyes. Thought of his old, boring life once more. Wished he could go back there.

SIMON RAN. LUCKILY he'd kept his trainers on in his room, another mini-rebellion against Ludmilla's house rules: shoes off at the door, no marking the polished floors or expensive rugs. Yeah. Last laugh.

He had no idea where he was running to, only from. He kept within the shadow of hedges, avoiding passersby, even though there were none. The trees and bushes and fields felt all wrong to him. Simon should be back in London, where he belonged. Look what happened when you moved to the country. Look . . .

He ran on, the initial adrenaline burst dissipating, leaving him a little lethargic and conscious of the biting cold. His sweatshirt might have been enough for London at night, but not this barren, bleak, backward land.

He felt a pain in his right ankle but didn't dare stop. *Shit.* Was it broken? Could you do that and still run on it? He had jumped out of his bedroom window. The bushes in the garden border underneath had broken his fall while ripping at his clothing and flesh. There had been no time to stop and think about what was going on inside the house, only time to get up and run. *Run.*

Get help. But where and from whom? He knew no one, had no idea where he was, especially at night. He needed the police, even though his dad had told him to keep away from them. But Dad told him to keep away from everyone. Just till they got settled, he said, until they knew what was what and who was who.

Well, Simon had seen what was what. And who was who. And now he needed the police.

He took the new iPhone from his pocket. Two bars. Would that be enough? He dialed.

Spoke.

Then Simon West collapsed.

IT WAS NO LONGER A LIVING ROOM. It was a dead room.

Mr. Punch stood in the center, surveying. The neat, designer furniture was unrecognizable; ripped, snapped, broken, smashed. Everything rendered down to its components. Down from split cushions floated in the air like funeral pyre ashes. Punch smiled.

"That's the way to do it."

Turnip Head entered. Sweat covered his bare hairy shoulders and arms. Breathing heavily.

"Done?"

Turnip Head smiled. Nodded. Rearranged the front of his trousers.

"Where's Judy?"

"Upstairs, still."

"Let's go then."

They walked into the hall. Nick West was curled up into a ball, broken in every possible way and sobbing. His body was blood-soaked, his face split open, skin peeled back to bone in places. His legs went in opposite directions, and his arms wouldn't move. He was a dead man who hadn't quite stopped living. They stepped over him, went upstairs.

Nick West's last words before his mouth was too damaged to speak: "The boy's got . . . what you want . . ."

After that, it just became a party.

"What'll we do about the boy?" asked Judy, standing in Simon's bedroom, pointing at the window.

A dark cloud hovered over Punch's features as he crossed to the window, looked out and down. Saw the ruined bushes where the boy had landed.

"We can wait and see where he goes or what he does. Who he talks to. We'll get him, though, one way or another. He can't hide from us."

The Horse passed the room on the landing, head back, neighing. Its once-white shroud was now decorated by sprays of blood.

"Horse is happy," said Judy.

"Wouldn't you be?" said Punch. "Doing what you love best in all the world?"

"Know the feeling," said Turnip Head. He let out a low, guttural sound that could have been mistaken for a laugh.

Punch stepped onto the landing, walked into the bedroom where the still bodies of the woman and girl lay. Naked and brutalized, blood pooling and congealing around them. He smiled. They had done a good job.

"Time to go," he said. He led them downstairs. Nick West hadn't moved. Couldn't. Judy pulled Nick's head up, looked into his eyes.

"He still there?" asked Turnip Head.

"Not for long," said Judy.

"Want me to do it? Suppose it'll be kinder."

Judy stood up, let Nick's head drop to the floor with a thud. "If you like."

Turnip Head stepped up behind him, straddled the body, fist back, ready to administer a fatal blow to the head. But before he could move, the Horse appeared, dancing in front of him. Barely breaking step, the Horse applied its booted hoof to Nick's head. Again and again. Neighing and whinnying all the while, head back, jaw open. Job done, the Horse stepped back. Shook its mane, fell silent and still.

"Sure, steal all my fun," said Turnip Head.

The Horse said nothing.

"Let's go."

They walked out the open front door, leaving the bodies behind them.

The gravedigger's song had been sung once more.

Darkness swallowed them.

PART TWO
TURNIP HEAD

2

"NO, OF COURSE IT'S NOT RACIST to say that. Or right-wing or Far Right, whatever. You see, that's the problem. Ideas, words even, that only a few years ago were used commonly, now we can't say them at all. Or if we do, we're called racists."

"Political correctness, you mean."

"Not at all. A lot of people have got that wrong, too. The way I see political correctness—and I think the way it was intended—is an attempt to talk inclusively about everyone without being offensive. To treat everyone equally with respect. And what's wrong with that? No, the only people with a problem about political correctness are the real racists. Not me. Not people like me."

With his strong build, tall frame, and tied-back blond hair, Arthur King, the speaker on TV, looked like a handsome, charismatic Viking. By comparison, the talk show interviewer appeared small, almost insignificant.

"Take that attack recently," the Viking continued. "The multiple murders in that house in Falmouth. No motives have been given."

"And who do you think is responsible?"

"Well, sadly, you just have to look at the facts. A rich family *moves into an impoverished area. Keep themselves to themselves, don't mix. They don't want to mix. Naturally, that's going to breed resentment among the locals."*

"So you're saying that they deserved what happened to them?"

The Viking looked appalled. *"Not at all. What I am saying—and this is where some people in your profession try to twist my language—is that an attack like that in an area like this isn't entirely unexpected. Incomers, not contributing, not mixing, seen rightly or wrongly, as leeching off the area, the people, giving nothing back."*

"So you're saying—"

"I'm saying that people need to stand up for themselves more. Stop blaming others for their misfortunes. Take pride in themselves, what they do, where they're from, who they are. That's not racism. Or nationalism. That's pride. There's a big difference."

"Just one final question. Is Arthur King your real name?"

The Viking laughed. *"What's real? What's myth? Which one matters? I'm here and that's what my name is. And that's—"*

Click. The TV turned black.

"Thank you," said Tom Killgannon.

"You're welcome," said his host. "Last thing we need is another nationalist snake oil merchant."

"Couldn't agree more."

Tom's host poured him a glass of wine.

"We don't drink, as I'm sure you know. So we only keep it here for the guests. Hope it's OK?"

Tom took a sip. He had tasted better vinegar. "Fine." He managed a full swallow. "Yeah, good."

His host smiled, topped up his glass. Tom managed to return the smile and, knowing that he was being watched and judged on his response, took an even larger mouthful.

"Lovely."

"I'll leave the bottle there for you. You may as well have it. It'll be wasted otherwise."

"Oh, don't worry." Had he said that too quickly? "I've still got to drive home tonight. Don't want to, you know. Get into any trouble."

"I would have thought with your contacts you'd be able to sort all that out."

Tom frowned slightly. Was that a dig? He smiled in response. "I don't know what you've heard, but that's a bit of an exaggeration. Well, a huge exaggeration."

His host laughed. "Dinner won't be long. But I'm glad we've got this opportunity to talk."

Tom sat back in the armchair, waited. Here it comes. The real reason for the dinner invite.

The living room was pleasantly but conservatively decorated. Like the whole house. But that was to be expected. The Mirzas were a wealthy couple, both in good careers. Faisal Mirza was a psychologist with both a private and an NHS practice. His wife, Karima, was a lawyer. Their daughter, Anju, was studying with Lila at Truro College. They were both eighteen, and Lila was the nearest thing Tom had to a daughter. She was also Anju's girlfriend. Tom hadn't known what to expect when the invitation for dinner at the Mirza household was made. His initial response had been to turn it down. But Anju had told Lila things would be a lot easier in the long run if they accepted. So there was Tom at the tail end of January, the most austere month of the year, sitting in an expensive house-cum-mansion on the outskirts of Truro, pretending to enjoy some truly shocking red wine.

Faisal poured himself a Diet Coke and took the armchair adjacent to Tom. They were in Faisal's study. The placing of the chairs, the room's decor, told Tom he liked to bring his work home with him. Framed certificates on the walls, a huge desk, filing cabinets, and bookcases. He was sure Karima had a similar room of her own. He couldn't imagine the Mirzas slumping down into the sofa after a day at work. The fact that Faisal was still wearing suit trousers and a dress shirt reinforced that. It made Tom—in his plaid shirt, worn-in Maple motorbike jeans, and Red Wing boots—look like the hired help.

Faisal took a sip from his glass, replaced it on a coaster on the desk. Lined up the edges. "I wanted to have a talk with you, Tom, before dinner. Just us two."

Tom had expected something like this. "OK," he said, grateful for an excuse to set aside his glass of wine.

"It's about . . . well, I'm sure you know what it's about." Faisal offered a weak smile.

"I'm guessing it involves Anju and Lila to some degree."

Faisal nodded. "Of course. I'm a liberal man, Tom. Really, I am. And I have no problem with Anju seeing Lila. Honestly. None at all. I don't see myself as a traditional Muslim father. You know, locking up the daughter until she has to have an arranged marriage with a cousin she's never met from the subcontinent. Keeping her away from evil Western influences."

"Glad to hear it," said Tom, for want of something to say.

"I mean, in my line of work it would make me a hypocrite of the highest order. No. Gender is what it is. And if Anju is happy with Lila and vice versa, then great. You know?"

"Couldn't have put it better myself."

"Good." Faisal nodded, a serious frown creasing his brow, at odds with the lightness in his voice. "Good."

Tom waited.

"It's the other thing that worries me."

"The other thing?"

"The . . . well, how can I put it? We both know what happened to Anju and Lila last autumn. The house invasion. That person who pretended to be a friend of yours and then . . ." Faisal tailed off, sighing.

"I know," said Tom. He was an ex-undercover police officer who, for his part in putting away a notorious Manchester gang leader, was now living in Witness Protection in Cornwall. But his old bosses weren't averse to using him when they wanted to. Which they had done several months prior. And it had made Tom, or rather the people he loved, a target. "I had no idea anything like that would happen."

"No, no. Obviously not." The frown was still there. "It's just . . . It's your past, Tom. I know I'm not supposed to know about it. And that's fine. I don't know all of it, and it's not for me to pry. The part I do know I can keep quiet about. As can Anju. So no worries for you there."

"But?"

"Well, it makes one think. You know? I don't mean to be negative, but every time she leaves here to go over to your house to see Lila, we worry. Is the same thing going to happen again? Will there be some armed and dangerous madman from your past forcing his way in? Will she, I mean, will she just . . . not come back one night?"

Tom took a drink. Vinegar or not, he needed it. "Look, Faisal, that was a one-off. I was forced back into a job I'd left behind years ago. It wasn't my decision, and I wish there had been some way I could have said no. And I'm truly sorry for the way it turned out. I won't be doing it again. And they know it."

Faisal stared at Tom. Those events had only been three months previous, and the injuries he had endured hadn't entirely faded. The scars, the bruising, were all still there. Literally written on his face. And a promise from a man who looked like that . . . Tom put himself in Faisal's position. Smiled. "You might not believe this, Faisal, but I came here for a quiet life."

Faisal laughed, ice broken. The smile quickly faded. Ice refrozen. "But you can see my point, surely?"

"Absolutely. And I don't know what more I can say to reassure you. The thing is, Faisal, if you stop Anju from seeing Lila, they'll just do it in secret. They'll both see it as a challenge."

Faisal looked slightly affronted that Tom could make this judgment on his daughter, but the addition of Lila's name somewhat placated him.

"Faisal, I love having Anju around the house. She and Lila are great together. They make a good couple. Bring out the best in each other."

Faisal seemed like he wanted to say more but gave a tight smile instead. "Well, I'm glad we had this chat." He slapped his hands against his thighs, stood up. "Let's rejoin the ladies. See where dinner is."

Tom stood also, smiling inwardly. The men chat, the women make dinner.

Not that liberal, then, he thought.

PEARL SMILED AS HE ENTERED THE KITCHEN. He knew that smile. It wasn't a good one.

"You boys been having fun?"

"We have," said Tom, trying to communicate with his eyes. Being separated by gender was something he knew Pearl would hate.

"You left your wine behind, Tom," said Faisal.

"Oh."

"I'll get it for you. And bring the bottle."

Faisal left the room.

The kitchen was like something from a restaurant or a TV cookery show: huge and gleaming stainless steel. And the aromas from the food cooking were wonderful. All vegetarian: shahi paneer, black dal, dum aloo, eggplant dhansak, onion bhajis, mutter paneer, and—Tom's favorite—chana masala. In addition, there were paneer-stuffed naans and brinjal pickle. All home-made. Tom felt immediately ravenous. Karima stirred pots, tasted things, chopped ingredients, checked the oven, fried things—seemingly all at once. She glanced up at Tom and smiled.

"We've just been talking," said Pearl, leaning up against what might have been the fridge and cradling her wineglass. Tom noticed not much had been drunk. "I said we should get Karima in the kitchen at the Sail Makers. Would bring in a good crowd."

Karima gave a self-deprecating laugh. "Oh, I'm not a professional. And there just aren't enough hours in the day."

Not a professional, Tom thought, but clearly could have been had she wanted to. The kind of high achiever who wholeheartedly committed to whatever she started, determined to rise to the best.

"So how soon is dinner?" asked Tom. "Should I call the girls?"

"I don't think we need to trouble them just yet," said Karima. "I'm nearly there."

"Can I do anything to help?" Tom again.

"Pearl's already offered. I'm fine."

"You boys been chatting about anything interesting?" asked Pearl.

"Oh," said Tom, trying to let Pearl know exactly what had been discussed but not wanting to go over it again. "Man stuff. You wouldn't be interested."

Pearl looked like she either wanted to laugh or hit him. Or both. "Really?"

She smiled. He returned it. Both trying to read the other's unspoken words.

She couldn't keep up her mock anger. Her free hand reached for his, held it hard. Their smiles deepened, eyes locked. This was all still relatively new. And so good.

Three months now since they had officially been an item. There had been months before that of fumbling, trying to get together. An item—God, how old was he? But then what was he supposed to say? It had been so long since he'd been in a proper relationship that he was almost unsure how to proceed. Some things came back to him quickly. Others took longer. And the two of them had been through a lot together in a relatively short space of time. The kind of events that could bind people together or send them spiraling apart. For now at least, they were bound together.

"Come on, young lovers," said Karima, laughing, "dinner's ready."

LILA AND ANJU JOINED THEM FOR DINNER. Tom smiled at Lila, who arched her brows and rolled her eyes in response. She had been dead set against Tom coming here tonight. Hated even the thought of it.

"It's so embarrassing," she had said. "Like your parents meeting your partner's parents. Kill me now."

"You can see their point," Tom had replied. "They just want to make sure their daughter's safe with . . . well, me, mainly, I think. Most parents wouldn't want their kid to visit again after what happened with Anju that time she came to our house."

"Doesn't feel like that. Like I'm being vetted."

Tom had smiled in an effort to placate her. "Put yourself in their place. They want the best for their daughter—"

Lila had tried to interrupt, Tom had silenced her and kept going.

"The best for their daughter. They're very accepting of the fact that their daughter's gay. Great. Some parents wouldn't be. But they're more concerned by the fact that the object of their daughter's love—"

Lila blushed and began to object. Again, Tom ignored her, kept going.

"That she's a teenage runaway living with an older man who isn't a relative and who has a shady past." Tom smiled as he spoke. "That's more concerning, I would think."

Lila had broken into Tom's life over a year ago. Literally, he found her one night in his kitchen, trying to steal food. She had run away from a hellish home life and succeeded in getting herself into an even worse situation, which Tom had managed to help extricate her from. When she had nowhere else to go and nowhere to live, Tom had taken her in. It was an unconventional surrogate father/daughter relationship, but it was working. They brought out the best in each other, putting their individual damage aside in order to help the other with theirs.

"But it's not like that," said Lila. "That's not what our life's like."

"No," said Tom, "but that's what it looks like to them. And that's why they want to meet us properly. Why not ask Pearl along?"

"What, to play happy families?"

"Why not? We deserve a bit of happiness."

Lila couldn't argue with that.

So now they sat around the Mirzas' dining room table, eating, making small talk.

It wasn't the worst experience of Tom's life; the food was too good for that. But it wasn't the best either. He was aware, without it being overtly acknowledged, that the three of them were being judged. For Lila's sake, he would tolerate it. Tom knew how much Anju had come to mean to her in such a short time. And he had meant it when he told her she deserved happiness after what she'd been through in the previous few years. He was doing this for her. Pearl was doing this for him. That was how relationships worked.

Tom and Pearl drank only the politest amount of wine, both claiming they had to drive home later. Then came the goodbyes. Faisal shook Tom's hand.

"Thanks for the chat earlier," he said. "Hope you can get a bit of peace and quiet now."

"The past is the past. I'm not that person anymore."

Faisal studied him, gave a professional appraisal. "You're an interesting man, Tom. I'd like to talk further with you."

"I already have a therapist."

Faisal laughed. "Just get to know you better."

"Let's do it, then."

They agreed to keep in touch, then, along with Lila and Pearl, Tom got into the Land Rover and drove away.

"Well, that was an interesting night," Tom said once they had pulled away.

And with those words, the night was dissected in full. The recap kept them entertained all the way back to the cottage.

Tom pulled off the main road, drove down the steep, winding slope to the old stone cottage in the bay. He felt the pull of the house he'd come to call home. Despite some horrible events that had happened there since moving in, it still felt like his retreat, a place cut off the rest of the world.

He had told Faisal the truth. His other identity, and the

baggage that went with it, was in the past. He planned for just a quiet life from now on, a future with Pearl and Lila. He'd realized how important all that was when he'd come close to losing it all. For the first time, Tom felt close to finding some kind of contentment with life. This was a new and novel experience. And he wasn't going to let anyone or anything take that away from him.

So the police car parked in front of his house was an unwelcome sight.

3

THE SILHOUETTE OF A SINGLE FIGURE in the driving seat of the
car was illuminated against the porch light on Tom's cottage.
From a distance, it was impossible to tell whether it was male
or female.

Silence descended abruptly in the Land Rover. It might be
nothing, said a small optimistic part of Tom's mind. No, the
rational part replied. Police didn't stop by for nothing. Not at
this time of night.

Pearl and Lila's faces echoed his thoughts.

"Do you both want to stay here while I go and see what
this is about?"

"No," said Lila, immediately angry. "Might not concern
you, might it? Could be, I don't know, something else."

"No," said Pearl. "We'll all go." She looked to Lila for confirmation. Lila nodded.

Tom pulled up alongside the other vehicle. Killed the engine.
They all got out. As they did so, the interior light of the police car
went on, and they saw who was behind the driving seat.

Officer Chris Penrose.

Tom felt partial relief. As someone living in Witness

Protection, he needed a liaison within the local force, someone assigned to him to ensure nothing happened that could compromise his new identity and ensure he was adapting to his new way of life. The previous liaison officer hadn't worked out for various reasons, all of them criminal, and he had been without a replacement for a while. Chris Penrose had been appointed before Christmas and had called around to introduce himself, bringing Tom a bottle of whisky. This endeared the officer to Tom. But now, walking toward the house and seeing Penrose's silhouette backlit by the porch light, he wondered whether the gift had been meant as a down payment from Penrose for services not yet rendered.

"Hello, Chris."

"Tom."

They shook hands.

"Been here long?"

Penrose shrugged. "I knocked, and you weren't in. Thought you wouldn't be long or you'd be working in the pub, so I waited. Not long, really."

"Why didn't you come to the pub?"

Penrose stumbled over his words. "Wasn't the kind of thing . . . just thought it was best to talk to you at home. Rather than disturb you at work."

"We've been visiting friends in Truro for dinner."

Penrose frowned. Was there something he didn't know about Tom? Some people he knew that may be a threat or a risk to his new identity? Did they need to be vetted before Tom could have dinner with them? Tom smiled at his reaction.

Penrose's remit covered Witness Protection in the whole of Cornwall. He worked out of Truro, government cuts meaning it was just two of them in an office with an ancient computer and a petrol allowance. He was young and keen and new, eager to make a good impression. At first he'd tried too hard, comporting himself as if he was some kind of swaggering TV detective, looking for trouble or a huge conspiracy everywhere. He had soon been disabused of that approach when a superior officer started calling him Hot Fuzz.

The four of them entered the house, Tom leading them to the kitchen. Pearl and Lila shook off their coats. Penrose, following, did likewise.

"Tea? Coffee? Something else? Or are you on duty?"

"Well, kind of on duty, really."

"So this is work? Sitting outside my house all night?"

"I was told to talk to you as a matter of urgency."

Tom exchanged a glance with Pearl. A shiver ran through him. "I'll get the kettle on."

Penrose's youth and general eagerness rendered his every pronouncement overearnest. Consequently, Tom didn't always take him as seriously as he should, but this time the officer's tone told him it was different.

Tom made coffee and tea while Pearl asked Penrose about his parents, his brother. His older brother, Sean, had been a semi-regular in her pub before the Upheaval—that was how the events that almost tore the village apart were being referred to by locals. In the wake of the Brexit result and the realization that Cornwall was overdependent on soon-to-be-canceled EU grants, the village of St. Petroc, where Pearl lived and Tom worked, came to a collective decision to take drastic, desperate action. A kind of collective mania had gripped the village which had very nearly led to a blood sacrifice. Even after some people vanished overnight and others were arrested, the village never quite recovered. Ironically, by trying to capitalize on the horror of what happened, enterprising locals had opened up a new but precarious revenue stream.

Coffees and teas made, they all sat down around the ancient farmhouse table. Sturdy and scarred, it had served generations. Barring accidents, Tom imagined it would out-live him.

"So." Tom poured himself a companion whisky from Penrose's gift bottle, sat it next to his mug of coffee, "What's this matter of urgency you need to talk to me about?"

Penrose looked between the three of them, back to Tom, hesitant to speak.

"Don't you think . . . Maybe we should be alone to talk about this."

"No, they stay. I've been caught before like that. Police turning up to ask me something, then almost losing—not to be too dramatic—my life as a result. No offense to you, of course."

"None taken."

From the corner of his eye, Tom noticed Lila smile at that.

"So what have you got to say?" he asked Penrose.

The officer looked around once more, mouth open, then down to his mug as if expecting to draw strength from there. Then back to Tom.

"Well, it's not me exactly. As I said, I've been asked to relay a message—more of a request, really."

Tom waited. Sensed this wasn't going to be good news.

"They . . . my bosses. They need your help. Again."

"No."

"Look, please, Mr. Killgannon, please, just—"

Tom stood up, circled the table. "Whatever it is, whatever they want, whoever *they* are, no."

"But—"

"Last time I tried doing one of your lot a favor, I nearly died." He looked at Lila and Pearl. "*They* nearly died. Nice talking, Chris. Drink your tea, and off you go."

Penrose looked down at his mug of tea. Shoulders slumped, stomach out. He looked like he was about to cry.

Pearl placed her hand on Tom's arm, looked up at him. Eyes kind. "Hear him out, Tom. Then say no if you still want to."

Her words warmed the room. Tom resumed his seat. He picked up his whisky glass, drained it. Went to the bottle for a top-up, then thought better of it. "OK," he said. "Ask me."

Penrose looked up, wary. "I've got . . . in here . . ." He reached down to the large pocket on the side of his trousers, pulled out several sheets of folded A4 paper. Scanned them.

Tom waited.

"I've . . ." He cleared his throat. "There's . . . I don't know if you were aware, but there was a serious attack at a house in the south of Cornwall just before Christmas. Did you see it on the news?"

"Couldn't miss it," said Pearl. "Big house, wasn't it? Somewhere down past Falmouth? A whole family murdered?"

"Nearly. One survived."

"So what happened?" Tom asked.

"The Wests had recently moved in, both to the house and the area. Ready to celebrate Christmas and then . . ." Penrose looked up, nervous about continuing. Everyone waited. He went back to the paper. "Someone broke in, destroyed the house, raped"—he swallowed the word, blushing as he did so, glancing between Lila and Pearl—"the women, then killed them. Ludmilla and Angelica, their names. And then the father. They killed him as well. Nastily."

"And the survivor?" asked Tom.

"The son, Simon. He escaped. Jumped out of his bedroom window, ran away. Called us, the police."

"And this concerns me because?" asked Tom.

"Right. Well. Nothing directly. But . . . let me just tell you a bit more about what happened. Give you some background."

They waited. Tom assumed Penrose was pausing for dramatic effect, but the shuffling and dropping of papers said otherwise.

He found the right one. "Right. Here. Simon West won't say anything. Or can't say anything. The shock of what happened to him . . . He doesn't remember anything, really. Some vague things, some singing, then waking up in hospital."

"What? Carol singers did this?" Tom almost smiled.

"Like a high voice, singing a song, and bells. Jingling bells. Then like a horse, neighing."

"What?" said Lila.

"Oh," said Pearl.

"Three different voices, maybe four. He's not sure."

"A horse at the door?" said Pearl. "A real one?"

"Apparently not," said Penrose. "There's no evidence of a horse being in the house. Apart from the noises, that is. But the kid kept mentioning a horse."

"Not an 'Obby 'Oss, was it?" asked Pearl.

"What?" said Tom.

"Old Cornish folklore," said Pearl. "It's a May Day thing, over in Padstow now, I think. There's a big parade, and these two 'Obby 'Osses go around town after the maidens."

"*After the maidens?*" said Lila, clearly unimpressed. "#MeToo."

"Yeah," said Pearl, "it can get a bit like that. But there's this whole festival, bands, and everything. What's that got to do with Christmas? And all this?"

"The horse didn't just appear on May Day," said Penrose. "Used to come around Christmas time too. Traditional thing. Someone would dress up with a horse's skull on a white shroud thing and be led around to people's houses."

"Really?" asked Lila. "That used to happen around here?"

"Years ago," said Penrose. "Kind of died out here, but still big in Wales, I believe."

"Yeah, that makes sense," said Lila.

Penrose smiled. "It's one of the theories we're working on. The detectives in charge thought the same and checked out the local folklore. A horse would be led to someone's house, then there'd be a battle of song and poetry before they'd be allowed in. There's also something about Punch and Judy being there too."

"That would explain the singing. Any leads? Any arrests? What did they get away with?"

Penrose looked thrown by Tom's onslaught of questions. "No arrests. It's like they just disappeared afterward. Forensics say four people entered the house, but they left behind no DNA, no fingerprints. Footprints, yes, but the snow melted afterward. We're stumped. No one's talking. And another thing. Nothing was taken."

"So just a random attack?" asked Tom.

"Well, we're not so sure about that."

"Where's this boy now?"

"We've got him in a safe house. But he can't stay there indefinitely."

Tom sat back. The purpose of Penrose's visit became clear. "I get it. Now I know why you've come to see me."

Penrose looked slightly ashamed. "It wouldn't be for very long. We just need somewhere temporary where we know the boy will be looked after."

"And that's me, is it? Promoted to babysitter."

Penrose nodded, seemingly not wanting to make eye contact. "No one would know where Simon West is. It's strictly need to know."

"Yeah, I've heard that one before. So how long's this for?"

Penrose swallowed hard. "Until we find him somewhere more permanent."

"You're making a lot of fuss for this one kid," said Lila. "What makes him so important?"

Penrose folded up his sheets of paper and neatly stowed them away. "Because Tom's not the only person around here in Witness Protection."

4

Tom stared at penrose, who swallowed hard, like he was expecting to be punched.

"Right," said Tom. "Who do we know around here who's an ex-cop? What about Killgannon? Isn't he in Witness Protection himself? Yeah, he is. Isn't that even better? Yeah, double protection. Saves on the budget too. Perfect. That how the conversation went?"

"I . . . I don't know . . ."

"No. Like you said, you're just the messenger. Doing their dirty work for them. *Them* again. Always *them*." Tom took another drink. It calmed him. "Look, I know it's not your fault. And I'm sorry for taking it out on you. But they must have known what my answer would be, which is why they sent you in the first place."

Penrose looked like a kid who'd been overlooked again for the school football team despite secretly practicing in his own backyard. Set up to fail, still believing he could have done better.

"Thank you, but it's not *them*, like you said. You're not my only client. Simon West is as well. I was trying to help.

Thought you would too." He placed his papers back in his pocket, drained his mug, rose to leave.

"*Whoa* there," said Lila.

Penrose looked up. Lila glanced between Tom and Pearl, who both looked at her quizzically. With the room's spotlight thrust on her, she seemed hesitant to continue.

"What?" said Tom, voice flat, near irritated.

Pearl reached over a hand, placed it on Tom's forearm. "Hear him out, Tom. He's come all this way to see you, been invited into our home, then you just shout at him. I know you're upset and I can see why, but Jesus, at least let him finish what he came here to say."

Tom sighed. "OK, Chris. Sorry. Go on."

Penrose resumed his seat reluctantly. Once more, he took his papers out of his pocket, smoothed them down.

"Nicholas West. That's the name of the male victim in Falmouth—was, rather. Witness Protection." The longer Penrose spoke, the more confident he became, the more he sounded like police. "West was a lawyer for some very dodgy people. One of them was a Mr. Raymond Bain, a big shot on this side of the water."

"This side?"

"Part of his company's activities was bringing in migrant labor from Europe. But they were really human traffickers, selling women into sexual slavery and men to gang masters who worked them on farms, building sites, whatever. The workers were never paid. Instead, they put them in hock to the bosses, gave them debts they could never pay off. The usual."

"How'd they get caught?"

"Nick West blew the whistle on them. He'd fallen for one of the migrant girls, left his wife for her. After the trial, they had to move from London and ended up here. Well, down near Falmouth."

"But someone found out where they were," said Pearl. "And got even."

"That's what we thought at first. But Bain's locked away. He's been questioned, all of his chain of command have. They're as surprised as us at what happened. They're not sad, of course, but as far as we can tell, we're not looking at them for this."

"You sure?" asked Tom.

"Sure as we can be. Like I said, the boy's in a safe house at the moment, just in case. We had him in hospital, but he was discharged when he recovered from his injuries. Twisted ankle and shock. He jumped out of a window. But he still can't or won't tell us anything. We don't know what to do with him, really—what's for the best."

"No other family?"

"None we can find."

"And no one's come after him?"

"He's been under really close surveillance. If someone was after him by now, we would know." Pride for the force he was part of was evident in Penrose's voice.

"So you want Simon West to come here and . . . what?"

"We thought this kind of environment might get him to open up. Somewhere more like a family home, sort of, with people who might understand a bit of what he's gone through. Or at least appreciate it a bit more. Just 'til he's eighteen. Only a couple of months. And then, you know, he can do as he likes. He'll be discharged from Witness Protection. With his family dead, he's no longer deemed to be in danger. We know that from what Bain said."

Lila stood up. "Can I talk to you in private, Tom?"

Tom seemed surprised. "Yeah." He glanced at Pearl who shrugged. "OK."

Lila went into the hallway, waited for Tom. Closed the kitchen door behind them.

"I know what you're going to say," Tom said. The door was heavy old oak but he lowered his voice, just in case the two in the kitchen overheard. Unlikely, as he could hear Pearl making small talk with Penrose to distract him. Good teamwork. "Just say it."

"Do I need to? Do I have to spell it out?"

Tom knew that look. Knew she was thinking of the time he had helped her out. He sighed. "This is different."

"Tom, you took me in, even after I stole from you. No, more than that, you came to find me when I was in trouble."

"Yeah, but that was for—"

"Getting your stuff back that I'd nicked, yeah I know. But you brought me back, and you didn't need to. And then you put a roof over my head. Gave me somewhere safe to live. You didn't have to do any of that but you did."

"Yeah, but—"

"So, what? You just help me, then pull the ladder up afterward, is that it?"

"This is different."

"How's it different?"

"I don't know this kid. What sort of state he's in. He might be a danger to himself, to us even. He'll have, I don't know, PTSD, as well as this amnesia thing. Shock. I'm no professional, I can't sort all that out for him. Neither can you. Not to mention if someone's still after him. It's too much."

"Too much effort? Tom wants a quiet life?"

"Something like that, yeah."

A smile played around the corners of Lila's mouth. "You're

just going to be a bird-watcher or something? Spend your Sundays counting grebes and gannets and whatever, yeah?"

She knew which buttons to push. "Why d'you think I'd do that?"

"You wouldn't. You'd be bored shitless by the first afternoon. Be like retirement. I don't see you wearing trousers with an elastic waistband."

"You need a bit more normality as well, though, don't you?"

"Yeah. But that doesn't stop us helping someone. And I know you. If you don't have something to occupy your time and your mind, you get restless. You've got the pub, but that's hardly rocket science, working there. And you're good at looking after people."

"We've just been to dinner with Anju's parents, and I had to promise him there would be no more trouble here and it would be safe for their daughter to come over. I can't do anything to jeopardize that, can I?"

"How is this jeopardizing anything? You're helping someone. And you're good at it. You can give someone space when they need it and talk to them when they need that. And it's only for a little while." She grabbed his arm. "Come on. That poor kid. His whole family wiped out, no one to turn to . . . He needs help."

Tom studied her face, her imploring eyes. Eventually sighed. "All right then. Let's talk to Penrose."

They went back into the kitchen.

5

SULLIVAN PULLED AT THE MEAT. It came away from the bone with little effort. Not really chewy. Not as bad as it'd tasted before. Connective tissue not too stringy. It was an old badger, so the meat would be past its best as far as tenderness went, but it wasn't inedible.

The firepit was behind his caravan by a vegetable patch, the badger supplied from one of his traps in the surrounding forest. He never ate anything he hadn't grown or caught and killed himself. Too many chemicals. Too much processed shit. And too much money. This was by far the best way.

It was dark out but keeping him lit and warm while he ate were—along with the fire—oil lamps fashioned from old spirits bottles hanging from the caravan along. Everything he needed was in or around the caravan. His whole life. He would only leave to fulfill a need. Or to work. But that fulfilled a basic primal need in him too.

Occasionally, like tonight when the weather was good enough, he sat outside. He didn't care what he looked like, all beard and hair, his oversized body roped with muscle, chewing away. He just observed. Not surveying nature or admiring his surroundings, his place in them. No. Seeing if there was somewhere he hadn't thoroughly checked out, where an intruder could creep up on him. There weren't. The traps he had laid should take care of that, but he could never be too careful. He trusted no one. His father had instilled those words, that creed, into him. Beaten it into him. The field was large enough, his caravan central enough, and the trees and bushes distant enough, that Sullivan would swiftly spot anyone's approach.

Like Marx, his recent visitor, the one who'd originally offered him the job.

"You only got three of them at the house," Marx had said, looking at the Turnip Head mask lying on the table. It stank, like the rest of the caravan, of decay and old sweat.

Sullivan had shrugged. "The boy got away."

"That wasn't the plan."

"Did what I were told to." Sullivan was economical with words, like each one cost him. His voice cracked from lack of use, as lilting as rocks being ground down. "Boy wasn't there, boy wasn't there." Sullivan shrugged. His visitor didn't scare him. His visitor knew that.

"Well, lucky for you in a way."

"Why lucky?"

"You're still in work. The boy, I know where he is."

No surprise there, Sullivan thought. Not with Marx's connections. His face betrayed no expression. Beard and hair near covered it. "You want all of us? We work as a team."

"Just you this time. Not the two freaks, not the Horse. Stealth job. Your specialty."

Sullivan was thoughtful again. "This boy got something you want?"

Marx kept his expression blank. "Let's just say it's a confluence of interests. I want this kid Simon. Alive."

Sullivan nodded. A light in his eyes glittering in the darkness of the hair around his face. "How alive?"

"Alive."

Marx had supplied him with information, told him where the boy was being kept. Sullivan hadn't asked how he knew, not that Marx would have told him. He paid him half his sum up front—in cash, as Sullivan liked. It was rumored by some that Sullivan had a fortune stashed away somewhere in that caravan. Someone had even been stupid enough to try and find it once. No one would make that fatal mistake again.

Sullivan ate, recalling that conversation with Marx. He left the tastiest bit of meat for last: the badger's head. There were five different tastes and textures in there: tongue, eyeballs, connective tissue, muscle, and, of course, the brain. He kept that for the very end. Looking forward to sticking his knife in the hole at the back, rooting around, pulling it out. Sucking it down.

He smacked his lips in anticipation.

Lovely.

6

THEY WOULDN'T FIND HIM HERE. He had made it his secret hiding place, somewhere away from the rest of them, away from the house. Where he could think, be himself.

The snow had long gone. The surrounding branches, hedgerows, and fields had turned from picture-postcard John Constable to black scratch branches and mud-slush Francis Bacon. Given everything he had recently experienced, it felt to Simon West like a metaphor for his world. How he had thought it looked transformed into what it was really like.

Now he sat—among that mulch in the forest by the river, fast-flowing from melted snow and winter storms—feeling the pulse of the world. Above him, the bare branches bronchial fronds sucking down oxygen to give them life once more. The river beside him pumped circulatory blood. The rushing water was desperate to be somewhere, anywhere else. He could empathize.

That night before Christmas never left his head, but there was a huge black hole in his memory from storming upstairs, slamming the door to his bedroom, to coming around the next day in an Accident and Emergency cubicle in Falmouth Hospital. He'd told the police he had heard voices, shouting, screaming. And weird singing. Beyond that, Simon wasn't sure.

Bells. He'd heard bells. And a horse's neigh. What was that all about?

He woke up with police and doctors around his bed and was told that his father, sister, and stepmother were dead. Murdered. Did he remember anything before that? He didn't know. Coming around in the hospital was a series of jump cuts—time elastic, sometimes taut and stretched, sometimes slack and short—as he washed in and out of consciousness on a tide of prescribed drugs combined with his body protectively closing down to heal itself.

They questioned him repeatedly, but his memory wouldn't cooperate. Numbness enveloped him, narcotic and otherwise. The jigsaw puzzle had too many missing pieces. Not only was Simon's memory of that night missing, but there were big chunks gone from the weeks leading up to it. When he tried to think back, it was like trying to recall the plot of a movie he hadn't paid attention to. Finally, he'd been released from the hospital and taken to this safe house. For his own good, the police said.

Amnesia and insomnia kept him lying awake at night, depressed and anxious. The doctors and nurses gave him pills but after the occasional good night of sleep he felt guilty, like he deserved to suffer, so he'd stopped taking them.

They talked to him, tried to *get through* to him. Help him. Or maybe they just wanted his full memory returned so he could provide them with answers leading to an arrest. The only thing he knew for sure was that this spot by the riverside, away from the safe house with its constant guard and questions, with only its canopy of dripping branches, was the only place he could go to feel like himself. Or whoever he was now.

He wished his mum was still here. But she never would be.

He stared at the water. Wished he was part of the river, flowing along, rushing away. Not thinking, just moving. Cleansed, leaving everything behind. Simon was still too numb to mourn the loss of the rest of his family. He was ill-equipped to take on that burden of grief on top of everything else. It would come, he knew, and the thought of that terrified him.

So he sat. Watched the river. Listened.

And then a rock moved beside his foot.

Simon jumped, almost cried out, then felt foolish. It wasn't a rock at all. It was a . . . toad? Frog? Frogs were green and smooth, he thought. This was rough, brown, and warty. A toad. Yeah. He smiled.

The toad didn't move, barely breathed. Simon studied it. Glistening from the water, its skin shone like living stone. Its slow-blinking eyes gave away nothing about what it was seeing or experiencing as a human would. Totally alien.

Simon slowly reached down and picked it up.

Its legs thrashed uselessly, as if trying to use the air around it to swim away. Its features remained expressionless. Simon brought the creature up to his face. Smiled. Stared into its eyes. Tried to see what was going on in there.

He was rapt with fascination. Then something else crept into his expression. Something cruel and twisted. Compared to this tiny creature, Simon was big and powerful. In charge. For the first time in months, perhaps years, he controlled the destiny of another living thing. Let it live, let it die, and everything in between. See how much he could hurt it before it screamed out. Did toads scream? He didn't know. Now was his chance to find out. Could toads plead for their life, even with those inexpressive eyes?

"Simon? You there?"

Simon froze. Had they caught up with him? Were they going to give him the same fate as his sister, his father, Ludmilla?

"C'mon, Simon, time to head back now."

He relaxed. It was Judith, one of his handlers. A psychology-trained police officer who babysat him during the day, leading their conversations in subtle directions that she didn't think he noticed. She used what she thought were triggers to bring back his memory. Simon wasn't stupid. He knew what she was doing.

He wasn't supposed to be this far away from the safe house but flouting the rules was in part why he'd wandered off in the first place. And Judith was the kind of person, if he told her about this, she would want to come and sit here with him, asking more stupid loaded questions. No.

He looked down at the toad, relaxed his grip.

"Your lucky day, mate," he said.

The toad jumped from his grasp, hit the water, and was swiftly pulled away in the current.

Simon stood, stepped away from the river's edge, and onto the small path through the woods.

"I'm here."

She confronted him. "You know you're not supposed to be where we can't see you."

Simon gave a petulant teenage shrug, kept his expression sullen.

"Come on. You've got a visitor."

Simon followed her, the pain in his ankle gone, thinking of that toad. Long gone, now. Borne away. He envied it.

7

SHELAGH LOOKED OUT OF THE WINDOW, up the street, down again. Beyond quiet. Proper zombie-apocalypse empty. She yawned into her mug of coffee. Hardly worth opening the gallery. But she would anyway. Ever the optimist.

She turned the lock of the door, slid the bolts back, top and bottom, catching the old-fashioned brass bell as she did so. Turned the fancy hand-painted sign from Closed to Open. Took her coffee back behind the till, sat on the stool. And waited.

It was a new year and a new start and all that. Shelagh had imagined setting up in a pretty old Cornish village, putting her art on the walls, making new stuff—either paintings of sunsets, buildings, and clifftops; black-and-white photos of craggy old local fisherman faces; or repurposed bits of old driftwood—selling it to incomers and tourists as authentic, rustic, local, artisanal craft. And maybe she would, when the summer came and tourists began turning up. But not at this time of year.

The shop had been a bargain. An old family-run butcher's, closed down when, the estate agent said, the latest generation of the family decided to go and do something else with her life instead of being stuck in the backwater that had trapped the rest of her family. He hadn't said that in so many words, of course, but he hadn't needed to. The estate agent's relieved smile when she had taken it might have set off alarm bells in someone else. But not Shelagh. She had done her research and she knew this wasn't the usual surfing-and-cream-teas kind of Cornish tourist village. This was St. Petroc, where witchcraft and paganism thrived. Where they still practiced human sacrifice.

At least that was the legend. The truth, of course, was more complex and painful than that, but at least the Upheaval, as locals called it, now brought in tourists. Or a certain kind of tourist: the prurient, and even ones who should probably be on some kind of register. But money was money, and there were plenty of locals ready to take it from these rubberneckers. That was why the local shops' meager tourist knickknacks tended toward the grisly and the garish. There were walking tours around particular sites and sights: "This was to be the sacrificial altar where the young girl would be drained of blood!" "See here's the entrance to the old mine workings where she was kept prisoner. Can't go down it just at the moment for reasons of health and safety. Wouldn't want to lose yourself down there. We lost one person and never found them again! You can still hear their cries and wails on nights when the wind is just right and the sea is calm, as they try to find their way out . . ."

After a mouthful of coffee, she took a look around the shop. No, gallery. She had gutted the remains of the butcher's shop, left nothing behind. It wasn't her first instinct. She had been tempted to keep the white tile walls and exposed brickwork. But she wasn't in the city anymore. There were rules about these things, even in pagan St. Petroc. So pale colors and painted wood it was. Calming, like some hippie retreat. Somewhere tourists could momentarily indulge their middle-class bohemian side, then walk away with something to hang on their wall and brag about its authenticity. She had reached out to local craftspeople and displayed their scarves, mugs, plates, jewelry. It wasn't all about human sacrifice.

Shelagh turned on the radio. Places like hers usually went in for Radio Four or Three, but she didn't like classical music and people's voices all day bored her. She had it tuned to Radio Six Music for the small stab of excitement the indie and hip-hop gave her. What she hoped the customers might expect an artist to listen to.

She had started drinking her coffee out of one of the fancy mugs she sold. Normally she would have been drinking out of an old chipped one, or to demonstrate that she may be a creative person but she wasn't precious, a Sports Direct one. She had read somewhere about Damien Hurst attending college carrying his art supplies in a co-op carrier bag, and it had inspired Shelagh to do the same. She had soon discovered just how impractical that was and stopped. But she still kept the cheap mugs. Not as an affectation but, she told herself, because it kept her unpretentiously grounded during the creation of art. She'd see how long the fancy mug would last.

Radio Six Music played something modern and abrasive. She checked her watch. No one would be by today. It would take a miracle, and St. Petroc didn't hold with that Christian stuff. Knowing that in the unlikely event of a customer the doorbell would alert her, she left the till and went in back to her studio. It was as easy to work here as anywhere else. She also had a tiny studio in the small house she had recently bought, but she felt her potential customers might be more invested to make a purchase if she was an artist working right in front of them. She wouldn't let them actually watch her work, of course, but they'd catch a glimpse of an easel, a stretched canvas. That should be enough.

There were no artfully arranged pieces of driftwood back here. No pastels. No cute mugs. The light wasn't great but with the addition of two large strategically positioned IKEA spotlights to cut down the shadows, it was serviceable. She put them on, illuminating her work in progress: a painting.

Against a dark winter background was a horse skull wearing a rope around its neck, as if in defiance of the hangman. Its eyes were decorated with two large green fake jewels. Winter blooms were entwined in a crown on the top of its skull, the petals brittle and rotten and falling like dandruff. The shift from the neck down had originally been white, but it was now gray with dirt and other darker splatters. There was clearly a figure beneath this shift, operating it, but the painting became deliberately vague at that juncture. The creature's glowing green eyes drew the viewer in. Light made them glitter with life and shadows gifted them intelligence, a cunning malevolence, a dark intent. The painting went beyond a simpler represen-tation of subject matter. It possessed a presence as if the ghost horse possessed a life of its own and might gallop straight out of the canvas.

Shelagh took a sip of her cooling coffee and went back to work.

8

SULLIVAN WATCHED, GAUGED, JUDGED. He squatted among wet trees, his booted feet squelching in mulch and mud, spying on a terraced row of run-down houses. The village had tried to extend but had just reached out and died, these houses marking the boundary. They were so cheaply constructed it looked like they'd begun their decay even as they were being built. No one, not even outsiders with money to burn and looking for do-it-up opportunities, would touch them. That made them the perfect site for a safe house.

The boy was there. And two handlers. Both women. One definitely police, maybe the other social services or a head doctor or something. The boy had been out recently. Sitting by the river. Sullivan had been hiding nearby, ready to rush up and snatch the boy, then get out of there. He'd deliver his cargo and return to his caravan, money in his personal bank once more. And if there were complications? He fingered the old well-used hunting knife in the oiled leather holster at his side. Just in case.

He watched, fascinated, as the boy picked up a toad, studied it, played with it.

Sullivan almost smiled at that. Brought back memories of his own childhood.

Then came a call from the house. The boy dropped the toad, stood up, went back.

Now. Follow him. Don't let him get there.

For such a big man, Sullivan was remarkably light on his feet, leaving hardly a trail, making barely a sound. And he was almost invisible; skills honed from a life spent in hiding, observing. Hunting.

The boy reached the back of the house.

Now or . . .

A woman appeared at the corner. With her was a tall man wearing a leather jacket, plaid shirt, jeans, boots. Longish hair, bearded.

Sullivan froze. Blended back into the rain-black trees and bushes. Watched.

The man was introduced to the boy. The boy didn't seem happy to meet him. They went inside, closed the door behind them.

Sullivan stayed where he was. His first idea: rush the place. Knife out, break the door down, take them all, element of surprise. Snatch the boy. Didn't matter how much blood was spilled, he was wearing black and slick from the rain. It wouldn't show on him, so that was no problem.

But.

Were they armed? Expecting an attack? He didn't think so, but that didn't mean they weren't. He usually did a thorough risk assessment before contemplating a change of plan as drastic as this. It was how he'd survived so long.

And there was something else. Sullivan recognized a peculiar kinship with this leather-jacketed newcomer. Like a predator or hunter scenting another in the wild, Sullivan had gotten all that from just one look, an instinct developed into a skill. It had never led him wrong. That was why he was stepping this operation down.

For now.

He waited for the man to emerge. He did so, the boy alongside him, carrying a bag.

Sullivan reached into one of the flaps of his jacket, brought out his cheap burner phone, one of his few concessions to connection with the rest of the world, used for work and nothing more. With its camera he snapped photos of the boy and the man, trying to get them from all angles, building up as much of a composite image as possible. Satisfied he had taken enough, he replaced the phone and watched as they got into a Land Rover parked at the front of the house. Sullivan tried to make out the registration plate, managed only a partial but that was something to work with. The man and boy drove off, leaving the woman behind. The kid's bag suggested a permanent move to a different location. Sullivan's car was hidden nearby. He'd follow.

He smiled.

The hunt was on.

9

LILA FELT LIKE she was about to meet the Queen.

Not that she knew what *that* felt like—to meet the Queen, or even if she really wanted to. But she imagined getting dressed up, waiting with a fixed smile, straight back and legs primly crossed, something like that. Afraid to move in case her poise disappeared, her frock creased.

Not that she was actually wearing a frock. Or sitting with her legs daintily crossed. Or even with a straight back. But the waiting probably felt the same.

Simon West. The lost boy. His arrival, supposedly imminent.

Lila had cleaned the house, vacuumed, dusted, and even put away the dishes. Like we're expecting royalty, she'd thought, and the phrase stuck in her mind. So even slumped in an armchair with one leg dangling over the arm and wearing her usual hoodie and ripped jeans, she still felt that heightened sense of nervous anticipation.

Tom had phoned an hour or so ago to let her know they were on their way. So with not enough time to do anything— watch a film, read a novel, go for a walk—Lila sat in the living room, coffee at her side, waiting.

Tom's Land Rover came down the hill toward the house.

Lila stood, remembered Tom's leaving words: "Be kind. He's been through a lot."

She didn't have to be told.

She watched from the window as Tom got out of the car. The boy slowly removed himself.

Lila opened the front door. Got her first look at Simon West.

Her first thought: his face was blank. Like a mask, but with eyes alive and screaming behind it. She remembered an old horror movie she'd watched a few months ago with Tom, one of the old favorites he kept returning to: *The Mummy*. The main character had a flashback where he remembered being wrapped in bandages until he couldn't move or speak, and then he was buried alive. All he could use to communicate his fear were his eyes. Watching the film hadn't scared her, but those eyes haunted her later that night in bed. They were eyes like Simon West's.

"In you go. Living room's this way. We'll get your stuff."

His belongings were pitiful. A tiny bag, all he had left in the world. Lila could empathize. She'd spent years on the run, even when she hadn't really been moving anywhere. Always fleeing something, never headed toward anything better. Her belongings had been few, able to be shoved in her backpack for a quick departure. But she was changing, beginning to put down roots, both emotionally and materially. She had acquired possessions that meant something to her. Kept them in her room, cherished them. She would look at them, examine them when she was alone. Connect them to the memories associated with them. Relive moments in contemplative solitude. In safety. Good moments led to good memories.

Simon was in the place Lila had been before meeting Tom: running away, not moving forward.

Tom left Simon's bag in the hall, led the way into the living room. Simon, still dragging his ankle slightly, entered, head down, unsure whether he could look around.

"I'm Lila, hiya."

He nodded. "Simon." Said like he was still getting used to the name.

"Sit down," she said. "Take your coat off. Make yourself comfortable."

His head wobbled, the instructions too much to take in at once.

"D'you want a cup of tea or anything? Coffee?"

Simon shook his head.

"Water? I'll show you where the kitchen is in a bit. And your room."

Simon sat.

"I'll put the kettle on." Tom left for the kitchen.

Lila watched him go. Maybe she was speaking too hastily, but Tom seemed somewhat closed off. Smiling, welcoming, but reserved. Not giving much of himself to their guest. She thought back to her introduction to him. Breaking into his kitchen, stealing his food because she was starving. He had seemed much more friendly to her. Or was she remembering it wrong? Is that what she wanted to believe? Memory played tricks.

"Do you want to see your room?" Lila asked Simon.

"Yeah. Sure."

"Come on, then."

She led the way out of the living room. Simon, still wearing his coat, followed her up the stairs, onto the landing. Lila pointed out where her room was, Tom's room. The bathroom, too. "And you're in here." She opened the door to the spare room. There was a small double bed, wardrobe, a dresser that could be used as a desk, and a chair all stood in there. Like a country cottage B&B, clean and anonymous.

"Not much of a view, mind. You just look out at the garden. Not at its best at the moment."

Simon looked like he didn't care one way or the other. "Thank you," he said eventually.

Lila smiled. "No problem." She sat down on the edge of the bed. Indicated for him to do likewise. He did so slowly, carefully, as if by moving too quickly the world around him might shatter and break.

"I just want to say, you know, that this is going to be difficult, what you've been through, what you're going through. Tom and I both know that. I don't mean we've been through the same thing, 'cause we haven't. But we've both been through bad stuff. And . . . I just want to say, you're welcome here. And this is your room. And you're safe in it." She shrugged. Smiled. "That's it, really."

Simon tried a smile in response. "Thank you."

Lila nodded.

Before she could move, Simon's hand had shot out, reached her chest.

Lila froze and stared at him.

His eyes weren't on hers. They were lower down. She followed his gaze, panic welling inside her.

That's not right, he's touching me. I can't have this, he's got to go. I don't care what he's been through, I'm not . . .

"That's lovely."

"Oh." Lila saw what he was doing. He had reached for her necklace, was holding it in his hand, staring at it. "Yeah." A solid silver Hand of Fatima: small, exquisite, beautiful. Lila found herself reliving its associated memories.

"It was a Christmas present."

"From Tom?"

She smiled. "Tom buying jewelry? You're kidding, aren't you?"

Simon smiled too—a little less forced this time.

"From my girlfriend," said Lila.

Simon's smile disappeared, replaced with confusion. "*Girl-friend?*"

"Yeah."

"Oh."

"What's wrong with that?"

"Nothing, just . . . surprising."

Lila nodded, suddenly uncomfortable alone in the room with him.

She stood. "Let's go back downstairs. Tom might have made tea by now."

Simon said nothing, just rose and followed her from the room.

Back downstairs in the living room, Tom handed out mugs. "Just in time." Then to Simon, "You getting settled in? Lila been showing you around?"

"Yeah," Simon said, "thank you. For this, I mean." His head dropped. "Thank you."

"No problem," said Tom. "Right. I'd better drink up. Got to go to work soon."

Simon and Lila sat down. Lila said nothing. Just took her mug.

She wasn't sure, but when Simon lowered his head after speaking to Tom, had he just smiled to himself? Or had she imagined it?

And if she hadn't imagined it, what did it mean?

10

ST. PETROC HAD BEEN OVERLOOKED by everyone. On a coast that boasted waves crashing from the Atlantic, surfers chose Constantine Bay. For somewhere to eat and buy overpriced tourist stuff, there was Padstow. And for somewhere offering a more authentic Cornwall village for holidaying, there was St. Agnes. St. Petroc, harder to reach than those other places and consequently more disappointing upon arrival, had never become a destination for anything. It was the small apple on a branch that withered and died while the rest of the tree grew big and healthy at its expense.

The Sail Makers Arms was at the bottom of the road, down toward the cove of St. Petroc. It was the only place open and enduring the early February wind and rain. The only folk, aside from local workers, venturing out on the North Cornish coast at that time of year were surfers defined by an unhealthy relationship with both the sea and themselves. Even the board and equipment shop on the bayfront was closed at this time of year. Everything in St. Petroc was battened down, waiting for the storm to pass, the sun to return—and with its return, whatever tourists the locals hoped to attract to revitalize an ailing economy.

Pearl Ellacott was behind the bar. She had dusted and cleaned and was now counting stock in the refrigerators, finding things to do to justify staying open. A few regulars were dotted about the premises, as always, ready to outsit the evening as it became nighttime. She was grateful for them, their custom, the fact that they still maintained the pub as a central hub of the community.

Things were improving for the village as the events of the last year, the Upheaval, faded. Everyone collectively worked to put it behind them, to rebuild what they'd nearly lost. It was never discussed, not openly, but was always there—behind eyes, in unspoken words, in memories of people or particular places—and Pearl imagined it always would be.

The one good thing to come of it was the tourism, even if it was of a prurient and grisly sort. Pearl knew it was in the heart of humanity to be interested in the macabre, as long as those professing interest in the dark side were not themselves directly affected. Or if they were, they didn't hang around for long.

Inventory made, she set down her notepad by the till, looking around for something else to do. The book she'd been reading was on the side of the bar, close to being abandoned as it hadn't gripped her. She was in that kind of mood. She should be happy. And she was, for the first time in a long while. Tom and she were still in the honeymoon period of their relationship. People might hate to be around them and their public displays of affection, but they didn't care. Still, something ate away at her. Something she couldn't talk to Tom about. Something she hadn't even fully acknowledged to herself. Plus, part of her didn't like to be seen reading in the bar. She felt it was unprofessional.

"Oh God, not him again."

Pearl looked to see where the noise came from. One of her customers watching the TV. Old enough to look like they'd built the pub around him and with a strawberry nose to show where most of his money had gone. Arthur King was on the screen once more, spouting his nativist nonsense.

"I know what you're going to say," King said, talking over an interviewer attempting to speak. *"My argument is nationalistic—specifically, English. Well, why not? I mean, the Scots have their own identity, don't they? The Irish, even the Welsh. But if you say you're white and English and proud of it, you're called a racist. It's madness."*

"Reckon he's talking sense," said her customer.

Pearl listened in to the conversation between her two regulars, as well as what King was saying.

"Going about it in a daft way."

"Not a politician, though, is he? That's why you can understand him."

King continued. *"What white English working-class people need once more is a sense of pride. A sense of belonging. Being able to love their country and know their country loves them back. Now, that's not racism, is it? It's common sense."*

"Right enough."

"I mean," said King, *"that's why I chose this name. Heritage. Myth. Legend. English heritage. We all need something, someone we can unite behind. To feel pride. To continue with what we believe in. We're not going to find it in Westminster or the BBC or anywhere like that. It's going to come from here. From us."*

"From you?" asked the interviewer.

"Why not?"

The bar's door opened, and a woman entered. Middle-aged and attractive. Like she had the money and the time to take care of herself. Dressed in white middle-class bohemian fashion, she looked vaguely familiar to Pearl. She must have seen her in the village.

The woman smiled as she came up to the bar. Shook rain

off herself while uncoiling her scarf. Pearl was grateful for the intrusion.

"Chilly out there, isn't it?"

Pearl agreed. Smiled. "What can I get you?"

The woman's eyes scanned the shelf behind Pearl's head. Ran her eyes along the bottles.

"I'll have a . . ." She paused, face screwed up in what she must once have assumed was an adorable fashion. "Rum, I think. That'll be warming. And Coke?"

"Coming up."

"Too cold for gin. I'll look forward to that in a few months' time, though. My summer drink."

"You from around here, then?"

"I am now."

Pearl looked up quizzically, encouraging the woman to continue.

"Not so long moved in. I've taken the old butcher's shop in the main street. Turned it into a little gallery."

That was where Pearl had seen her. She'd walked past as the woman was setting up, arranging framed pictures and other doodads. Pearl had seen her painting the outside of the shop pastel blue. It stood out against the surrounding drabness, like a drag queen at a Brexit Party meeting. *Good luck*, Pearl had thought as she had watched her labors. *You'll need it around here.*

"Oh, nice," said Pearl. "How's it going? I'm Pearl, by the way."

"Shelagh." She took the proffered drink, paid for it. "Well, I'm sure it'll take off when the tourists arrive in the summer."

Don't count on it, thought Pearl.

"I just wanted to get established in the village first. Get to know people. My new neighbors. My new friends, hopefully."

"Well, you've come to the right place."

"Good." She looked around the bar, then back to Pearl, still smiling despite there being only a smattering of people, and most of them agricultural workers or locals, none of them likely potential customers or friends to artistic Shelagh.

"It gets a little livelier as the night wears on," said Pearl. "Don't worry."

The two regulars finished watching the TV, discussing what they had just seen.

"Got a point though, hasn't he?" said the strawberry-nosed customer. "Things used to be better."

"What, in King Arthur's time?"

"Yeah. Much better."

Pearl tuned them out. The pair looked old enough to have been around in King Arthur's time.

Shelagh kept smiling at her. She sipped her drink, seemed loath to sit down. She spied the book on the countertop. "What you reading? I presume it's yours?"

"It's mine." Pearl went to fetch it. "Hilary Mantel. *Wolf Hall*. I felt like the only person not to have read it."

Shelagh glanced over at the two old men. "What, even in here?"

Pearl smiled at the joke. "Well, maybe not in here."

"You enjoying it?"

"Yeah. I mean, it's a great book, but I'm not sure I'm in the mood for something too thinky at the moment. Could probably do with something a bit more chick lit-ey."

Shelagh frowned, ready to speak. Pearl immediately regretted her words, realizing she had just invited Shelagh to have a conversation of some depth with her. Pearl was casting around for some kind of distraction when the door opened once more.

"Tom, hey."

Tom Killgannon entered.

"Hey yourself. You OK?" He crossed to Pearl.

They kissed—one of those PDAs she knew must annoy people but she didn't care about.

"Yeah." Pearl was pleased to see him. For the diversion, as much as anything. "How was your day?"

"Oh, you know . . ." Tom said, then realized there was someone else there listening.

"This is Shelagh," said Pearl. "She's just moved in. Taken the old butcher shop and turned it into a gallery."

Tom looked surprised. "Good luck." He smiled. "You'll need it."

"So people keep saying, but you never know. I've got a feeling it's going to be a success. Wouldn't have done it otherwise."

"That's the spirit. We need more like you around here."

Pearl looked at Tom, clearly wanting to say more but knowing she couldn't. "Everything OK? Everything went well?"

"Yeah, fine," he said. "I'll tell you about it later."

"Good."

"I'll just go and get rid of my coat." Tom walked into the back of the pub.

Shelagh turned to Pearl. "He's nice. Does he come with the pub?"

Pearl felt herself blushing. "He's my . . ." She rarely stated what she and Tom actually were to each other. The words *boyfriend* and *girlfriend* seemed slightly absurd. *Partners* sounded like businessmen or American cops, so she usually just introduced him by his name.

"Other half?"

Pearl smiled. "Suppose so."

Shelagh was trying to get a glimpse into the back where

Tom had gone. "Pity. I could do with someone like that around. Been a bit lonely since the—well, you know."

"Divorce?"

"Something like that. Has he got a brother?"

"'fraid not. But . . ." She looked around. "You never know . . ."

Shelagh laughed. "No, you never do." She took her drink, went and sat by the fire. Tom emerged.

"Ready for duty, boss. Just tell me what you want me to do for you."

He smiled at her. She tried to return it, but it wouldn't reach her eyes. Not wanting him to see, Pearl turned away. Went back to work.

She didn't notice Shelagh staring at the two of them.

II

SIMON SAT ON THE CLIFFTOP, staring out at the sea. Knees drawn up to his chin, arms wrapped around them, rain battering his face and body. He still wore his city clothes because he had no country ones yet. He wondered if any other person had ever sat here, thinking the same thoughts as him, having experienced similar actions or emotions. No way. For definite. He was unique. And for all the wrong reasons.

The cliff he sat on was about a mile away from Tom's house and even farther from the village of St. Petroc. Far enough to provide solace, if that's what was wanted. To feel alone against the world. He hadn't intended to end up sitting here on the cliff edge, staring at the tumultuous waves below. He had gone for a walk, and the dark had arrived quicker than he expected. So he'd sat down, watched the sun disappear behind clouds. He was totally alone in the dark. He'd thought it would be quiet in the country, but it wasn't. The constant sound of the sea was like listening to an untuned radio on full volume. But that was good; it would stop his thoughts from becoming too deep. When the rain came, his mood darkened with the night around him.

He was freezing. Shivering, teeth chattering, but he wasn't going to move. The waves were hypnotic, building like a huge intake of breath, crashing on rocks with the kind of cathartic thrill that smashing up a room gave his raging teenage heart. One of his dad's rooms. Or even better, Ludmilla's. Like he'd done in the past. Simon sighed. He wouldn't be doing that any more. But he didn't know whether that made him happy or sad.

Sad, he decided. At least doing something bad had gotten his dad's attention. Now he had no dad and never would again.

Sorrow and rage built up inside him, crashing like waves against the rocks. He might have been crying. Cold rain on his face made it impossible to tell.

He gripped his knees tighter. He would sit here until it was fully dark. Then he would walk home along the cliff path and maybe fall off. Crash onto the rocks. Not the worst thing that could happen. Might even be the best.

Home.

But it wasn't and never would be. He had been there nearly a week now. Tom and Lila seemed OK. They were doing their best. Not pushing him or asking him questions, like at the safe house. Just letting him be himself, whoever that was. Giving him space. He could tell they had been through things of their own, the kind of things that left scars that only showed when you got to know them. That should have made it easier for Simon to talk to them, or at least relax. And maybe he would. Or maybe he never would.

There was also that thing about Lila being gay. She didn't look gay. Yeah, she was a bit scruffy, but she was good-looking. He imagined what his mother would say. Living in a house with a gay girl. A gay girl with an Asian girlfriend, apparently. She wouldn't have been happy. At least he didn't think she would. Now he'd never know.

He shuffled closer to the cliff edge. His feet went over, dislodging pebbles that tumbled down the cliff face. He didn't hear or see them land. The sea, the jagged rocks, absorbed them into its noisy mayhem. That could be him. It would be easy. Just keep edging forward and soon all the massive, soul-deep, crushing depression would be gone. Forever.

Heart beating faster, he moved closer to the drop.

It was fully dark now. He wouldn't even see what would happen to him. And it would be over so quickly that he wouldn't even feel it. Or maybe for a little bit, on the rocks, but then once the waves hit and dragged him off, there would be nothing left to feel. Ever again.

Closer to the edge. Feet dangling right off it now.

They tingled in the empty air. His whole body joined them, stomach flipping, like the feeling he got at the top of a tall building, that all-over-body shiver. He had read somewhere that no one was ever truly scared of heights. They were just scared about what they might do to themselves when they were up there. Yeah, that sounded right.

Bit farther . . .

So easy. Just shuffle himself forward . . .

"Simon?"

Hearing the voice over the noise of the sea was like an electric shock pumped through his seated body. As he jumped, he screamed. His arms flailed, legs kicked out, scrambled, finding fresh air instead of land. His body began slipping, panic taking any decision away from him. The sea became louder. Rocks illuminated by flashes of foam appeared through his vision in the darkness.

"No . . ."

His heart skipped several beats. His arms windmilled wildly. Instinctively, he grabbed the ground at his side for support, realized he had moved his body too far toward the edge. What stones he could grab crumbled away due to erosion.

He flung his body backward, hit the ground. Turned over, and began desperately to pull himself forward, legs bicycling in the air, grasping for sodden stones and mud. Breathing so hard he felt he would pass out.

Then there were hands on his arms, pulling him forward. Two sets, one on each side. Yanking him away from the edge.

"Simon, you OK?"

He opened his eyes. A flashlight was being shone on him. He squinted.

"Simon?"

His heart was hammering so hard he couldn't make out who was speaking. He thought he recognized the voice, but—

"It's OK, Simon, we've got you."

He began to calm down. Adrenaline-pumping heart began to slow. He breathed in deep. Out again. Recognized the voice.

"Lila?"

"Yeah. What are you doing out here? And in the rain? It's treacherous."

He sat up. There was another girl. He looked from one to the other. The smartphone light was lying on the ground, its beam casting upward.

"Hi," said the second person. "I'm Anju."

Lila sat down next to him. "So what you doing here, then?"

Simon tried to recover himself. "Just sitting. Thinking. You know." He looked at the other girl. Was this her girlfriend?

"In the dark?" Anju this time.

He was grateful to be rescued but didn't want to show it. After all, they were girls. He was instantly defensive. "Yeah, so what?"

"I'm just saying it's dangerous here, that's all," said Anju. "Especially if you don't know the area."

"Even if you do know the area," said Lila.

"True."

"Come on." Lila tried to help him up.

He shook her off. "I can manage."

He got to his feet. A look passed between the two young women. In that look, he knew what they were thinking. They had realized what he was doing out here. Why he had come. Even if it had taken him a while to figure it out himself. Sitting too close to the cliff edge had not been an accident. It was a way of building up courage. In that moment, he felt like they really saw him for who and what he was and felt ashamed.

He dropped his head. Said nothing.

"We missed you at home," Lila said. "I got worried. So we decided to come looking for you, see if you'd got into trouble on your walk."

Simon nodded, feeling suddenly angry. And tearful. And that was something he definitely didn't want these two to see. He turned away from them.

"Come on back to the house," said Anju. "Lila's cooking, but don't let that put you off."

Lila mock-hit her. Anju acted mock-injured. Simon know this was all for his benefit so he forced a false smile.

"Come on," said Lila. "Let's get you home."

Home. It sounded better when she said it, he thought.

12

THE ROMANIAN SHOVED A STICK of wood between the dog's teeth. It clamped down hard. He shook the stick, ensuring the dog attached itself even firmer. Then he held the dog up by the stick, looked at his host. "Strong enough for you, Mr. Marx?"

Marx's expression gave nothing away. "We'll see what he's like after the roll."

The Romanian let the dog down slowly. Tried to pull the stick from its jaws but it wouldn't let go. He pulled harder. The beast held on and started shaking it, enjoying the challenge, aggression rising. The Romanian smiled. "See? Natural fighter."

Marx said nothing, just watched.

The Romanian hit the dog on the back, shouted something in his native language at it, and the dog let go.

"You said something to him in your language," said Marx. "I don't speak your language and I'm not going to learn. Will that be a problem?"

The Romanian smiled. Marx saw glints of precious metal.

"No problem," he said. "You train him, you get him to understand you. This dog is just . . . what is the word? Potential."

Marx nodded. "Okay, let's get the roll started."

All the Romanian's previous dealings with Marx had been through third parties or over the internet. This was the first time he'd met Marx face-to-face. He'd been led to believe that Marx was a fearsome figure and was now disappointed at the sight of him, amused even. Here was this slight, long-haired man wearing glasses, dressed in a woolen sweater and shapeless jeans, one boot built higher than the other, walking with a pronounced limp and supporting himself on a wooden cane. At first, the Romanian had thought he'd come to the wrong place. Upon meeting, he'd stifled a laugh. But after one long gaze into Marx's reptilian eyes, the Romanian realized there would be no laughing today.

Marx lived in a sort of ecosurvivalist compound. The land was ringed by tall fences of concrete and razor wire, which in turn were camouflaged by leylandii and laurel. Into those were woven indigenous hedgerow plants and flowers, to attract birds and insects. The gate into the compound looked from the outside like thick aged wood, but that hid reinforced steel—maintaining privacy while appearing nonthreatening. Discreet CCTV cameras were strategically placed. Anyone who managed to scale the outside fence would be greeted by barking dogs.

With Marx hobbling on his cane and leading the way, the Romanian pulled his dog past other dogs in pens, who threw themselves at their cages, growling and barking. An old well-used Land Rover Discovery was parked in front of the main house, which resembled an overgrown wooden shack with clapboard sides, a porch, and a tiled roof. It looked like it had been assembled out of repurposed and recycled material and attached to a flat pack industrial unit. Solar panels were attached to its roof, and rain barrels positioned under drainpipes at two back corners. To the side of the house was an extensive vegetable garden. Fruit trees flourished behind that. Another section of land was devoted to solar panels and wind turbines. Surrounding them were newly planted trees. There were two big hangar-like structures dominating the land with other similar smaller buildings dotted about. Marx pushed open the door to one of the big hangars.

"In here," he said.

The floor was smooth hard-packed earth. At the center of the space was a square enclosure, its wooden sides pitted and discolored, like fresh meat had been violently flung against it. Fresh meat with claws and muscle.

"Stick him in there."

The Romanian picked up the dog, placed him in the arena.

Marx scrutinized the animal. Scars around his muzzle and forehead. Patches of hairlessness, scarred skin stretched tight. He stood firm on his four legs, unmoving, eyes unreadable, more like a living engine than an animal.

"He is young," said the Romanian. "Has many years before him. A champion."

"Bloodline?"

"Bred from Soldier." He shrugged. "Not Chinaman but pretty close."

"A Bully Kutta. What else?"

"Crossed with Presa Canario. Fierce but loyal."

"Loyal to who?"

The Romanian smiled, held up his arms in a shrug. "Whoever's boss. He's just what you wanted. What you asked for."

"Name?"

"Bully. Means same in any language."

Marx kept staring at the dog. Eventually, he nodded, turned, called. The sound of a slavering dog being barely restrained came closer, paws and claws eager to get into the arena. The man who entered was older, burly, muscle gone to fat. Baseball cap pulled low, tracksuit and trainers, barely retaining a grip on the wooden flirt pole, the dog straining against the rope noose around its neck.

"This is Iceboy."

Marx gestured to the overweight bloke who moved to a trap at the side of the arena. The Romanian climbed into the arena, began unchaining his dog.

The dogs scented each other. The fat guy gave a couple of smacks to the head of Iceboy, who growled in response, tried to go for his fingers. He pulled them out of the way, kept up a litany of hatred to the dog.

"Fuckin' 'ave him, get 'im, tear the cunt apart . . ."

The dog growled, jaws gnashing, legs ready to launch himself forward.

In the ring, the Romanian was doing something similar with his dog. It had the same effect.

Marx nodded. The two men let the dogs go.

Bully and Iceboy sprang at each other like two walls of muscle colliding. Straight away Bully opened his jaws, attempted to latch on to Iceboy's neck. Iceboy twisted away, not ceding ground, and went for the top of Bully's head. Bully shook him off, again dived for the neck.

"Good fighter, yes?" said the Romanian. "Good instincts?"

Marx said nothing, kept watching.

The dogs locked jaws with each other, both trying to dominate and throw the other around the ring, but finding their opponent matching them move for move, bite for bite.

"How many fights?" asked Marx.

"Four. Last one went for over an hour and a half. Tenacious—is that the right word?"

"Did it win?"

"You think I'd sell you loser?"

Marx turned to him, gave him the scrutiny he had been giving the dogs. "It would be a bad idea if you did."

The Romanian had dealt with some of the most vicious and violent people in the whole of Europe and managed to conduct business while not being hurt. But something about this slight, limping man with those deadly eyes told him he was in a different league of dangerous.

He swallowed. "My word is my bond. Ask anyone. They will tell you."

"I did. And they did. Lucky for you."

The Romanian expelled a breath he wasn't aware he'd been holding.

"You seen enough?"

Marx gave the overweight man a nod. The man entered the arena, break stick in hand, and began separating the two dogs.

The Romanian also entered the arena. He carried a choke chain that he slipped around his dog's neck, which was now slick with blood. Eventually, the dogs, torn but defiant, were parted. The overweight man led Iceboy away. Marx turned to the Romanian.

"Bank transfer, as agreed?"

The Romanian nodded. He wanted to get out of that compound as quickly as possible.

"It'll be with you in an hour."

The overweight man returned to the barn, took the chained dog, and led him away.

The Romanian managed a smile. "Pleasure to do business with you."

"Robert will open the gate for you," said Marx. He turned and left the barn.

The Romanian followed. Already, the overweight man, presumably Robert, had placed the dog in one of the pens and was walking toward the gate. Business seemingly concluded, the Romanian walked over to his car, got behind the steering wheel. Started the engine, ready to leave.

As he did so, another car entered. Old and Japanese, its original color was almost impossible to make out due to a patchwork of different colored replacement sections, rust, and thick gray primer. It pulled up in front of the house as the Romanian left, grateful to be out of that compound, unnerved that someplace so open could feel so claustrophobic.

As the patchwork car came to a halt, a young woman wearing leisurewear appeared in the doorway to the house. Marx walked up the steps toward her.

"What's that on your face?" said Marx.

She was made-up, her hair styled. She tried to smile for him. It barely left her lips, certainly never reached her wide, fearful eyes.

"I . . . I did it to look pretty for you."

Marx sighed. A change came over him. He wasn't the same person with the girl as he had been with the Romanian and the dogs a moment before. He shook his head sadly. "Wash it off. Please. You don't need that."

"But Aiden—"

He took her chin in his hand, tilted her head toward him, stopping any more words from her as he did so. Smiled. "Just wash it off. There's a good girl."

She was about to answer, but a glimpse into his eyes disinclined her to do so. She bowed her head. Nodded.

"There. That's better." He still held her face in his hand,

his eyes locked with hers. She couldn't bear the intensity and looked away. She went back inside to do as she'd been told.

He smiled, watching her walk away, then turned his attention to the car that had just arrived. Two men got out, both stocky, one with a beard.

"Well?" Marx said as they approached, his manner changing again. All business now.

"He got the message." The beardless one smiled. "Won't be slinging his filthy, foreign muck around here ever again," he added, his voice high and singsong.

Marx nodded. "I saw it on the news. Good job."

The two looked pleased to have been commended.

"Any more? Or are we going public now?" asked the clean-shaven one.

"Couple more to go first. Don't worry. You'll enjoy them." Marx gestured toward another barnlike building. "In there. Let's talk."

In their pens nearby, the dogs growled and howled.

13

Simon looked down at his hands, finding no solace or answers there. He wasn't sure the person in front of him could provide any of those things either. But he'd reluctantly agreed to give it a try.

The man sitting opposite him smiled. "I'm Doctor Mirza. Faisal, you can call me. And may I call you Simon?"

Simon nodded, still staring at his fingers, noting the way they coiled around each other, wrapping and unwrapping like writhing flesh-colored snakes.

"Good." Faisal leaned forward in his chair. "Now, I know this will be difficult for you, Simon. So I want to make it as easy as I possibly can. I'm here to help you. That's all. Not to find things wrong with you or report anything to someone else. I am here to help you feel better, to be able to move forward from here, OK?"

Simon nodded again, his fingers loosening slightly.

"Good. Treat this space like it's soundproof. No sound can get in, none can get out. And it's safe, as well. Safe for you to say what you want to. Express yourself in your own time and your own words. OK?"

Another nod.

"Good. Then let's start."

Simon glanced up, took in the room once more. It was meant to be comfortable. There was a desk and filing cabinets pushed to the back wall, but most of the space was taken up with two chairs on a brightly colored rug, not quite facing each other. It wasn't overly lit like other offices Simon had been to. More subdued. More grown-up.

Tom had said Simon might find it beneficial to talk to someone he didn't know or didn't see every day, someone who could keep a secret and who might actually help him. Tom knew about the night on the cliff edge even if he hadn't said anything directly to Simon about it.

Simon had shyly agreed, not wanting to ever again feel like he had on that cliff. It was only on the drive over that Tom had told him the doctor was Anju's dad. He hadn't had time to think about his response to that, so he'd just gone along with it. And now here he was. He didn't know where to start, or even if he wanted to.

"You're Anju's dad. She's going to know I'm here."

"Well, I suppose she does. Is that a problem?"

"She'll tell her girlfriend what I say. Or Tom. Or . . . I don't know. Anyone."

"No, she won't," said Faisal. "Because I won't tell her anything, and it's none of her business. These sessions are private and confidential." He smiled in what he supposed was a reassuring way. "And, anyway, if I started telling my daughter—or anybody for that matter—about what goes on in here, I wouldn't have a job for much longer. No one would come to me."

Simon nodded. He felt a slight lift in what was weighing him down. But it still wasn't enough. "Won't people think I'm mental for talking to you?"

"Not at all. Lots of people get counseling, therapy, all sorts. They're not crazy, they're just trying to understand themselves better. This is a good thing, Simon. It helps a lot." A smile. "I wouldn't do it otherwise."

Since he'd agreed, Simon would have to go through with it. Give it a go, Tom had said, see what you think. He thought again of that clifftop in the rain, his feet losing their grip, his cry for help becoming a real scream. He nodded at Faisal.

"Good. So the first thing I should ask is, how are you feeling?"

"I'm . . ." Down to his fingers again.

"No hurry. Best to give an honest answer than a quick one."

His gaze moved beyond his fingers, down to the rug. Trying to make order out of the random pattern on it.

"I'm . . . sad. And scared." With those words, Simon felt like he had just stepped off that cliff and was in free fall.

"Scared about what, Simon?"

Faisal seemed genuinely interested. He had a way of listening, an open manner, which made Simon want to keep talking. "Because they might come back for me. Whoever . . . did that. And angry. Because I ran away instead of . . ." He sighed. "And guilty because we'd just . . . I'd just . . . I was angry."

"Right." Faisal was about to speak further but Simon interrupted.

"Why did I run away? Why didn't I stay and fight? I hate that I'm a coward. I should have stayed and done something."

"Your house was taken over by violent intruders. You ran to get help. The bravest thing isn't always to stay and fight."

He felt anger rising within. "Didn't do any good, though, did it? I didn't help them."

"You did your best."

"You don't know that. You can't say that."

"The fact that you're here now tells me that. And you weren't to know what would happen. No one blames you for not staying in that house."

"I do." His voice was as small as the statement was huge. Simon hadn't known he was going to say it until the words left his mouth. It was the first time he had articulated what he felt about that night, even to himself.

"Why?"

"Because I do."

"Sometimes it's difficult being the only one left when such an awful occurrence has happened. Like a train crash or what you've been through. Survivor's guilt, it's called. And it's easy for me to say you shouldn't blame yourself because you will. So let's look more closely at this."

Simon waited.

"Has any more of your memory come back from that night?"

"Just the argument. With my dad. That was why I was upstairs, the last thing . . . Oh, I don't know."

"And does that argument add to the blame in your mind?"

Simon thought. "You mean, would they still have died if I hadn't gone upstairs? If I'd been there when the door was opened?"

"Do you feel that?"

Simon thought. "Maybe." Again, he was facing things he hadn't even been able to say to himself. He had the feelings but not the words.

"We all think like that, Simon. If only. If only I'd been there. *If.* It's a great word, a powerful word. One of the most powerful in the English language. It can make so many things happen. If I just do this, what'll happen, you know? This is how great advances are made. But it's also destructive. *If.* If only I'd thought about this thing or that thing sooner. If only that hadn't happened, or this thing had happened instead. And there's nothing you can do about it. But look at *if* itself. The word. That upstanding *I*, that's always about you and you alone, then that letter *f* curled over"— he mimed the action with his hand—"so it can get its claws into you. And stay there. And hold you back. That one little word. But it's only powerful *if* you let it be."

Simon nodded. He put his hands to his face. They came away wet.

14

TRURO IN THE RAIN IN FEBRUARY—not the loveliest of places to be, but Tom had no choice. He was waiting for Simon to finish his session with Faisal.

He'd parked in a multistory car park, walked Simon to Faisal's office beside the cathedral, then went to a coffee shop to wait. Truro had never been his favorite place; it had small pockets of beauty and history, but even in sunlight there was something depressing about it. It was another small Cornish city that had allowed its quirky individual soul to wither and die after leaving itself at the mercy of chain stores and thuggishly unsympathetic town planners. It had once been as pretty as its coastal neighbors but the characterless high street chains had doomed its independent cafés, restaurants, and businesses. Any progress to return it to its former glory was going to be a massive uphill struggle. If it had a coat of arms, the crest would be crossed antidepressants.

Lila had told Tom about Simon's cliff-edge brush with death.

"I just—We couldn't tell if he was trying to jump on purpose and he scared himself or what," she'd said later that night in the kitchen, after Anju had gone home and Simon was in bed.

"You did the right thing," said Tom. "Didn't scare him, made a joke, got him to come back. I'm proud of you."

She tried not to smile. "Piss off, Dad."

His turn to smile then. "No, you did a good thing. It can't be easy having Simon staying here."

"No it's all right, it's just sometimes . . ."

"What?"

Lila hugged her late-night hot chocolate, not wanting to continue.

"You've said it now."

"Yeah. I don't know. Maybe I'm imagining things, but . . . I dunno. He seems a bit . . . Well, he gets a bit creepy when Anju's around."

"He's probably never met a queer couple before. Of girls. Or ones that he knows about. Certainly not his own age."

"Then he's the only boy in the country who hasn't. Different world out there now, Granddad." She moved her mug around on the wooden tabletop. Smearing the drying milk ring it left. "Maybe he's never met ones in real life, but he'll have seen plenty on porn sites."

"Oh, come on, give him a break," said Tom. "Poor kid. Lost his family, now he's stuck in a house with me and a queer couple. It's bound to be a shock to his system."

"Yeah. Maybe."

Tom took a swig of the whisky he had been nursing. Lila wasn't a drinker, just the opposite. He admired her for that. It would have been easy to use it as a crutch, considering everything she'd been through in her young life. When he had mentioned it, she had just laughed and told him, once again, that he was out of step with young people.

That's when Tom asked Lila whether they should involve Faisal in a professional capacity. She'd thought it a good idea, so the next morning Tom contacted him, telling him the police would be footing the bill and making a mental note to inform Penrose of that. Faisal had agreed to see Simon. Then came a harder part. Tom approached Simon, took him for a walk, put it to him. Eventually, the boy agreed.

In the car on the way there, Simon had looked terrified. Tom worried that if they were stuck at traffic lights too long, the boy's fear might get the better of him and he'd be out the door and away. The one thing that might stop him, Tom reasoned, was that the poor kid had nowhere to run to.

But Simon stayed where he was. Seemingly hating every single second.

At the coffee shop, Tom had a view of the doorway to the Georgian office building, watching for Simon coming out, to be ready if the boy ran. The coffee shop Tom sat in was close, but it was covered by scaffolding to the front, obscuring a full view. But it would have to do.

Then someone caught his eye.

A man stood out from the crowd. Tom spotted him straight away. He carried himself all wrong. Not a city dweller or a farmer. Not just from the country but of it, like his city surroundings were incidental, and he was stalking through a forest.

Tom scrutinized him: tall, burly, dark wild hair. Beard. Wearing black camo trousers and boots, an ancient black waxed jacket over the top. He paced back and forth in front of Faisal's building too many times, hands deep in his pockets, trying not to pay attention to the doorway, unaware he was being observed.

At first, Tom dismissed it. He told himself he was caffeinated and on high alert, unconsciously falling back into his training, looking for bad actors just for the sake of it. Making a quick risk assessment of each one who came near the doorway to Faisal's building. Just keeping his skills honed, passing the time more than anything.

But something persisted within, an instinctive acknowledgment. And over the years he had learned to never ignore those instincts. He waited until the man strolled past one more time—making this his fifth pass—then stood up, left the café.

Out on the rain-sodden sidewalk, Tom watched the man disappear around the corner. Tom stood behind the scaffolding, trying not to get in people's way. Waited. Soon the guy returned from around the corner, walking back toward Faisal's building.

Tom saw the man fully from the front. The beard and hair covered most of his features, but he could make out dark oily skin and deep-set black eyes. He emanated contained violence. Other pedestrians, without knowing why, instinctively moved to let him pass.

Intercepting him might go south quickly. The man hadn't done anything wrong yet. He could turn it around, make Tom out to be the dangerous one on the street. But then he would also know Tom's face. Not a good idea.

Or Tom could keep watching him, see what he did, where he went. As long as he didn't allow the man to get to Simon.

However, before he could decide, the decision was made for him. The man looked over the road and spotted Tom. He stopped walking, stared. Even from the other side of the road, Tom could see the anger in his eyes.

Neither moved, each waiting for the other.

The man suddenly turned and ran.

Tom gave chase. Due to the scaffolding, the pavement was clogged with pedestrians, and pushing his way through was difficult. He heard angry cries behind him as he tried to navigate a route through the press of bodies around him. Eventually, Tom emerged from the scaffolding tunnel, looked around. The man was nowhere to be seen.

Tom crossed the street, found the corner the man had repeatedly walked around, ran up it, eyes scanning both sides. No sign of him. He checked shops, cafés. Pubs. Nothing.

Like he'd just disappeared.

"So how did it go?"

They were in the car, Tom driving back home.

Simon thought before answering. Weighing what to tell, Tom thought, deciding what tone to take.

"OK."

"Good. Feel like you want to go back?"

Another pause for thought. "Yeah." Another pause. "Yeah."

"Pleased you got something from it. Hope it helps."

"Me too." And a smile.

That's a first, thought Tom, returning it. Long way to go yet though.

As if reading Tom's mind, Simon's smile disappeared.

Tom wanted to talk more but knew there was a thin line between being concerned and prying. Too much could set back any progress he had made. Too little might make Simon feel he didn't care.

"You want the radio on, or some music?"

"Your music's weird."

Tom laughed. "You been talking to Lila?"

Simon hid a smile, shrugged.

Good, thought Tom, putting the radio on.

As Radio One took over the atmosphere in the car, Tom zoned in to what had happened previously. The stalker.

Had he and Simon been followed after leaving Faisal's? Were they being followed now? He didn't think so. He'd checked carefully when he left the parking ramp. He'd even taken a different route out of Truro, following tiny one-track roads where it would be easier to spot a tail. No sign.

He drove on, Radio One blaring. Simon was either listening or in his own world.

Tom was uneasy. What he'd feared might happen seemed to be happening.

Now he just had to decide how to deal with it.

15

THE BELL RANG as Pearl entered the shop—*er*, gallery. She had to get used to calling it that. It wasn't the butcher's anymore.

"Hello, stranger." Shelagh looked up from the counter where she sat reading *The Guardian* and drinking what smelled like coffee from a Sports Direct mug, glasses on the end of her nose. Michael Kiwanuka played in the background.

Pearl smiled. "Thought I'd come and see where *you* worked for a change."

Shelagh took off her glasses, placed them on top of the newspaper. "As you can see, I'm rushed off my feet."

"Had any visitors yet?"

"Visitors, yes. Customers, no. They're a bit harder to come by."

Pearl looked around. It was about what she'd expected. Driftwood sculptures from local artists, watercolors of sunsets and stranded fishing boats. Framed black-and-white photos of men in big jumpers, frowning at lobster pots. Mugs and fridge magnets. Painted clay lighthouses.

"What d'you think?" asked Shelagh.

"Very nice."

Shelagh smiled. "*Nice*. Hate that word. But yeah, you're right. Nice is what it is. Nothing here to frighten the horses, so to speak. Not my taste, but . . ." She shrugged. "What can you do? It's what sells. Or so I thought."

"No *Poldark* stuff?"

Shelagh laughed. "Finished on TV, hasn't it? Didn't want to get in on the tail end of that. End up with boxes of tat I can't shift. No, I think that'll all go the way of Flat Eric furries and 'I Shot J.R.' badges."

Pearl shook her head, smiling. "I have no idea what you're talking about, but I get your point." She paused, looking around once more. "So what would your taste be, then? Why not stock that?"

"Remember what I said about frightening the horses? Well, that."

"Oh I don't know," said Pearl, picking up a painted lighthouse. "Sometimes I think the horses could do with a shock."

Shelagh seemed focused on something far away. "I've had quite enough of those, thank you very much. I'm looking for an easier life now."

Pearl nodded. "Know the feeling."

Shelagh nodded to herself, her mind seemingly made up about something. "Let me put the kettle on again. You've got time, haven't you? The thirsty of St. Petroc can manage without you for a bit?"

"I've got someone watching the bar. I don't want to—"

"Coffee? Tea? It's no trouble, honestly. Glad of the company, to tell you the truth."

"*Erm*, coffee, please."

"Right you are."

When Shelagh went into the back of the gallery, Pearl caught a glimpse of something behind the curtain, something very different to what was out front, but the curtain fell back into place, cutting off her view.

"I'm glad you popped in," Shelagh called as she made coffee. "You're the first friend I've made since coming here." She emerged holding an unplunged cafetière, a mug, and a plastic container of milk. Placed them on top of the newspaper. "If you don't mind me calling you a friend, that is."

"*Erm*, no. Not at all." Pearl might have considered the word *friend* a bit strong, especially when she didn't really know the woman, but Pearl stood here in her gallery and Pearl had called on her, so the feeling must at least be partway to being mutual, she rationalized.

Shelagh smiled once more. "Good." She looked at the cafetière. "Here's a tip. Never plunge this until all the coffee grounds are thoroughly soaked. That way it goes down smoothly." She laughed. "And who doesn't want to go down smoothly?"

Pearl smiled. "Oh, and I'll take this." She placed a painted mug by the till. "I'll have my coffee in this, then take it with me."

"Oh, don't be—"

"No, it's only fair. You come in and drink at my place, don't you?"

Shelagh nodded. "Fair enough." She rang the mug up in the till. Pearl paid contactless. Shelagh gave her the receipt, smiled. "My first friend is my first customer." She poured the coffee. "So what brought you in here?"

"I was just . . ." Why had she come in? Curiosity? "You know how it is. You get bored with talking to farmers and surfers in the pub all the time. The few that are there."

"Everything OK?"

"Yeah. Sure. Fine."

"You should be. You've got it all going for you, haven't you? Run your own business, it's profitable—or at least for around here—you've got a great bloke, if you don't mind me saying so."

Pearl reddened.

"So good for you, girl."

Pearl nodded. "So how are you finding life here? The village been welcoming?"

"I suppose so. I don't think any small village likes incomers. Not the ones who stay, anyway. It's a bit of a strange place, though, isn't it?"

"You could say that."

"I mean, given what happened here recently."

"That's why the tourists, or what tourists we get, come. We kind of need them."

Shelagh's eyes lit up. "What was it, paganism or something? Black magic, ritual murder? I mean, that's exciting. You can have a whole tourist industry built on that." Before Pearl could answer, Shelagh continued. "You were here for all that, weren't you? What was it like?"

Pearl paused before speaking. "Not as exciting as you made it out to be."

Shelagh looked deflated. "Oh. Sorry. I suppose it must have been different for you."

"It was like a collective madness gripped the village. A desperation. And yes, if I'd read about it somewhere else, then I'd have been excited by it. But when it's happening to you and people you—" She sighed. "Never mind." She sipped her coffee. Bitter. But welcome.

"Sorry. It must have been hard for you. That was insensitive of me."

"It's OK. I mean, it happened. I can't pretend it didn't. Everyone was led to believe that ritual sacrifice would make St. Petroc prosperous again. And to be in the middle of it, to witness everyone being swept up in this madness and not being able to stop it, was horrible. But like Voltaire said, 'Those who can make you believe absurdities can make you commit atrocities.'" Another pause, another decision made by Pearl. Maybe she really did need a friend after all. "That's why my parents left. They ran the pub, I just worked for them. They were . . . involved, shall we say. Heavily. And they couldn't stay around afterward. So off they went."

"And you never heard from them again?"

"Oh I hear from them. They're sorry for what they did, they hope I can understand why they thought it was for the best, they hope I can find it in my heart to forgive them, all of that. Even asking me to go and join them. Not that they ever tell me where they are."

"And would you?"

Pearl didn't answer straight away. "When they started contacting me, letters and that, I always said no. Never. They were responsible for what they'd done, and they had to spend the rest of their lives living with it. But . . . I don't know." She gathered her thoughts. Maybe she had actually come here today to say all this. To speak to someone she didn't really know. Someone who could listen without involvement. "What d'you think of this village? The people in it, how they look at you, talk to you? What d'you really think about it?"

"I . . . well, like I said, it's a small place, not very welcoming to outsiders. At least, I hope, just not at first. I'm sure they'll welcome me eventually."

Pearl nodded, thinking before replying. "It's changed. For me, at any rate. From what it was. Oh, I don't know, maybe I've just opened my eyes to what it's really like after having had them closed for so long. You know, like you're growing up and don't know what the world's really like so you think everything's wonderful. Then as you get older you realize that isn't the case. Maybe that's what's happened to me here. It's like . . . the Upheaval, everyone tried to forget it, go on like it had never happened, business as usual. Except for the tourist trade, and even that's started to become something a bit separate. You know, stories to tell. Like Robin Hood. Or the Salem witches."

"Well, isn't that a good thing?"

"Yeah, but it hasn't been addressed. What caused it, what led to it. It pulled the village apart, set neighbor against neighbor. People were close to dying. To being killed. And then . . . nothing. Like it's this vast wound that's just had a plaster put over it. It hasn't healed, it might never heal. It's still there, festering."

"What d'you propose? Mass counseling? Sorry, that came out flippant. I didn't mean it to."

"No, that's OK. You're probably right. That's what we could do with. Won't happen, though. And every day I have to go to work and look at their faces, know what they were planning to do and who they were planning to do it to. And they look at me, knowing which side I was on, what I thought of it. And them. And what I did about it. And they say nothing. And I say nothing. And I have to live with that. Just get on with it." She fell into silence.

"What about . . . Tom, is it? He seems like a good man. Worth hanging on to."

"Yeah, he is. Absolutely. No doubt. I can trust him, no problem."

Shelagh smiled, mainly to herself. Looked like she was thinking. "But?"

"Is there a *but* there?"

"You tell me."

Pearl sighed once more. "He seems to attract trouble.

Violence. He doesn't mean to, and he definitely doesn't want to, it just sort of . . . happens. He's the same as me. After everything that's happened, he just wants a quiet life as well."

"Are you sure about what he wants?"

"Yeah. Definitely. But the quiet part never seems to happen."

A smile from Shelagh that Pearl couldn't read. They drank their coffee.

Shelagh spoke after a while. "I can't speak for Tom, but you just get on with things, don't you? No matter what's happened in the past, you try and make the best of things now. Whether it's an abusive relationship or what happened here. You just . . . keep going."

Pearl looked at her. "Is that why you're here?" Before Shelagh could answer, Pearl felt embarrassed for her directness. "I'm sorry. I didn't mean to pry."

Shelagh's expression changed swiftly. Like the curtain falling on the back of the shop, uninviting further investigation. "No, it's fine." She forced a laugh. "But it's a long story. I'll tell you sometime if you like. When we can drink properly and not at either side of a bar."

Pearl nodded. "OK, then." She looked at her watch. "I'd better be getting—"

"Sure. Yes."

"Thanks for the coffee."

"No problem," said Shelagh. "Let's make a night of it next time."

"Sure."

Pearl let herself out. Shelagh watched her go. Mug to her lips, eyes never leaving Pearl's departing figure.

16

Sullivan watched. sullivan waited.

It wasn't going to be easy. This guy who had taken in the West boy knew what he was doing. The stone cottage was at the bottom of a hill beside a small inlet with a concrete slipway leading into the sea. It had good views of its bare, exposed surroundings. Anyone approaching by road would be instantly spotted. Similarly, anyone making their way over the rough ground down the hill would stand out. And approaching by boat would be the most obvious way of all. Killgannon had known what he was doing when choosing this place.

Not easy, thought Sullivan, but not impossible. Not to a lifelong hunter such as himself. There were patches where the rough bracken on the hillside was slightly deeper than others. Patches where a patient man could make a nest for himself while watching, waiting.

He always thought of his father when embarking on a mission like this. The man who'd taught him all he knew about living on the land, off the grid. Making a successful life for yourself without doing what *they* wanted you to do. Joining the masses. The sheep.

It wasn't a commune he was brought up in. More like a camp. His parents had moved there when he was little. He might have had biological brothers and sisters, but there was no way of knowing. Raising children was the collective responsibility of the women. The men trained, hunted. Fought. He couldn't even isolate his mother either. She had joined the rest of the women: cleaning, cooking, child-rearing, servicing the men in whatever way they wanted. The way women should be, Sullivan had been brought up to believe.

The camp trained them for the war that was coming. Living apart from the rest of the herd, ready to defend themselves if need be. Sullivan loved it. Loved pleasing his father, the other men. Demonstrating how well he could fight and hunt. He even kept the other kids in line who didn't respond as well as he did. He enjoyed that. Dishing out punishment beatings on the orders of the adults. Made him feel powerful. The more the other kids cried afterward, the stronger it made him feel.

When he was seven, it all ended abruptly with a police raid. Sullivan was taken to a children's home along with all the other kids. Sent to doctors, psychiatrists, social workers who assessed, prodded, examined, talked and talked. Made to play with toys like a baby and tell them what he was doing. He fought them every step of the way. Used all his training on them. Made them pay for what they'd done to him. He hated that, wanted to go home. He never saw his parents again. Wasn't allowed to contact them.

The children's home couldn't cope, couldn't contain him. He was placed in a secure unit until he was eighteen, then allowed to leave. He returned to where the camp had been—a remote part of Cornwall—but it was long gone, razed to the ground like it had never been there. Rage built up inside him at the empty site. Anger, hatred, self-pity. That day, it felt like he had walked into a forest and never returned. It took something special to coax him out again. Very special.

So he thought about his father. Wondered where he was, if he was still alive, even. And Sullivan prepared to do his job.

The house was in near darkness. The downstairs lights were all off, only a faint light from one upstairs window remained on.

Simon West was in there, he was sure of that. He'd glimpsed someone of his shape and size against the upstairs window. The boy didn't seem to stray far from his bedroom. But that light was now out. A woman had turned up at the house, along with the man. They had entered, neither left. His wife? Girlfriend? Quite pretty. Might have some fun with her later.

He would wait until the light went off, until he was sure they were all asleep, then enter the house. Despite its strategic location, it didn't appear to have any complex alarm systems. Not even a dog. He checked his weapons. This wasn't a job for guns. Or bare hands. It was a stealth job. A knife job. The biggest one was strapped to his right thigh. Recently sharpened. A backup was strapped to his ankle; another sheathed in the small of his back. And a spring loader attached to his wrist. He had spent hours making sure that it worked, that just the right finger to palm pressure could make it jump into his hand without snagging on or tearing the sleeve of his camo jacket. Or slicing up his fingers. It was a last resort but a good one. He pressed his fingers to the hidden pressure pad on his palm, testing it. The knife jumped straight into his hand. Sullivan smiled, reset it. Ready.

The upstairs light went out. Sullivan smiled to himself. Not long now.

"WHAT WAS THAT?" Pearl's eyes opened with a start. She sat straight up in bed. Tom was slower in waking.

"What?" he asked.

"I heard a noise downstairs. Like glass breaking."

Tom was fully awake now. Was it the traps? He had been reticent to leave Simon on his own in the house or just with Lila and Anju for company since the incident in Truro the week before. But having to work, he had no choice. He could have taken the boy to work with him, but that would likely raise questions he didn't want to answer.

Pearl and he had also had sex for the first time in what felt like a while. They had both been tired from working but each seemed to feel an instinctive need of the other. Even so, there'd been something perfunctory about it, and afterward, Pearl had lain silently. Mind elsewhere, edged away from him. Unlike her, thought Tom. He was reticent to ask her if anything was wrong in case she gave an answer he didn't want to hear. The kind that would break his heart. So he left her to her own thoughts.

And now this.

Tom jumped up, grabbed his jeans from the end of the bed, pulled on a T-shirt. Trying to make as little noise as possible while doing so.

"Stay here," he said.

"What are you going to do? Phone Penrose?"

"See who it is first." He reached under the bed, brought out a heavy wooden baseball bat. An emotion he couldn't read passed over Pearl's features as he hefted it within his hands.

"Be careful." She turned away.

Hoping he was overreacting, he opened the bedroom door as silently as he could and made his way out into the hallway.

SULLIVAN CURSED HIMSELF and his stupidity.

There had been alarms, just not the kind he was expecting.

More benign versions of the kind he had at his caravan. Empty tin cans and glass bottles strategically arrayed at windows and doors, unseen from outside, placed where they could make the most noise possible.

He had thought the sash window in the kitchen would provide the easiest access. It opened with the minimum of persuasion and, on reflection, that should have been a warning. But Sullivan, riding his luck, went in. That was when he discovered the noisy glass bottles.

He paused, one leg inside the kitchen, the rest of his body outside, not knowing whether to progress or retreat. Listening for sound, any sound.

Nothing.

Tentatively, he reached inside the window with his right hand, put it down on the sill to give him leverage.

And felt pain shoot through his fingers.

He nearly cried out, not because the pain was so intense, but because it was so unexpected. He looked at his fingers. A rattrap held his middle and index finger captive, the metal bar designed to break a rodent's back nearly succeeding in breaking his fingers.

He tried to balance himself on the sill and use his other hand to remove the trap as quietly as he could. His freed fingers painfully throbbed. They'd be useless for a while. He felt anger at his own stupidity, cursed himself for making the kind of mistake he had thought he was above.

He fought down the anger. Tried to reach a decision. Go further or get out. If he went inside, continued with his original plan, someone could be waiting. He didn't expect that anyone would be a threat to him, not with all his knives, but if that guy had been alerted and had a shotgun, then that would be no match for his knives, no matter how sharp. There was also the possibility he might phone the police.

Alternatively, if he turned around and left, he wouldn't be able to use this plan again. They might move the boy somewhere else, and Sullivan could lose him. He had his professional reputation to consider.

His mind was made up. He'd go on.

And improvise if he had to.

Ignoring the broken glass and wary of any other traps, he hauled his body through the window, pivoted, then landed on the floor. His feet crunched on broken glass. To Sullivan, it sounded like it echoed beyond the kitchen. He unsheathed his largest knife, moved as stealthily as he could toward the kitchen door. Stood behind it, waiting. Ear pressed up against the wood, he was trying to listen, silence his own heartbeat, breathe.

Nothing. Gripping the knife in his right hand, he stretched out his left and turned the handle on the door. It came free. He slowly pulled it back, hoping it wouldn't squeak. It did. He pulled it slower, hoping the noise would reduce.

Eventually, the door was fully open. He waited once more, trying to control his pounding blood, his heavy breathing, and listened, hearing nothing.

He carefully stepped into the hallway, alert for any more cans or bottles.

His eyes, accustomed to the darkness of the hallway, began to pick out shapes, objects. He saw the silhouette of the newel post and banisters against the far wall, the open doorways into the rooms. The rooms themselves were shrouded in shadows. He couldn't make out anyone in them.

Wary of creaking boards beneath his feet, he slowly walked the hall, making for the stairs. Listening as he went.

He reached the bottom, made to put his left foot on the step.

The sound almost came too late for him to react. Anyone

else would have missed it, but Sullivan wasn't anyone else. A noise came from behind him, from the open living room doorway. He managed to turn just in time.

A baseball bat, aimed for the back of his neck, instead came down on his left shoulder. It hurt, but not as much as it should have.

He turned. Tom Killgannon, the man Sullivan had seen in Truro, stood there, bat in hand, ready to go again.

"Let's have a look at you," Killgannon said, turning on the light switch.

Sullivan hadn't been expecting that. The light was sudden and bright. He closed his eyes, blinked several times. His assailant was ready and made the most of these few seconds of confusion. The baseball bat swung once more, this time connecting with the knife in his right hand. It clattered to the floor, his hand falling painfully dead.

The baseball bat swung again. Sullivan was again taken by surprise as it struck him in the neck, making him trip over the end of the first stair and stumble down to the floor.

The man stood over him. Ready for more.

"Why were you watching us in Truro? What are you doing here?"

Sullivan just stared at him, said nothing.

"Who sent you?" the man shouted, clearly angry.

The man was allowing emotion to get the better of him. Sullivan could use that anger to his advantage. To Sullivan, this was just a job. And he was good at his job.

The man drew back the baseball bat, intending to swing it once more, telegraphing the move. Sullivan was ready for him. He pressed the pressure pad in his palm, felt the spring-loaded knife appear in his hand. Before the baseball bat could fall once more, he slashed at the man's leg. Connected.

"Shit . . ."

Blood spurted through the gash in the denim. The man stopped, knew he had been hit.

Sullivan slashed again. His assailant was ready this time, moving backward out of the knife's arc. Sullivan used that moment to get to his feet. The baseball bat swung once more but with less power behind it. Sullivan managed to duck beneath it. He ran for the kitchen.

Panicked voices were heard from upstairs, lights coming on. Shouts to call the police. It was no good. Sullivan had failed.

He scrambled for the kitchen window as Killgannon ran after him. The cut in the man's leg slowed him down, but he managed to reach Sullivan just as he was crouching on the window ledge ready to jump into the garden. The man picked up a glass bottle from by the sink and brought it down over his head.

"*Arrgh . . .*"

That hurt. The glass didn't break. He knew from experience that it wouldn't. Films weren't real life. But it seriously hurt. Sullivan tried not to black out, to keep the momentum going in his body, get as far away from the house as possible.

He landed in the garden, seeing double, and began to run, retracing his path.

He rounded the front of the house. The man was waiting for him.

"You can't escape, fucker," he said, swinging the bat once more.

Sullivan ducked, quickly reaching for the hidden knife at the small of his back. In one movement he pivoted and sliced the back of the man's hand. Killgannon screamed, dropped the baseball bat.

Knowing an exit when he saw one, Sullivan turned and ran.

17

Tom STARED AT THE WHISKY in his hands before him, tried to focus only on that. Think for himself.

The circus had arrived at Tom's house. After their intruder had fled, he'd phoned Penrose, told him what had happened. Within half an hour, what seemed like every police officer in Cornwall descended on his doorstep. Two cars of uniforms, Penrose, a couple of detectives. Plus paramedics. The house's inhabitants had been herded into the living room while condom-suited CSIs had gone about their business, gathering any evidence the intruder may have left behind. Tom didn't think they would find any. The man had managed to ditch Tom in Truro. He was a professional.

Tom's hand and leg had been bandaged up by paramedics. He was given a supply of painkillers and told he was lucky that the wounds weren't any deeper or he would have needed stitches. He was taken outside to the front of the house, away from the rest of the inhabitants, and interviewed by the two detectives on the scene.

Tom told them what had happened, recalling as much as he could remember, from Pearl waking up to phoning Penrose.

He was adrenaline-pumped but tamped it down, remembering his training: give detail, build evidence. Tom closed his eyes as he described his attacker, blocking out everything happening around him, concentrating on getting his facts right. After agreeing to work with an e-fit artist to build up a fuller picture, he was dismissed. He went to the living room where the rest of the house's inhabitants had been corralled, poured himself a whisky, and sat down among them.

They had all been shocked into wakefulness. Lila and Anju huddled on the sofa together, holding onto each other, both terrified. Simon sat on his own, staring straight ahead. Tom wouldn't have liked to guess what the boy was thinking about.

Pearl stood by the window, looking out. She appeared very tired.

Tom sat, his hand and leg bandaged, his body bruised and aching, nursing his whisky. He was aware of Lila looking at him.

"Look," she said, "they might not have been after Simon. Maybe it was a message from Dean Foley."

Foley was a Manchester gangster that Tom had put away, the man who'd initially caused Tom to take on a new identity and move to this remote part of the country. A man who'd subsequently escaped from prison and disappeared into the night, presumably assuming his own new identity.

"Unlikely. Foley promised to leave me alone."

"Yeah, until it suits him not to."

"I don't think it was Foley. Not his style. He'd have just turned up himself."

"So who?" asked Anju.

"Well, whoever it was," said Pearl, turning into the room, "it's déjà vu, isn't it?" she said, a note of anger in her voice.

Tom returned his gaze to his whisky.

"So come on, Tom, who was it this time?"

Tom stared at Pearl, unable to answer straightaway.

She continued. "What, don't you know? Are there that many people wanting to attack you that you can't answer?"

Tom sighed, took a mouthful of whisky. Felt it burn all the way down.

Pearl kept talking, staring straight at him. "Supposed to be safe here, isn't it? Yet here we are again. Another unwelcome visitor. For someone who's supposed to be in hiding, you manage to attract them. Maybe we should just put a big neon sign up on the main road. 'Tom Killgannon's house down here. Feel free to break in and attack us.'"

"All right," said Lila, "let's not. Please."

Lila glanced over at Simon. The boy wasn't looking at anyone. He just sat with his head in his hands. Reminding the rest of them that he was there defused some of the room's tension.

"If it's anyone's fault, it's mine," said Lila.

"How is it yours?" asked Anju.

"Because I insisted that we have Simon here. And if it's someone after him, then I'm to blame."

"That's not fair," said Pearl, anger subsiding. "You weren't the only one saying that. We all agreed."

"Yes, but—"

"Let's talk about this later, shall we?" said Tom.

"Hello?" Penrose's voice echoed down the hall.

Tom stood, glad to be leaving the room and this discussion.

"Here!" Tom's voice carried all the way down the hall, louder and perhaps more aggressively than he'd intended.

Penrose was waiting by the front door. "I didn't know whether to come in or not, because—"

"What's going on?" asked Tom.

"Well, *erm*, we're combing the area but we haven't found any trace of the intruder. Perhaps it was—"

Tom lowered his voice in case anyone from the living room had followed him out and was listening. "It's because of Simon, isn't it?"

"We don't know that for sure but—"

"Come on, Chris. An armed maniac bursts into my house and stabs me. It has to be for him. I told you last week that I chased someone away from where Simon was in Truro."

"I know you did, and we've been keeping a discreet eye on your place ever since because of that."

"But not tonight, apparently." Tom felt his anger rising.

Penrose's eyes flashed in a rare moment of anger. "We're still not sure the guy was after Simon, are we? I mean, you can hardly say this hasn't happened to you before, can you?"

"So it's just coincidence?"

"We don't know yet. We'll have to investigate."

Tom knew Lila and Pearl's words had hurt him, and he was taking that anger out on Penrose. He felt slightly guilty about that, so he tried to rein it in. "Investigate in what way?"

"Whoever it was seems to have vanished into thin air. Maybe he was some kind of outdoors type? A survivalist?"

"Well, he survived," said Tom, "and he's outdoors now." Tom spoke before Penrose could speak again. "What are you going to do about Simon? Leave him here in my house tonight?"

"We could move him to a hotel. Or another safe house. But if he was the subject of the attack, that means our intel has been compromised. Strange though it may sound, he might actually be better staying with you, yes."

Tom made to argue, but he could see the logic in it. His house probably would be the safest place for Simon right now. The intruder wouldn't be back. At least not tonight. "And what about long term? This survivalist knows where I live. Knows where Simon is. We're sitting targets. He might get lucky next time."

Penrose chewed his bottom lip, thinking. "We'll have to move him somewhere else. Shame, poor kid. He was making good progress here. You were helping him."

Tom said nothing. Just stared at the ground. He felt he was letting the boy down by agreeing to him being moved. But he tried to rationalize that by thinking of Lila, Pearl, and Anju. "Maybe when . . . I don't know. Could he move back later? When you've found whoever was after him? When it's safe?"

"You taking in waifs and strays? I don't know, Tom. You know how these things work."

Tom nodded.

"We'll move him tonight. Say your goodbyes if you want to."

Tom wasn't looking forward to that. "And there's something else. I want to pay a visit to Raymond Bain. He's the guy Simon's dad ratted out, right? Where is he, which prison?"

Penrose stared at him. "You can't do that."

He turned, looked at the house, then back to Penrose. The implication clear. "You owe me."

Penrose said nothing, only dropped his gaze. Tom took that for assent.

"Thank you."

Tom looked away, saw Pearl at the window. She turned away when their eyes met.

Behind her sat Simon, looking lost.

18

SHELAGH STOOD BACK, admired the painting. She had definitely captured something. Another aspect of the horse.

In her studio, late at night, her angled poise lamps were focused on the canvas, lighting it up as if it were being displayed in a gallery—a proper gallery, though, not one with shitty driftwood sculptures.

Music played in the background. Vaughan Williams. It felt appropriate somehow.

Glass of red wine in hand, she scrutinized her work.

It was much more than just a skull. The horse's sockets were deep-set indentures, and the green jewel eyes in those holes could have given a cheerful, happy image. Instead, there was just enough darkness surrounding the glinting light to impart a sense of hooded malevolence. That shine spoke of a cunning intelligence. Instead of white, the bone was a sickly yellowish color, dead or diseased. A necklace of flowers ringing the base of the skull was old and withered, desiccated gravestone blooms. The sheet obscuring the human form beneath looked like an ancient, exhumed funeral shroud. The background of the painting was deliberately distant, like the horse loomed from somewhere shadowed and indistinct into the viewer's contemporary reality, an image of evil conjured from myth or nightmare.

Shelagh nodded. Just right.

She looked again. Not perfect, though. There were things she hadn't got right, a few petals were flawed, their brush-strokes showing through too much. Likewise, the sheen on one of the jeweled eyes. And she could have spent more time on the corners of the funeral shroud. So that presented her with two options. Keep working on it, try to get those details correct, aim for perfection, or to leave it as it was and move on to the next project.

She could keep working on it, sure, and she may well get those details perfect. But there was always the chance, as there was with any act of creation, that the whole thing could become unbalanced in the process. Artists, she'd read somewhere, often had to have their work taken away from them to stop them from self-sabotaging in their quest for perfection. The more proficient she became with the brush, the more the message hit home. She would leave it as it was. Acknowledge its imperfections and move on.

But she kept staring at it. Smiling as she did so.

This was part of the process she had come to enjoy. Of course, the actual act of creation, the painting itself, was the most important thing. But just looking at what she had achieved came a close second.

Wonder what Tom Killgannon would make of it?

Shelagh actually jumped as if she had been touched. Where had that thought come from? Tom? The guy in the pub?

She smiled. Told herself not to be so surprised. She had been watching him since her arrival in St. Petroc. Hard to take her eyes off him, really. Even getting friendly with Pearl, asking questions about him, finding out about her relationship with him. And it all sounded encouraging. They seemed happy enough, but Shelagh knew Pearl was having problems.

Not with Tom, but that could be arranged. Shouldn't be too hard to stick a wedge between them. Exploit Pearl's doubts. And then . . .

She sat down on an old armchair, still looking at her painting.

Yes, it would do. She stood up, removed the canvas from the easel, and set it down at the side of a cabinet by the wall where she kept her paints.

She picked up a blank prestretched canvas, placed it on the easel, stared at it. The picture was already forming in her mind's eye. Just like the last one did, just like they all did. It would then be her job of rendering what was in her mind on the canvas. She had done it before, she could do it again. And better this time. Always better. Otherwise, what was the point?

She thought of Tom Killgannon once more. Smiled.

He'd like the painting Shelagh had just completed. She was sure of it. Could imagine him complimenting her on it, his eyes crinkling up in the corners as he did. Smiling all the while. She imagined him with her in her studio, sharing a bottle of red wine, discussing her art and the effect it had on him.

Then discussing her and the effect she had on him.

Shelagh swigged from her glass until it was empty. Put it down among the paints on top of the cabinet. Picked up a pencil. Studied the canvas.

Oh yes. If he liked the last painting, he would love what was going to happen next.

19

THE TWO DOGS WERE LOCKED TOGETHER by their jaws. Both pulled backward, neither giving ground. Both were so exhausted they were ready to drop. But they kept going.

Their claws skittered on the blood-soaked concrete of the pit floor, too slippery for them to stand, losing balance whenever they tried to move. Only the sheer solidity of muscle combined with their low centers of gravity kept them upright. Their indoctrinated rage, pride, and viciousness kept them fighting.

Aiden Marx watched, arms folded, face impassive. Bully, his new dog, was in there. It was the dog's first competitive fight since buying him from the Romanian. And the hard-muscled beast was doing good. Excellent instincts. Powerful. Wouldn't give in. A good investment.

Marx checked his watch. The fight had been going for over an hour, and the dogs were tiring. Robert stood by the barrier, ready to jump in if anything happened; if the dogs needed separating or one took clear advantage and began to tear the other to pieces. The crowd, all men, were used to playing the long game, their initial calling and shouting having died down.

Now they watched, gave the occasional exclamation, but mostly kept their eyes on the dogs. They would claim, if asked, that they were interested in tactics, a good contest. Working the odds, betting on a favorable outcome like any other sport. But it was the blood, the violence, that held their fascination.

Bully bit down harder onto his opponent's head, tried to shake him. Kaiser, the other dog, tried to pull away. Bully sensed that, pushed Kaiser back. Bit harder, growling as he did. Kept trying to maneuver his teeth away from the other dog's skull and down toward his neck where he could sink his teeth in and inflict more damage.

Marx admired the dog's initiative. The fact that Bully didn't want to let go of the hold he had in case Kaiser tried to do the same demonstrated intelligence. This dog could go a long way. Bully was going to be a champion.

If he got through this fight.

Kaiser renewed his assault, growling, biting down harder, jaws locked and pushing. As determined as Bully not to cede ground or show even the tiniest weakness. But Bully had the superior breeding. Bloodline was everything, Marx always said. Time for him to demonstrate it.

Robert was shouting his own words of encouragement to the dog.

"Come on, Bully, get the fucker, Bully. Get him. Bite him, you cunt, do it. Hard. Fucking hard. Go on . . ." Growling nearly as much as the dogs were.

Kaiser's owner was doing the same. The dogs responded in kind: growling, biting, pushing.

Marx kept away from the pit-side activities. He preferred to watch from a distance.

"Come on, Bully, fucker's weakening . . . come on, kill him off . . . you can do it . . ."

Bully responded to Robert's words, renewing his attack, pushing harder. Growling. Kaiser matched him move for move.

Until something gave.

Kaiser slipped on a patch of blood, his back left leg going down, the rest of his body following. Bully took immediate advantage. He unlocked his jaws from the top of Kaiser's skull, taking whatever flaps of skin and flesh his teeth had dislodged with him, moved swiftly down to the other dog's neck. Kaiser, sensing what was happening, tried to dodge out of the way and attack Bully once more, but couldn't right his body quick enough. Bully clamped his jaws on Kaiser's throat. Bit down hard.

Kaiser let out a strangled whimper, tried to pull away, shake the other dog off. Couldn't. Bully's jaw was clamped. Immovable. Adrenaline once more coursing through his veins and with renewed aggression, Bully shook the other dog, biting down farther, ripping out whatever he could.

Marx watched impassively.

The crowd was as reenergized as Bully. They jumped to their feet, shouting encouragement to both dogs and, depending on where their money was, hurling abuse at the other.

Bully renewed his attack. He pushed Kaiser toward the far wall of the arena. Kaiser, visibly weakening, ceded ground. His owner screamed at him to keep going, threatening him with punishments if he stopped fighting.

It was no use. Blood gurgled and spurted from the wound in Kaiser's neck. His owner called for the fight to be stopped. Robert stepped into the ring with his wooden separator, pushed it between the dogs, dragged Bully away by his collar.

It was too late for Kaiser. He tried to stand, made a halfhearted attempt to go after Bully, but his body didn't have the strength. He slipped in his own blood, fell sideways to the concrete floor. His owner stepped into the ring, picked up the dog, carried him out. The crowd, sportsmanlike to the last, applauded.

Robert took Bully away to his crate, forced him to stand still, checked his injuries. Began patching up what he could.

Marx's phone rang. He took it out of his pocket, put it to his ear. Didn't speak. Just waited for the caller to identify themself. To match the name that had appeared on-screen.

"You there?" No reply. "All right, I take it you are. Listen. Got some bad news for you."

He listened.

And the triumph he felt at Bully's success drained away.

20

AFTER LEAVING KILLGANNON'S HOUSE, Sullivan returned to his hidden car and drove away, keeping as near to the speed limit as possible, not wanting to attract attention from the police he knew would be on their way. Angry with himself, he pounded the steering wheel as he drove, not believing he'd made such a basic mistake. And been bested. That did not happen to Sullivan.

He pulled up outside his caravan and made the perimeter patrol around the field, quicker than usual, running, checking that his traps and sensors hadn't been tripped. Everything was as he'd left it. He disarmed the alarms and locks—some to just deny entry, others to permanently disable—and entered the caravan, closing the door behind him.

He looked around. Tried to plan. Marx had contacts in the police. He would know by now that he had failed in his mission. That he didn't have the boy. Not only that, but the local police now had a full description of him. Sullivan had to get away and lie low for a bit. Be forgotten.

He'd need money.

He stood immobile, breathing heavily and weighing his

options, aware of the seconds, minutes, running out. He had only so long before Marx's reckoning. Get his money, get out. Quick.

He knelt in front of the built-in sofa, took a knife from his pocket, prized off the wooden paneling. There, close to the ground, was the first of his hidden caches. He reached inside, drew out neatly stacked bundles of notes, shrink-wrapped into hard bricks. He flung them behind, into the room. The first of the pile.

He worked his way along the paneling, wrenching off the wood, not caring how neatly he did so, bringing out the bricks until the front of the sofa was gutted. Then he turned his attention to the walls. He reached for the doors of the cupboards above the sink, put his knife down on the draining board, and, using both hands, pulled one of the doors off its hinges. He took his knife and forced it into a tiny, paper-thin gap in the fake wood. Pulled away the top layer, revealing a grid of thin bricks of money, even higher denominations than the sofa haul. He repeated this with all the cupboard doors until before him, on the center of the floor, was a substantial pile of cash.

Breathing heavily from the exertion, he swiftly moved into the bedroom, down under the bed, drawing out a heavy canvas bag. Back into the living room, he hurriedly tossed the money into it.

A quick check of his watch, balancing how much time he had left to collect the rest of his money against how much time there was before Marx's foot soldiers arrived. Sullivan was under no illusions. He was good at what he did, but Marx had people on his books that scared even Sullivan. It was not so much what they did, but how they did it. Punch and Judy, for a start. He'd seen them reach levels—or plumb depths—where even he wouldn't go. They'd gotten along on a work basis, and

Sullivan even considered them friends, but he would never cross them. He'd seen what happened to others that had.

And then there was that fucking Horse . . . the worst of the lot, no doubt about it. The Horse was insane. Chilling and freaky, even for the people who worked alongside it.

Let it not be the Horse, he thought. Please let it not be the Horse . . .

He looked at the money crammed in the canvas bag. Calculated. Not enough to get as far away as he needed to.

Back into the bedroom, he knelt on the floor and, with his knife in his hand once more, stripped back the flooring. Welded into the underside of the caravan's floor was another hidden recess. He reached around his neck, took off the chain that he always wore. A key hung from it, which unlocked the hidden chamber. He turned it. A hinged metal door flipped open, revealing more bricks of money, along with a plastic-wrapped automatic and several fake official-looking documents. He picked up the documents, including a passport and driver's license, and stuffed them into his combat jacket pocket. The gun went into another pocket. The money was taken to the canvas bag on the living room floor. That was better. Looked more like a decent amount now.

He zipped up the bag, flung it over his shoulder. Gave one final look around. He would never see this caravan again, his home for most of his adult life. He had no time to grieve, if that was what he wanted to do. He just had to go. Now.

And then he heard it. Outside.

The jangle of bells.

Fuck . . .

Sullivan didn't move, like trying to hide in full view.

It came again. That jangle.

He stood so still he didn't dare breathe. The blackout

blinds stopped him from being seen from outside, but his car was parked there. They knew he was inside.

Another jangle, followed by an irritated voice: "Look, you going to open this door, or do we have to fuckin' sing for it?"

21

Tom walked into the bedroom—*his* bedroom or *their* bedroom, as he was beginning to think of it—to find Pearl throwing her clothes into a holdall. The intruder, Simon leaving, now this.

"What are you doing?"

Pearl didn't look up. Her eyes couldn't meet his. "What does it look like?" Not said maliciously, just a matter of quiet fact.

"Why are you—Where are you going?"

"Home." Said without stopping what she was doing.

"Home? You mean the pub?"

"Where else?"

"But why?"

Pearl stopped and looked up. Tom saw the pain in her face, the hurt in her eyes. She looked away again. "Tom . . . look, I . . . there's lots of things, but—"

"Like what?" Said quickly and too loudly, and instantly he regretted it.

She stared at him, clamming up where she had been about to talk.

"Sorry," he said. "I shouldn't have . . . but what things? What's wrong?"

"Just . . ." She gestured around the room. "This. Tonight. What happened." Another sigh. "D'you really need to ask?"

"But . . ." He crossed the room, tried to place his hand on her arm. She shrugged him off.

"Please, just . . . Don't touch me." Said more in pain than anger.

Tom said nothing.

Pearl dropped the piece of clothing she had been holding. Just an orange T-shirt. He had liked her in that. Remembered her laughing joyously once when she wore it. He'd taken a photo of her in it.

"I . . . don't feel safe here. Anymore." She picked up the T-shirt, placed it into the holdall, her movements now heavy and weary.

"Safe?" said Tom.

"Yeah, safe. After what happened tonight?"

"I know, but . . . Simon's going to leave. Faisal's coming for Anju. It will just be us. And Lila. We'll be safe."

Pearl didn't answer.

"But this is, this is sudden. This is— Why not think about it?"

"I have thought about it. It's not sudden."

Tom had never been good with words in relationships. It was why he hadn't had many successful ones. His relationship with Pearl was the best he'd ever had by far. And even now he didn't know what he could say to change her mind, what he could do.

"If it's . . . if it's about being safe, then I can protect you."

Pearl stopped, looked up, her eyes wide with amazement. "Protect me? Is that what you think I need?"

"Well, yeah. I can protect you against . . . things like what happened here tonight. I've done it before. I'll do it again."

Pearl almost laughed. "Is that what you think? Seriously? Tom, I don't want protecting. I shouldn't need to be protected."

Tom just stared at her.

"Why can't we just have a normal relationship? Just you and me, watching a film or going out to dinner or having people around or going to a party. Or taking holidays together. Why can't we have that?"

Again, Tom couldn't find the words.

"Why does it have to be like this all the time?" She stared at him until he felt he had to answer.

"I . . . I don't know. I want those things as well. Just a normal life. All the things you said, just like you do."

Pearl's expression changed, hardened. "Do you, though? Do you really?"

Tom made to answer but hesitated.

Pearl smiled, which seemed to cause her pain. "You can't answer, can you? Can't say it."

"I just—"

"No, Tom, you don't want a normal life. You might say you do because you think that's what I want to hear, but you don't really. If you're honest with yourself. And if you're honest with yourself, you should be honest with me."

Tom opened his mouth to answer but couldn't. He couldn't find the right words. The ones that would tell Pearl she was right. Or the ones that would prove she was wrong.

"Just admit it, Tom. Say it." There were angry tears in her eyes as she spoke. "Because that's fine for you to say it. It's what you're like. You love all this." She gestured around the room. He knew what she was referring to. "This chaos. This . . . aggression. This violence. You love it. Or part of you does. Part of you thrives on it, needs it."

"But I'll—Look, Pearl, I can't—"

"I saw you, Tom. The way you looked after our intruder left. The look on your face. It was like you'd become someone different. Someone . . ." She sighed. "You weren't my Tom Killgannon."

Tom sighed, about to speak.

Pearl shook her head to stop him. "I know, you try to be him: this gentle person who's in front of me now. I know. But you can't, can you? Because there's that part of you that only comes alive when it's dispensing violence."

Silence. Until Pearl spoke once more.

"No, it's not a part of you, is it? It's the old you. The person you used to be. Who you told me you were trying to escape from. Trying to get rid of. But you can't escape, can you, Tom? The old you is still in there. That is still you."

When Tom spoke, his voice was small. "It's part of me, Pearl. I know that. It's a part I'm fighting against."

Pearl's voice was shot through with sadness. "But you can't fight against who you are. Who you really are."

"There was a time when we came together, when we first met, that you liked that side of me."

"Yeah," said Pearl, anger tingeing the sadness. "You're right, I did. A little. And I even joined you in it for a while. But I can't live like that, Tom. Never being able to sleep, in case I wake up with a mad knifeman standing over the bed. Or not being able to go to work, in case some maniac comes in, waving a shotgun." She sighed. "I can't. I just can't . . ."

She zipped her bag closed, picked it up. Slung it over her shoulder.

"Bye, Tom." She couldn't face him as she spoke.

Tom said nothing. Did nothing. Just watched her leave.

He heard her go down the stairs, open the front door, close it, get into her car, and drive away.

He stood there. He'd been unable to find the proper words to stop her. And even if he could find some, Tom didn't know if he would mean them while saying them.

So he let Pearl go.

22

"Sullivan . . ." the voice was singsong. "We know you're in there."

Holding tight to the bag over his shoulder, he looked around frantically, then stopped, frozen in place.

"Sullivan." The voice was impatient now, the accompanying jumble of bells erratic. "Open the door."

A thrill went through Sullivan. Punch and Judy hadn't tried to open the caravan door because they assumed it was booby-trapped. It wasn't. He had been too busy to rearm it after he'd entered. All they had to do was open it, and they'd find out for themselves. He needed to distract them while readying his escape route.

He moved silently to the door, studied its locks and armaments. Could he manage to lock and rearm without them noticing? It would buy him a little time. Also, it was his only option.

He leaned against the door, hands on the lock.

"What d'you want, boys?" His fingers turning the lock as he spoke, hoping his words were loud enough to cover the action.

"Come on, Sullivan, just let us in, mate. You know we have to talk."

"I know your idea of talk." Another part of the armament in place.

A laugh from the other side. "You forgot to lock the door, Sullivan?"

Sullivan looked at the door, the majority of locks, the lethal ones, were still not primed. "It's locked now."

A pause while Punch digested that information.

Sullivan thought of something. Two of them. One at the door, one . . . where?

He looked around quickly. The blackout curtains were drawn. He couldn't see if Judy was prowling around, looking for an opening while Punch kept him talking.

All the more reason to get out now.

"It's locked," Sullivan said. "Try it if you don't believe me."

An unamused laugh came from the other side. "Like I'm going to do that." A pause. "Listen, Sullivan, you messed up, but it's not the end of the world. You just need to have a chat with the boss man, get it all sorted. Come on, you're part of the gang. He won't get rid of you."

Part of him was desperate to believe Punch's words. Because he was right. Sullivan had worked for Marx a long time. He was part of the gang. Had been since back in the fight club days when Marx first met him. And Sullivan had been reliable. Effective. So a chat, an apology, lay low for a while until it all blew over, then come back and start again. It all sounded reasonable. *But.* Sullivan knew what had happened to others who'd screwed up. Ones who had previously been reliable, effective parts of the gang. Sullivan knew because he'd been the one to deliver the lethal message.

He forced a laugh. "You forget that I've stood right beside you when you've made the same speech to some other gullible idiot. And now you're making it to me? Well, I'm not falling for it. No, thank you."

Silence from the other side of the door. Even the bells had stopped jingling.

As Punch would be thinking his options, it was time for Sullivan to move.

But all at once the caravan shook, rocked as if by an explosion. Brightness cut through the night, bursting inside around the blackout curtains. Sullivan crossed to the front, pulled one back, looked out. Outside, his car was in flames.

He dropped the curtain back into place. Taking a deep breath, he held it, let it out slowly.

He lifted the table away from its booth, bringing a section of the flooring with. He placed it in the center of the caravan. The exposed flooring showed the caravan's metal base. Into the floor had been cut a square. He pressed hard on a corner of the table. A hidden compartment sprung out. Inside was a key. He took the key, fitted it into the lock on the square. Opened it to reveal a metal-walled shaft with a steel ladder attached to one side. He stood up once more, reached farther into the table's hidden compartment. Took out a black metal square box with a red button in the center. He crossed to the TV set, pulled it away from the wall. A matching button was there. He pressed it. A red light next to the button lit up. He looked around for the last time. Smiled sadly. Then climbed into the metal shaft.

Sullivan had known that at some point his home might very well come under attack, and he'd have to strike out on his own. He just hadn't thought the sudden move would be triggered by the people he worked with. He'd considered other options—the government coming for him, post-Brexit civil war, the European Superstate Army invading—but never this.

He would be sad to see his home go, but it had served its

purpose. He had to move on. Survive. Like a good survivalist.

At the bottom of the ladder, the metalwork stopped. It was replaced by a tunnel cut through the earth, propped up at intervals by sturdy beams of wood. A tiny homemade mine shaft. Sullivan picked up a headlight that was already placed there, put it on his head, switched it on. With no room to stand upright in the tunnel, he slung the bag onto his back, began to crawl.

Eventually, he reached the tunnel's end. Another ladder awaited him, leading up. This one was wooden; the shaft it sat in, rough and unfinished. He'd done that deliberately. Anything more polished might have attracted attention.

He reached the top of the ladder. Stopped. Put his ear to the hatch above him. Listened hard. There was a grill in place on the hatch to keep the tunnel aired, to stop mold and rot. He kept listening but heard nothing.

He took the key that he had opened the hatch in the caravan with, now fitted it into this lock. Turned. Sullivan turned off his headlight, took a deep breath, let it go.

He opened the hatch.

Outside was still darkness, but the surrounding forest was alive with nighttime sounds. He listened harder, unmoving. Identifying the sounds he heard. Branches in the breeze. Creatures in the undergrowth. No breaking twigs or heavy breathing. Movement of clothing. No bells. Slowly he hoisted himself out of the shaft, stood up. His eyes were accustomed to the dark. Breathing as slowly and shallowly as possible.

He had practiced this. Knew which route would get him through the forest to where he needed to go, which was as far away as possible. Out of the surrounding area, out of Cornwall itself. Maybe even out of the country.

He kept breathing, kept scanning the surroundings for movement, voices. Nothing. He had done it. He had beaten them.

He took the small metal box out of his pocket. It didn't feel so bad now, what he was about to do. Now that he was through the tunnel and out the other side, it felt like a part of him. His old identity, Sullivan, had been shed the further along he had come. Now he was out, into the fresh air, a new man with a new name. New possibilities. A whole life before him. He looked at the button.

Yeah, it wasn't so bad after all.

He pressed the button.

Nothing happened.

He looked over to the approximate area where his caravan was, expecting to see an explosion. Expecting it to shake the forest, send sleeping birds skyward. But it didn't happen. He only saw the outline of his burning car at the far side of the trees. He stabbed the button once more. Nothing. Then again and again. Nothing.

"Just can't get the craftsmen these days, can you?"

He turned to his left. Sullivan knew who it was without seeing: Judy.

Laughter came from beside Judy, accompanied by the tinkling of bells. "Out of puff after that run," said Punch. "I disarmed the caravan. Good job you did, really. Plenty of money left in there. Don't want to see that go to waste."

Sullivan had nothing to say. He'd been caught.

"Judy's been waiting for you right here, in case you were wondering. This was the plan all along, see. Get you to scurry through your tunnel out here." Punch cocked his head forward, a hand to his ear. "What's that? How did we know about the tunnel? You think we're stupid? Everyone knows about your tunnel. It's the worst-kept secret since Jimmy Savile's sex dungeon. Mind you, you took some persuading, didn't you? Had to blow your bloody car up to get you moving."

He saw they were both in costume again, etched against the trees. Looking like they belonged to the woods, to the dark.

"Come on, boys," Sullivan said, surprised at the desperation in his voice. "You're not going to let it go like this, are you? Not us. We go way back. Remember the fights? The club? We were untouchable. The Gladiators. Remember?" He glanced in the woods, then back at the two. "This is Turnip Head here in front of you."

Punch and Judy shared a look.

"Come on, lads."

Punch smiled. "You finished?"

Judy began jumping up and down. "Do it, do it, do it."

With just one way out, Sullivan reached toward his pocket and the automatic.

"He's predictable, isn't he?" Judy giggled.

"Too bloody predictable," said Punch, drawing a gun of his own and firing.

Sullivan barely felt the first bullet. But he felt the next one. And the one after that.

Through the pain, he observed Punch standing above him, still pointing the gun at him, hand to his mouth, mock-yawning.

"Boring way to go. But never mind. Can't stand here all night. Places to go. People to see."

Sullivan's body had spun and buckled with the force of the gun. He lay on the forest floor in a twisted, tangled heap. Wetness spread around him, inside him. He found breathing hard.

He watched Punch and Judy walk away.

Then . . . nothing.

PART THREE
PUNCH AND JUDY

23

BEFORE THE POLICE TOOK AWAY SIMON, Lila had gone to talk with him in his bedroom.

He had withdrawn into himself. He was sitting on the bed, legs drawn close, head on his chin, face buried underneath his bangs, rocking back and forth. Bag packed once more.

"Hey, it's me."

No response.

She kept staring at him without getting a response, so eventually she sat down next to him.

Questions ran through her head, each triter and more pointless than the last. How you feeling? You OK? Can I do anything? Knowing how useless they would be, she didn't ask any of them.

"Look, I'll just sit next to you, OK? If you need me, I'll be here. Yeah?"

She thought, somewhere inside his rocking and his slowly swishing bangs, that he nodded.

"OK."

So she sat next to him. And after a while, she became aware that he was crying. Lila didn't know what to do. But she couldn't sit next to him and do nothing. Slowly she reached across, placing her arm around his shoulder.

Immediately, he stopped crying. Or tried to. It was like an electric shock had shot through his body. She removed her arm straightaway. Wrong move, clearly. So she sat next to him in silence until Penrose put his head around the door, told Simon to get his stuff, he was leaving.

Simon stood up, grabbed his bag, and wordlessly left the room. Not looking at Lila once.

With no one else around, she had gone to bed and lain awake most of the night feeling something broken inside her.

FOR THE NEXT COUPLE OF DAYS, it was just her and Tom. Like it used to be.

But nothing like it used to be. Both of them, wallowing in sadness, feeling Pearl's absence, and Anju's absence, since Faisal would no longer allow her to come to the house. Lila and Tom barely spoke. The loss of a sense of security.

Tom, sitting in an armchair, mug of tea in hand, had constructed around him a seemingly unbreachable barrier. He stared at the tea, through the tea, miles away. Lila took a seat opposite him. She wasn't even sure that he was aware of her presence.

"D'you want me to leave?" she asked.

Tom looked up as if woken from a deep sleep or emerging from a fog. "What?"

"I said, d'you want me to leave?"

Tom frowned. "Why?"

"Because you don't seem to want me around. So I just thought . . ."

He shook his head, looking amazed she could even think

that. "No. 'Course not. This is your home. Our home. Why would you say that?"

Anger welled within her. She tried not to let it all out in one huge unfocused wave. "Because it feels like I'm not here. I try to talk to you, but you don't even register me. Ask you questions—nothing. So since I may as well not be here, I thought I might make it official." She paused, waited. "That's all."

Tom took in her words, sighed deeply. "I'm sorry," he said. "Everything's gone wrong, and it's my fault."

"Why is it your fault?"

"Because . . . I let Simon stay here. I gave Faisal my word that what happened before wouldn't happen again. And so I put you at risk, and Pearl. And now she's . . ." He couldn't finish.

Lila felt hot tears form in the corners of her eyes. "If it's anyone's fault, it's mine. I talked you into letting Simon stay. I twisted your arm. *Me*." The tears came. She put her head down, tried to fight them but failed.

Tom put his tea down. It looked like he wanted to come over to her, comfort her, but hesitated. Probably, she reflected later, for the same reason she had been unsure how to comfort Simon.

He waited until her tears subsided, then spoke. "Pearl's right. She said that part of me enjoyed it. And I did. You know I liked the danger, the fight. I can't deny it. And I've tried to be different, I've tried to be this . . . new person, this Tom Killgannon, but it looks like I just can't do it."

"But Tom, you haven't given it long enough yet."

"You even said it yourself when you were trying to persuade me to take in Simon. If I stayed here, worked in the pub with nothing else to do, I'd go insane. You said I need excitement. And you're right, I do." His voice trailed away.

They sat in silence for a while, then he spoke.

"How's Anju?"

"Fine. Talked to her this morning. Don't know if she'll be coming over here too soon, though."

Tom nodded, understanding.

More silence. Broken by Lila this time.

"You going to work later?"

Tom shook his head. "Pearl's gone. And my job's gone with it. She's made that clear. Anyway, bar managers are ten a penny."

"Give her a few days."

"No," said Tom, staring once again at his tea. "I think that's the end of that."

"Just give her a few days. Please. Then talk."

Tom said nothing.

"Have they caught him yet?" asked Lila. "The guy who broke in?"

"If they have, they haven't told me. I've asked a favor from Penrose, though."

"What?"

"That he goes with me to see the person that Simon's father's testimony put inside."

Lila couldn't believe what she'd just heard. "What? Why?"

"Just to look at him, see him for myself."

"But Simon's gone. It's over. What's the point of that?"

"I just want to see him for myself. Put my mind at rest. And also tell him not to send anyone else if it was him. Tell him the boy's gone, and we don't know where."

"Surely if he's the bad guy who set it up, he'd know that."

Something dark slipped into Tom's eyes. "It might be more convincing hearing it from me."

Lila noticed the look. Didn't reply.

AND THAT WAS HOW SHE'D ENDED UP at Anju's house. With Simon gone, Pearl back at the pub, and Tom going away for a couple of days, Lila hadn't wanted to be by herself. And Anju couldn't let her be either. But Lila still felt alone. She probably would no matter where she was or who she was with.

Karima was calling. Dinner was ready.

Slowly, Lila stood up. Checking that her Hand of Fatima necklace was on, she left the guest room and went downstairs.

24

GRANT TRENT SAT BACK ON THE SOFA, sipped his champagne, smiled. Checked his watch. Wouldn't be long now.

The heating in the room was turned up full and it still wasn't that warm. Trent wore only a silk dressing gown and was determined not to put anything else on. *No.* This was his night. His fun. And nothing would get in the way of it. Even a drafty old flat with rattling windows and poor heating. As the local member of Parliament, he should do something about it, investigate the landlord, perhaps. But as the decrepit place's landlord as well, he was inclined to just leave it as it was.

Another sip, another check of the watch. Tibor was sure taking his time. Didn't usually take him this long to meet his connection and score. Not to worry. He'd be back soon. Hopefully with a friend, as promised. Then the fun would start.

Grant Trent knew he had to be careful. Others in his position had done similar things, procured boys, got them to score cocaine, had sex with them in exchange for money and party favors, and they had ended up in scandalous headlines in the tabloids. Lost their jobs too. But he worked hard at a high level, so he had to let off steam. His wife knew all about it—or some of it anyway—and turned a blind eye, as she'd always done. As long as she was kept in the manner her parents had accustomed her to, she didn't complain. And his spoiled daughters need never find out. So what he did was a victimless crime, really. Everybody got something from it; everybody was happy in the end.

He had the kind of urges that if uncovered would put *Daily Mail* readers off voting for him, and with caution and perseverance, he had managed to successfully hide them: a false name given, a false occupation. These boys weren't the type to be up on current affairs. Several rendezvous had been arranged in his own slum-landlord flats, and there he was. Satisfied.

Up to a point.

The initial thrill of getting away with it was starting to pale. He'd tried doing a few new things to spice up these evenings. Not using a condom for sex was one. The thrill of wondering whether he would catch something from one of these boys—lying awake afterward next to his wife while she pretended to sleep, trying to work out which one was most likely to give him which STD— had been fun for a while. But that too had paled. Then drugs began to play an increasingly large part. Mainly cocaine, but he was open to anything. He'd discovered ketamine was a lot of fun. But still, Trent found the highs increasingly harder to hit.

On some level, he knew that it would always be this way. Giving in to urges, feeding addictions, the highs taking longer each time to reach what had once been so sweet and easily attainable. And he was getting sloppy, taking stupid risks and chances, almost as if he was asking to be caught—the way, he thought, laughing to himself, that serial killers operated. But Trent wouldn't let things go that far. He wouldn't.

He checked his watch again, took another sip. Christ, it was bloody cold in here. His boy had better hurry himself up and he had better have someone with him or this night was going to be very dull.

And that was something Grant Trent wouldn't stand for.

THE PATCHWORK CAR WAS PARKED OUTSIDE a block of run-down flats in Old Hill in Falmouth. Its two occupants watched the first floor flat in front of them. Waited.

"Supposed to be one of the most run-down areas in Cornwall, this," said Judy.

Punch grunted in response. "So?"

"Well, that fucker inside should be doing something about it. Instead of milking it for himself, like."

Punch sniffed. "All the fucking same though, aren't they? Never trust politicians. Any of them."

There was a pause. They kept looking.

"Turnip Head's a miss, isn't he?" said Judy eventually.

Punch turned, looked. Smiled. "Really? You miss having that sweat-stinking hulk breathing his bad breath on you from the back seat? That fucking rotting vegetable on his face?"

Judy's face was half hidden in shadow, expression unreadable. "Sullivan was our friend. Whatever else he was."

"And look what he did at the end. Ran out on us, just like the others." He turned to face Judy. Streetlight glinting off his small cruel eyes. "It's you and me. Always has been. Always will be. Family. All you can rely on." He turned back, kept staring at the flats opposite.

Silence fell once more.

"I've been reading this book . . ." Judy shifted uncomfortably, putting the words forward tentatively.

"Oh yeah?" said Punch, barely listening.

"Yeah. It's a thriller, like. About this bloke who wants to be a woman. Or thinks he does. So tries to steal a baby because his partner wants them to be a proper family. But then this bloke realizes he isn't a real woman and never will be one, and that he doesn't want to be one anyway . . ." He trailed off.

"So what happens?" Punch, again, barely interested.

"Dunno. Haven't finished it yet."

Punch shook his head. "So what you telling me for?"

Judy tried to speak, couldn't find the right words. Shrugged, instead.

Punch didn't reply. There was activity on the street. He pointed. "There he is. Come on."

Punch got out of the car, his bells jangling. The road was deserted, apart from the twitchy pretty boy on the opposite pavement. Hearing their approach, he looked across. Stopped in his tracks.

Judy smiled, the novel forgotten. Ready for fun.

ANOTHER GLANCE AT HIS WATCH, another mouthful of champagne. No. The glass was empty.

Grant Trent stood, walked into the kitchen, opened the fridge, took out another bottle. He was wrestling with the cork when there was a buzz at the door.

"About bloody time."

He put the bottle down, went to the intercom, buzzed the door open. Went back to the kitchen, resumed what he was doing. The front door opened.

"I'm on the second bottle now, and it's all your fault." He walked into the living room. "So don't blame me if I—" He stopped dead. "Who the hell are you?"

Punch and Judy stood there, Tibor held firmly in front of them. The boy's forehead was bleeding.

"Don't blame Tibor," said Punch. "We made him let us in. He didn't want to, but . . ." Punch sighed. "We had to get persuasive. Didn't we, Judy?"

Judy giggled.

"What the hell do you people want? I'm going to call the police."

"I don't think so, Mr. Trent." Punch smiled. "I think the police are the last people you'd like to see here."

"Apart from us." Judy giggled.

"True, Judy, very true. Apart from us."

"What d'you want? Money?"

"We know you can give us money," said Punch. "And if we separate you from what you have on you, along with all the sweeties young Tibor here has on him, that'll be lovely. But that is not actually why we're here."

Despite their ridiculous appearance, Trent was terrified. He'd craved excitement, but not this kind. Please God, not this kind.

"Just . . . please. Take whatever I've got. Just . . . don't hurt me. Please."

Punch laughed, his bells jingling as he did so. Judy joined in the laughter.

"We're going to do more than hurt you," said Punch. "Consider this an early by-election. A bye-bye election, in fact. Consider this you being voted out of office. Permanently."

Understanding dawned in Trent's eyes. "No, no . . ."

Punch shoved Tibor in the back, sent him sprawling on the ratty carpet. "And I'm afraid young Tibor here's got to go as well."

Tibor looked up in horror. "What?"

"Sorry, Tibor, old boy," said Punch, his accent exaggeratedly English upper class to contrast with Tibor's East European pidgin English, "But it's wrong time, wrong place for you, I'm afraid."

Before Tibor could move or speak further, Judy brought the hard wooden handle of his broom down on his head. He flattened onto the floor, his hand to the injury, let out a gasp of pain. Judy did it again. And again.

"Stop, stop!" Trent waved his arms around ineffectually, as Tibor's writhing body came to a halt and collapsed, a pulped mess.

"*Shh*, Mr. Trent," said Punch. "Don't want to alarm the neighbors, such as they are. Although knowing you, there probably aren't any neighbors, am I right? Now." He drew out a huge knife that had once belonged to Sullivan. "Are we going to do this the easy way or the hard way?"

Trent fainted.

25

Tom threw his holdall on the hotel room bed, sat down next to it. He surprised himself; it was much nearer to the floor than he had expected. He spread his fingertips, felt the mattress. Far less comfortable than he was used to. Sheets and bedding one step up from a detention center. The cheapest, most basic of the budget hotel chains. Amenities as spartan as a prison cell. Apt, considering where he was going.

He had spent most of the day in Penrose's Toyota Prius, the police constable driving so he could claim for petrol on their return. Out of Cornwall into Devon, hitting the M5 all the way to the M42, then cross-country to the M1 northbound, taking that to Yorkshire and HMP Lazenby. By the time they arrived, they had missed prison's visiting time, but a stay in a chain hotel had been budgeted for. An extremely basic chain hotel.

Radio Two played in the background: Adele, turning misery into money. On the ride up, the atmosphere between the two men in the car had been tense.

"What made you choose the police force, Chris?"

Penrose became thoughtful. "I know you laugh at me. Think I'm a joke."

Tom didn't know how to reply.

"You don't need to deny it. I know they all think I'm young and keen and eager. Too keen. Straight out of college and eager to impress. Show them what I've learned and how I can put it into practice. Well, yes, maybe that's me. Maybe I am."

The car sped up as Penrose's body tensed, responding to his words. He gripped the wheel tighter.

"Chris—"

Penrose laughed. "And they gave me you to babysit. *You*, with your track record!" He gave a grim laugh. "Someone must really hate me."

Tom said nothing.

"Well, think what you like. I'm in this job because it's right for me. And I'm right for it. I know what I'm doing. Oh, you might be like the rest of them, laugh at me with my criminology and sociology degree. But I don't care. I'm putting into practice what I believe. If you want to understand people, understand crime. And vice versa."

Silence in the car. DJ Ken Bruce prattled on in the background.

Penrose smiled. Then laughed and said, "Get a bit carried away sometimes."

"No, passion is good. Never be ashamed of it."

Ice broken, they continued.

"What about you?" said Penrose. "Ex-job and all that."

"Came out of the forces, joined the force. It was that or go to a university, get a degree. And that seemed like hard work. Anyway, long story short, I found I had a talent for undercover work. And I got too good at it. And, since you're my assigned officer, you know the rest."

Penrose nodded. Something from the '90s came on, an Oasis song Tom had never liked but it carried with it a sense of nostalgia nonetheless.

"You ever wish you were back on the job?" Penrose asked.

Tom felt his sore knuckles. "A few more nights like the other night and I'll think I am." He paused. "I just want an easy life from now on." Even as he said the words, Tom felt they were unconvincing. But maybe he'd start believing them if he said it often enough.

"So this guy, Raymond Bain," said Tom eventually, a few kilometers down the road. "Give me what you've got on him."

"I thought you already knew everything," said Penrose. "That's why you wanted to come on this trip."

"I'm on this trip to make sure my life and Lila's life are not in any imminent danger from him. I'm sure there's stuff you've got on him or heard about him that you haven't told me. If all we're doing is eliminating him as a suspect in my break-in, then I think you can tell me."

"Raymond Bain. Human trafficker. It's how he wound up inside. Gareth Mundy—alias Nick West—was his solicitor. Made a lot of money off Bain. Gave him plenty of advice. Bain brought over seasonal workers for farms and construction jobs. Advertised in Eastern Europe. Mundy handled the legal side of things. Then workers didn't want to come anymore because of Brexit, and feeling unwelcome by British people, they thought, screw that. Not coming."

Tom smiled to himself at Penrose's reluctance to swear.

"So with the legitimate market for workers drying up, Bain turned to other revenue streams. Prostitution: bringing women here from Eastern Europe, Africa. He'd promise them work as au pairs or jobs in the fashion industry, all that. Then he'd take their passports away and imprison them in a flat above some

Chinese takeaway or something in Poole or wherever, put them in debt, and beat them if they didn't make his customers happy. Lovely."

"But Mundy fell in love," said Tom, "which put an end to Bain's empire."

"We think so. Or hope so."

"Was Bain into other stuff? Drugs? Guns?"

"Probably, from what we can gather. But it's the human trafficking we got him on. He might have people still out there, working on his supply routes, keeping money aside for him when he gets out. But it's going to be so long until he does, that money's not going to be worth much by then."

"What about Mundy? Was he working for anyone else?"

"Undoubtedly, but we haven't really looked into it yet. Bain was the focus of the investigation. He says he has nothing to do with Mundy's murder or the attack on his son at your house. Which is why I don't understand why you want to see him."

"Because he might have been asked to send me a message by someone else, Chris. You've read my case files. You shouldn't have to ask."

TOM WAS LYING ON THE BED when his phone rang. He picked it up.

"What's your room like?" asked Penrose.

"Exactly the same as yours, I imagine. If I rub my hands on the carpet, my hair stands on end."

Penrose laughed. "Just wondered if you fancied a drink. I'm in the bar here."

The bar. A beige alcove consisting of two beer fonts, neither of which Tom would ever willingly drink, and a sad collection of spirits along the back wall and a smattering of uncomfortable-looking seats paired with stained tables in front of it. A loud TV playing Sky Sports News 24-7.

"You're all right, Chris. Got a bit of reading to do."

Penrose sounded disappointed but didn't push the matter. "OK, then. See you at breakfast. Have a nice evening."

Tom replaced his phone on the bedside table—if he could stretch the description of the small plank of veneer jutting from the wall that far. The display faded to black. The room was in darkness. He had lied to Penrose. He had no reading to do. He kept staring at the scarred black carapace of the phone.

No word from Pearl. No attempt to call him. He hadn't called her either. Not because he didn't want to, but because he didn't know what to say. He was more hurt than he was willing to admit. Too much to say anything out loud. Or even know how to say the right thing. And not just because she left him, but because he feared that everything she'd said might be right.

He lay back on the uncomfortable bed, stared at the ceiling. Thinking what a long night he would have ahead of him.

He picked up his phone.

"Chris? Yeah, me. Hey, still fancy a drink?"

26

SIMON WANDERED THE STREETS of Falmouth aimlessly, looking for something, anything, to break his mood. He searched for omens. Counting seagulls and crows, making up what each bird stood for. Tendering out his happiness to external influences, even if it had no effect on his situation, pretending it did. Making deals with his subconscious if a certain number was reached. If he saw seven gulls in a row, that meant all this would be sorted out and he could go home. Then, counting the birds.

Six . . . no. No seventh bird. And no home to go to.

He turned away from the seafront, slowly made his way back up the hill, the wind at his back, coming in from the sea, carrying with it the threat of sharp salt rain.

There had been swimmers in the sea. Parking up, crossing the road before stripping down to bathing suits. Then running over the shingle into gray water, pausing as the first freezing waves hit them, forcing themselves to become acclimatized, then diving into the swell, swimming out. Simon, bundled inside his parka, couldn't fathom what was going on in someone's mind to want to attempt that. Like things weren't bad enough in your life without stripping and throwing yourself in the freezing cold sea. For fun.

Back up the hill, he headed toward the town center. It was a long walk, but that didn't matter. He had nothing to do, no pressure on his time. Free to go where you like, Mr. Knox had told him. Free. Yeah, right.

Whether cooped up in a strange home, Tom's cottage, or here in the open space, Simon felt anything but free. He was in the world's biggest outdoor prison. His body could move, but there was nothing free about what was inside him.

He had been taken to Mr. and Mrs. Knox's foster home. No one seemed to know what to do with him. He was seventeen, almost an adult. He should have been studying for A Levels, but Simon didn't have anywhere to go. He wasn't in Witness Protection anymore, but he also was not allowed to return to any of the family he had left behind. Social workers were supposedly having meetings about him, but in the meantime, he was in the foster home. There had been underpinnings in place all his life, taken for granted, always holding him up. Now he felt himself slipping through them all.

When he got there, the Knoxes already had two other teenagers staying with them: a boy, Darren, and a girl, Taylor. They seemed wary of Simon, suspiciously sizing him up.

"This is Simon," Mr. Knox had said, "he'll be staying with us for a while. Just till they decide what to do with him. Show him where he'll sleep, Darren. Make him welcome."

Darren had taken him upstairs, pointed to a single bed in the same room as his.

"Where you from, then?"

Simon remembered what he had been told to say by the Witness Protection people, the cover story drummed into him. Did it still matter now?

"Hertfordshire," he said. "Bishop's Stortford."

Darren nodded, not interested. "What you doing down here?"

Simon didn't know how to respond. He felt suddenly alone. He had been so busy moving forward, responding to everything that had happened recently, he hadn't had time to think, let it settle in. He wanted to be somewhere else. Even back in that office, talking to Faisal again.

"Things . . . went wrong." It was all Simon managed to say. He hoped it was enough.

Darren nodded. "None of us would be here if that hadn't happened. Your bed is there. Don't fucking snore."

He left Simon alone in the room.

He sat on his bed, felt like bursting into tears: screaming, shouting, throwing everything around—furniture, bed, the lot. Feeling the impact as objects hit the walls and floor, the vibrations going back up his arms into his chest. More screaming. Ripping his clothes apart and off. Smashing the windows with his fists. Punching the wall until his knuckles were broken and the blood ran down his wrists.

But he just sat there, sadness pressing down on him like a weighted blanket.

He couldn't do that. So he got up, walked out. Shouted in to Mr. Knox that he was going for a walk, didn't wait for any acknowledgment.

He walked through the Old Hill area, where police tape marked off a street. A white tent was erected in front of a run-down block of flats, a couple of police cars parked up front. A uniformed policeman stood at the front door. He stared at Simon, so Simon went the other way.

Eventually, he hit the town center. The front street seemed to have been designed to tempt the tourists in. Old buildings turned into quirky shops, encouraging tourists to feel bohemian for two weeks of the year. There was nothing for him there.

He found a square, saw shops with names that he recognized. He liked that. It made him feel more anonymous. Less conspicuous. He bought a pasty from a bakery, sat on a nearby bench to eat it. He felt numb, a horror-movie zombie, walking through life, no longer living, aware of nothing but the most basic needs. But that was how it had to be because if Simon started to think about much more than that, he'd fall apart.

But other thoughts seeped in. Living at Tom's place hadn't been so bad. People not judging him, letting him be himself, if he knew who that was. Even Faisal seemed all right. The things he'd said were sensible. But that was all gone now.

Anger was pushed down hard inside him, but he knew it was there. After what happened at Tom's, he thought Tom should have fought more for him to stay with them. He would have fought harder if it had been Lila, no doubt. But not Simon. If Tom cared, like he'd said he did, he would have tried harder. But he was just another liar. Like his dad. Like . . . all of them.

He finished his pasty, threw the wrapper in a nearby bin. He took his iPhone out, the expensive gift his dad had given him, useless now because he had no one to call. Except Faisal or Tom. And he couldn't bring himself to do that. So he pocketed the phone, stood up, and started walking again.

He didn't get far. Farther up the street was some kind of commotion, shouting or something going on. He went to investigate. Someone had set up a small stage with posters and balloons fluttering in the drizzle-filled air, and there was noise and movement around it.

Two lines of men emerged from behind either side of the display, dancing—skipping really—all big and ungainly, each with a wooden sword. A troupe of Morris dancers in negative. White men dressed in black. Bowler hats, shirts, trousers, and shoes, with bells attached to their lower legs. One played an unrecognizable tune on an accordion, and the rest made attempts to dance in time to the resulting clamor. They went into a prerehearsed routine in front of the stage, gathering a crowd of watchers the longer they danced.

They looked to Simon burlier than most Morris dancers, with faces like ex-boxers, all mashed noses and cauliflower ears. Black ink tattoos poked from collars and cuffs. But they were all dancing seriously, their eyes incongruously, larcenously hard. The audience smiled and laughed as they cavorted. It was a spectacle, but to Simon it appeared a joyless one.

The men's swords intertwined into something that looked like a medieval star that one of them held aloft while the rest of the troupe orbited. Climax reached, the audience applauded. The men disentangled their swords and split into two lines, standing on either side of the small, raised platform. They seemed more at home there, ready to sort any trouble. A Praetorian guard on a hair trigger.

Simon watched a tall, muscled man with long blond hair tied loosely back, appear on the stage. He wore clothing from ancient times: a tunic, boots, and buckskin trousers. He had a huge sword by his side and rested on it like a walking stick. He looked like Thor from the films come to life. The audience applauded. He acknowledged it, hands raised, smiling.

Simon had never before seen anyone like this man. He stared, open-mouthed.

"Firstly, thank you to my Morris men for that great introduction. And yes, it's me. You've seen me from the telly," said Thor. "My name, if you don't know it, is Arthur King. And I'm here to deliver a message to you."

Arthur King. Simon smiled. Almost laughed. Very clever.

"What's the message? It's this. We've all had enough. Of broken promises. Of lies. Of politicians telling us one thing, then doing another. Doesn't matter what side they're on—or what side they tell you they're on—they all do it. And the bigger the promise, the bigger the lie. Well, let me tell you this. There's going to be a by-election coming up here because of the sudden and unfortunate death of our local MP, Grant Trent. And though it's sad for Mr. Trent's family, we should also seize this opportunity to move forward. To bring forth a new kind of politics. And that's why . . ." He picked the sword up and held it aloft, as if in triumph. "That's why I'm standing for election!"

Some of those in the small crowd cheered and clapped. Simon joined in, smiling to himself, then he stopped, looked around, self-consciously. Maybe the clappers had been planted in the crowd. Preplanned. He suddenly felt stupid.

"If you've seen me on telly or heard me speak, you know what I stand for," said Arthur King. "If you haven't, let me tell you now. It's a new kind of politics that isn't new. Instead, it's a return to tradition. It comes, everyone, from the past, from when England had myths and legends." He paused. "There were heroes . . ."

Another sprinkling of applause. Simon didn't think that one was faked.

"Yes, ladies and gentlemen, England used to be a land fit for heroes. But it's been sadly run down since then. Degraded. Now, I'm not a racist. I think racism, in any form, has no place in our society. Live and let live. I'm not a fascist. I'm not Far Right. I'm not like the other political parties that appear and trade on those things. I'm nothing like that. I'm here as part of a new party. The Heritage Party." Another swing of the sword, another round of applause. "We want to be proud of who we are, of where we came from. Proud of our heritage. You don't have to be racist to do that. You just have to be proud of who you are and where you come from. You don't have to hate Europe. You just have to love England."

Simon looked around. People had stopped shopping, were gathering closer to listen. His words resonated with them.

"Patriotism, the guardians of our civilization tell us, is backward-looking," he continued. "Reactionary. Dangerous. We're all one, they tell us. We're progressive. We're moving forward, leaving all that nonsense behind." He waited, ensured his words connected. "But that's wrong. They say that magic and mystery, wanting to belong to our land, to our history, is wrong. We shouldn't do it, they say, that's the past, not the future. Well, I say, why shouldn't we be proud of where we come from, of who we are?"

Another round of applause. Simon couldn't help himself. He joined in this time, not caring if anyone was watching.

"Do you feel like you don't fit in?" Arthur continued. "Like this isn't your world anymore? Even though they're telling you that you should be just fine fitting in. And if you don't, the problem's yours. Really? Is that right? Is that how our politicians, our newspapers, and TV stations treat us? They're meant to serve us, not the other way around. Not us serving them."

Stronger applause this time.

"Scottish people are proud to be Scottish. No one calls them racists because of it. Same with the Welsh. And the Irish. But we can't. They're small countries in one big one. Why not the biggest one, why not be proud of being English? You see, we have to ask ourselves something. Something important. What does it mean to be us? To be English, right now? It's a difficult question to answer because of—and I'm not being racist here, I'm just stating a fact—because of migration. And we have to acknowledge that. But what we don't do is allow all that hate that goes with it to take over. Because that's what's been happening recently, isn't it?" Arthur King scanned the crowd as if waiting for an answer, then continued before he got one.

"Here in this town, the MP was murdered. An MP who, despite promises, did nothing about immigration. Before that, an African was beaten to death in his restaurant. An African. In Falmouth. And up the road in Redruth, a Polish shopkeeper was burned alive in his shop. All racially motivated attacks. But I say to you, the people that have committed these atrocities can be reached. They can be turned around. They don't have to behave like that. They can be shown that pride is a good thing, a positive thing. It stops us from carrying out attacks like that. These people, these angry people can be shown it's the wrong way to go about things. We can harness that power. Use it for something good. For all of us."

Another pause, letting his words sink in.

"And before that, at Christmastime, that poor family from somewhere outside the region, blowing into town. Look what happened to them."

Simon froze. He knew who Arthur was talking about.

"That poor family." Arthur looked sincerely sad. "They weren't immigrants. They were English, as much as we know— or most were. But things have gone so far that even people from different parts of the country moving somewhere else are attacked. That poor family."

Simon felt himself tearing up. Someone properly understood him.

"I ask you all, are you ready to be counted?" Arthur King's voice boomed. "Are you ready to stand beside me and live once more in a land of heroes? Are you ready for a Britain of legends?"

The applause was not staged. Nor were the accompanying cheers.

Simon smiled. Joined in. For the first time in ages, he felt like he belonged.

27

Walking through the doorway, Tom froze.

He should have expected something like that. Feeling nothing, he had walked toward Her Majesty's Prison Lazenby with Penrose, the bleak high-walled edifice rising out of the mist like an ancient fortress. But as soon as they walked through the gates and he was actually inside, his heart started hammering, and he couldn't move.

"You OK?" asked Penrose.

"Yeah . . ." Tom tried to breathe normally. "Just . . . bad memories coming back."

"You're on the other side of the door this time, Tom. You're going home today."

The last job Tom had undertaken involved going undercover in prison. He'd been lucky to escape with his life. He wasn't looking forward to going back inside, even as a visitor.

Penrose flashed his warrant card at the officer on the gate. They were expected. They waited for an escort, then were led to an empty room on one of the wings and left to wait once more.

"Nothing happens quickly in prison," said Tom.

Eventually, the door opened, and Raymond Bain was led

in. The officer instructed him where to sit. Bain complied. The officer told them he would be right outside if they needed anything, closed the door, and left.

Tom studied Bain, who he was sure was studying him in return.

He appeared to have been carved from a potato. Lumpen and stocky, his hair cut short, his face pockmarked, skin various pallid shades of pink and yellow. Tom recognized the pale, unhealthy indoor pallor of a wing tan when he saw one. Nose was like another potato stuck on his face, ears the same. His tracksuit-clad body was spud-like as well. But two hard, unpleasant little eyes peered out from that starchy face.

"Raymond Bain," said Penrose, opening the file before him. His further speech was cut off.

"Who's this?" Bain pointed a stubby thumb at Tom. "You're filth, but he's not. So who is he, and what's he want here?

"My associate," said Penrose. "We have some questions to ask you."

Bain kept his gaze fixed on Tom. Tom didn't flinch. Just returned the stare, arms folded, giving nothing away. A small smile appeared at the corners of Bain's mouth. A twitch, nothing more. Tom knew he'd been made. Not who he was, but what he was. Copper. Even an ex-copper. Bain had answered his own question.

"What questions?" Bain couldn't have sounded less interested if he tried. "And what's in it for me to answer them?"

Penrose ignored the interruptions, continued. "Your solicitor was a Mr. Gareth Mundy, correct?"

Bain sat back, folded his arms. "This about him? I already told the others. What happened with him and his was nothing to do with me. But I'd like to shake the hand of whoever did it. Just a shame they didn't do it sooner."

Penrose looked down at the file. Tom hoped he was using it as a prop and taking note of Bain's body language and intonations. They were here to study him.

"There was an attack on Mr. Mundy's son a few nights ago."

Bain shrugged. "So?"

Tom studied his reaction.

Penrose looked up, directly at Bain. And in that look Tom saw just how good a copper Penrose really was.

"A vicious attack on a boy, Mr. Bain," said Penrose. "Directed, we think, solely at him. Anything to say about that?"

Bain gave an elaborate sigh. "No."

"You want to shake his hand as well?" asked Tom. "The person who attacked his son?"

Bain looked slightly surprised when Tom spoke, but he managed to cover it well.

"No answer?" said Tom.

Bain's arms dropped to his side. He sat forward. "I don't care either way."

"Did you do it?" asked Penrose, staring straight at him.

Bain smiled. Like a spade slicing through a potato. "I was in here, wasn't I?" Laughing like he'd just told the best joke ever.

"Hilarious," said Tom, his face saying otherwise. "Did you send someone to do it? You hated Mundy enough after what he did to you."

Bain just stared at him. "He recorded our conversations. That shouldn't have been allowed in court. Privileged information."

"Apparently not, considering what you were discussing."

"You think I was the only one?" said Bain, anger welling. "If Mundy did that to me, he did it to others."

Something sparked behind Tom's eyes. He hoped Bain didn't notice. He quickly glanced at Penrose. He had experienced something similar.

Penrose continued, suppressing a smile. "So Mr. Bain, you're not the only person who employed Gareth Mundy?"

"'Course not. He was the go-to lawyer. Everyone knew that."

"So he shared his gifts around among your fraternity."

Tom turned to Penrose. "And recorded other conversations, presumably."

Penrose didn't bother to hide his smile this time. He looked at Bain.

"So did you send someone to take care of Mr. Mundy's son or not?"

Bain sat back, folded his arms. Said nothing. Smiled.

Penrose closed the file in front of him. "Thank you, Mr. Bain. We'll be off now."

Bain looked aggrieved. "That's it?"

"You've told us everything we need to know."

"What d'you mean?"

Penrose allowed himself a smile. "I know you only saw us today because you thought you could get one over on us. Think yourself some kind of master strategist. Make the law squirm. Well, Mr. Bain, you're not. You see"—Penrose leaned forward—"we asked you whether you or someone you know was responsible for the attack on Mr. Mundy's son, and you declined to answer. You think your silence makes us assume you either did it or know who did. And gives you power over us. But it does quite the opposite, in fact. It shows us that you have no idea who carried out the attack." Penrose leaned back into his seat once more. "You don't know anything."

Tom was impressed. Now was the time that Bain, if he knew

anything, would say so. Penrose had damaged his pride with that speech, and pride was all Bain had left.

"But thank you for suggesting another avenue of investigation to us," said Tom. "Assisting the police is always looked on favorably come parole time."

Bain's head dropped. "I want to go back to my cell."

Tom and Penrose both stood.

"Thank you for your time, Mr. Bain," Penrose said before departing.

28

THE YACHT LOOKED LIKE it had been moored, tied off, and abandoned. Two of those things were true.

Its original owner had paid a lot of money for it at a time when money wasn't something to be worried about. But the worldwide financial crash of the late 2000s had changed all that. It had once been moored at a private marina on the River Kenwyn near Truro alongside plenty of other expensive status symbols, and it had belonged to a second-home-owning banker who believed his life was charmed. After the crash, this marina became a Sargasso Sea of floating extended-credit cautionary tales as one after another of the yachts' owners cut their losses and left their boats to rust and rot rather than try and salvage what they could from them materially and financially. Their losses were others' gains, as the more enterprising of those left destitute and homeless by the financial crash got the engines started and piloted these crafts away to less public waters where no questions would be asked. These became their new homes.

A rusting yacht was moored alongside an old towpath beside a closed and rotting soap factory on an industrial estate at the other side of Truro. In its living quarters, Punch lay on the sofa, smoking.

Judy peeked through the curtains. He liked watching the few pedestrians who used the towpath walk by. The place was unrecognizable from its earlier incarnation. Dishes and take-away cartons were piled high in the sink of the galley kitchen, mugs and plates covered every surface of what had been the lounge. Everything was so filthy and mold-encrusted, it could have been a chemical weapon development site. As filthy as the rest of the yacht, the two men's costumes hung on the back of a doorway leading to the bedrooms.

"See anything you like?" said Punch, blowing smoke at the sickly yellow ceiling.

"That blond's gone past again. Yeah. Every day like clock-work. Look at her. Those heels and that skirt."

"Fancy a ride like, do you?"

Judy let the curtain drop, turned back inside. "Yeah, right. Here would be the first place they'd look, wouldn't it? Too much trouble." Judy sighed. "Nice, though."

"Way out of your league. Don't even think it."

Judy didn't reply, just sat down, picked up the novel he was reading. He found his place, tried to read. Couldn't concentrate. So he got up, walked to the kitchen area, looked for a clean or at least less-dirty mug, put the kettle on. Before it could boil, the phone rang.

Punch sat straight up. Judy moved away from the sink. Like they were both in the army, waiting for inspection by a superior officer. Both stared at the phone, wanting the other to answer it. Eventually, Punch picked it up.

Marx spoke straight away. No pleasantries. "The law've found Sullivan's body."

Punch looked at Judy, mouthed the word *Marx*. Judy

nodded, stood there like Marx could see and hear him.

"You both there?"

"We are, Mr. Marx," said Punch.

"Put me on speaker so I can talk to both of you then."

Punch did so, and Marx's voice filled the room.

"Now think hard. Did you leave anything or see anything on the scene that might link Sullivan to me?"

"Of course we didn't," said Punch. "We were careful, just like always."

"You threw Sullivan's dead body in the caravan, then set fire to it?"

Judy looked like he wanted to say something, but Punch refused to catch his eye.

"Yeah," said Punch. "Exactly that. *Boom*, up it went. I mean, his body had bullet holes in it, but there's nothing we could do about that, was there?"

Both Punch and Judy held their breath while Marx was making up his mind whether to believe them or not. They knew that if they spoke before he did, he wouldn't be pleased. And they also knew what happened to people who displeased Marx.

"Right," he said eventually, and the two brothers heaved sighs of relief. "Just wanted to let you know. Give you time to think in case there was something you feel the need to share with me. Because if there is, now's the time. There won't be another."

The two remained silent.

"You sure?"

"We're sure," said Punch. "It went just like we said."

"And anyway," added Judy, "if we have fucked up, you've got plenty of coppers on the payroll to sort it, don't you?"

"Something to tell me, Judy?" Menace dripped from Marx's voice.

Judy swallowed. Hard. Something was lodged in his throat

and he kept trying to clear it. Punch stared at his sibling, eyes wide in horrified disbelief.

"Judy?" growled Marx. "Anything you want to tell me?"

Judy was aware of Punch staring, eyes boring into him like laser death rays. He dropped his head, shook it. "No, Mr. Marx. Nothing. Everything went like we said it did. I only said it because—"

"Let's hope so, for your sake," said Marx. The phone call ended.

"What the fuck did you have to go acting like that for?" asked Punch after putting down the phone. "Fucking idiot. Now he thinks we're hiding something."

"I'm sorry, I was just—"

"You were just being fucking stupid, that's what. You should have kept your mouth shut. How many times?"

Judy's head dropped. "Sorry."

Punch took control of his anger at Judy, his fears of Marx. He stood, paced the room. When he felt mentally prepared, he stopped in front of Judy and said, "Marx doesn't need to know about the money we took. It's none of his business. Sullivan wouldn't care, and he's not here anymore so he can't use it. Marx already has plenty. This was meant for us. So keep quiet about it, right?"

Judy said nothing.

"Got it?"

Eventually, Judy nodded.

"Good." Punch stood back from Judy. "You still making tea?"

29

THE WORLD WAS MONOCHROME. It was daytime, but the weather hadn't been informed. The trees were black against the gray sky, the green-and-yellow grass of the field trampled away to nothing. Rain poured, turning already marshy ground to mud. Tom walked slowly through the clearing, wet earth pulling his boots as he went, sucking him down with every step.

What remained of the caravan was ahead. A police tent covered it and that, along with the border of crime scene tape, looked as out of place in the countryside as a Motörhead fan at a Vivaldi gig. No, thought Tom. That was stereotyping. Motörhead fans could enjoy Vivaldi, just as murder and arson weren't primarily urban phenomena.

"Now don't say anything," said Penrose. "Strictly speaking, you're not meant to be here. We could have done all of this at the station. Or at your place."

Tom winced slightly at the mention of his place. It wasn't somewhere he liked spending a lot of time at the moment, with Pearl and Lila both absent. "Here's fine," he said. "Besides, don't you want the benefit of my years of expertise?"

Penrose struggled to find the right answer. "Just keep quiet, that's all."

They approached the crime scene. The huge tent looked like a grim wedding marquee. They ducked under the tape.

"This way," said Penrose, showing his warrant card to the unlucky, water-soaked officer on sentry duty. Tom nodded and followed him into the tent.

Inside, well-lit against the tent's white background like some contemporary art installation, was a caravan. Or what was left of it: a blackened burned metal skeleton, the remains of charred fixtures and fittings hanging unidentifiably from occasional joints. The grass around it was scorched away and a black greasy surface covered the mud. Next to the caravan was a burned-out car.

"From what I hear," said Penrose, "the caravan doesn't look much different to how it was before the fire. Or the car, for that matter."

"Was that a joke, Chris? There's hope for you yet."

Penrose blushed, tried to say something clever in return but couldn't find the words. Instead, he opened his briefcase, pulled out a file.

While he shuffled through papers, Tom's concentration slipped.

Still no word from Pearl. He'd texted her the day before, thinking that maybe enough time had passed for her to at least speak to him again. Or even learn if he could get his old job back. There was so much he wanted to say, but he thought it best if he didn't put any of that down. Not yet. Just keep it open. Businesslike.

Hey, he texted, heart hammering and fingers trembling, *just wondering if you need me for tonight's shift. Let me know.*

Then signed it *Tom x.*

Then took off the *x.*

Then waited.

He had never felt like this over a woman before. There had been relationships with women in his past, but none lasted. His job put paid to that. Sometimes he had even had girlfriends as part of a cover story. Sometimes they had been other officers, most times not. And when it came time to leave them, he had. It wasn't him who had fallen for that woman, he always told himself. It was the other fella, the persona he adopted as part of his work. Not him. When the job finished, the relationship ended. And Tom walked away a different man.

That he had experienced nothing like this before was strange, in a way, because Tom Killgannon was just another assumed identity—one he hoped to be inhabiting for some long time—if not indefinitely, but still a new persona. And it was *this* person Pearl had fallen for.

Tom was glad Penrose when spoke to him, pulling him back to the present.

"Here we are: Duncan Sullivan," he said, pulling out a sheet of paper. "One of life's more colorful chaps, it would seem."

Tom took the paper, read it.

"You got to the survivalist bit?" asked Penrose.

"Yeah," said Tom, reading on, "son was a chip off the old block."

"He certainly was. His place here, the techies tell us, was like a booby-trapped fortress."

"So he got clumsy and set them off himself?"

"I think that's what we were meant to believe, and we just might if it weren't for the bullet holes in his body."

Tom stopped reading. "Oh."

Penrose was visibly excited, getting into his story now. "As far as we can gather, Sullivan tried to leave the caravan by his escape route."

"Escape route?"

Penrose smiled. "Never watched *Doomsday Preppers*? It's on Netflix. Highly recommend it. Sullivan excavated a tunnel from underneath his caravan into the woods. We found his bag out by the opening. He was prepped, all right."

"So what went wrong?"

"He made it to the end of the tunnel but it looks like someone was waiting there for him. They pumped five rounds into him, then dragged him back to the caravan, left him inside, and detonated the whole place. He had it wired with explosives, of course."

"Of course. So you don't think he did the detonating?"

"Looks like his dead body was tossed into the fire. The pattern of destruction, from the little that remains of the place, would suggest someone went through the caravan first."

"Looking for what: money?"

"Presumably. His bag, when we found it, only had papers in it: passport and the like. New identity. But no money. Which seemed strange. And we've found no record of a bank account. So we think he stashed the money here, in the caravan."

"So someone killed him for his money?"

"Our first thought. And then we found a photo of him. He was on file already. Want to see?"

"I presume that's why I'm here."

Penrose slid out another sheet of paper, handed it to Tom. "Duncan Sullivan, I presume?"

The pic was taken a few years ago, and his hair was shorter, the beard not quite so long, but the similarity was striking. "Yeah. That looks like the man in my house. And from Truro."

"You sure?" Penrose could hardly keep the excitement out of his voice. "Take your time."

"It's a few years old, but . . ." Tom kept studying it. "Yeah. Could well be him."

Penrose smiled.

"What made you think of Sullivan for the break-in at my place?"

"I don't believe in coincidences. Very little like this happens around here. Something as extreme as what happened to the Mundys, then this? Of course, I'd always look for a connection. My theory is that Duncan Sullivan messed up the job at your place and came back here, planning to bug out. But before he could, someone stopped him, killed him, then took all his money."

Tom thought. "Sounds plausible. Which leads to more questions."

"Like who was Sullivan working for? And what was so important that he got killed for it?"

"Exactly. I think you and I should be the ones looking into this," said Tom.

"Why?"

"Come on, Chris, you know why. We've come this far. We're just getting started. Just you and me, on the sly. What d'you say?"

Penrose didn't answer. They stared at the caravan in silence, the rain hammering on the tent's roof.

Tom took Penrose's silence as a yes.

30

LILA WENT INTO ST. PETROC as little as possible. The village held too many bad memories. Also, she felt the locals staring at her as she walked the streets, went into shops, or called in at the Sail Makers pub. Or used to work at. Or would work at again in the future, if Lila had anything to say about it.

She stood outside the Sail Makers, looking up at the window of the apartment above the pub. It was lit, and it was Pearl's night off working the bar, so Lila expected she was at home.

On one side of Lila, just down the winding road to the cove, waves dramatically crashed against seaside rocks. At her other side were the lights of the village. Anju had dropped her off after asking if she needed her to come in as well.

"You need me for support?" asked Anju. "Strength in numbers, you know."

"Thanks, but I think I'd better do this on my own."

Anju understood. "Call when you need me," she said and drove away.

The pub was old stone, had been there centuries. Supposedly, it had smugglers' tunnels going from behind the bar to the caves in the cove. Supposedly. The structure appeared it would be there for centuries more. Permanent. And that's how Lila had started to regard Tom and Pearl's relationship.

It had been a difficult start. The attraction between them was obvious to anyone with eyes. But it had taken time for Lila to fully accept Pearl, for reasons that were bound up with her uneasiness at coming into St. Petroc: the Upheaval. She feared that Pearl might hurt Tom. And that was something she wouldn't put up with. Tom had given Lila a second chance at life, and she wasn't going to let anyone spoil it. Not for her, not for him. However, since then Pearl had more than proved her friendship to both of them, and Lila had come to regard her as part of their dysfunctional family unit. This blowup had upset Lila nearly as much as it had upset Tom. So if there was anything she could do to keep them together, she would make best efforts.

She opened the pub door, entered. Went up to the bar. Someone she didn't know was working it. A middle-aged woman with nicely dyed hair—not too dark, not too light, but covering up the gray—smiling. Lila could imagine her being popular with the clientele.

"What can I get you?" asked the woman.

"I'm here to see Pearl," said Lila. "Is she in?"

The woman's smile slipped slightly but she recovered. She made a play of thinking. "I . . . think so. I'll just go and see. Who shall I say wants her?"

"I'll just pop up. I know the way. We're old friends."

The woman's smile froze in place. "All the same, I think it's best if I check first."

"It's no problem. I'll just—"

"I've just started here, love. All due respect, I don't know you. Wouldn't be doing my job if I just let anyone walk about the place, would I?"

"Suppose not," Lila said reluctantly.

"Won't be a mo." She turned, walked behind the bar. Lila heard her going upstairs.

Lila no longer had the element of surprise. If she'd just walked straight in, Pearl wouldn't have been able to stop her. Now she could pretend not to be in or refuse to see her. She felt angry with herself. And whoever this new woman was.

As Lila waited, she kept her eyes averted from the rest of the customers. Anything she had to say to these people, she'd already said.

Eventually, she heard footsteps on the stairs. Two lots. The barmaid reentered, followed by Pearl. Neither were smiling. Pearl walked straight to the counter.

"Thank you, Shelagh."

The woman took that as a dismissal and disappeared. Lila imagined her eavesdropping from somewhere nearby. She seemed the type.

Pearl looked tired. But more than that, it appeared that a great sadness or depression had settled on her. She tried to give an impression of strength, but it was visibly costing her.

"How you doing?" asked Lila.

"Fine," said Pearl, clearly lying. "Did he send you?"

Lila was taken aback by Pearl's abruptness. "*Erm*, no. He doesn't know I'm here. I just . . . came to see you."

Pearl kept staring at Lila. The facade was close to crumbling.

"Pearl—"

"If you've come here to ask me to go and see him or take his calls or answer his texts or whatever, then you may as well just leave. I don't want to talk to him."

"But Pearl—"

"Is that all you came to say, Lila?" Pearl was trying to sound tough, but it just came out as weary.

Lila looked around, knowing they would be attracting attention. "Can we go somewhere a bit more private to talk?"

"If that's all you've got to say, you can go."

Lila studied Pearl. She was hurt by her reaction. And surprised at its vehemence. "Why are you acting like this? It's me you're talking to."

At those words, it seemed like Pearl might break down. Her hard mask, not firmly in place to start with, was slipping.

"Lila . . ."

Lila waited.

"Pearl? You busy?"

That woman again. At the sound of her voice, Pearl snapped out of her mood. The ice-cold mask fell back in place.

And again: "Pearl?" Pleasant but insistent. The kind of voice that wasn't used to being ignored.

"Yes, Shelagh. In a minute."

Shelagh stood by the doorway, no longer bothering to hide her presence. Staring at Lila. So did Pearl.

"What were you saying, Lila?"

No, Lila's anger was mingled with sadness. She felt she was losing one of her best friends.

Shelagh walked up behind Pearl, placing her hand gently on her back.

"I think you'd better go," she said to Lila.

Lila stared back at this interloper, still hoping Pearl would say something, come to her senses.

"Go on now," said Shelagh.

"Pearl?"

Pearl turned away.

With no other choice, Lila turned and left.

Outside, while phoning Anju, she looked back in through the window. Pearl was still standing where she'd been, slumped against the bar like a puppet with her strings cut. Shelagh had her arm around her shoulders and appeared to be whispering to her. Pearl was nodding, clearly holding back tears.

Lila turned, angry but not really knowing who at, and walked away to meet Anju. Remembering, as she walked, a phrase from an old play or poem or something she had studied in English, something about having poison poured in the ear.

31

SIMON KNOCKED on the old steel-framed door, waited. He used the time to straighten his hair, plastering his bangs to one side, huffing into the palm of his hand to check again that his breath was fresh. He held leaflets and a clipboard and had a smile ready for whoever opened the door.

The door opened, and an obese middle-aged white man stood before him. Face as red as his vest was white. Zip-fronted cardigan over the top, joggers on his legs. He stared at Simon. The smell emanating from the interior of the house behind him told Simon the front door hadn't been open for some time.

"Yeah?"

"Hello," said Simon, taking a leaflet from his collection and holding it out. "I'm from the Heritage Party."

"Oh God, not another one," the man said, about to close the door on him.

"Arthur King?" said Simon. "You know him?"

"No." The door stopped as the man thought. "Wait a minute. Arthur King? Is he that long-haired bloke on the telly? Swinging a sword around?"

"That's the one."

"And he's what, what you here for then, what you selling?"

"Well, you know, the by-election is coming up and—"

"The what? By-election? What, around here? What for?"

"Your local MP has unfortunately died. And now there's an election to find a replacement. And Arthur King is standing."

"Oh, right, yeah." The man seemed interested.

Emboldened, Simon continued with his speech. "Can I just take a few minutes of your time to tell you about the Heritage Party and what we stand for? And Arthur King himself?"

"Heritage, eh? Go on then, son."

"We're a party for everyone. And, er . . ." Simon tried to remember the script he had been drilled on. "We, we have to move forward, or rather if we are to move forward we have to acknowledge our collective past. Our history. Our heritage. Relearn who we are as a people. As a race."

The man stared at him.

Simon took the man's silence for encouragement. He continued. "Reestablish a connection with our past. Not just our history but our . . ." Think, Simon. ". . . our myths and legends. And not just the legends, but the facts. No, not just the facts but the dreams. Of who we once were, and could be again. The dreams of Albion." Simon finished, waited.

"This Arthur King, he's all for sending them back, isn't he?"

Simon stared, didn't know what to say.

"That's what he said on the telly, anyway. The Muslims, and that. Sending them back. Yeah well, I'll vote for him. Seems like a good bloke. And you're a good lad as well." The man smiled and closed the door.

Simon was confused. He'd never heard Arthur King say anything of the sort. In fact, Simon was sure he had said the exact opposite. He walked away from the house, frowning.

"You OK, son?"

Simon looked up. Arthur King's agent, Raheem Nazir, was standing there on the sidewalk, his Crombie overcoat collar pulled up, gloved hands slapping his sides to keep warm.

"Yeah," said Simon, puzzlement showing on his face. "I just gave that speech, you know, the one we talked about, and then he just asked if we were going to send them back."

Nazir smiled. "And what did you say?"

"I didn't say anything."

"Is he voting for Arthur?"

"He said he would."

"Then what you worried about? Job well done."

"Yeah, but—"

"Simon," said Nazir, taking him by the arm and walking him along the wet pavement, "a vote's a vote. That's all that matters."

"But Arthur never said anything like that. Never."

Nazir shrugged. "Worked though, didn't it?" He studied Simon, choosing his next words carefully. "Come on, Simon. If Arthur doesn't get in, then he can't do anything, can he? Can't make a difference. So if we have to get someone like that nasty man to vote for him, we'll figure out a way to do it. Sort the niceties out later. Yeah?"

Simon still frowned. "Yeah, but—"

"No *buts*. There it is. Now, where to next?"

After seeing Arthur King's speech onstage, Simon had tried to approach him. He ended up speaking to Raheem Nazir, who took his contact details and asked his age. Eighteen, Simon had said, adding a few months. Nazir shrugged as if to say he didn't care one way or the other, and said he'd be in touch.

Simon was contacted at the foster home and told to come to the campaign headquarters for a volunteers' meeting. It was the most positive, exciting thing that had happened to him in ages.

He turned up at the given address to find a disused retail unit away from the main shopping area, surrounded by run-down and empty shops and closed takeaways. But one storefront had its windows full of Arthur King posters. He slipped inside. There were a few desks and lots of campaign literature, flyers, and posters. People sat at the desks, talking on phones. The shop's old shelving had been moved to the sides of the room, its till to the back. When Nazir spotted Simon, he came over and greeted him, told him to go through to the back room.

The front room looked luxurious by comparison. Back there were old mismatching plastic chairs and a cracked sink and draining board with a kettle on it. A flip chart had been set up. There were others gathered in the room's seats. Simon felt anxious, thinking this might have been a bad idea after all. However, Nazir took that moment to enter, and he told Simon to sit down.

They were briefed about the campaign, told to stress the pride and patriotism angle, say that Arthur was going to be a voice like no one had heard in politics before. Representing the people no one listened to, that everyone else ignored. He took them through scenarios of what to do on the doorstep when meeting antagonism, what to do with an undecided voter, or even an enthusiastic one. Simon—despite or perhaps because of everything he had been through recently—enjoyed it. Glad he had come after all.

They were then assigned their areas and told to go out, put leaflets through doors, stop and talk to certain addresses. How would we know which was which? Simon asked. Nazir told them they would be given a list to work from. When one volunteer asked how the list had been compiled, where they got the names from, Nazir had smiled, said it was a secret.

Simon had a new life.

As he walked beside Nazir, he thought about what the fat man on the doorstep had said.

"Raheem, are you Muslim?"

"Born Muslim, yeah. Why?"

"Well, that guy I just spoke to mentioned sending back Muslims. Doesn't that annoy you? Working for Arthur as well?"

"Why should it?"

It wasn't the answer Simon had been expecting. "Because you're a Muslim."

Raheem smiled. "You're white, yeah?"

"Yeah."

"Christian, non-religious, whatever. But white. Do you walk down the street and see every other white person and smile at them? Or think you've got something in common with them because they're white?"

"No, course not."

"Then why d'you think I should feel that way about Muslims? Couldn't care less, mate. They're not my brothers and sisters any more than they are yours. D'you care about Muslims?"

Simon frowned. "I've never really thought about it."

"Then don't." Nazir smiled. "Good lad. You'll go far with us, I can tell."

He escorted Simon down the street to the next address.

32

With the late winter rain hitting hard and the wind off the Atlantic pummeling even harder, Newquay was positively ugly. But Tom was biased against the place. He had history in Newquay. Not the happy kind.

Lila had been imprisoned by a drug gang there and had, with his help, fought her way out. It hadn't been pleasant, and they'd both vowed never to go back there again if they could help it.

But Tom couldn't help it.

Newquay might have been charming in its heyday, but that was long past now. The old-fashioned seaside town had died and returned as a destination for stag and hen parties. Tom had found the place already rough and impoverished, and the consequent refocusing of the bars and restaurants to chase this new clientele had only resulted in a further coarsening, as well as deepening resentment between the residents and the tourists whose money they relied upon.

Driving through the seemingly arbitrary one-way system in the town center and taking in all the failing businesses and semi-thriving themed bars, Tom thought it was the kind of place you had to be off your face to tolerate, never mind enjoy.

He blocked out the past and concentrated on the present, on why he was there. Slowing down, he checked the satnav on his phone: the woman lived just around the corner.

Claire Hightower was the name Penrose had given him.

"Why are you telling me this?" Tom had asked the previous day. "Surely she's been interviewed already?"

Penrose had come around to Tom's house the day before, after making sure no one else was there first. He was out of uniform, trying to be as plainclothes as possible.

"Yes," Penrose continued, "Claire Hightower has been questioned. She's a prostitute in Newquay. Sullivan used to meet her in the pub there, or at her place, do . . . what he wanted, then go home again."

"That's generally how it's done, I believe."

"I mean, she didn't have a relationship with him beyond that." Getting slightly angry at Tom's dig.

"But you think there's more she has to say."

"She didn't respond too well to the police, and we got nothing. She doesn't like coppers. You might have more luck. Worth a try, anyway."

Tom pulled up in front of an apartment block that held a dying dream behind each door. He locked the Land Rover and checked the notes on his phone for her apartment number: eight. He walked up to the main door, rang the buzzer. Waited. Eventually, a tired voice answered.

"Claire Hightower? Could I have a word?"

A pause. "You police?"

"No, I'm not police. But I do want to talk about Duncan Sullivan. Could I come in, please?"

"What d'you want to know?"

"It'll be a lot easier if I come in."

Another pause. Tom could almost hear her thinking, calculating. *Was this going to be worth money?* He'd expected that.

"I'm willing to pay for your time."

The door buzzed open.

He made his way down a corridor that stank of neglect and sweated-out linoleum. At number eight, he stood in front of a plain door and waited. When it opened, he saw that Claire Hightower looked as tired as her voice had sounded. She looked fifty, but Tom was sure she was younger. Had a hard paper round, as his sister would have said. Her gray roots showed, and her face held ingrained laughter lines from a joke that ceased being funny years ago. Despite all that, Tom still glimpsed the ghost of the girl she'd been, which made her current state all the sadder.

"How much?" The phrase came easily to her lips with a well-practiced resignation.

"Fifty. If you've got something to tell me."

She paused, calculating. Tom expected she'd think up something to tell him.

She nodded and beckoned him inside.

The flat was furnished in a style he recognized from his own upbringing. An off-brand wide-screen TV and a dirty faux leather cream three-piece. Glass topped occasional tables that had given up waiting for occasions and now held overflowing ashtrays. He sat down on the sofa.

Claire Hightower wore jeans and a sweatshirt. Her face was composed, stiff like a death mask. Nothing could penetrate, make her feel anything. She sat in the armchair opposite him. Lit a cigarette, exhaled. Didn't offer him one.

"Money first," she said.

Tom handed over a fifty-pound note. She made it disappear. Settled back.

"What d'you want to know about Sullivan?"

"He broke into my house a few nights ago. Came at me armed with a knife. I had to fight him off. Did the police tell you any of this?"

She blinked. "No. They didn't. I haven't seen him for a while."

"What did the police say to you about him? What did they ask you?"

"When I last saw him. Who his friends were. If I heard anything about his death." Her breath caught on that final word.

"And?"

Hightower took a moment to remember. "I saw him over a month ago. I don't know who his friends are. I don't know anything about anything else."

"When you saw him, you . . ."

"Had sex, yeah. And he paid me for it. Want to make some snide comment like those coppers did?"

"No. That's none of my business. I just want to know about the man who broke into my house and attacked me. What did he say when you last saw him?"

"What d'you mean? Like, sex talk? He wasn't much of a one for that."

"Did he mention other people, things he'd been up to, that kind of thing?"

"You didn't know him. If you did, you'd know how ridiculous that question is."

"Not much of a talker?"

"The strong silent type where sex talk was involved. Which was a relief. You wouldn't believe the bullshit some of them come out with."

"I can imagine."

She gave him a look that hovered between pity and contempt. "I don't think so."

Tom felt himself reddening. Tried again. "How did you meet him?"

"He came into the pub I drink in. People know it's the place to come if you want some business. He wanted business."

"And you were happy to go with him?"

She gave him that look once more.

"Right," said Tom. "And Duncan Sullivan never told you anything about himself? Where he lived even? What he did?"

She drew down smoke, thought. "He would talk once the sex was over and done with."

"What kind of things?"

"About himself, mainly. Like how he lived off the grid. His words. Was cash rich. Didn't trust banks. Kept it somewhere no one could find it. Maybes he was showing off, telling me that. Only said it once. Mostly he said nothing, just turned up when he was in the mood. Got what he wanted and left again." She frowned. "But sometimes, after a couple of drinks, he would start on about his philosophy."

"Which was?"

"England for the English, and all that. Don't trust the government. Any government. Our history, our heritage. I didn't ask him about it. I wasn't interested. It sounded like he'd heard someone else say it and was repeating it."

"What makes you say that?"

Hightower almost smiled. "He wasn't a great thinker."

Tom processed what she had told him. "Cash rich," he said. "What from? Did he say what he did?"

"Not really, but once when he was drunk, he said he was a dangerous man."

"A dangerous man?"

"Yeah. Who worked with other dangerous men for an

even more dangerous man, and he said that it paid well and it was for the greater good."

Tom wondered what Sullivan had thought was "the greater good." He asked, "Was he dangerous when he was with you? Were you afraid of him?"

She smiled. Back on solid ground once more. "*Nah.* Some are scary, but not him. He was like a kid. Like he'd hardly ever been with a woman. Didn't know what to do. Just a need he had to take care of, then off he'd go."

"Was there a pattern to when you saw him? Number of weeks or something?"

"Not really. Not . . . Well, he always said he'd just done a job when he came to me. Had some cash. Whatever he did must have made him horny."

Tom thought of the attack on the Wests. "If I gave you some dates, would that help?"

She reached over to the overflowing ashtray, stubbed out the end of her cigarette. "Not really. I'm not big on diaries. I'm not Heidi fucking Fleiss."

Tom smiled. Hightower joined in. The atmosphere in the room had changed just slightly. For the better.

She kept smiling, this time at a memory. "He asked me to go away with him, you know."

"When? Where?"

"The last time he came to me. Said he was making a lot of money, doing some work that he enjoyed, that he was good at. It would pay well enough for a holiday. Asked me to go with him."

"And would you have?"

"If he was paying and it was to somewhere decent, why not?"

"And he never mentioned Tom Killgannon or breaking into my house? Never mentioned any other names?"

She thought again. "Just one. But not really. Well, kind of."

"What d'you mean?"

"He wanted me to go somewhere else with him, to see someone. This was a couple of months ago. Don't know what he'd been doing, but he was on a real high from it. Pounded the fuck out of me that night. Like he had something inside him he wanted rid of."

"So what was the name?"

She screwed up her face, thinking. Tom said nothing, not wanting to break her concentration. Eventually, she found a name. "Tarpley. That was it." She opened her eyes, pleased with herself. "Tarpley."

Tom thought. "Tarpley? Doesn't . . . no. Don't know that one."

"Ben Tarpley, that was his name."

"Why did Sullivan want you to go and see him?"

"He's a professor at the university. Falmouth, I think. And he gives talks on that stuff Sully liked. England for the English, that kind of thing."

"A political meeting? That's what he wanted to take you to?"

"Sully said it wasn't like that. It wasn't like Tommy Robinson or Nigel Farage or anything. The man was a professor. It wasn't racist, he said, just a new way of thinking, of being patriotic."

"Ben Tarpley, University of Falmouth." Tom made a note in his phone. "And did you go?"

"'Course not." She lit another cigarette. "Not my kind of thing. I mean, there probably is too many immigrants, but around here we need them, don't we? So what d'you do?"

Tom didn't answer. "Was there nothing else he said? No other names he mentioned?"

She thought but he could tell what her answer would be. Whatever moment they had shared, it had now passed.

Tom stood. "Thanks for your time. If there's anything else you think of, anything at all, no matter how insignificant it might be, give me a call." He handed her a card with his phone number on it.

Hightower took it and smiled. "Want me to give you a call, do you?"

Tom didn't know quite how to answer.

"Just joking with you," she said, but there was a sad tone to her voice.

He smiled. Made his way outside.

Out of Newquay as fast as possible.

33

ANOTHER NIGHT AT ANJU'S PARENTS' HOUSE, and Lila tried to work out how she was feeling.

She felt like part of the family in a way, but in other ways, she felt like she would never be, no matter how long she stayed there. She was an outsider for many reasons, not just her skin color. There was her religion—or lack of it—but mainly it was because Lila's life experiences had shaped her so much that she thought she'd always be an outsider . . . anywhere apart from at home with Tom. They'd been two outsiders together.

She understood why she was still at Anju's—with the potential for another house attack it wouldn't be wise for her to stay there—but she wanted to go home. She wasn't good at living on someone else's terms, not even the fairly liberal ones Anju lived under.

She was trying to make the most of it.

"Faisal, can I have a word?"

Sitting in the living room after dinner, Faisal looked up from his newspaper, *The Guardian*. He was one of the few people to still take their news from the printed word. And proud of it, he'd told her. "Yeah. Sure." He folded the paper, waited.

Karima had gone out to a spin class—or was it a book club, Lila couldn't keep track—so there were just the three of them in the house. Anju knew what Lila wanted to say and was conveniently absent.

Lila sat in the armchair opposite him.

"It's Tom," she said. "Well, it's not really. It's Pearl, actually."

"The two of them still not back together?" asked Faisal.

"Yeah. That's what I wanted to talk about." Lila took a deep breath. She wasn't good with authority figures, and Faisal, no matter how friendly he was to her, was just that. "I know he said Pearl doesn't want to see him anymore. Because she saw him, well, defending himself, and she went off on him."

"She said what she saw in his eyes scared her," said Faisal, gently, "so much so she wasn't sure she could be with him any longer."

Lila felt slightly deflated at the correction, but she persisted. "Well, do you think that's fair? I mean, they've been together a while, and look how they came together. It's not like this is news to her. Or it shouldn't be, should it? So why now?"

Faisal thought before answering. "In relationships, it's not always as clear-cut as that. A person may change, evolve in a way their partner does not. Or perhaps something that once attracted them to their partner is now the thing that repels them. There's no simple answer."

"Yeah, but Pearl was all for taking Simon in. And me too. Tom was the one who had to be talked into it. And he didn't want to, in case something like . . . what happened happened. So Pearl can't claim it was unexpected, his response to that."

"You think there's another reason?"

Lila thought before answering. Faisal waited.

"I went to see her the other night."

"Anju said."

Lila paused, momentarily annoyed. Had her girlfriend betrayed her confidence?

Faisal sensed her discomfort. "Anju didn't tell me anything more than that, and I didn't press her. She said only that the visit hadn't gone well. Is that right?"

"Yeah. There was this a woman there, the barmaid called Shelagh. At first she didn't want to let me see Pearl. But she did, as long as it was in the bar, in public. And I just know she was hiding somewhere when Pearl and I spoke, listening all the time. Basically, this woman Shelagh wouldn't let me talk to Pearl, not even just to see how she was."

"And how did she seem?"

"Pearl? Awful. Like she could barely hold it together. In bits. Like she was just a doll and this woman was working her. And she seemed to be running the pub too."

Faisal thought. "And how did this woman seem? Like she was a friend, a confidante?"

"Nothing like that. I didn't get a good vibe from her. I feel like she's using Pearl in some way. Like she wants something."

Faisal became thoughtful once more. "There's not a lot to go on, really. What do you want me to do about it?"

Lila was surprised at the question. "Well . . . can't you, I don't know, stop her? Talk to Pearl, tell her what this woman's doing, make her see?"

"And go back to Tom?"

Lila dropped her head. "Yeah. That too."

Faisal gave a sad smile. "It's not as easy as that. I can't do anything unless Pearl comes to see me and asks for my help. And before that, Pearl must come to the realization that what you say is true, that, let's say, she's fallen into a kind of abusive or at the least unhealthy relationship with this woman Shelagh, that she has a hold over her and that

Pearl wants to get away from her. Then I could put together strategies to help."

"But can't you just go and see her? See for yourself what she's like? She'll listen to you."

"I expect she'd treat me just the same as she treated you. I'm sorry, Lila, I know you wanted me to give you a different answer, but I can't. Perhaps Tom could go to see her?"

"She won't see him. Or answer his calls or anything."

"Then we have to hope that Pearl changes her mind. Or that this woman Shelagh isn't all that bad and actually wants to help her."

He saw the look on Lila's face. Impotent anger crossed with a heartbreaking belief in goodness.

"I'm sorry," he said. "Really."

Lila thanked him and left the room.

She closed the door of her bedroom and worked through everything that had happened, along with all the attendant emotions.

Nearly an hour later, she smiled. Her mood had lifted. Lila had a plan.

34

THE COFFEE SHOP in the University of Falmouth was a glass-and-steel rectangle with open metal supports and glass windows overlooking the campus on Portland Square. The only thing giving it any character were the students. A sunny day saw the braver of them venturing outside, optimistic and coatless, while others populated the blond wood chairs and tables, along with a few lecturers. The words EAT and DRINK hung on banners either side of the entrance, an instruction more than an invitation.

Tom Killgannon sat alone, nursing his white Americano. He checked his watch. Slightly early. Good. He'd be able to spot Ben Tarpley when he arrived.

After meeting Claire Hightower, Tom had thoroughly researched him. There was plenty to read. So much so that Tom wondered why he hadn't heard of him before. But perhaps it wasn't so strange. He was reaching an age when some huge cultural things were beginning to pass him by. He hadn't heard of Stormzy until fairly recently and that was only through Lila. Understandable, because he was hardly the man's target demographic, but he was gladdened by the discovery. Tom had liked what he heard by Stormzy. What Ben Tarpley said, not so much.

His interviews and speeches were all depressingly familiar. He was a rabble-rousing blowhard of the first order. Apparently, he'd spied a gap in the hate speech market for someone to articulate and boost the signal of those with unpleasant and abhorrent far-right opinions, making their words palatable and even acceptable for a mainstream audience—while, of course, monetizing his ideas in the process. He was an articulate Nigel Farage with a degree, a cut-rate Jordan Peterson wannabe, all the while hiding hate speech behind the banner of free speech.

Tarpley's rhetoric was the usual demagoguery: demonizing foreigners, especially nonwhites and those of different religions. A belief system where all that fear could be externalized and utilized without any thought or inner reflection. Doubts erased, questions ignored. A terrified, and terrifying, luxuriance of hatred. And Tarpley's Get Out of Jail Free card? It couldn't be hate speech because he was a well-educated and well-spoken academic.

Clever but limited, thought Tom. He'd come across Tarpley's type before in his undercover work with the police. They fleeced their followers and acolytes for every hate-tinged penny they could get while only truly believing in the money that fattened their bank accounts and the gullibility of the marks providing it. It was all an act, a game as realistic and honest as professional wrestling. And people fell for it. Embraced it and believed in it.

Tom didn't have long to wait. Ben Tarpley entered the coffee shop as if expecting to be seen, disappointed if he was ignored. No one paid him any attention, Tom noticed. He stood poised like a Soviet-era poster come to life: back straight, deportment slow, head held high, jaw firm, resolute even. His frame was slight but his self-confidence radiated an impression of strength. He dressed like a successful bank manager or talk show host, not a university lecturer. He made his way straight to Tom. Stood over him.

"Mr. Killgannon?"

Tom looked up. "That's me. Ben Tarpley?"

Tarpley remained standing, completely still as if expecting Tom to rise to greet him. Compelling him to do so, even. Suspecting this, Tom stayed seated.

"Pull up a chair," Tom said.

Tarpley, not wanting to appear bested and giving the impression it had been his idea all along, did so. He studied Tom, a quizzical expression on his face, arms folded across his chest.

"I must admit, your request to see me made me curious."

"Why's that?" Tom stretched back in his chair. If Tarpley was going for rigid and formal, Tom would do the opposite.

Tarpley leaned back, checked his watch. Smiled. A game player, thought Tom.

"I'm looking into Duncan Sullivan's life. I heard that you know him."

Tarpley frowned. "Duncan Sullivan? Don't recall the name. Was he a student of mine?"

"Not as such, no. Not here, I mean. At the university."

Tarpley's eyes narrowed. "Can I just ask you where you're from or who it is you're representing? You were vague on the phone."

"I'm representing myself, Mr. Tarpley."

"I got the impression you were a . . . private detective?" He loaded the phrase with as much irony as he could manage, even going so far as to raise an eyebrow.

"I'm investigating something, yes. But I'm not a professional investigator."

Tarpley sighed, rolled his eyes. Gave an insincere smile and made to stand. "Have a good day, Mr. Killgannon."

Tom stayed where he was. "Duncan Sullivan broke into my house. He assaulted me, attempted to kill me with a knife. I managed to overpower him, and he escaped. The caravan he lived in was later found burned, with his body inside. He'd been shot."

Tarpley stared at him. Tom could almost see the machinations of his mind expressed on his face: whether to deny he knew the man, walk away, or sit back down and tell Tom what he thought he would want to hear.

Tom waited. Tarpley, he could tell, would do what was best for Tarpley.

He sat down again. "Murdered, you say." His features composed themselves into concerned shock.

"That's right. Just after Sullivan paid me a visit." Tom said nothing more, just looked at the other man. Waited.

"And what has this to do with me? You think I murdered him? The police haven't been to see me."

"No, but they will when I tell them what I know."

Tarpley smiled once more, nodded. "You think you can blackmail me, is that it? Say I knew the man or put him up to it or something. How preposterous. How tedious."

"Not at all," said Tom. "I just want to know who sent Sullivan to my house and why. I want to make sure they leave me alone in the future. Interesting the way your mind works, though."

Another smile from Tarpley, one that said he was back on familiar ground. "What do you know about me, Mr. Killgannon? About my work?"

Tom stared evenly at him as he spoke. "You're a far-right

mouthpiece that makes a living from exploiting the scared, vulnerable, and ignorant. And because you've got letters after your name, you think you should be given a platform and your opinions taken seriously."

Another raised eyebrow was the only visible response. "Interesting but inaccurate, of course. I'm not Far Right, as you would have it. I'm proposing a new kind of national pride. We aren't saying our culture is better than anyone else's. No. We're just saying this is our culture. And we're proud of it."

"And you say all that with enough spaces in between for people to fill in their own twisted opinions for themselves. For people to use your words to excuse and encourage—to justify even—racial violence."

"That's not my intention. You can't blame me if that happens."

"You're a white supremacist, though. You can't deny that."

Tarpley shrugged. "I'm an advocate of and a believer in the indigenous British people. They're white. They—*we*—are the dominant culture in the land. And we celebrate and take pride in that fact." He sat back, firmly in his own territory. "Did you come here for a debate, Mr. Killgannon? Because I'm happy to provide one. And I'll win, of course."

Tom was tempted to take him up on that; the man had annoyed him. But he swallowed his emotions, fell back on his training, kept to what he was there for. "Some other time, perhaps. I just want to know about you and Duncan Sullivan."

Tarpley shrugged once more. "Ask. I'm an open book."

"Sullivan could quote your speeches. He used to attend meetings you held. Fascist meetings. Rallies. That kind of thing."

Tarpley opened his mouth to speak.

"Don't bother to deny it, it's a matter of record."

Anger flashed in Tarpley's eyes. "I have held forums for a

free exchange of nonmainstream views. There's nothing secret about that."

"Yeah, and all these views happened to be on the Far Right. Holocaust denial, eugenics, white supremacism, the usual stuff. Even legitimizing the QAnon fuckwits. And all as far away from the campus as possible."

Another glare.

"I'm sure they like having you here or at least tolerate you, bit of notoriety and all that, but even you wouldn't shit on your own doorstep."

Tarpley stood up. "This conversation has run its course."

"Fine. I'll let the police know, then. University might not like that kind of publicity, though. Controversial lecturer in murder inquiry . . ." Tom gave a grim smile. "There's tolerance, and then there's dragging their name through the mud."

Tarpley sat down again. Tom was certain the man wanted to kill him. Or at least do him serious harm. "Ask your question, then leave."

"Sullivan attended your meetings. That's a fact. I want to know who he met there, what he did. I want to know all about the membership and what you were planning. You must have been planning something. Someone like you doesn't start holding meetings like those without an endgame in mind."

"We attract disparate people," said Tarpley. "There is a need for the meetings. A yearning in the area. We want to take people's anger at seeing other less deserving sorts get further ahead. We try to mold that anger, channel it into something positive."

"A political party?"

"The Heritage Party. You may have heard of it. It's putting all our beliefs into practice."

"And you're behind that?"

Tarpley paused. "I dissociated myself from it."

"Why?"

"Because—let's just say there was an element beginning to emerge there I didn't like."

"Or couldn't control."

"What we were doing wasn't enough for some. They wanted to go further. Take to the streets. Confrontation. Physical action. Violence. I'm against that in any form. That isn't what my work is for. And I remember Sullivan's name. He was one of those most enthusiastic about the aggression, shall we say."

"Who else was?"

Tarpley made a play of thinking then sighed. "I don't know. I can't recall all the names. Sullivan got together with that element, like I said, and they started—well, it was strange what they wanted to do."

"Like what?"

"We'd discussed myth and folklore, how we had to regain it, harness it for our movement, take pride in it. These fellows took it . . . not further but sideways, I suppose. They began dressing as the characters. Enacting scenes."

"What kind of scenes?"

Tarpley stared at him. "Fight scenes."

Tom smiled. "Folklore fight club? Really?"

Tarpley didn't smile. "You have battle reenactment societies. They're very popular around here. These men dressed as characters from popular myth and folklore. Who they felt best represented them. That they could in turn represent. There's no difference."

"Except they were doing it for real."

Tarpley nodded. "Exactly."

"Did they meet anywhere special for this? A specific location?"

"I have no idea. This was a bastardization of my work, so I severed all connections to it."

"And it still goes on now?"

Tarpley shrugged. "I have no way of knowing. As I said, I no longer have any connection with the Heritage Party. I may agree with them in spirit but not in practice."

"And have you a list of names of those involved in your meetings?"

"Yes."

"Could I have it?"

A triumphant smile crept over Tarpley's face. "No. You'd need a court order for that. Or the police will have to compel me to part with it. As you said, you're"—he raised his shoulders in a shrug—"nobody, Mr. Killgannon." Tarpley stood. "I hope you've had an enlightening meeting."

And he was back up the stairs and away, head held high, smile in place as if acknowledging applause only he could hear.

35

NIGHT FELL HARD ON ST. PETROC. The paucity of street-lights, the lack of illuminated front windows in the center of the village, and the absence of nearly anything open at night meant that shadows were cast long and deep. The streets, never very busy during daylight, were deserted in darkness. Down an unlit cobbled alleyway off the main high street, something moved in the shadows, careful not to be seen by any curious eyes, no matter how unlikely that was.

The shadow turned left, moved along another unkempt back alley, home to abundant weeds and hidden piles of dog shit. It stopped in front of a wooden gate and spoke in hissed, urgent tones.

"Listen. I thought I heard something."

Lila sighed. "You might have. We're not the only living things out here tonight, you know."

Anju fell silent, still nervous. Anxiety emanated from her like radio waves.

"And this is definitely the right place. And she's definitely not in."

Lila sighed. "If you didn't want to do this, you should

have let me come on my own."

"Yeah. And be worried sick about you the whole time."

"Then stop worrying. You're here. You've come with me. Head in the game now. Yeah?"

Anju nodded. "Yeah."

"Good. Come on."

Lila had discussed her plan with Anju the previous night. No surprise: Anju had not been impressed.

"You're going to break in to this Shelagh woman's place? Her gallery? What . . ." She shook her head, pacing her bedroom. "What for?"

"Because there's something off about her, and I need to find out what. She's already poisoned Pearl's thoughts; I want to figure out what she's up to. See if there's anything in there that might give us a clue."

"So what do we do if there is? We can hardly go to the police and tell them, can we? 'Sorry, Officer, we broke into her house because we thought she was a wrong 'un.' What would they say to that?"

"We don't go to the police though, do we? We don't need to. We talk to Tom. He'll know what to do. Then he can go and see Pearl, confront her with what's going on."

Anju stared at her, saw the desperate hope in Lila's eyes, wanting to believe that her actions could bring Tom and Pearl back together again. Focusing all her energy, her blame for their breakup, on this Shelagh woman. Hoping that with her out of the way, everything could go back to what Lila clung onto as normal. Anju sighed. It was heartbreaking to see the girl she loved so desperate for her family.

"You won't be talked out of it, will you?"

Lila frowned. "Why would you want to do that?"

"Because that's supposed to be my job. Be my father's daughter

and say this is a terrible idea. That it won't help, won't change anything, and might make things worse. Especially if you get caught."

"I won't get caught." Eyes still downcast.

Anju had sat down next to Lila on the edge of the bed.
Taken her hand in her own. "No, you won't. I can't talk you
out of it, so I'm not going to let you do it on your own."

Tears had crinkled the corners of Lila's eyes. Anju hugged
her so she didn't have to see those tears fall.

AND NOW HERE THEY WERE, about to enter the gallery from
the back entrance. Anju, heart racing, hands shaking, wished
she hadn't been so keen. She took a deep breath, tried to steady
herself.

"Right," she said. "Head in the game. Let's go."

The back alley looked to Anju like something out of *Cor-
onation Street*: a row of old brick-and-stone walls, overhead
height, interspersed with doors. Some doors were heavy metal,
padlocked. Others, wood. Behind those doors, the backyards
were virtually nonexistent as the owners of the properties had
extended out to the back gate.

The gallery was no different. The back gate led to a
one-story extension at the back. One small window in the
center, just underneath the roof's apex.

"That's where we get in," whispered Lila.

Anju knew Lila had made a thorough reconnaissance of
the area, worked out the best way to get inside at the best time.
Anju would have said the door was the best bet, but it was
one of the padlocked metal ones, a hangover from the gallery's
butcher days.

"Give me a hand."

Anju knit her fingers together, braced herself for Lila's

weight. Lila placed her foot there and, clasping an external drainpipe, pulled herself up the side of the building.

Anju's heart started hammering. If someone spotted them, would she run and leave Lila? Or wait for Lila and risk being caught as well? She hoped she wouldn't have to find out. She would hate to be tested in that way.

Lila reached the window, stretched out an arm toward it, her foot sticking to the wall for balance, her other arm and leg still wrapped around the pipe. Her hand reached the frame. She grabbed on hard, brought her leg over to the sill, stretched, found purchase. Gripping tightly, she let go of the pipe, brought her other arm and leg over to the sill. Made it.

Watching her, Anju's heart skipped into near meltdown.

Lila balanced herself on the sill, worked her fingers along the joints of the window, looking for a way in. She took something out of her pocket, worked it between a joint in the sash window. After what seemed an eternity, the window gave and opened. Lila looked down, gave Anju a thumbs-up, and slipped inside.

Anju exhaled a breath she wasn't aware she had been holding. And waited.

It wasn't long before bolts and locks on the metal door were being undone. It swung open and there stood Lila.

"Enter," she said.

Anju didn't have to be told twice. She closed the door behind them. They were in a darkened passageway. No amount of renovation could mask the ingrained smell of meat. Lila took her hand, led her along until they were in a room that reeked of paint.

"This must be her workshop," said Lila. She pointed ahead of her. "Through there's the gallery."

"Do we need to go in there?"

"Doubt it. Anything she has to hide would be back here or upstairs. Let's start upstairs."

They found the stairs. Lila took out her phone, turned on the flashlight. "We're far enough back to use this now."

The stairs were bare wood. The walls bare also. The relocation of the front of the shop didn't extend this far. They reached the top of the stairs. Lila pointed. "This room's the toilet, this is the bedroom. Spare room, living room."

"Where do we start?"

"Bedroom, I think."

They entered the main bedroom. The curtains were drawn so Lila put away her flashlight, turned on the light.

"Jesus."

"Looks like someone beat us to it," said Lila."

It took Anju a few seconds to realize that was a joke. But only just. The place was an absolute tip. Clothes were strewn and discarded on every surface, both fresh and soiled. Bottles and jars of creams and makeup were left open on the dresser. Old tissues, wine glasses, bottles, and ringed coffee mugs were dotted about. On the bed was a laptop and what looked to Anju like an expensive camera. A lead connected the two.

"Let's take a look," said Lila.

She pressed a button on the keyboard, and the screen lit up. It opened straightaway to the Photos feature.

"No password?" asked Anju.

"She's either very sure of herself or very stupid," said Lila. "Either way, good for us."

Anju sat next to her on the bed, mindful not to further disturb the chaos of the room. She looked at the screen. Most of the photos were landscapes. Sunrises and sunsets. Fields and trees. Pastoral settings. Coastal pictures of cliffs and crashing waves, of dramatic cloud formations and rock faces. Then there were some of buildings, close-up architectural features, things that had clearly caught her eye.

Lila shrugged. "All art stuff. Boring." Then she stopped. "Oh."

The landscapes stopped. In their place was shot after shot of 'Obby 'Osses. Some from celebrations in Padstow, others taken from archived newspaper articles. Some apparently taken by herself.

A shiver ran through Anju as she gazed at them.

"Not what I was expecting," said Lila.

"Didn't Simon say something about hearing a horse? You don't think . . ."

Lila didn't answer. "Let's keep looking."

The numerous horse photos ended, their place taken by what looked like surveillance photos. The photos focused on one man, someone Anju had never seen before: inconspicuously dressed, supported by a cane. Walking around a town, getting into and out of his car. Waiting in his car while two huge gates opened for him, driving in.

"Any idea?" asked Lila.

"None."

They kept scrolling. Anju's stomach turned. She knew Lila's would as well.

There was a photo of Tom Killgannon coming out of the Sail Makers. Then another, going into the pub. Then another, getting into his car. Pulling up at home. Reemerging once more. Surveillance photos, like those they had just seen.

"Shit," said Anju.

"Knew there was something creepy about her."

They scrolled through the rest of the photos, but they had reverted to landscapes.

"Want to check anything else?"

Lila looked at her watch. "We'd better be going. She'll be back from the pub soon. Wouldn't want this to be the one night she leaves early. Come on. Let's try to leave everything as we found it."

"Shouldn't be too difficult . . ."

They made their way downstairs once more and were about to head for the back door when Anju stopped Lila, placed a hand on her arm.

"What?"

"We were in her studio, but we never looked at her paintings," said Anju.

"Probably boring old landscapes. Come on."

"Give me a minute." Now that they were nearly finished, Anju, feeling some kind of bravery, turned and walked into the studio. Ensuring that no one passing would be able to see farther than the gallery, she switched on her phone's flashlight. And stopped dead.

"Lila . . . you might want to see this."

Lila entered, saw where Anju was pointing.

"Shit . . ."

A painting of the 'Obby 'Oss. And another.

These paintings weren't the kind to go in the gallery at the front. For tourists. These were different. They conveyed a sense of threat, a kind of darkness. They both felt it.

"Let's get out of here," said Lila.

Anju didn't have to be told twice.

36

JUDY WALKED SLOWLY along the towpath by the estuary, back to their moored home. Trees overhung the path, and intermittent lighting made it ripe for any activity that would be frowned on in the daytime. Warehouses and industrial units were to one side, water on the other. The kind of place to hide or be forgotten about.

The night was quiet and cold. Judy wasn't in costume, and it felt strange to be dressed normally. If *normal* was the right word. Judy's skirts felt more normal to him now. He had on an old zipped-up parka and cargoes, walking boots on his feet. He carried two pizzas as flat as he could, aware that if he didn't hurry up they would be cold by the time he got back. Part of him didn't care because he had other things to think about. That was the same part that was tiring of being bossed around by Punch.

Punch. Judy. The brothers had proper names once, names given at birth. But no one used them anymore. Hadn't for years, even before all this started. Their parents had seen to that. He had seen something on the telly once on second children, how they were treated differently from the firstborn. Taken less seriously, more a figure of fun. Yeah. That's why he'd ended up being called Judy. Being second place to Punch. He'd endured it for so long that it had become unremarkable. But reading books recently, thinking about them and the lives described in them, was making Judy ponder his own life. And how he was mistreated by his brother.

Dad had been a Punch and Judy man on Torquay Beach. They were all called *professors*. And Mum was his bottler: the one who stood at the side of the tent, drumming up an audience, keeping up a noisy running commentary, getting the kids in the audience to shout along. And then, most importantly, after the show, forcing the children or their parents to part with money. And Mum did it dressed as Judy: bonnet, skirt, makeup, the lot. Dad had dressed up as Punch for a while, but there was no point, seeing as only his arms were visible.

But he put on a full show: the old-time one with the baby, the crocodile, the policeman, and the hangman called Jack Ketch. It was always the same story. Punch and Judy appeared, seemed to be in love for a while, then a baby came along. Punch was supposed to mind the baby while Judy went off, but it never went well. Punch became so infuriated, he attacked the baby, hitting it with sticks and eventually putting it into a sausage machine. Judy returned and attacked him, and the fighting between the two of them intensified. A policeman arrived, who, in turn, would be assaulted by Punch. A crocodile would attempt to eat sausages that had been made from the baby, and Punch, for his crimes, would be hanged by Jack Ketch, coming up against the devil and repenting for his crimes.

Their real father and mother had drunk and fought even before their kids came along. When they'd arrived, it intensified their conflicts. "We're just the baby that got made into sausages," Punch had once said, and Judy never forgot it. Judy still had scars that had never healed from their dad. Punch had plenty too. And that was without even taking into account the psychological abuse both had received from their drunken, loudmouthed, vicious mum.

And that was their childhood.

In the summer, the brothers would get bored watching the show and wander off, seeing what trouble they could find in Torquay. There was plenty if you knew where to look. They broke into places, stole from tourists, fought, and tried to get with girls. Those youthful days were the best time of Judy's life. Just him and his brother, away from their parents, living life how it should be lived.

It didn't last.

When summer ended, their dad always had trouble finding work. As the years went by and his drinking became more of a problem, employment became even harder for him to come by. Their mum's shouting and bullying, the constant shrill cries about what a failure their father was, finally got to him. One day, in the garden shed, Dad made his own appointment with Jack Ketch.

Judy found him hanging from a beam in the shed's roof. He'd assembled the Punch and Judy theater before him, the puppets laid out with a front-row view of this final performance.

After that, Mum took over. They didn't know how she brought in money during the off-season, but she did. And when the next summer season came around, she tried to run the Punch and Judy theater herself. The boys were put to work as bottlers. Punch wore his father's discarded costume and Judy wore his mother's. Punch found it easy to stand and shout, to rope in kids. He was outgoing and commanding, with a cheeky charm. Judy was the opposite: the straight man—or woman—to Punch's comedian. And the more Judy stood there, doing nothing and looking genuinely like he wanted to be somewhere else, the more people in the audience roared with laughter. Punch played upon it, making it part of the act. Having no option, Judy played along. And they were set for the summer.

Except they weren't. Mum couldn't do the show properly. She couldn't get the voices right, even with the modulator halfway down her throat, couldn't time the action on the stage. That meant no laughs from the crowd. Which meant she'd get more and more angry, especially when she saw how well her sons were doing. She took it out on them both.

But by then, Punch and Judy were in their late teens, big enough to stand up to her. So they did. And she crumpled before them. Punch had an idea: take over the show, Judy works as bottler, leaving their mother out of it. Punch told her they had no more use for her in their lives, and she may as well go and live somewhere else. Broken, she did. They never heard from her again.

Their show was a success. For one summer.

But trouble had been building. Judy's brother became more closed off. Judy wanted to talk about their father and his death, share the burden of finding him dead with someone close, explore the blame and guilt he felt, but Punch wouldn't listen. He was becoming volatile, taking after their parents, his temper flaring, lashing out at Judy. The more he worked the puppets, the worse he became. It was like seeing Dad come to life again, with their still-living tyrannical mother in there somewhere too. Judy decided it was the show's fault. The show had possessed their father and now it was possessing his brother. The show had to go. And it did, up in flames.

At first Punch was furious. But Judy was adamant. It had to go for him to be saved. For them both to be saved.

They were at a loss about what to do next until Judy remembered the fight clubs. They had found something even better.

Walking the towpath, Judy looked up. Home was in sight. The light from inside the boat told him that Punch was waiting for food.

Don't know why he couldn't go and get it sometimes, Judy thought. Always has to be me. He's more than capable of doing this himself.

Judy was looking forward to going to bed and reading. That was his new thing. Punch laughed at him for it, but only because he could hardly read. Judy took no notice of him.

He had started reading books recommended by the professor they used to go and see, but they were long and boring. Judy preferred novels, stories in which people's lives made sense. He wasn't brave enough to go into a bookshop so he bought them at charity shops in Truro. And they had opened up new worlds to him, where he could lose himself and be someone else.

He boarded the boat, opened the hatch, went downstairs.

"Finally!" said Punch, swinging his legs down from the sofa he'd been lying on. "Bet this fucker's cold by now. Where you been?"

"Just coming home."

He handed him the pizza. Punch opened it. Smelled it.

"Lovely. Good old-fashioned English food. Can't beat it. Spicy pepperoni and meatballs."

Judy didn't correct him. He knew pizza wasn't really English. It was American. And that knowledge made him feel superior to his brother for once. He moved to leave the cabin.

"Where you going?" his brother asked.

"In my room. To read."

Punch shook his head.

"Do your fucking head in, that will. Get us a beer from the fridge when you're done."

Judy turned, wanted to scream at him: *Get your own fucking beer, you lazy cunt.* But said nothing. Instead, he went into his room, ate his pizza, read his book. And went to another, better world.

37

Tom was at the kitchen table late, making notes in one of Lila's old exercise books, writing up the interviews and events of the previous few days. Seeing if any clues or anomalies might emerge from the testimonies. Identifying threads he could go back and tug harder at, forcing secrets to unravel. This felt like what he was supposed to be doing. Forcing truth from lies. Creating narratives out of obfuscation and misdirection. And Tom was good at it. He'd forgotten how much purpose it gave him. Better than working behind a bar, better than hiding away. Instead, confronting events of his life on his own terms, being reactive, not passive. He felt energized.

And it took his mind off the painful absence of Pearl. The failure to care for Simon West. Now he had a puzzle to solve. One that could have a profound impact on his life.

When there was a knock at the front door, he checked the time. Eleven thirty. Good news never knocked at that time of night. He had been so self-absorbed he hadn't even heard a car approach. He closed the exercise book, took a mouthful of the whisky he'd been drinking.

His first thought: whoever had come for Simon West was making another attempt.

His mind quickly rejected that. They wouldn't have knocked, they would have just come straight in. As noisily as possible.

His second thought: Pearl was back.

He drained the whisky glass before making his way to the door. Standing before it, hand outstretched, he took a deep breath, another, then opened it.

"Hi."

A woman he didn't know stood just outside. Middle-aged, good-looking, she was smiling at him.

"I'm Shelagh. We've met before."

Tom said nothing. If that was the case, he couldn't remember. "Right."

She looked around, a slightly embarrassed smile on her face, as if regretting the visit.

"I work with Pearl in the pub. I run a gallery in the village. Art gallery."

Tom thought. Perhaps he had seen someone like her in the pub, but working there? That was new. And a gallery in St. Petroc? But one word stood out for him.

"Pearl sent you?"

Another half-apologetic smile. "Not quite. Can I come in, please? Easier to talk than standing out on the doorstep."

Deciding he had more to gain from talking to her than turning her away, he let her in, closing the door behind her.

"D'you want a drink?"

She shrugged. "If you're having one. What are you having?"

"Well, I was on whisky, but I could—"

She smiled. "Sounds fine to me."

He took in her slightly too-wide smile, her slightly

unfocused, glassy eyes. Whisky wouldn't be the first thing she'd had to drink that night.

"Coming up." He gestured to the living room. "Just in there."

Tom went to the kitchen, picked up his glass, another for Shelagh, and the bottle. Dalwhinnie. Winter's Gold. It was near the bottom of the bottle and a favorite that he didn't like sharing, but he didn't have a choice. In the living room, Shelagh had made herself comfortable on the sofa, boots off and legs tucked underneath her. She smiled as he entered.

"Really nice place you've got here."

"Thank you." Tom poured out the whisky. Handed her one.

"Thank *you*."

Her fingers touched his as she took the glass. Accompanied by another smile. Tom felt suddenly wary. He sat away from her.

"How's Pearl?"

She took a heavy mouthful of the whisky, hid a grimace as it went down. "She's as well as could be expected, I suppose."

"Is she—"

"It's over, you know." Shelagh suddenly looked and sounded sober. "You and her. She's told me. Never wants to see you again."

Tom said nothing. Just felt like he had been punched.

"Sorry," she said. "It's hard to hear it like that, but it's for the best."

Tom stopped himself from speaking. He didn't know this woman or anything about her. He wasn't going to expose himself emotionally in front of her. He took a drink, replaced the glass on the arm of his chair. "What can I do for you, Shelagh?"

"Pearl told me about you," she said, taking another gulp, almost draining the glass. "Quite a bit, actually."

Tom waited to see where this was going. "Like what?"

Shelagh smiled, tossed her hair back. Tom noticed the

curve of her breasts against her open top. She was an attractive woman.

She looked directly at him. "She told me you have a violent past."

"Did she now."

"But context is everything," said Shelagh. "She told me why. She talked about your strength. Your positivity. Your . . . physicality." Shelagh smiled. "Well, I can see that for myself."

He felt her eyes run over his body. His response shocked him. He thought he would have been angry. But he found the action unexpectedly, shockingly stimulating.

"My glass is empty." She looked toward the bottle. "May I?"

"Help yourself."

She did. Tom did likewise. The bottle was nearly empty. He checked his watch. She saw him do it.

"So is this visit about Pearl, then?"

Another drink before answering. Something in Shelagh seemed to be shifting with each mouthful. She slowly shook her head, her body's rhythms tuning in to the amount of alcohol consumed. "No. Not Pearl. She's gone. Forget about her."

"Gone where?"

"From your life. Whatever." Another drink. "I came to see you."

"What for?"

"Because I want to tell you a story." Her words were slightly slurred.

Tom knew he should ask her to leave, but something stopped him. Her top seemed to have fall open even farther too. Tom couldn't pretend that he hadn't noticed. The primitive, reptile part of his brain responded to what he saw.

"What kind of story?"

"About a woman who loved a man, or thought she did.

No. Rather, she thought the man loved her. And she had a son with this man. And then the man made her see that he didn't love her. And he was cruel to her. And he took the son away." Another drink. She held the glass out to him. "Can I?"

"Help yourself."

She drained the bottle.

"So who is this man?" asked Tom. "Do I know him?"

Shelagh frowned. Physical actions seemed to be taking longer for her to accomplish. "I don't know. You might."

"So what's this got to do with me?"

"I'm coming to that. But first I have to tell you more about this boy and this man. And this woman. You see, the woman really loved her son. She'd do anything to get him back."

Shelagh leaned across to the armchair, placed her hand clumsily on Tom's knee. Tom once again found his body responding. Love had nothing to do with it. Pearl had nothing to do with it. But the loss of her did. The aching gap left in his life by her departure did.

She removed her hand. Took another drink.

"This woman wants to find her son. Needs to. Because she loves him, and she knows he loves her and not his father who cruelly took him away. A son needs to feel his mother's love. Only she knows how to look after him properly. And she knows where he is. It's why she came here. But here's the thing. She can't do it alone. She needs help." She looked at Tom, stared right into his eyes, unblinking.

"I see," said Tom.

"Do you? Really?"

Shelagh slid off the sofa, onto the floor. Knelt there, back straight, breasts out, thighs open.

Tom took a mouthful of whisky. Drained the glass.

Shelagh moved toward him, still on her knees. She placed

a hand on either of his thighs, knelt between his legs. Looked up at him, eyes wide, staring. Her breathing heavy, breasts rising and falling.

Tom was breathing heavily too. He felt as if he was on a precipice about to step off. He hoped he would land somewhere safely but knew he wouldn't. Still, something inside told him to do it, to jump and face the consequences later.

"Pearl told me all about you. How strong you are. How capable you are. You're what I need right now. Who I need."

She looked intently into Tom's eyes, trying to see behind them. Tom stared back, felt his body responding. Realized he was still holding the empty whisky glass.

"I've got another bottle in the kitchen."

With what felt like a superhuman effort, he managed to get to his feet. Shelagh watched him. Smiling at the bulge in his jeans.

"Hurry back," she said.

He almost ran into the kitchen, breathing hard, trying to get some sense back.

"Don't do this . . . don't do this . . ." Mentally repeating his mantra, he grabbed another bottle of whisky, turned, steadied himself, and returned to the living room. Ready to ask her to leave.

And stopped dead.

Shelagh stood in the center of the living room, naked. The room was now lit only by a couple of small table lights that accentuated the curves of her body. She closed her eyes.

"This is me. This is who I am."

Tom didn't move, didn't speak.

"D'you see my scars? Do you?" She held her arms out, rotated them. The dim light picked up raised, jagged sections of skin. "He did this. Why I always have to wear long sleeves. And here." She ran her hands over her stomach, her breasts. "More scars. Knives. Cigarettes. Whatever was on hand. D'you see?"

Tom knew he had to speak. "I . . . see."

Her eyes found his in the darkness. "I used to hate them. My scars. But I don't anymore. I think they're beautiful. Because they're me. My body. My soul. They're who I am now. Don't you think so? Don't you think I'm beautiful?"

Tom couldn't answer.

"We're all scarred. Whether we admit it or not. I'm just showing you mine." She stepped toward him. "I want to find my son, and I need you to help me. And I'll do anything. For you. *Anything.*" The final word whispered like the darkest secret Tom had ever heard.

He felt his body responding, rising. His rational, responsible mind was being dragged into deep darkness and replaced by something raw, primal. He moved toward her. She moved toward him.

And the door opened.

"Tom, listen, I've got to talk to you. I saw the light on, and I—"

Tom turned. Lila stood in the doorway. She stared from Tom to Shelagh, from Shelagh to Tom.

He hadn't heard the car. Or the front door. The blood had been pounding too hard, too fast within him.

Lila kept staring, mouth open, too shocked to speak. Then she turned and ran.

The spell broken, Tom called after her. "Lila, come back. It's not . . . not . . ."

Tom scrambled to get to the front door, but she was gone. The taillights of Anju's car disappeared up the hill.

38

SIMON WAS FEELING GOOD. He was doing something worthwhile. Important. And his work was valued.

He blocked his grief, anger, and unspent emotion; instead, he poured everything into campaigning for Arthur King. And it was paying off. He was much more confident on the various doorsteps he visited—eloquent even, Nazir had said, making him glow with pride. His arguments were subtle, persuasive. Standing up for the beliefs he believed Arthur King held. He made converts, turned opponents into potential voters. He had found the thing he was good at.

Campaign headquarters treated him as a valued member of the team. A lot of the volunteers he had been inducted with had fallen by the wayside, finding the work too challenging or arduous. Not Simon. He was in the campaign headquarters back room now, getting a new supply of leaflets for the morning, drinking tea, and chatting with Nazir and his new friends. They were a disparate bunch, all ages, mainly men, and not perhaps the sort of people Simon was used to mixing with. But like Nazir had said, it was like going to church. You have a calling, you meet the others likewise inclined. And you're welcomed into the fellowship. That's how Simon felt. Like he belonged somewhere.

"Got a surprise for you," said Nazir as Simon took the tea bag from his mug, squeezed it, and dropped it into the bin.

"Oh yeah?"

Nazir's smile always verged on the smirk. Like he knew something you didn't but desperately wanted to. "We're having a visitation tonight."

Simon frowned, then understood. "You mean—"

Nazir nodded. "Arthur, yeah. The man himself, coming here this evening. Rallying the troops. Told him to keep his eye on you."

"Yeah?" Simon couldn't keep the astonishment out of his voice. Simon had met Arthur King in passing during the campaign but had never dared speak to him.

"You'll go far, kid." Then another smile. "All down to me, of course. Taught you everything you know." Nazir laughed when he said it, but Simon had no doubt he meant it. "So don't rush off early. You got anywhere special to be?"

Simon thought of his depressing foster home. "Nowhere special."

"Good lad."

It seemed like only seconds after Nazir spoke that the door opened and Arthur King paused in the doorway, ensuring that everyone noted his arrival. The workers at their desks looked up from whatever they were doing, and the candidate smiled. The handsome man radiated charisma.

"How's my people doing?"

The volunteers spontaneously broke into applause. Or Simon thought it was spontaneous: one glance at Nazir and he saw who'd started it. But that didn't matter. The group's appreciation was heartfelt and it was right.

"Is the town ours yet?"

More laughter.

Simon studied Arthur. He didn't have the black-shirted Morris men accompanying him tonight. Critics had pointed out that they looked like his own fascist guard, but he'd laughed off the insinuations. "Public Enemy, remember them? The rap group? They had the S1Ws onstage with them. Black men in military uniform, doing complicated dance routines. Why would you complain about me doing it and not them? Because I'm white and they're Black? What's the difference? They put on a great show. So do my boys." Any dissension got lost in the applause.

Simon was disappointed to see Arthur dressed normally in jeans and a parka. His blond hair was still tied back and he wore an Aran sweater.

He wasn't alone. A smaller man followed the candidate into the room. Wearing nondescript clothing, he was supported by a cane, throwing his right leg out with every step. His eyes darted across the room, not missing a thing. Despite his innocuous appearance, something powerful emanated from him. Simon didn't know what it was, but he felt it.

"Right then," Arthur called, knowing he had everyone's attention. "You've all been working hard, putting in the hours and then some, so I want to show you I really do appreciate it. So dinner. On me."

Another round of applause, this one more spontaneous.

Nazir smiled at Simon. "Told you to hang around, didn't I? Get your coat."

SIMON WASN'T A PARTICULAR FAN of Indian food, but everyone else seemed to like it. When ordering, he couldn't differentiate between taste and heat, so he played it safe by choosing chicken tikka masala and hoped he could cope with it.

Nazir sat next to Arthur, Simon next to Nazir. The small man with the cane and the piercing eyes flanked Arthur on the other side. The restaurant table was round—of course—and the rest of the volunteers and workers took their places around it. Arthur held court, telling stories, asking others about their jobs and families, paying interest in their answers, laughing uproariously at the slightest joke. Simon saw the effect it had on people. They felt special, noticed, needed. Arthur had charisma to burn. Diners at the restaurant's other tables also noticed. Kept looking over, nudging each other, trying not to stare. This must be what it's like to be famous, thought Simon.

Nazir and the man with the cane had been in deep conversation across Arthur all evening. Heads down, chatting in low, conspiratorial tones. Whatever they were discussing, thought Simon, it looked important. More important than what Arthur had to say, really. Simon overheard the odd word or phrase, meaningless without context, but given the seriousness of the demeanors, he assumed that strategy was being discussed.

Thankfully, when the food arrived, Simon found his meal wasn't too hot, and he quite enjoyed it. Looking up from his rice, he noticed that everyone around the table seemed deep in conversation but him. He glanced at Nazir, but he was speaking to Arthur. Simon was on his own.

Not quite: the man on the other side of Arthur was staring at him. His frank gaze unnerved Simon, and he had to look away.

The man leaned across, speaking to Nazir while still looking over at Simon. Simon tried to listen but couldn't make anything out. He figured the odd man was asking who Simon was, and Nazir was telling him. The nod the man gave and the way he sat back after the conversation seemed to confirm this assumption.

Looking again at Simon, he smiled. Simon, suddenly shy, looked away.

Food consumed, Arthur ordered drinks and coffees for everyone, and people moved about the table, chatting with those they hadn't been directly seated next to.

Except for Simon, who sat on his own, a cup of coffee that he didn't want cooling in front of him.

"Simon West, is that right?"

He looked up. The odd man stood to the side of him, leaning heavily on his cane. Smiling a kind of superior smile. Like Nazir's. This man knew something about Simon, something he might use against him.

"I'm Aiden Marx."

The man extended his hand, which Simon shook.

"Simon West." He blushed. "But you know that."

Marx laughed. It sounded genuine, and Simon thought maybe he wasn't so bad after all. "I do." He pointed to Nazir's empty chair. "May I join you?"

"Uh, yeah. Sure."

Marx sat, seemingly relieved to take the pressure off his leg. "Heard good things about you, Simon. Nazir tells me you're a bit of a star in the organization. That right?" Still smiling all the while. He didn't have Arthur's charisma, but he seemed pleasant. Simon felt he had misjudged him earlier.

"Well . . ." Simon felt himself redden. "I . . . I don't know."

"Don't be modest. I hear you're quite the doorstep warrior."

Simon felt uncomfortable but pleased nonetheless.

"Sorry, I'm embarrassing you. I just want to say it's been noticed. Keep it up, and you'll go very far in our organization. Very far."

"Thank you, Mr. Marx."

"Aiden, please." Another disarming smile.

"*Er*, Aiden. Right." He paused, felt like he should ask something. "Are you a friend of Arthur's?"

Marx laughed. "You could say that. Arthur and I go back quite a way." He looked around the table. "He's done well for himself."

"Yes. He's . . . I really like what he has to say."

"Good."

Simon was about to launch into what he loved about Arthur and his policies, but Marx cut him off.

"Where are you staying at the moment?"

"Staying?"

"Nazir tells me that you're living in what sounds like an awful place. Is that right?"

"It's a foster home, yeah. Just temporary, though, 'til I'm old enough to leave."

"Sounds like hell from what Nazir's told me."

Simon frowned. Had the two men really been discussing where he was living?

Simon shrugged.

Marx smiled once more. "Listen. I know this might sound a bit odd, seeing as you've only just met me, but I can assure you it's not meant to be taken that way. I've got a place that I think you might be happy in."

"What?" Simon was confused.

"Please don't think I'm being weird or anything. I just want to help you out. I've got a . . . well, it's kind of a spread in the country. It's quite safe, don't worry. A rural retreat. I live there with my . . . partner and my dogs. D'you like dogs, Simon?"

"Yeah, I do. We never had one at home, but I always wanted one."

"I love dogs too. You can always tell what a person's like by how they treat their dogs. Now you don't have to take me up on it, but I can guarantee it's better than where you are now. Your own room, no one telling you what to do. And of course you could still come down here to help with the campaign. What d'you say?"

Simon was dumbstruck. He couldn't answer. Just then he noticed Nazir looking at him. He nodded toward Marx, smiled, and gave Simon a thumbs-up.

Nazir's response helped him make up his mind. "Yeah. Thank you. Yeah."

"Done. Well, I'll come and get you in the morning. How about that?"

"*Er* . . . yeah. Thanks."

"Good." Marx pulled himself to his feet, walked off. Nazir, hovering nearby, hurriedly took the empty seat.

"What did Aiden say?"

"He offered me somewhere to stay. His place. Says he's got a big house or something."

"Told you you'd been noticed, didn't I?"

"But you said Arthur wanted to speak to me tonight. Who's this Aiden?"

"Never mind Arthur. Aiden's the guy to keep in with around here. Trust me. Do what he says and you'll go far."

"People keep saying that."

"There you go, then. Don't worry. Just relax. You've got a glorious future ahead of you."

Simon looked around the table, saw everyone talking, laughing. Maybe they weren't who he would choose to mix with or to be close to. Some of them he might even have avoided if he'd seen them on the street. But now they were his new friends. New family, even.

Simon tried hard to feel he was where he belonged.

39

"YOU ALL RIGHT? Look miles away."

Tom looked around, momentarily puzzled. "Sorry, what were you saying?"

Penrose bit back his exasperation, but Tom noticed. He tried to pull himself together, get his mind focused on the conversation they were having, not what had happened the previous night.

The two men had arranged to meet in Grounded, a coffee shop Lila and Anju often went to. Small but fashionable and in the artist's quarter of Truro, it had a relaxed feel. Tom thought it would be the kind of place where he could have a clandestine meeting with Penrose and anyone spying on them would be easy to spot. Plus, Lila said, it did great chocolate brownies.

But Tom wasn't hungry. He and Penrose sat on industrial metal stools at the shelf along the front window, looking out onto the street. Tom had an Americano, Penrose a cappuccino.

Penrose was looking quizzically at Tom. "I asked you, what did you discover?"

And Tom was back in the present.

Tom told him what Claire Hightower had said concerning Sullivan.

Penrose listened, frowning. "Should I have heard of this Ben Tarpley?"

"Lecturer at Falmouth Uni. Fancies himself as an alt-right intellectual. If that's not a contradiction in terms." He told Penrose about the meeting.

"This fight club thing he mentioned," said Tom. "Masculinity and identity wrapped in a kind of English heritage folklore thing. Sounds ridiculous, but I think Tarpley has more to do with it than he made out."

"What makes you say that?"

Tom sipped his coffee. It was just as good as Lila had said it was. "Because he was too insistent he didn't know much about it. Got that vibe. He's definitely worth looking into."

Penrose shook his head. "For what, exactly? You think this university lecturer was behind the break-in at your house or the murder of Duncan Sullivan? What would a lecturer have to do with any of that? He's got a steady job, and it sounds like he's got influence of a kind, an audience. Why would he bother?"

"I'm not saying he is. I'm just saying he's worth looking into."

"Just because he's right-wing?"

Penrose's words had made Tom defensive. "Well, put like that it sounds ridiculous but there's a link, don't you think?"

Penrose's expression hardened, making him look more like a police officer despite his tender years. "He'll be looked into. I'm sure the detectives in charge of the investigation will be thrilled with that lead. Thank you."

Tom sat back, looked at Penrose. "I thought we were looking into this together? Going places where the official investigation couldn't. Now I've got you a solid lead—which none of your lot managed to get, by the way—that's it? You hand that over, thanks a lot?" He shook his head. Angry. "Cheers."

Penrose sighed. "That's not how it is, you know that. I just don't think we can go any further. We have to hand stuff over."

"Why? Been getting in trouble with your line manager? Been seen as too ambitious? Again?"

Penrose flinched. Tom had hit a nerve.

"Time to put Officer Penrose back in his box. I get it." Tom drained his coffee cup.

"I'll get another coffee," said Penrose.

"Don't bother." Tom stood up.

"Where you going?"

Tom shrugged. "There's no point hanging around here. I thought we were trying to see who was behind the attack on my house, but apparently I was wrong. I'll see you around."

When Tom grabbed his coat, Penrose placed a hand on his arm.

"I'm sorry. It's just become difficult at work. They don't like uniforms trying to muscle into ongoing investigations."

Tom was all wound up. He'd been harsh with Penrose. He had a job to do after all, people he was accountable to.

Penrose spoke again before Tom could apologize.

"Let me see if I can get information out of the official investigation that I can pass onto you. OK?"

Tom felt embarrassed about his earlier outburst. He nodded. "OK."

"Good."

"And I'm sorry for what I said before. I know you've got a job to do."

"It's OK. You have a lot on your plate."

Tom looked at the other man's honest and open face. For

a few seconds, he wanted someone to confide in and share his troubles with: a friend. He shoved that feeling away.

"Tell you what you could do," Tom said.

"What?"

"This fight club thing. Someone on the force must know about it."

"Noted. It'll be looked into," Penrose repeated.

"Yeah. But don't you think it would be better if you had someone visit, someone on the inside?"

Tom smiled.

Penrose didn't.

40

PEARL HAD HAD ENOUGH.

For the fifth day, Shelagh hadn't turned up to work, and she was left to look after the Sail Makers alone. For the first time ever, she was glad of the pub not being too busy. Pearl had to do everything: tend bar, restock, gather and clean glasses, serve food. At least the cook had turned up. She would have been in serious trouble if she went missing too.

In her rare down periods, a reflectiveness captured her mood. At the moment she didn't want to be running this pub, not like this, not now. She wanted to be anywhere but behind this bar in this village. No. That wasn't true. She wanted to be back upstairs wrapped in the duvet, curled up on the sofa, letting someone else make all her decisions while she atrophied in front of Netflix and kept the outside world at bay.

It was Tom's fault. Shelagh had regularly reinforced that fact. Letting Pearl down, not being the person she thought he was or needed him to be. And Pearl had believed her, blaming Tom for her unhappiness in the village, running the pub, everything. Even her own internal conflict over the contact her parents had made. If Tom had never shown up in St. Petroc, according to Shelagh's logic, things would still be just fine between Pearl and her parents. They'd still be here, running the pub, their lives unchanged. Their disappearance was Tom's fault too.

Pearl wanted to believe her, found that position easy to fall into. Instead of taking personal responsibility or engaging in any kind of self-examination, scapegoat someone else for every difficult emotion, every perceived personal failing. And in doing so, Pearl now realized, she had handed over control of her life to her absent barmaid Shelagh.

Shelagh's absence had forced Pearl to reluctantly go back downstairs and resume management of the pub, the last thing she wanted to do. But it also led her to question Shelagh and why the woman kept pouring poison into her ear. What did she gain from it?

Shelagh hadn't answered or returned Pearl's calls and texts, and Pearl had been too busy to go to the gallery and confront her. But now, after leaving the pub in the hands of temporary bar staff, she decided she felt well enough to find those answers for herself.

It was a quiet Friday afternoon on St. Petroc. Usually, there would be that collective sigh of relief as Friday afternoon slid into Friday night, as work stopped and leisure began. But not here. Not enough people engaged in enough activities to make it so.

But that didn't explain why Shelagh's gallery was closed.

Daytime was drawing to a close, the streetlights were on, darkness lengthening and flattening shadows until they became dominant. Pearl looked through the glass door, cupping her face with both hands to try and see better. She made out silhouettes of sculptures against the walls, angular frames of deeper darkness where paintings hung. But there was no sign of movement. She knocked on the glass.

No response.

Her breath fogged the glass. She wiped it with her coat sleeve, squinting to see farther.

She saw something. Movement, shadow on shadow. Behind the curtain at the back of the shop. She narrowed her eyes further and made out a faint light from somewhere deep within.

Pearl's heart quickened. Shelagh was in there, hiding from her. Or from someone. No, her. It had to be.

"Shelagh? Shelagh, I know you're in there."

No response. The light blinked out.

"Right," she said under her breath. Pearl hammered on the door harder, not caring who else heard the commotion.

She paused and heard a noise as faint as the light had been. It came from the back of the building. Looking quickly around, Pearl saw the alleyway at the side. Ran down it.

She reached the back of the building and worked out which gate led to the backyard of the gallery. She was about to try opening it when it opened inward.

Shelagh stopped dead when she saw Pearl. Pearl gathered her wits about her fast. A look that Pearl couldn't read passed over Shelagh's face. Whatever emotion it was, it wasn't pleasant.

Pearl noticed the suitcase in Shelagh's grasp and tried to gain the upper hand, not letting her speak first. "Shelagh, off somewhere?"

Shelagh looked as if she'd been caught stealing.

"Just . . . away for the weekend. Couple of days. Thought I'd see a bit more of Cornwall." She attempted a smile. "Might go surfing."

"You coming back?"

Shelagh's eyes widened. "'Course I was. My gallery's here. Why would I just up and leave?"

Anger rose within Pearl at the other woman's answers. "I don't know, Shelagh. Why would you? I mean, why would you spend all that time getting to know me, practically running my pub for me, just about taking over as my manager, controlling my life, and then suddenly, without any warning, just disappear? Not to mention leaving me short-staffed." Pearl's voice rose along with the anger. She tamped it down. Didn't want to give the other woman the satisfaction of seeing she'd been hurt. "And then you ghost me when I try and contact you? Why?"

Shelagh placed her suitcase on the ground, sighed as if about to unburden herself of some great personal tragedy that had been weighing her down. "I'm sorry about that. Truly. But I had no choice."

"Really." Pearl's tone of voice showed she didn't believe her.

"Yes, really." Shelagh's eyes were pleading, wanting to be believed. "I had no choice. Something . . . Well, under the circumstances, I thought it best to not contact you."

"And what circumstances?"

Shelagh looked down the alley. Almost smiled before turning back to her, eyes brimming with emotion. Later, Pearl would think Shelagh had been gathering herself as an actor would about to play a scene.

"It was . . ." Shelagh looked at the ground. "Tom." Then eyes back up, hooking on to Pearl's.

That answer surprised her. She frowned. "Tom?"

"Yes," said Shelagh, more confidently, "Tom. Your . . . I don't know, ex? Whatever. Boyfriend. Because of him."

"Why?"

Shelagh's eyes dropped once more either from shame at what she was about to admit or a liar getting her story straight. She looked up again. "He tried to rape me."

Pearl felt like she was having an out-of-body experience,

looking down on someone playing her part. She couldn't believe what she was hearing. She noticed Shelagh's hands were shaking.

"When? When did he . . . When?"

Shelagh gave another weight-dislodging sigh. "The other night. I'd just finished my shift and was going home when I got a call from him. Asking me to go over and see him. Well, I told him no, obviously. But he persisted. Sounded drunk. And very upset. Kept mentioning your name. So I . . . Well what could I do? I was worried he might hurt himself or something. I couldn't leave him like that, could I? So I went to see him."

Pearl now felt numb. "And what happened?"

"Well, I went to his house. And as soon as he answered the door, I could tell he'd been drinking. And crying by the looks of it. I went in. He offered me a drink, I said no and asked him what this was all about. He started talking about you, about how heartbroken he was over you, you wouldn't call, all of that. And what was he going to do now? That's what he kept saying, what was he going to do now? Well, I couldn't just leave him like that."

"So . . ."

"So I went and sat next to him on the sofa. A shoulder to cry on, you know? Literally." Her eyes dropped once more. "And that's when it happened."

Pearl didn't trust herself to speak, to ask another question. She didn't want to hear the answer.

"He . . ." A shaking hand moved her hair over her ear. "He was all over me. Hands, arms. He's strong, and I . . . I fought him off as best I could. But he . . ." Tears were starting now. "He tore my clothes off. Literally tore them off me."

"And . . . did he . . ."

Shelagh shook her head. "Someone came in before he could . . . A girl. She saw what was happening, screamed at him, and left. The spell was broken after that. I managed to gather up my clothes and get away." She shook her head. "And that's why I haven't been in touch with you since. Because I didn't know what to say. And I couldn't *not* tell you. So I stayed away. I thought it for the best." She looked up, reached out a hand to Pearl. Touched her on the wrist. "I'm sorry."

Pearl nodded, felt emotions she once more couldn't describe well up inside her. She looked at Shelagh, this broken woman before her, and felt she had to say something.

"How did he get your number?"

Shelagh looked startled at the question. "What?"

"Your number. You said he phoned you. How did he get your number?"

"He . . . he must have asked for it in the pub one day. Maybe, I don't know, wanted to ask about shifts or something? I don't know. But he had it."

"And how did you know where he lived?"

"I . . . He gave me directions over the phone when he called. Otherwise, how could I have known? But the main thing is Tom, your boyfriend, tried to rape me. That's what you should be thinking about."

Pearl was thinking about that. But she was also thinking about Shelagh's response to her questions. "I don't believe you. Whatever else Tom is, he's not a rapist."

"A few days ago I would have agreed with you," said Shelagh, voice tinged with anger. "Just shows, we never truly know anyone else, do we?" She looked at her watch. "Look, I'm really sorry you had to hear it this way, but I have to go. I'll call you when I get back. Sorry." She managed a smile then scurried off down the alleyway.

Pearl just stared after her, thoughts coming faster than she could process.

41

"Here it is: your new home."

The morning rain had held off, and the sky was unseasonably blue for February. These factors mitigated the effects of the drab winter scenery surrounding Aiden Marx's compound. Simon looked around. The grass would get greener once spring took the mud away. Trees would be lush again once their leaves returned. Perhaps even the ramshackle, squat house in the center of the compound might then look less like a prison or an army barracks and more like someone's home.

"Is this a farm?" Simon asked. He could hear barks and whines coming from the outbuildings.

Marx smiled. It didn't look natural. "That'll be the dogs you can hear."

"Can I see them?"

Another stiff smile. "Later. I'll show you around."

Marx had turned up in his car at the foster home to pick Simon up. No one came out to ask who this person was, where he was going. He hadn't told them he was leaving. He doubted they'd even notice he had gone. At least not until their payments for him were stopped. He loaded his bag into the trunk of the car and got in the passenger side. Checked his phone. Nothing. No calls, no messages.

"Nice phone," said Marx as they headed off. "Yours?"

"Present. From my dad. The . . . people made it pay as you go so they could keep in touch with me. But they never do."

About an hour later they were at the compound.

Simon looked at the hangars where the whining was coming from. There were pens to the rear. Even far away, he could smell the animals. There were also rows of vegetable plots, winter-barren fruit trees, wooden fences waiting for vines to grow once again up and around them. And dotted about the place were what looked like random pieces of sculpture.

"What's that?" asked Simon, pointing at the one before them. It was a framework of bars at a weird angle: small at the bottom, larger at the top, like it was being looked down on. And a figure inside was curled up on the floor, holding its head like it was in pain.

"Art," said Aiden, smiling.

Simon hadn't really got along with art in school, but this wasn't like the art they'd studied in school. For some reason it made him think of his father and sister. And mother too. And himself. And he felt a tingle inside he'd never before experienced. He understood the sculpture, maybe not on a conscious level but an emotional one.

"Did you make it?" Simon asked.

Marx laughed. "I just bought it. Like the other sculptures around here. Like the paintings indoors."

They walked on, Marx leaning heavily on his stick as they went.

Simon tried to concentrate on what the man said, but his mind was reeling at how much his life had changed in such a short period of time. Like it had happened to someone else, and Simon was just a spectator, watching it happen.

They reached the back of the compound, where there was a small brick cabin, its door securely locked, windows shuttered.

"What's in there?" asked Simon.

"That's the mad dog." Eyes flat, blank. A warning behind them. "Just keep away. Don't go near. Let's go back to the house."

Once back at the house, Simon asked, "Will I be going out canvasing today?"

"Not today. In fact, you may not do it ever again. There's a place for you much higher up."

"Doing what, though?" He was really curious to know. He'd liked canvasing, was good at it. "No one'll tell me what I'll be doing."

"It'll be taken care of. Until that happens, just make yourself at home and relax. Come inside."

Gazing at the single-story building, Simon's heart skipped a beat when a face appeared at the window. It was a girl with long hair and haunted eyes. Then, quickly, she was gone. So fast it shocked him. Made him doubt he'd even seen her.

"You all right?" asked Marx.

"I thought I saw a face at the window . . . but it disappeared. Like a ghost."

He looked at Marx, expecting to be ridiculed. But Marx did no such thing.

"No ghost. That's my girlfriend. Michelle. She's shy. I'll introduce you."

They stepped inside. Simon no longer had specific expectations so he wasn't shocked or comforted or disappointed by what he saw. A functional living room with a big TV and white leather furniture. On the walls were paintings. Abstracts. He couldn't tell whether they were good or bad. It looked comfortable, that was what he cared about. From a corridor off to the side, a shadow emerged.

"This is Michelle," said Marx. "Say hello to Simon. He's come to stay with us."

"Hi," said Simon.

Michelle stayed where she was, nodded, kept her distance.

"But don't worry. I'm sure you'll become friends. Michelle, make Simon a cup of tea." He turned to Simon. "D'you want tea?"

"*Uh*, yeah. Thanks."

The action, the words, took him back to a similar situation a couple of weeks ago: Tom Killgannon and Lila asking him the same thing. It seemed so long ago. And something inside said that he missed them. But now he had Arthur King and this whole new community.

Don't think about them. Move forward.

"Sit down."

When he sat, the sofa moved beneath him, welcoming his body. Relaxing him.

Michelle returned with a mug of tea, passed it to him. Her eyes briefly met his, then darted away. "Thank you," he said.

She barely acknowledged the words.

"Right," said Marx. "Here we are. I'll let Michelle show you to your room. Make yourself at home. She'll show you the ropes. Where you can and can't go. I've got some work to do. I'll see you later."

He left the room, down the corridor Michelle had emerged from, shutting a heavy door behind him at its far end. Michelle sat across from him, saying nothing.

"Nice place," Simon ventured.

She nodded imperceptibly.

He thought she was barely older than he was. Early

twenties, he reckoned. And she looked fragile, washed out. Like life had been drained from her. He drank his tea without another word. Eventually, Michelle reached out for the TV remote, turned the TV on. Stared at whatever came up.

Simon took his phone out, looked at the screen. Nothing from anyone. Old life or new. He began to feel uncomfortable and looked up. Michelle was staring at him, maybe had been for some time. Or more precisely, she was staring at his phone. Like she'd never seen one before.

Feeling guilty without knowing why, he put the phone away in his coat pocket.

"He let you keep it?"

"What?"

"Your phone. He took mine away. Told me I didn't need to talk to anyone anymore. To see them. He would do everything for me."

Simon didn't know how to respond. "OK."

"Why have you got yours?"

Simon shrugged. "Dunno."

"Have you got anyone to call?"

Simon stared at the phone. "No."

She settled back, seemingly satisfied with the answer.

He felt uneasy. Who was this girl, and why was she here? More to the point, was she here against her will? Was she a prisoner? Was he?

Simon felt panic rising.

He wanted to go home. But he couldn't. Ever again.

So he just drank his tea, watched the TV.

42

"You're the one who wanted to come," said Punch. "Let's go in."

The night was still and cold as Punch and Judy parked their patchwork car outside an abandoned factory in Camborne, once one of the greatest manufacturing towns in Britain in the days when Cornwall prospered from tin mining. The factory had once manufactured railway equipment for the mines and employed hundreds of proud men in a job for life. Now it stood empty, eaten away by years of neglect until it was just a rotting brick shell. Others like it had been sold off, renovated as luxury flats to entice younger people into the area. This one hadn't been given that upscale makeover, but it had been repositioned. Where working-class men would have once found pride and identity working in such a factory, they now attempted to regain something like that inside its crumbling walls. This was the venue for the Fear Machine, the official name of their fight club.

From the passenger seat, Judy stared at the entrance. Imposing double doors, nearly denuded of paint and sprayed with graffiti, gave no hint of the goings-on inside. He was angry. In the past, coming here angry had given his brother and him not just an outlet, an expression, but a new avenue of income. But he didn't want to enter. Not tonight. He'd rather be back on the boat, reading his books. They also made him angry, but they made him think too, offering ideas on how to channel his anger into something more than fights. Or at least better fights.

Punch was impatient. "Judy, come on. You ready?"

Judy looked at his brother behind the steering wheel. His makeup done, the same old stained costume dragged on. Even his jester's cap. And Judy had been talked into wearing his skirts and bonnet once more. But he'd refused to put on makeup. He wasn't in the mood tonight.

Judy looked away from the entrance, down the street. In the distance, lights were on in homes. People with normal lives. Could have been a world away. He looked back at Punch, sitting behind the wheel of the car.

Judy gave his skirt a flick. "I don't want to do this"— another flick—"anymore."

Punch frowned. "What you talking about?"

"I don't want to be Judy anymore."

Punch shook his head, baffled. His bells rang as he did so. "But that makes no sense. It's who you are. I'm Punch, you're Judy. Come on. Let's go in."

"You're not listening. I don't want to be Judy anymore."

Punch's exasperation was transforming into anger. "Well, who d'you want to be, then?"

"Who I am." Spoken so loudly they both jumped.

Punch smiled. "But that's Judy. That's who you are."

"No. I'm tired of dressing up. Of being Judy."

Punch thought for a moment. "Who would you be, then? You can't be Punch because I'm Punch. And you wouldn't want to be the baby, would you? The crocodile, is that what you mean? You want a crocodile costume?" He became thoughtful once more. "It'd be hard to fight in."

"No," Judy said indignantly. "None of them. No stupid costumes."

Punch turned to Judy, vibrating with anger, bells jangling. "I'm getting really tired of this. Gonna smack you one myself before we get in there, if you keep this up." Then slowly, as if explaining something complicated to an imbecile, "Judy is who you are, who you've always been ever since you were little. It's like I can't stop being Punch. You can't just stop being who you are and be someone else now, can you?"

Judy felt the conversation wearing him down. "You can try."

Silence. Eventually, Punch sighed, spoke. "Come on, we've come all this way, let's get in there."

Punch opened the door, grabbed his heavy fire iron, got out. Judy, seeing no choice, did likewise.

"Look at the state of that," said Penrose, smiling as he spoke.

Tom and Penrose sat in Penrose's car. They were parked down the street from the old factory, hidden between the pools of two streetlights. They watched as Punch and Judy stomped up to the old double doors of the factory.

Punch and Judy. That rang a bell in Tom's mind. Also, a literal one: the chiming of Punch's jester hat carried in the still, cold night air. He turned to Penrose. "Didn't Simon say something about ringing bells the night his family was attacked?" He nodded toward the figures in front of him. "You think it might be those two?"

Penrose shrugged. "Could be, I suppose. You think they look like a threat?"

"They're carrying weapons. Or things that could be construed as weapons. And they're heading off for a fight. I don't think it's a huge stretch of the imagination to say they might be involved in the violence at Falmouth. If not them, then quite possibly someone in there like them."

"What, like the Morris dancers we saw going in earlier?"

"Always something dodgy about Morris dancers."

Inside was where Tom itched to be. It was useless, sitting outside watching. He needed to see the place and its clientele for himself, then decide on next steps.

Penrose had struck it lucky finding out the location of the fight club. The Fear Machine, it was apparently known as. An informant giving up a local drug dealer to one of Penrose's colleagues had mentioned the place and Penrose, even though it wasn't his jurisdiction, had managed to get the details. They were in luck. Tonight, one of the club's regular events was planned.

"I know what you're thinking, Tom," said Penrose, "but there's no way to get in, I'm afraid." Invitation was strict; only current participants were allowed to invite newcomers.

"Isn't there someone on the force who might get me in?" Tom had asked.

"Probably. But they wouldn't want it publicized. Might even come here on their night off."

As they sat staring at the doors, waiting, Penrose said, "You know, I come from around here."

"Yeah?"

"Yeah. One of the most deprived areas in the country, this is. Never mind just Cornwall. All the industry went when the mines closed. Never replaced. Like this factory here. But at the same time, it's one of the most beautiful parts of the county. When I was a kid, I could be on my bike in a rural heaven

within minutes of getting out of my horrible housing estate."
He sighed. "But you can't live on scenery."

"Fight club here makes sense, then."

Tom flexed his knuckles. The club had more than one attraction for him. The last few weeks had left him frustrated, angry.
He'd tried running along the cliff-edge path to get it out of his
system, tire himself out, but it wasn't enough. He needed something more, something physical. Walk into a ring, fight. Either
beat his opponent or get beaten by him. Then leave. The way
he was feeling, the emotion pent-up within him, it would take
more than a man in a jester's cap with a stick to take him down.

He wondered what Pearl would have to say about that,
then pushed aside the thought.

They sat and watched. And waited.

43

THE MIRZA FAMILY AND LILA were having a quiet evening in. Sitting around in the living room, watching TV. Rare, Lila thought, for them all to be together. Usually, Faisal or Karima would be out for the evening, undertaking extra work or classes, but recently they seemed to have made cancellations to spend time with their daughter. And her girlfriend.

At first Lila thought it was because they didn't trust her, or that beneath their liberal skins they found something distasteful about their daughter choosing another girl as a partner. But no. She now thought they were staying in to keep an eye on them. Not to stop them having sex on the pristine furniture—the other kind of keeping an eye. Making sure they were safe.

Making sure that no one brought trouble to their front door.

They were half watching the news, the two girls both studying their phones for a counterpoint to the stories presented to them, when there was a ring at the front doorbell.

All four jumped as if jolted by electricity. Eyes on each other, fears rising.

Faisal stood. "I'll go."

The other three said nothing. But strained to hear what was being said in the hallway over the TV.

"Come in," Faisal said from the hallway. Curiosity increased, they all stared at the door.

"This way." Faisal entered the living room, followed by Pearl.

She looked terrible, Lila thought. Thinner than before, gaunt even, and like she hadn't slept in ages. Pearl summoned a pathetic smile. Spoke hesitantly. "Sorry to break up your evening like this but . . ." A sigh. "Can I have a word with Lila, please?"

The other three looked between them, Faisal and Anju on the verge of insisting they accompany her.

"Please . . . Just a word."

When Lila stood, receptive to the idea, Faisal said, "Use my study."

The two women went into the study and closed the door behind them.

Pearl sat in the armchair, looking exhausted. "How . . . how you doing?"

"Fine," said Lila automatically. Then thought. "Well no, not fine, actually. A long way from fine."

Pearl nodded. "I just wanted to say sorry. For how I've been recently. For . . ." Her expression changed. "I need to talk to you. About Tom."

"Of course," said Lila, the words out before she could stop them. "Why else would you come to see me? Not to see how I'm doing, clearly."

Pearl's head dropped. "I deserved that. I haven't been a good friend to you. To anyone really." Tears formed in her eyes.

That made Lila angry. She didn't want Pearl's self-pity. She had enough to deal with. Tom had tried to contact her after *that* night. And she had ignored all his messages. She didn't know what to say to him, what to even think. What she had seen him doing had broken her heart. Especially with her. *Her.*

"Look," said Pearl. "I've spoken to Shelagh. I think it's the last we'll see of her. And I'm glad. She was, I don't know how to say it. She . . . wasn't a good person."

"I tried to tell you. I tried to tell Tom."

"I should have listened. I'm sorry."

"You keep saying that." Lila was surprised by the hardness in her voice. "Is that what you came here to say—that Shelagh was rotten?" She thought of the creepy horse paintings. The photos of Tom. "Because I already know."

"I confronted her. About other stuff but she . . ." Another sigh. "She said Tom had raped her. And that you had seen it happen."

Lila stared at her, unable to believe what she had just heard. She didn't blink, didn't even breathe for a few seconds. "She . . . what?"

"Said he raped her."

Lila regained control. And laughed. A bitter bark. "Raped? No." She shook her head. "No, that's not what I saw."

Pearl asked what she had seen. Lila told her. The memory etched onto her brain like fork lightning. Shelagh naked, kneeling in front of a fully dressed Tom. Tom staring down at her. She had thought about that night so many times, wondering what she had actually walked into. Tom's messages said that the woman had turned up at his house drunk and then stripped off when he left the room, said she would do anything for him, and that he was as surprised as Lila had been. And Lila hadn't known what to believe.

"I didn't see any rape going on," she said.

Pearl, head down, nodded. Sounding relieved. "I knew he

couldn't have done it. Not really. But she was so convincing. She almost made me believe it."

"Why didn't you just call him and ask?"

"And what d'you think his answer would have been?"

Lila nodded. "So you came to see me. Eventually."

"Sorry."

Lila remained wary, wanting to protect herself, but since Pearl had made the first move, it was up to her to make the next one. "Maybe it's time we both talked to him."

Pearl nodded.

"Together."

"And I've got other stuff to tell you about that woman as well," said Lila.

"Like what?"

"Let's have a cup of tea. This may take a while."

44

Judy banged the double doors open, marched out of the dank factory. Cold night air hit him, but he took no notice. He pulled off his bonnet, threw it on the ground, and kept walking, riving the dress from his chest as he went. The old worn fabric tore easily.

Behind him the door banged open once more. "Judy? Judy . . ."

Punch ran after him, placing a restraining arm on his shoulder, which Judy violently shook off.

"Hey, no need for that . . ."

"Just fuck off." Still ridding himself of his garish worn garments, Judy kept walking away.

"Come on . . ." Punch's voice was unusually wheedling, whining.

Judy channeled his rage into his clothing: ripping, rending, pulling off an old skin to reveal a new one beneath.

"Judy, listen . . ."

Judy stopped, turned. His eyes murderous, his voice was barely controlled when he hissed, "Don't call me that fucking name ever again."

Punch smiled.

"You think what you tried to do to me in there is funny?"

"Oh come on, that was just a joke." Punch's eyes glittered with a dark, maniacal light.

"That was no joke. What you tried to get them to do to me wasn't a joke."

Judy's wrists caught on the cloth of the sleeves. The more he pulled, the angrier he got, the more trapped he found himself.

The humor disappeared from Punch's face. His eyes turned to stone.

"Yeah," he said, "you're right. It wasn't a joke. You needed to be taught a lesson."

Judy stopped, stared at Punch. "What kind of lesson?" he asked his brother. "A lesson in what?"

Punch moved closer until they were face-to-face. "You've been getting a bit uppity lately. Getting ideas into your head that you shouldn't be having. You need to be put in your place."

The penny dropped for Judy. "That's why you wanted to come here tonight. You tried to make me think it was my idea, but you had it all planned what was going to happen to me."

Punch smiled once more. "Yeah."

"Except I wouldn't let it happen." He moved his face even closer. "You cunt." Hissed.

Punch stood his ground. "Remember what we did to Sullivan when he fucked up? Keep going the way you were, with your books and your big ideas, you'd have been next. And I didn't want that. So I arranged something to break you down a bit, get you back onside."

Judy just stared, eyes like embers.

"I did it for you, Judy."

He responded slowly, his words dripping venom. "Don't call me that name ever again." Arms free of the material, he started pushing off his skirts.

"Come on," said Punch. "We're brothers."

Judy removed the dress fully, threw what was left of it at Punch. He stood in the T-shirt, jeans, and trainers he'd been wearing underneath.

"I don't have a brother. There's just me from now on. Just me."

He walked off.

"Judy? Come on . . . Judy . . ."

But Judy didn't look back.

"HELLO," SAID TOM, observing the peculiar scene, "that's an interesting development. What d'you think? Should we follow?"

"Which one?"

He looked between the two of them. The one previously dressed as Judy was striding away. The one dressed as Punch stared after him for a while before slowly making his way back to his car.

"Let's follow Punch," said Tom. "Got a bad feeling about him."

"Punch, it is," said Penrose.

"Wait a minute," Tom said, gazing at the warehouse.

"What?" said Penrose.

Tom was opening the car door as he spoke, "The guy left the door open. No one's come to close it."

"You can't just—"

"Never mind about me. Follow the twat in the hat."

Tom ran across the road, leaving Penrose alone.

Judy stalked the streets without direction or purpose, words muttered with every angry step. Imaginary conversations in his head, all with the same outcome: a bad ending for Punch.

"Excuse me."

At first he thought he was imagining things. Hearing voices.

"I said, excuse me."

No. It was real, and he turned to see a woman standing beside him. She looked like she didn't belong in the area. Well-dressed, middle-aged, and attractive. But not a prostitute. So what did she want with him?

"Yeah?" No sense of an invitation in his words. Right now he didn't need any more complications or distractions.

She approached him, standing beside him on the sidewalk. Her perfume smelled nice. "I heard you arguing. Sorry. Couldn't help it. Sound carries at night. I was worried about you and followed. That was Punch, right?"

He nodded. "Yeah. My brother . . . or he was."

"And you're Judy?"

"Not anymore."

"Right. And you're angry with him, are you?"

"Yeah, I'm— What d'you want?"

She smiled. Good teeth. Nice mouth as well.

"I'm angry with somebody myself, and I think it might be somebody you're angry with too."

"Who?"

She gestured behind them. "My car's just here. Why don't we go somewhere and talk about it? Maybe we can help each other."

He looked around. Was this a setup? Maybe another of Punch's rotten surprises?

"I'm on my own," she said, as if reading his mind. "I just want to talk, that's all."

The cold hit him now. So did the harsh realization that he had nowhere to stay. He couldn't go back to the boat, possibly ever again.

"OK, then."

Another smile from her. "Good. My name's Shelagh, by the way. What's yours?"

He thought for a moment. "Not Judy."

She laughed. "Well, Not Judy, let's see if we can help each other." She placed her hand on his arm. He thrilled at the feeling of her warm fingers on his cold flesh.

"And I should say, that if you can help me, I'll do anything for you." She gave his arm another squeeze. "Anything."

For the first time in what seemed like ages, he smiled.

45

Tom pushed the heavy door open. He heard shouting and chanting coming from the corridor in front of him. Beneath that was music, heavy, beat-laden, aggressive. He moved forward.

An old plastic garden table and chair were inside the doorway, but no one was currently manning it. Tom didn't have to give some elaborate code or password to get in. A metal cashbox sat on the table next to a rubber stamp and ink pad. Tom picked up the stamp, rolled it in the ink, and stamped some kind of old Norse or Viking rune on the back of his hand. That fit, he thought. The Far Right had co-opted Norse mythology and imagery for their own ends, the blond, blue-eyed Viking an ideal they aspired to.

The hallway he stood in would once have looked impressive in a Victorian Gothic way, but years of neglect had taken their toll, as had opportunistic gentrifiers, stealing decorative tiling from its walls and floors and even some of the heavy old wooden doors from their frames. Along the ceiling was a looping string of bare bulbs leading in a straight line. Tom followed the lights.

They went as far as a double doorway, original doors still

intact. All the clamor came from behind those doors. Tom, poised and wary of a challenge to his presence, put his hands on the old wood and pushed.

Sweat, noise, and heat hit him, as if his senses had been cranked up. The room was spotlighted by arc lamps, heavy rubber cords snaking away to hidden generators. Huge speakers from a hidden sound system were at one end of the room. In the center, a makeshift arena was contained by chain-link fencing pulled into a rough circle. The fencing was tall—double height—welded together, and topped by razor wire. A doorway had been cut into it. Most of the arc lights in the room shone down into this central area. Surrounding it were men, chanting, baying. Above Tom, he saw stone walk-ways and old metal gantries, also filled with more overexcited hooligans. No one paid him any attention.

He made his way through the crowd. They were all men, all white. Different ages, different sizes. Some in full cosplay. There were a few homemade attempts at a Viking look, with the side inspiration of biker gangs. Skinheads. Nazi regalia. Full camo survivalists. Black-shirted Morris dancers. Heritage Party T-shirts and badges, swastika armbands pulled on over normal clothing. No one holding back, no one hiding. Safe in their environment, comfortable in their hatred.

He reached a spot in the cheering crowd with a better view of the cage. Inside were two fighters, one a long-haired Viking, the other looking more like a wrestler gone to fat. Both went at it, tearing into each other, a lack of skill supple-mented by enthusiasm. The crowd, having chosen their favor-ites, jeered and cheered every punch, kick, gouge, headbutt. Violence as celebration, as catharsis. The audience could have been regulars in Sail Makers; they could have been neighbors down the street. Ordinary, normal people. No one was anyone special, but because they were part of something bigger than themselves they all felt like they were special.

The Viking landed a fist in the ex-wrestler's face, and he went down, blood arcing from his shattered nose as he did so. The crowd bayed as the unsteady Viking tried holding his weary arms victoriously high. He was swaying and about to join his unmoving opponent on the concrete floor when one of the black-shirted Morris men stepped into the cage, propping him upright. He shouted into a microphone, "Let's hear it for Thor!"

The crowd cheered and jeered, louder this time. Thor was helped out of the arena. His unconscious opponent was dragged out.

Through a microphone, the bowler-hatted ringmaster addressed the crowd.

"Collect your winnings, if you've got any, from the window. No refunds. If you backed the wrong one, tough."

Some of the crowd laughed. Unpleasantly.

"We've seen some good stuff tonight, haven't we?" shouted the ringmaster.

There was a roar of approval from the crowd.

"And we know why we're here, don't we? In the Fear Machine?"

Some actual answers were shouted out, but none that Tom could make any sense of.

"We will let them know that together we're more powerful than they are!" said the ringmaster.

More cheering. The words were too much for some of the crowd; they couldn't contain themselves, and—their blood up—they began fighting with each other. Those small brawls drew their own cheering, chanting audiences.

"That's it! That's it!" shouted the ringmaster. "Get stuck in!" He waited until the fights wound down, the men wore themselves out, then spoke again. "You know who we're up against, don't you?"

Another cheer.

"The liberal elite. The ones who say you can't live your lives the way you want to."

Another cheer.

"The government who've abandoned all of us."

Cheering and booing.

"The Blacks and foreigners who took our jobs. Who stopped decent, hard-working white men from doing an honest day's work and bringing in an honest day's pay to their families."

More cheering.

It was a malevolent pantomime, thought Tom.

The ringmaster waited until he had a semblance of hush. "Remember, vote for Arthur King. He'll sort things out."

Another cheer went up. Chants of "Arthur, Arthur," echoed through the large space.

The ringmaster nodded. "That's right." The chanting continued. "Then we'll have a voice, then they won't be able to ignore us any longer!"

Cheering once more.

"In the meantime . . ." He waited for quiet once more. "We've got some more entertainment for you. We already had Punch and Judy, with all those boys showing Judy what they wanted to do with her . . ."

More cheering and jeering, mixed with sexist and homophobic chants.

"And we've just had the clash of the titans. Well now, here's something unexpected. We've got a special guest here tonight."

The ringmaster gestured to someone on one of the metal gantries, and Tom felt himself suddenly squinting. A spotlight had been turned on him. Beyond the glare, he saw the ring-master point at him.

"We've got a spy in the camp, lads. He's not one of us."

The crowd turned and looked at Tom. They moved in on him, crushing him.

"You know what we do to spies, lads, don't you?"

The chants went up straightaway.

"Kill! Kill! Kill! Kill!"

Numerous arms manhandled him, propelling him toward the cage. There were too many; he could only be swept along by them. He was pushed up against the cage, the metal digging into his face, bending his nose sideways.

"Get him inside."

He was hauled to the gate, thrown in. He sprawled on the floor, jarring his knee on the concrete. The gate was bolted behind him. He looked up and saw a familiar face on a gantry. Didn't have time to register whose.

The ringmaster looked down at him and smiled. Then looked toward the gate, beckoned. "Come on in, lads. It's your lucky night."

The gate was thrown open. In walked three men, all built like battleships, all wearing executioners masks.

"He's all yours," said the ringmaster, exiting.

Tom barely had time to look up at the three men before they attacked.

PART FOUR
INSIDE THE FEAR MACHINE

46

THE BARKING DOGS woke Simon again. Either hungry, angry, or both. He sat up in bed, rubbed his head, feeling anything but rested. The walls of the bedroom were bare, the furniture functional. His two unpacked bags were on the floor, clothes spilling out like slit guts.

"This is your own room," Aiden Marx had told him. "Do what you like with it."

Two days later and Simon had done nothing with it. Because it still didn't feel like his space. He had moved around so much recently, he was reluctant to get too used to any one place. He hoped that would change. These were now his people, this was where he belonged. He repeated that mantra over and over. If he said it enough times, it might become the truth.

The dogs went quiet. The miserable fat old bloke who looked after them, Robert, must be feeding them. He had ignored Simon when Simon had tried speaking to him the previous evening. Just kept doing whatever it was he did, red-faced and angry looking, shuffling around like he was stumbling through a heart attack.

Simon had wanted to make friends with the dogs, but

Robert had warned him off. And the dogs themselves weren't given to being friendly. As soon as Simon approached them, they threw themselves at the bars of their cages, their scarred snouts pushed through the metal, teeth bared, snarling and barking, trying to reach him to rip him apart. Simon left them alone after that.

He checked the time on his phone. Seven thirty. He never got up at this time unless it was a school day, and those had been forgotten about. No one had chased him, found him somewhere to attend. He replaced his phone on the bedside table.

No one knew where he was. At first that had been exciting. A secret life. But now he felt abandoned, cooped up in the compound with weird Michelle who hardly ever spoke to him and seemed to resent his presence. So he just walked around, feeling alone once more.

Alone.

Everything that he had been through hit him hard. Like he was standing on the shore beside where Tom Killgannon lived, down from the cliff he'd almost fallen off, while a huge wave, harder than stone and colder than ice and more powerful than anything he had ever felt before, smashed into him. He tried not to be swept away by it but was pulled under again and again. It was so difficult to fight.

He had cried himself to sleep that first night. Really sobbed, the duvet shoved hard in his mouth so no one else heard. Thrashing around, trying not to let that wave drag him under.

His father. His sister. Even his stepmother. He didn't know what had happened to them. Had there been a funeral? Burial, cremation? No one would tell him. It was like he'd just been abandoned, left to grieve on his own. He knew he couldn't go back, he just wished he had been able to say goodbye.

He picked up his phone once more, scrolled through. Saw

Tom's phone number. Should he call him? Why? To go back there? And Faisal too had tried to help Simon, even in that one session. Something deep within wished he was back there, talking to that man, listening to what he had to say. Faisal was calm. He was kind. He had helped.

Simon felt that wave building up again, getting ready to smash against him.

Instead, he threw back the duvet, got up. It was early, but he didn't want to lie in bed any longer. He had to do something. He'd find Marx, make him take him to Arthur's campaign. The election was just days away. Surely the campaign needed all the help they could get.

He got dressed, wiped any tears that might be forming away, left the room.

47

LILA STARED INTO HER CUP OF TEA. She was back in the cottage, waiting for something but unsure what. Tom coming home, perhaps. Their lives resuming. Anju coming to stay again. And Pearl. Everything going back to how it used to be.

After Pearl told her about her Shelagh, the two women had talked. Anju joined them, then Faisal and Karima did as well. Into the night, they discussed and analyzed the situation, seeking as much clarity as possible. The upshot: Tom certainly did not do what Shelagh had accused him of.

"He's a good guy," Lila had said. "Despite all his faults, his demons, whatever, he's basically decent."

Karima smiled. "Like most men, he's trying to be," she said. "And that's the main thing."

In response, Faisal just raised an eyebrow.

Lila decided to go home the next morning. She had tried contacting Tom but with no luck. She was getting concerned about him now. Hoped he hadn't disappeared or moved on. When she phoned him, her calls went to voice mail.

"I should be there, though, when he comes back," she told the Mirzas. *If* he comes back, said the unvoiced thought.

Faisal gave her a lift home, saying she could always stay with them if anything changed. But Lila, sensing relief in his voice, suspected he was just being polite.

Anju would visit, but only after her parents were sure everything was safe at Tom's. And life was getting back to normal.

Truth be told, Lila was also looking forward to some time to herself. Refocus on who she was, where she was going, who she wanted to be.

Pearl knew Lila was back, had come around to see her the previous night. "I'm not intruding, am I?"

"Not at all. Just started bingeing the new series of *Queer Eye* on Netflix."

Pearl had smiled. "Then it's a big interruption."

She came in. Lila made tea. "I haven't been back long," she said, pausing the TV. Jonathan's hands were raised in mid-explosion. "Didn't know what to do first, so I thought this was as good as anything."

"Absolutely."

"Want to watch it with me?"

"Maybe later." Pearl looked at the floor, as if searching for the words she wanted to say.

"What's up?" Pearl said nothing. Lila waited. Until she thought Pearl wasn't going to speak.

Pearl looked up. "I'm . . . thinking of going away for a bit."

Lila felt confused. "Even as you now know Shelagh has been lying to you about Tom? Why can't everything be all right with you two again?"

"I don't know that it will be, do I? I haven't seen him yet. I just didn't want this to be a shock. I thought I owed it to you to tell you first."

Lila was worried now. "Tell me what?"

"I've heard from my parents. And they want me to go and see them. Join them."

"Where are they?"

"Abroad." The word snapped, discouraging further questioning.

"Right." Lila's face must have betrayed her thoughts.

"I can tell what you're thinking," said Pearl. "That I should have nothing more to do with them. Especially after what they tried to do."

"Have me killed, you mean?" Lila felt herself tremble inside as she spoke.

Pearl's eyes dropped once more. She nodded. Looked up again, her eyes struggling to hold Lila's gaze. "It's why I wanted to talk to you."

Lila felt her anger rising. "What d'you want me to say? Yeah, go and see them. Send them my love?"

"They say they're sorry."

"Oh well, it's all right, then. I'll come with you. Make a holiday of it." Her anger was getting out of control. She tried to tamp it down. "D'you want to see them?" she asked.

"Part of me wants nothing more to do with them" Her look of anguish seemed genuine. "The other part . . . They say they're sorry, that they've thought about it and realized they were wrong."

"How long did they have to think to come to that conclusion? Really?"

Pearl said nothing.

"Maybe they're just saying what you want to hear to get you to join them."

Pearl fell silent. Lila, her anger subsiding, waited. Eventually, Pearl spoke. "At first I wanted to go. Yeah, they're sorry. Great. I get my mum and dad back again. When that man attacked the house here, then I decided I was definitely going to get out of here as quickly as I could. And then there was Shelagh." She stopped talking, looking out the window. "She manipulated me when I was weak."

"I tried to tell you."

Pearl gave a sad smile. "I know you did. And I'm sorry. But when you fall into something like that, it's hard to claw your way out. I'm just glad she left when she did. Made me realize what had been happening."

"Good."

She nodded. "And Shelagh actually got me thinking about my parents. Maybe they were like that too. Manipulative. Kept me where they wanted me. Here. At home. Running their pub for them."

"You think so?"

Pearl became animated. "I've been thinking about this a lot recently. I went away to uni, but they made sure I came back here afterward. And I told them it was only temporary, until I got a job somewhere else. But there was always a reason why I couldn't go. They always needed me to do something. Something that meant I had to stay here. Until they left for good. Then I had no choice but to stay here."

"But wasn't it different by then?" said Lila. "You had the pub, you had Tom . . ." She smiled. "You had me to watch Netflix with."

Pearl returned the smile briefly. "Yes. But then there was this horror show with Tom. And Shelagh. So now . . ." She shrugged.

"Now, what? You're going to see your parents?"

"No. They made their choice. They have to live with it."

Lila frowned, puzzled. "Right. So . . . what are you going to do?"

Pearl sighed. "Go and . . . see what's out there? Beyond the village."

"OK." She felt sad at the thought of losing her friend.

Pearl picked up on that. "Doesn't mean I won't be coming back. Just that . . . I'll go away to think for a bit. I'm not getting any younger. Stuck behind a bar."

"What about Tom?"

Pearl nodded, eyes downcast once more. "That's the thing, isn't it? Tom?"

THAT NIGHT, LILA WENT TO BED EXHAUSTED.

That was last night. In the morning, she took a mouthful of tea, thankful that Karima had given her a pint of milk and a loaf of bread to go home with. Doing a regular shop hadn't been top of anyone's agenda recently.

She played with the remote, thought of picking up on last night's episode of *Queer Eye* but decided she didn't have the energy to concentrate on it. While deciding what to do, she heard a car pulling up outside, then doors opening.

Lila went to the window. She didn't recognize the car or the men hurrying back to it. It turned, headed back up the hill, a spray of gravel in its wake.

She put down her tea, ran for the door. Opening it, she stepped out, looked down, and gasped.

A bloodied, battered body of a man lay there.

She bent, heart hammering so hard it almost leaped out of her chest.

She turned the body over.

Gasped once more, felt her heart skip more than one beat. It was Tom.

48

"YOU ALL RIGHT IN THERE?" came a call through the bathroom door. "Haven't drowned or anything?"

"Yeah. I'm fine." Judy sloshed around the bathwater to demonstrate all was well.

"OK." A pause from beyond the door, as if something more was about to be said. But when there was silence, Judy stretched out in the bath once more.

He couldn't just sit in the bath all day but getting out meant facing the women on the other side of the door. And facing up to what he had just done, where he was going next. The bath was a more appealing option.

The night before, Shelagh had brought him back with her to her hotel room in Falmouth. It was swanky, certainly by his and his brother's standards, and he'd felt self-conscious walking past the night clerk, trying not to stare at the over-sized leather armchairs in the foyer. He couldn't believe they were just for temporarily sitting down in. The comfort, the relaxation. It made him feel even more out of place.

They walked down a corridor designed to mimic that of a ship—round porthole windows showing views of the restaurant where people were finishing off food he couldn't recognize—toward the bar area. Again, it looked like a luxury liner. A bow-tied barman and Shelagh shared a smile. Judy stared at a shelf of spirit bottles.

Then down a corridor, huge coils of rope forming sculptures and handrails, the walls clad in cream-painted wood, more of a rustic Cape Cod vibe. When they reached her room, she turned and smiled.

"Here we are."

He nervously took it all in. A huge bed. Tasteful decorations. A doorway leading outside to a courtyard. A bathroom to the right. He sat on the bed. And could have immediately fallen asleep on it. But Shelagh was looking at him.

"Nice room." He thought that was expected of him.

"It'll do." She sat on the bed next to him. "There's a pool here. We could go for a swim tomorrow."

"I haven't got anything to wear."

Shelagh smiled. "Don't worry about that. You never did tell me your name. I can't keep calling you Not Judy."

Judy didn't know what to say. But felt he had to say something. "I was . . . My brother was Punch. So I was Judy."

Shelagh sat up again. "Your parents really named you both that?"

He shook his head. "It's complicated. We . . ." He sighed. ". . . used to dress up. And I had to be Judy. And it stuck."

"What, all your life?"

He nodded. "It's how we were known. In places like—where we were when you found me."

"I know about the Fear Machine."

He almost did a double take. "How?"

Shelagh lay back down on the bed. "Later." She patted the space beside her. "Let's get to know each other first."

Judy's heart was hammering as he lay down next to her. She turned on her side, stretched out a hand, started stroking his chest.

"So what can I call you, then?"

The touch of her fingers was the most sensuous thing he had felt for years, possibly ever. His mind seemed to drift away from his body. "I don't know. Everybody just called me Judy."

"But you have a real name?"

"I used to. But then I was Judy. And that was my real name."

Her hand moved upward, stroking his beard. He felt his erection almost spring through his jeans. Even violence didn't make his heart hammer this fast. "So what shall we call you, then?" she asked.

"I don't know."

Her hand was on his neck, slowly tracing up and down. "Who do you want to be?"

"I . . . don't know."

She moved closer. He felt her warmth against his. He had been with women before, but he had paid for it mostly. As a teenager, there had been tourist girls and day-trippers, but that was up an alley, on the beach, a quick fuck or blow job. Nothing like this.

Shelagh kept stroking. He had to respond. He grabbed hold of her, pushed her back on the bed. Started to pull at his jeans, push her clothes apart.

"Hey . . . hey . . ."

She pulled away, hitting him. Landed blows to his face, startling him to inaction.

"What d'you think you're doing?"

He stared down at her. She looked appalled, terrified. "I . . ." He lay back on the bed.

Eventually, she moved toward him. Her hand on his body once more. "Let's try it my way, shall we?"

He couldn't look at her. He closed his eyes. Nodded.

AND NOW HE LAY IN THE BATH. Afraid to come out.

He pulled the plug, reached for a towel. Stepped out. Cleaned away steam on the mirror, scrutinizing his face harder than he had in years. Nearing middle age, dark hair and beard obscuring most of his facial features. The beard was in defiance at being Judy. To stop anyone thinking of him as a woman. To ensure everyone knew he was just performing. But it became who he was. He remembered someone on TV once saying to be careful about the masks we wear because they become who we are. Punch had laughed like he laughed at everything, but the words made a lasting impression on him. Looking at his face now, he saw just how true they were.

I want a haircut, he thought. I want rid of this beard. I want some new clothes. I want to be someone else . . . It tumbled out of him like an emotional torrent. He left the bathroom.

Shelagh was lying on the bed, leafing through a magazine. She looked up when he entered. She was wearing a hotel-supplied toweling robe. Nice, shapely legs, good body for an older woman. Older than him, anyway. And something else. Patches of pink shiny skin on her body. He had been in such a frenzy the night before he hadn't taken anything in, but now he realized they were scars. She pulled her robe together as if suddenly conscious of his gaze.

"There you are," she said. "Thought you'd drowned." She managed a smile.

"I'm here," he said unnecessarily.

She moved so that her legs were tucked underneath her body. "Have you decided on a new name yet?"

He thought. He needed something that spoke of new beginnings, of putting the past behind him. Of being brave and unafraid. He had it.

"Jack," he said. "Jack Ketch."

Shelagh smiled. "Well, Jack, let's decide what we're going to do today, shall we?"

49

PENROSE COULD BARELY KEEP HIS EYES OPEN. He had sat for hours, staring at the tired-looking yacht moored just outside Truro. He'd parked up in a small clearing, hoping the twigs and branches of the denuded bushes would provide enough camouflage to stop the yacht's odd inhabitant from seeing him.

He'd followed Punch's beat-up car here from the old factory. Penrose had wondered whether the dilapidated vehicle would actually get the man home. He had stayed as far back as he could, risking losing him at times, due to the sparse nighttime traffic, but had stuck with him. Then Punch had pulled up alongside a boat, its degraded state matching the car's, and he went on board. A couple of lights turned briefly on, then darkness.

Penrose should have gone home then, slept, ready for work in the morning. But he didn't. He reasoned away his excuses for being late the next day or not turning up at all, and when he was sure Punch was out for the night, he settled back in the car to sleep.

The last few days had been the most exciting he had been through in his life. Being honest with himself, it was exactly why he had joined the police force. Ironically, he had had to go against orders to do this, but he reasoned that it was a risk worth taking. When he presented his and Tom's findings, that should be a commendation in the bag. Yes, he wanted to crack this case, do his job, but if he enjoyed himself along the way, what was the problem?

He woke before dawn, his neck fused to his shoulders, his legs aching from being curled into positions legs shouldn't be curled into. Checking that nothing had changed with the boat, he got out of the car, pissed up against the side of a tree. He yawned, smiled. A proper cop stakeout. Here he was.

He'd gotten no message from Tom. He decided against phoning him in case he was still undercover. He kept concentrating on the boat. And slept once more.

He woke again when dawn broke. No sign of movement in the boat. He doubted there would be for some time. Punch didn't seem like a morning person.

It was freezing in the car. Penrose pulled his coat about him, rubbed his hands together. Toyed with putting the heating on but decided against it. Didn't want to run the battery down. He checked his watch, called the office. Told them he was following up on something about the attack on Simon West and he would be in later. Conscience dealt with, he settled down to watch once more.

PUNCH WAS IN NO HURRY to get out of bed. Or wake up. They didn't have anywhere to be today. He and Judy could—

Judy. He remembered the club and the "surprise" he'd arranged. And how badly it had gone down.

He got up. Judy was bound to be back by now.

"Judy?"

He walked into the main seating area.

"Come on, it was just a joke. That's all. You'd have laughed any other time."

Angry now, he barged into Judy's bedroom, almost banging the door off its hinges. The bed, as far as he could tell in all the mess, hadn't even been slept in.

Judy had nowhere else to go but here. He had no other friends, no friends full stop.

He took out his phone and rang Judy's number, which went to voice mail.

He tried to see if he could find Judy's phone by using the GPS tracker on his phone. It started blinking. Punch smiled, but that faded when he realized that the signal came from the boat. Judy had left his phone at home.

He threw his phone on the tatty sofa. Sat down after it. Thought.

Had Judy gone back inside the club? Tried to get revenge on the men he had paid to pretend to rape Judy. Well, he had told them to pretend, but they weren't too good at following directions. Punch couldn't be blamed for that, could he?

His phone rang.

He jumped, grabbed it, hoping it would be Judy. Then he saw the display. He had to answer it.

"Might have a job for you and Judy." It was Marx.

Punch paused before answering. "All right."

Marx picked up on it straightaway. "What's the matter?" Voice deadpan, threat implicit.

"Nothing," said Punch too quickly.

"There a problem?"

"No problem."

Marx waited for Punch to answer.

"Judy didn't come home from the Fear Machine last night."

A pause from the other end.

"No worries," said Punch. "I'll find him."

"You will." Again, the unstated threat of what would happen if he didn't.

"Yeah. So what's this job?"

"Come to mine, and we'll discuss it."

"On my way." Another pause. "I'll find Judy when I get back." He made an ill-advised attempt at levity. Laughed. "Priorities, you know."

"Make sure you do."

When the line went dead, he threw the phone back on the sofa like it was suddenly hot.

Shit.

He scrambled to get ready and leave. Didn't want to keep the boss waiting.

PENROSE WAS ABOUT TO GIVE IN when, at last, there was movement on the boat.

Suddenly, he was wide awake. Conscious of not being seen, he slid down in his car seat.

Dressed in cheap trainers, joggers, and a jacket, Punch emerged from the boat and jumped into his junky car. After taking a while to start it, he sped off.

Punch was obviously going somewhere in a hurry. Thinking this must be something important, Penrose followed.

50

Tom opened his eyes. Turned his head. He saw Lila glance up at him, quickly put her book down, and cross to his bedside. He was in his own bedroom. He was home.

"What time is it?"

Lila checked her phone. "Just gone seven. At night. How you feeling?"

Tom gave the question some thought. "Terrible." He tried to take a deep breath and sit up but the movement set off small grenades of pain that exploded throughout his body. "*Ow.*"

"Take it easy," said Lila. "Try not to move."

Tom nodded. Tried to stay still. "What happened?" he asked.

"I was hoping you could tell me."

Tom nodded, the effort sending incendiary body waves from his neck. He tested himself, tried to move different limbs. Gauging his pain, wincing all the time.

"You were thrown out of a car to the front door," said Lila. "I was going to call for an ambulance, but you were insistent that I didn't. Gasping and shouting. So I managed to get you inside and up the stairs. Then you passed out."

"Have you called anyone? A doctor?"

Lila's expression became evasive. "Yeah. They said that apart from your ribs, which look cracked or broken, it doesn't look like there's any more serious damage. Lots of bruising. Like whoever did this wanted to really hurt you, not cripple you."

"How would you know that?"

Lila gave a grim smile. "Remember where I was living when you first met me. And who I was living with. This is not the first time I've seen this kind of thing. Hope it's the last, though."

Tom lay still for a while, letting his mind catch up.

Lila stared at him. Tears forming in the corners of her eyes. She angrily wiped them away. "You're a fucking idiot. What were you doing this time?"

"I . . . The Fear Machine. Where's Penrose?"

"No idea. Why, was he in on this too?"

"We were staking out a fight club, looking for the person responsible for the break-in here. I went inside." He sighed. It hurt. "There was a huge hall and a cage . . . Cage fighting. I was dragged inside it and . . ." He shook his head slowly. "That's it." He closed his eyes once more. "No. There was a face."

"Who?"

"Can't remember. Someone I recognized was watching."

They fell into silence as he struggled to conjure up the image.

"We have to talk," said Tom. "I tried to call you, but—"

"We'll talk about all that later. There's other stuff as well."

Tom sighed. "Thank you for coming back."

Tears threatened Lila's eyes once more. "You're a stupid twat, you know that?"

Tom gave a sad smile. "I know."

Lila forced herself not to cry. Eventually, Tom tried to sit up once more.

"What d'you think you're doing?" she scolded.

"Can't lie here all day. Or night. I have things to do."

"I don't think so. Nurse Lila says you need to rest."

Before either could say anything more, they heard a car pull up outside, the door open and close, and a knock on the front door. Tom gave Lila a puzzled look but she said nothing.

When the door opened, Pearl stood in the doorway.

Lila stood. "I'll leave you two to talk."

51

SIMON SAT ON THE CONCRETE front steps of the house, phone in hand, coat pulled around him. He had just returned from one of his many walks around the compound. Inside the house Michelle was lying on the sofa, staring vacantly at the television, clearly not wanting him in there with her. Outside on the porch, it was cold and threatening rain. When it started to fall, he'd go back inside to his room. One place was the same as another in this prison.

Several times each day, he walked around the grounds. Sometimes he ran, just to feel his body respond. The dogs barked and howled, and miserable Robert would go into the hangars to check on them, sometimes accompanied by Marx. Simon wanted to see them, but he knew he had to wait to be invited. It wasn't right to keep animals cooped up all the time like that. But it wasn't right to keep him cooped up either.

Twice a day, Marx walked out to the brick cabin at the back of the property. That was where the mad dog's howling came from. Simon had been told that this dog was so bad it had to be separated from the others. The howling seemed strange, barely doglike. When Simon had mentioned it one day to Michelle, she just shrugged. "Dog, innit?" she said.

Since Simon's arrival, the compound had only one visitor: a small ugly man driving an ancient, patchwork car. Marx and he had closeted themselves away in Marx's office in the house, too quiet to be heard. There was something familiar about this creepy man—his walk, voice, whatever. It kept niggling at him.

"Having fun?"

Simon jumped, nearly dropped his phone. He hadn't heard Aiden Marx's approach. For a man who relied on a stick, he could move quickly and quietly.

Simon thought of giving the kind of false, upbeat answer Marx expected. But thought again.

"Not really." Simon shrugged. "Nothing to do."

"You bored?"

He answered with another shrug, then thought it needed more. "When I came here, I was told I was going to do important things. But I've just sat here, doing nothing."

He didn't risk glancing up at Marx. Simon was frightened of the man whose maimed body seemed a frail cage for a violent soul. Simon sensed the man's stick was more than a walking aid. Maybe that's why he was reluctant to speak the truth to him.

Marx lowered his body next to Simon's, joining him on the steps. He smiled at him. Simon didn't know if he should be reassured or scared.

Marx sighed theatrically. "Simon, Simon, Simon, what are we going to do with you?"

Simon pushed his luck. "That's what I want to know."

"I'm sure you do. When I was your age, I couldn't wait to do everything, see everything, experience everything . . . you've got the whole of your life ahead of you for that. Don't rush it."

"So why am I here?"

"You'd rather be back in that foster home?"

"No." But maybe he would.

"Well, then. Just relax for the time being. You'll find out when the time comes. Gimme a look at your phone."

Before Simon could hand it over, Marx grabbed it from Simon's hands. He examined it, attempting to get whatever weak sunlight was hiding behind the clouds to glint off its edges.

"Nice," Marx said. "New one?"

"My dad bought it for me." A shiver of pain mixed with guilt rippled through him at the mention of him.

"Right." Still examining it, turning it over and over. "An iPhone. I've got a phone, but nothing as flash as this. Should I get one?"

"If you want one." Why was Marx asking him about this?

"What's it do, then? What makes it so special?"

"Well, it's just . . . an iPhone."

"Show me. Open it up."

Simon waited to be given the phone back, but Marx held onto it. Simon reached over, looked at the screen. It opened using facial recognition.

"Wow," said Marx. "So you have to look at it to get it to open? Yeah? Just you."

"Just me."

"And now what?"

"Then you've got all these apps. You press one, it does stuff. You've got photos, Twitter, Facebook, TikTok, all of that. Texting, FaceTime . . ."

"And of course, you can make calls with it?" Marx laughed as he spoke.

Simon felt himself loosening up slightly. "Yeah, that as well."

Marx began pressing apps, moving things. "You keep much on it, then?"

"Not really, I—"

"What's this here?" He pointed to a blue folder.

"Files. Never used it. You can make notes of things and keep them on here. Had a lot on my old phone. School stuff. Nothing on this one yet."

Marx pressed the blue folder. Something came up, an acknowledgment that a file was there. He closed it again quickly. "Well. Really nice bit of kit, that."

He handed the phone back to Simon. "Thanks."

"Called anyone since you've been here?"

Simon sensed a change in Marx as he spoke those words.

"I've got no one to call."

Marx nodded as if Simon had just given the correct answer, then looked across the field. Eventually, he spoke. "See that?" He pointed to one of the sculptures, of a man in a cage. It was the one they had stopped in front of the first day he had arrived. "Saved my life, that did."

"Really?" Simon looked at Marx in puzzlement.

"Yeah. Saved my life. I was a . . . well, suppose you'd say, a bad lad. In trouble with the law, that kind of thing."

"Did you go to prison?"

Marx laughed. "You don't mess about, do you? Yeah, I went to prison. Like I say, bad lad. Got in with some other bad lads. Had to pay the price. But him over there." Again, he gestured to the sculpture. "He saved my life."

"How?"

"Made me see things differently. That there was more to life than what I'd been doing. See this here?" He patted his damaged leg.

"Yeah."

"Police did this to me. When they caught me for burglary, they hauled me into the station. It's fair to say there was no love lost between me and the boys in blue, and when they got me on my own, well . . . they got carried away." Marx's voice took on an angry tone.

Simon couldn't think of anything to say.

"Made them pay for it later, though. Literally." He gave a bitter laugh. "Got me this place. I sued them. Well, my lawyer sued them. Said I could never work again. Which was true. Couldn't go back to my old ways as a cripple, could I? So I got a payout. A big one. And bought this piece of land. And had this all built. But it still wasn't enough. You know why?"

"*Er*, no."

"I'll tell you. I had money, but I still wasn't allowed into all the places money usually gets a person into. Couldn't join golf clubs 'cause I wasn't one of them. Mind you, couldn't play fucking golf, could I? Not with this leg. But that's not the point. They didn't want me. I wasn't one of them. But, idiot that I was, I kept trying. And then it all changed when I met a woman."

"Right."

"She worked in the arts, and she took a fancy to me. For who and what I was. Her bit of rough. I didn't mind. Take what you can get in this life, don't you?"

Simon, completely out of his depth, agreed.

"She and I got married. And suddenly people wanted to know me. Well, I thought I'd arrived. And because she was into art and that, I thought I'll give it a go. So I did. And you know what?"

"What?"

Marx laughed. "My work was shit. But that didn't matter. Because I'd invested wisely. I had money. And arty people always need money. So I became a collector. A patron. And all those golf clubs were now fucking begging me to join. And you know what? I didn't give any of them cunts the satisfaction." Anger entered his voice.

Wary, Simon was silent.

"Anyway. This sculpture here. I saw it and knew I had to have it. Because that was me. The old me. And I wanted a reminder of how far I'd come. And that's why he's there."

"Right." Simon nodded. But a fact stood out. "So what happened to your wife?"

Something unreadable passed across Marx's face. "We're not together anymore."

"Right."

Marx leaned in close. "Word of advice? Always go for the thick ones. Clever women bleed you dry, first chance they get. Think they're better than you. Know everything. And they won't take a telling . . ." He shook his head, off somewhere else. "Get one who won't answer back. You'll thank me for that one day."

Simon nodded, said nothing.

Marx struggled to his feet. Simon tried to help him, but he slapped his hand away.

"Come on."

"Where?" asked Simon.

"You wanted to do something, didn't you?"

"Definitely."

Marx frowned, as if trying to reach a decision. Smiled. "I think it's time you met the dogs."

52

Tom forced himself to move around the house. Up and down stairs, in and out of rooms, around the garden. Exercising his body, getting his muscles to respond and fight through the pain. In the three days, he'd been awake and up; his bruises were already changing from deep purple to pale yellow, like reverse-ripening fruit. His injuries hurt when he breathed, moved, or spoke, and his ribs were sore, but he thought there would not be long-lasting damage.

Was it a warning to stay away? He didn't know. Tom had never backed down from a fight before. A strategic retreat to regroup, come back stronger, yes. He had been trained for that both in the army and police force. But never give up and walked away. He was conflicted as to what to do.

Pearl's visit to his bedside the night before made his mind up.

She had stood there, looking uncomfortable. He felt something inside even harsher than his physical pain.

"Hi."

"Hi yourself." He coughed as he spoke and her expression shifted to concern.

She sat on the edge of the bed. "What happened?"

"You should see the other fella."

Her expression changed; proof of her doubts about him surfacing once more.

"Sorry. Joke. What you do in these situations." He propped himself up with a groan.

"What were you doing? Penrose said you just jumped out of the car and went straight into this old building where there was some kind of illegal bare-knuckle thing going on."

"Yeah, pretty much."

She shook her head. "This is what I meant, Tom. This is why I walked away. Why did you do it? What were you hoping to prove?"

Tom sighed. It hurt. "I wanted to make sure we were safe. You, Lila. All of us. That whoever broke into my house was finished with us. Looking into it led me there."

"And are we? Safe?"

Tom thought. Whatever was happening wasn't his fight, and there was no further need to get himself involved, his loved ones hurt. But admitting that aloud felt like an admission of failure, running away from a fight for the first time in his life. Not a strategic retreat, just a retreat. He was unsure how that made him feel. Or how it should make him feel.

Pearl answered for him. "You can't keep fighting the world, Tom. You have to make peace with it sometime. And with yourself too."

And my past, he thought. "Yeah, I know."

"Just let it go. Get on with your life."

Tom looked at Pearl—properly, for this first time since she'd entered the room. She looked drawn, distracted, like she had been engaged in a secret fight and didn't know if she was winning or losing. He wanted to ask her about it. Didn't know if she would answer. Didn't even know if he had that right anymore.

"I will," he said.

She scrutinized his eyes.

"I believe you," she said, smiling. "Either you're lying and hiding it well or you're telling the truth."

"I don't have the energy to lie, nor the creativity."

She kept smiling. "Good."

PENROSE ARRIVED while Tom was attempting to do sit-ups.

"Thought you'd have been here sooner," said Tom, getting up slowly from the living room floor.

"I waited until you were up before coming," he said. "I spoke to Pearl. She's been keeping me up to date on your progress."

"And what about your progress?'

"I followed Punch, the guy with the bells. He lives on a boat just outside Truro. I checked it out. It was abandoned years ago, the owners just left it."

"Right."

"I think he must have been living there with the one in the dress—Judy, we'll call him. But it looks like he's there alone now. Anyway, the day after we parted, I followed him driving into the country. He went to a private estate beyond huge gates, which slid back to let him in. Big high hedge—leylandii, I think—razor wire all around the top."

"Country house?"

"With razor wire? Hardly. More like a compound, a place where the Far Right or something would train. Or a cult would live. Something like that."

"Did you find out who owns the property?"

"It belongs to someone called Aiden Marx. Bit of a villain, nasty one. Sued the police for assaulting him a few years ago, even though he was guilty. Walks with a limp because of the treatment he received. Got a massive settlement, enough to buy that place and reinvent himself as a patron of the arts. Apparently, he's still dirty, though. Supposedly one of the biggest names in dogfighting." Penrose sat on the couch. "Dogfighting and the arts. How does that work? Anyway, question for us is, what was Punch doing there?"

Tom thought before answering. "No, Chris. Wrong question. What has this to do with us?"

Penrose frowned. "What d'you mean?"

"What's it got to do with us?" Tom said again.

"Well . . ." Penrose doubted what he was hearing. "It's what we've been working on. Our sideline. Our case."

Tom sighed. "There is no case, Chris."

Penrose looked hurt. "What d'you mean?"

"Whatever's happening in that compound has nothing to do with me. I went into that place, they beat me up."

"Which is all the more reason to keep investigating."

"No, it's not. It was a warning to leave off, and I'm taking it. I'm safe, Lila and Pearl and everyone else is safe. That's good enough for me. Whatever else is happening doesn't concern me."

Penrose's eyes betrayed disbelief. "What—"

"I'm sorry, Chris, but there's no point in me going on with this. You're police, you can. It's your job. But it's nothing to do with me anymore."

Silence fell between the two men. Eventually, Penrose stood up, tucked his shirt in even though it didn't need it. He looked at Tom, face impassive, eyes alive with something Tom had never seen there before.

"You feeling better, then?" the policeman asked.

"Getting there," said Tom.

"Good." Penrose turned, let himself out. Slammed the door behind him.

Tom felt bad damaging Penrose's evident enthusiasm. But he had no choice.

53

JUDY WAS DEAD. GONE FOREVER. Now there was only Jack Ketch. He was still getting used to the name but he enjoyed being someone else. It was like going to a place where no one knew you, talking differently, acting differently. Jack was never going home again.

A barber had shaved off his beard. He didn't recognize the face that stared back at him from the mirror. Even his eyes looked different. Then came a proper haircut. The barber asked him how he wanted it, and he didn't know. Shelagh had to give instructions. She had been right. The new cut suited him.

Clothes were next. They went on a shopping spree on Shelagh's credit card. No more charity shop jeans and joggers, Matalan and Primark when he had been feeling swank. He had always thought shopping was a waste of time. You bought new clothes when the old ones wore out. As cheaply as possible. Not so, said Shelagh. Clothes did much more than that. They were important, they told the world who you were. She took him to John Lewis, White Stuff, Debenhams. She made him try on things he would never in a million years have chosen for himself—or even looked at. Floral shirts. Suede shoes, brogues even.

Jeans that fit and accentuated his legs. Jackets, waistcoats, and fitted overcoats. Even a scarf. He stood in the changing cubicle with his new clothes on, his new haircut. It was like staring at a photo in a magazine. He no longer knew who he was, which scared and delighted him in equal measure. Because he was daring to like who he was becoming.

After Debenhams, they stopped for coffee. Jack was confused at first. Why would you stop shopping just to sit down and drink coffee and eat cake? He was inundated with bags and struggled to tuck them under the table, to prevent people from tripping over them and treading on his new clothes. He felt almost angrily out of place. But no one paid him or Shelagh any mind. There were young people working on laptops, mothers with babies in buggies. Couples just like him and Shelagh drinking, chatting. Normal people doing normal things. It was a different world from what he had been used to.

He panicked. The people around them knew how to sit, behave, talk. He didn't. He and his brother had never ventured into places like this. "Not for the likes of us," Punch had always said, voice dripping with acid. And Judy, doing what he was told, had gone along with it. Punch used to say that the kind of people who went into places like this or the shops he had been in were boring, Unimaginative. Dull. "Not like us," Punch said. "We're different. We're outsiders. We live lives they can only dream about."

Waiting for Shelagh while sitting at a table, Jack looked at other people in the coffeehouse. No one seemed to be dreaming about the kind of life he'd led with Punch.

He noticed something else too. Languages other than English were being spoken. One person sounded Eastern European, and he bristled when he heard the words, like a dog spotting an adversary in its territory. But this woman and man didn't look like adversaries. Just a couple with a small child in a pushchair, drinking and eating. He was mesmerized. Punch would have said they didn't belong there, that he had more right to this space than them. But Jack thought they seemed to fit in just fine. Knew where to sit, what to order, how to behave. They actually belonged here more than he did, a conclusion that came to him in a blinding flash. But instead of anger, he felt sadness.

Shelagh returned with coffees and cakes. Jack felt like a child experiencing things for the first time. The coffee was like nothing he'd tasted before—definitely not instant. The cake provided a massive sugar rush to his brain. He smiled to himself. This was the kind of life he'd always wanted but didn't know how to get. All he needed was someone to show him the way, someone like Shelagh.

Eventually, they went back to the hotel, both exhausted. She got him to try on all his clothes again. She smiled while he modeled them for her, looking at him, listening to him, seeing him. He had never felt like this before. She made him feel really special.

"I bought something for myself as well," she said. "Well, for you, really. Wait there."

She took a couple of the bags into the bathroom, closed the door. Jack was unsure what was happening. She took her time. He became nervous, angry once more, thinking she might be playing a trick on him. Like everything before had been to soften him up and she had Punch in there ready to jump out and show him what an idiot he was.

He had built himself up into quite a fit of anger by the time the door opened. It disappeared when he saw her. Shelagh stood framed in the doorway wearing the kind of underwear he had only ever seen in porn films. And it looked even better on her.

"Surprise," she said.

He stared.

She sighed, slight irritation showing. "Well, come on, then. Don't you want to open your present?"

Something shifted inside him. Something primal, alien to the new, polite Jack. He moved toward her and tore open his present.

54

THE DAYS DREW ON and Tom felt his body and mind improving. Increased exercise, coupled with spending time at home with Lila. And Pearl, although there was still some distance there. The events of the last week had shown him what was important in his life, what was worth fighting for, and more importantly, that there was more than one way to fight for it.

So it was almost inevitable something should happen to spoil everything.

Lila and he had eaten dinner, a simple vegetable lasagna Tom had made, experimenting in cooking without meat as Lila was toying with vegetarianism. They had both enjoyed it and were now arguing over what to watch on TV.

"You can watch that Netflix reality TV rubbish anytime," Tom said. "Let's watch something we both want to see."

"But it's not rubbish," Lila argued passionately, but Tom saw the glint in her eye. She would do this just for fun. It was often how they communicated. "All of life is there, Tom. Don't dismiss reality TV. It shows the everyday struggles that people go through, unscripted. It's real life."

"It's not and you know it's not. It's as fake as *EastEnders.*"

She shook her head sadly, her expression mock sympathy. "I just don't know what more I can say, Tom, how I can educate you. Yes, they might be people living on a luxury yacht, but they're the crew. It's set below deck, like it says. They do all the work, not the rich guests. They're the paddling webbed feet, churning away so the swans can glide gracefully on the surface." She sat back, pleased with herself.

Tom smiled. "Did you read that somewhere and memorize it?"

"Shut up." Also smiling.

"We're still not watching it."

"Fair enough." She threw the TV remote at him. "Have it your way."

He caught it. "Thank you." Pointed it at the TV, changing channels. "Let's have a look, then."

And stopped, stared.

"I know him," said Tom.

It was a Channel Four news show, and the subject of the interview was familiar to Tom. The suit, the smarm. The perfect hair. The condescending attitude and curled lip, like he was pitying the interviewer's inferiority.

"Is this what you wanted to watch?" said Lila. "Because it's boring . . ." The last word was drawn out in her faux-bored teenage voice.

"Just a minute."

She saw how serious Tom had become, realized it wasn't the time for jokes.

The TV interviewer, a man of Indian ethnicity, was doing his best to politely skewer the man, make him give himself away. The interviewee was dodging every parry.

"Wouldn't you say," asked the interviewer, *"that dressing up a political candidate in old English folklore is just pandering to an*

ethnofascist idea of what this country should be like? Hankering after a golden age that never truly existed?"

"Who's he?" asked Lila.

"Ben Tarpley. I spoke to him at Falmouth University. Didn't like him then, don't like him now."

Tarpley continued, *"Who says the golden age never existed? Who says Camelot was a myth? And who says we can't have that again?"*

"The Camelot we see in popular culture, films and TV, that one certainly never existed," said the host. *"There's even argument that King Arthur wasn't actually English, that he was Welsh. That doesn't help your English nationalist cause much, does it?"*

Again, the professor offered up his sanctimonious, pitying smile. *"Of course he was English. As all the history books will attest. All the ones that aren't revisionist left-wing propaganda, of course."*

"He's an arsehole," said Lila.

"No argument from me," said Tom.

Tarpley talked over the interviewer's next question. *"What's wrong with wanting to see a return to the mythic, the heroic in our country? What have you got against that? Don't you want us to be proud of who we are, where we came from?"*

The last few words dripped with wry disdain, given the interviewer's Indian origin.

He didn't rise to the bait. *"But aren't you just another racist apologist? Hiding your beliefs in fake patriotism?"*

Tarpley laughed. *"Not hardly. The party I'm speaking for, the candidate I'm speaking for, couldn't be further away from ignorance and racism. Haven't you heard a single word Arthur King has said?"* Tarpley smiled to the camera. And Tom felt a near electric shock course through him.

He remembered that smile.

Fight club. Inside the Fear Machine. Standing on one of the upper gantries, looking down at him in the cage. Smiling. One of the last things he saw before agonizing darkness had closed in.

"He was there," Tom said, getting up because the adrenaline moving through his body stopped him from staying still.

"What?"

"At the Fear Machine." Tom began pacing the room, feeling stronger than he had for ages. "That night, I saw him. I didn't remember until just now. But Tarpley was there. Looking at me. Enjoying himself as I went down."

"Is that bad?"

"He told me he didn't know anything about the place, that he was a supporter of Arthur King but nothing more. He was lying. He's right in it. Up to his neck. I'll have to phone Penrose."

Lila stood also. "*Whoa, whoa*, stop. Stop." She stood in front of him, placed her hands on his shoulders. "Why d'you have to tell Chris about this? What's the hurry?"

"Because Tarpley lied."

"So?"

"Chris needs to talk to him. Find out what else he knows."

"About what?"

"About Simon, our visitor, everything."

Lila kept staring at him. Eventually, Tom had no choice but to acknowledge her gaze.

"What?" More a statement than a question.

"It's not your fight, Tom. Not anymore."

Tom stared at her. The old energy back again.

"So Tarpley was there that night, so what? And he lied to you? Color me surprised. Big deal." She held him more firmly. "Let it go."

"It just feels like I should be doing something. That's all."

"Okay, so tell Chris. Let him deal with it."

Tom said nothing, turned his eyes back to the screen.

"All I would say," Tarpley was continuing, *"is if you're in the area and you're eligible to vote, vote for Arthur King this Thursday. You'll be part of the next exciting political wave to hit this country. This is going to be huge, I promise you. It's not just a little by-election in Cornwall. It's going to have major, national implications. This is only the start. Wait and see."*

At some point during the television interview, Tarpley had stopped answering the host's questions and started addressing the viewer directly. Tom shuddered with unease.

"Tom?"

He turned back to Lila.

Tarpley's face disappeared from the screen.

Another sigh. Of defeat this time. "I'll tell Penrose. Let him deal with it."

"Good." Lila dropped her hands from his side. "Let's watch something else. Cheer ourselves up."

Tom sat back down again. Let Lila choose her stupid show about the yacht crew.

He stared at the screen but didn't see any of it.

55

JACK KNEW HE HAD DONE WRONG. It just took him a while to work out what.

Shelagh hadn't spoken to him the morning after they had sex. Nor the rest of the day and night. Nor the morning after that. Or she had spoken, but in the most minimal way. Nodding or shaking her head, staring at something he couldn't see while he spoke to her.

Her behavior made him angry. He had heard that women weren't easy to live with and now discovered that was true. This was all her fault, and his anger was building, readying to explode. She wouldn't want to be near him when that happened. Oh no.

But like hungry snakes slithering into houses through the tiniest cracks in the floorboards, other thoughts crept in alongside his anger. Maybe it wasn't just her. Maybe he was responsible and didn't realize it.

Everything had been going really well until it wasn't. So what had changed? Shelagh's silences made him work to fill in the parts around them. His part in all this. He thought back to when Shelagh emerged from the bathroom wearing her present to him and telling him to unwrap it. He had. And everything had gone bad from there.

He didn't know what he had done. He'd responded to her the way he'd always responded to a woman dressed like that. Like he'd seen in porn films. Like he'd done with the women he had bought or Punch had bought for him, after Punch had first dibs on them. They'd always enjoyed it. Or said they were enjoying it, which was the same thing.

Shelagh hadn't. When Jack got going on her, she stiffened up. Closed her eyes. They usually put their head back and moaned loudly, but she lay still, unsmiling, as he worked his lust out on her body. And when he'd finished, he rolled off and went to sleep. Sometime during the night, he had woken up because the bed was shaking. He was surprised to find Shelagh crying.

Thinking she must be cold or something, he'd asked her what was wrong. She just looked surprised he was there and turned away. At least he'd thought it was surprise. Thinking back, he wondered if she had looked scared. He asked her again in the morning what had made her cry.

She shook her head. "Nothing."

He lay next to her, ready to be what help he could. "People don't cry for nothing."

She made a harsh sound that could have been a laugh or a cry, he couldn't tell. Then turned away from him and pretended to sleep.

Then the silent treatment started. And nothing he could say or do could get her to respond beyond a few mumbled syllables.

That dragged on all day and into the next. He kept himself busy by going for walks on his own, but he stopped because he feared that if he was too long away from the hotel, she might take the opportunity to leave him. Jack had done some deep thinking. He questioned what he was actually doing with her. She was paying, that was a big draw. And she wasn't bad looking—older than him, but she carried it well—and her scars were covered up for the most part. According to his brother, it was a well-known fact that older women were cougars, grateful for the attention and willing to do things to keep a younger man that a younger woman would not.

The clothes she had bought for him felt dirty, tarnished after her rejection, and he didn't want to wear them. Like they made her sad in some way. *That* was when the realization hit.

"Have I done something wrong?"

They were in the restaurant at the hotel, eating dinner. He had dressed up for her. She hadn't made much of an effort and appeared older than usual. She looked up from the food she had been moving slowly around her plate. "What makes you think that?"

"Because you're upset and won't talk to me. And I can't think why. But it was after we had that sex the night before last that you started crying. So it must be something to do with that. And if it is . . ." Here came the words he didn't want to say because he didn't know why he was saying them. ". . . then I'm sorry."

Shelagh almost smiled. She shook her head. There were tears at the corners of her eyes.

"I've done it again, haven't I?" she said to herself as much as to him. "Done it again." She shook her head. Wiped her eyes with the back of her hand. Looked at him properly for the first time in a while.

He smiled. It had worked. She was happy again. He had done it. *Jack* had done it.

"You've hurt people before, haven't you?"

It was not what he had been expecting to hear. He was too shocked to answer.

She spoke again. "Haven't you? Don't lie because I know you have."

His face reddened—from anger or embarrassment, he didn't know. "Yes," he said eventually.

"You and your brother both. That's what you do, isn't it?" Her voice crept up in volume, becoming shakier. "Don't lie. I know it is. I just want to hear you say it."

His head swam. Why was she talking like this? "I used to," he said, "but I want to change. Even before I met you, I was sick of all that. That's why I want to become someone new. With you. I'm Jack now."

She gave that noise again, which could have been a harsh laugh or a cry. "You weren't Jack the other night, were you?" Her voice rose again, becoming slightly untethered. "You were your old self again." Tears gathered once more, and she wiped at them angrily, as if they were irritating insects.

Jack stared at his plate, suddenly without an appetite. His mouth moved but no words emerged.

"Oh, stop that. You look like a masticating cow."

He frowned. Could cows do that?

"So you've hurt people. With your brother and others. And you've killed as well. Haven't you?"

Jack looked around the room. Was she wearing a wire? Were the authorities going to jump out from behind the bar? He readied himself to run.

"Relax, you idiot. I'm not police."

It was like she had been reading his mind. He stayed still.

She continued. "I made a mistake. That's all. I thought I could coax you into doing what I wanted. Ask you nicely." She looked down at the table, seeming angry at herself. "I shouldn't have bothered, should I? Should have just asked straightaway." Not angry, he noticed, sadder. "Would have saved me a lot of money."

"What are you talking about?"

She leaned forward. "I already knew about you and your brother. That's why I was parked outside the Fear Machine that night when I met you. Did you think it was a coincidence that we met?"

"Well, yes."

She shook her head. "It wasn't. You were my plan B. Either one of you would have done, or both, I couldn't be fussy. Someone else from that place might have done just as well. But when I saw you two arguing and you walked away, I knew you'd be perfect."

"For what?"

She almost laughed. "You never thought to ask, did you? After that first night when I said I needed help and I'd be grateful, you never asked what that was."

"I guessed you'd tell me when you were ready. And then all this happened . . ."

"The clothes, the hotel, this restaurant, I know. And you didn't say anything. But the other night when you . . . did what you did . . . I knew that none of my efforts had been worthwhile. I should have just asked." She shook her head. "You'd think I'd learned my lesson about men by now."

Jack was thoroughly confused. "What are you talking about? What do you want me to do?"

She moved her chair closer to his so there was no chance anyone else could see or hear what was going on at their table. "You hurt people. Even kill them. Good."

Jack felt uneasy. "No. I used to do that. That's not me

anymore. I don't— Sometimes I have nightmares. And I haven't had any nightmares this week with you."

She snorted. "Oh my God, he's developed a conscience. Well, I suppose that's my fault, isn't it?"

Jack just stared at her.

"Dear, sweet Jack . . ." Was she mocking him? He didn't like that. "What I need is for you to go back to your old ways. Get that killer glint in your eye once more."

He sat unmoving while her words settled in. And suddenly he no longer felt like Jack. That was a lie. He was just Judy in proper clothes, with a good haircut and no beard. He dropped his head.

"I don't want to go back."

"You have no choice."

"What d'you mean?"

"I know about your past. I could walk out of here, phone the police, and tell them where you are and who you are. And that would be the end of you, wouldn't it?"

Jack felt a great loss of control. He didn't know whether to be angry or scared. "Why would you do that?"

"I just said I could, not that I would. Because I want you to do something for me. You can keep the clothes. Don't worry about them."

Jack felt wary. The restaurant, the hotel, had turned into some kind of trap. He could try and physically stop her from leaving, but this place was too public. They would be on him straightaway. So he realized he had no choice but to listen to what she wanted. And probably do it.

"I'll pay you, of course," she said. "I should have made all that clear in the first place instead of all this playacting."

He thought. "So if I do this, then that's it? I can be Jack?"

"You can be whoever you want to be, darling."

He thought again. And spoke with something of a heavy heart. "OK, then. What is it?"

"You know Aiden Marx."

"Yeah, what about him?"

"He has something that I want. Something precious. I've been planning this for years, how to get near him. I want this precious thing back, and you're going to help me."

"How?"

"He's planning a party this week to coincide with the election."

Jack perked up. "Arthur King."

"That's right. You and me are going to go to this party. And that's when you're going to liberate my precious thing for me, preferably while inflicting as much damage to Aiden Marx as possible can. Deal?"

He would have to be Judy one more time. Or he would channel Judy while wearing Jack's clothes. Just one more time.

"OK, then."

"Good. That wasn't so difficult, was it?"

He nodded. "You still seem really angry with me. I said I was sorry."

Her eyes widened; her jaw dropped.

He thought for a moment. "When this is done, when I've got your precious thing out, and, you know, hurt Aiden Marx and that . . . When all that's done, will you and me still be a couple?"

Shelagh threw her head back and laughed.

56

MARX HAD GIVEN PUNCH A PROMOTION, and he was enjoying it. He was now at the factory, overseeing the dismantling of the Fear Machine, and he'd also supervise its rebuilding for election night in two days' time. Repairs and reinforcements were needed on the cage before it could be transported an hour away to the compound, and volunteer welders and metalworkers were hard at work. That was the thing. Even in a depressed area, people had skills, and they were more than happy to put them to use for a cause they believed in. Plus, it saved him having to do it. Punch looked around. The way everything was coming together helped take his mind off Judy.

When a loud boom echoed from the next chamber, he went to check. "What's happened?" His voice echoed around the brick-and-stone walls.

"Nothing," shouted one of the workers. "Just dropped some wood."

Punch wondered whether to shout at them, insult them, or urge them to work faster. But there was no need. Things were getting done, and he was a benevolent taskmaster.

They had the wooden pit packed up, ready for the

dogfighting. Punch loved that. The screams and snarls, the dogs going at it, money changing hands, the smell of blood and sweat, anger and fear. He was looking forward to it.

Went back to the main hall. The stage was packed up, ready to be moved out. The volunteers that had gathered were hoping Arthur King would pay a visit here. Celebrate his victory. Assuming he won, of course. Which he would. It was the culmination of everything they had worked for. Punch felt proud. But also sad. Judy should be here to share it with him.

He felt an unexpected hand on his shoulder and turned, fists ready. It was Nazir. The Paki looked alarmed for a few seconds. And well he should, thought Punch. Well he should.

"Sorry, mate, didn't mean to startle you."

Punch unclenched his fists. "S'all right."

Nazir gazed around. The gesture, to Punch, looked performative. Anywhere but at him. "Doing a good job. Going to be an exciting night."

"What you doing here? You got time off from leafleting or something?"

Nazir looked hurt. "Just checking in, seeing how it's all going. I'm invested in this as well, you know."

Punch looked at him. Behind his cocky veneer, Punch thought Nazir was just a scared little boy. Or maybe that's just how he was around Punch. Because he knew what Punch thought of him.

"It's going fine," said Punch.

"Great, great." Nazir nodded. "Any problems?"

"Like what?"

"You know. Unexpected visitors, that kind of thing."

"Not after last time. But if there are, I'll handle it."

"No doubt, no doubt." Nazir's fear was showing once more. "You needn't worry about anything else. All the payoffs have been made for the night, eyes looking in other directions. All taken care of." Nazir was good at that kind of thing. He had his uses.

"Well, that's your job, isn't it?" Punch kept his attention on the stage builders, hoping Nazir got the message and left.

"I'll leave you to it," he said eventually.

Punch nodded. "Yeah. On you go. Get the election won for us."

Nazir turned, took his phone out, and made a call as he walked away. Or pretended to.

Punch watched him go. He didn't like Pakis. Made no secret of it. Especially ones who thought they weren't Pakis. They were the worst of the lot. He put Nazir out of his mind, turned back to his workers. It was all going well. Right on time. He sighed.

Judy . . .

He shouldn't have done that to Judy. He saw that now. He was always pranking Judy like that, but this one had gone too far. He had expected Judy back now. Creeping onto the boat, letting himself in, a few days of silence in his room, then back to normal. That's how it had been before. He'd never stayed away this long.

At first Punch thought something must have happened to him and became worried. Even contemplated informing the police, but that would open him up to more questions than he cared to answer. He went looking for him, tried to retrace his brother's steps after leaving the Fear Machine. He called around. They didn't have many friends, but he asked the few people they knew if they'd seen Judy. No one had.

Worry morphed into anger. What was his brother playing at? Teaching him some kind of lesson? If so, well done. It had worked. Judy could come home now.

But he didn't.

So Punch was alone, even as he played an important role. He had taken Judy for granted, and now that he was missing, Punch was powerless to do anything about it. He hated that feeling.

Looking at the busy workers awaiting his next order, Punch wished Judy could be there to share all this with him.

Even if he would smash his face in as soon as he saw him.

PENROSE SPENT ANOTHER DAY parked in front of the Fear Machine, photographing everyone who went in or out, noting the times, and matching them up to file photos through the car's tablet. Checking car registrations too. A lot of recent activity. These people were gearing up for something big, it looked like.

Officer Penrose was there officially. After explaining the situation to his superiors, Penrose had been granted the rest of the week to conclude his inquiries. He started getting results. Names with outstanding warrants against them. No-shows at court. A few on the force who shouldn't have been there as well. A real rogues' gallery was emerging.

A guy leaving the warehouse caught his eye. Penrose had photographed him going in, and the man had stayed inside only briefly. Suited and booted, like he was in management, and he looked Indian or Asian—the last person he had thought they would tolerate in there. Penrose took a photo of the man's car, making sure the registration plate was visible.

This would be an interesting one.

57

"You all set for tomorrow night? It's the big one."

Simon and Michelle both looked up when Aiden spoke. It was unusual to see him in such a good mood. He was even smiling.

"What's tomorrow night?" asked Michelle.

"Election night," said Simon.

Michelle stared at him with more than the usual resentment in her eyes. It had worked its way up to hatred. He generally tried to avoid her gaze.

"See, Simon knows," said Aiden, laughing through the words. "Election night. Yeah, I know it's only a local by-election but it's going to have major repercussions. National ones eventually. But Arthur King's going to win. You can count on it. And that's good news for us all."

"Are we going to watch it from here?" asked Simon.

"Got something special planned. The crew'll be here soon to set up. A little celebration. You're invited. The dogs'll be doing their thing. It'll be a laugh."

Aiden had shown Simon the dogs the previous day. While Marx was with him, the dogs hadn't gone for Simon. But they'd made him feel unwelcome, afraid even. He watched them in their pens, snarling, staring, eyes white-hot dots of hatred. Standing ready, squat bundles of feral muscle, ready for the command. Ready to attack.

"What d'you think?" Aiden Marx had asked.

Simon hadn't been able to reply.

Marx had just laughed.

"Need to toughen you up, kid. You're too fucking soft."

Then there was the sound from the building at the back of the compound. The mad dog's howling.

"Why's that dog have to be kept separate?"

"Surely you know that by now. It's too dangerous to be put in with the rest. Has to be on its own."

The sound didn't strike him as the howl of a mad dog. More like a sad wail of an imprisoned creature. Simon could empathize.

Reverie over, something occurred to Simon. He asked Aiden, "Why will we be here on election night? Shouldn't we be with Arthur and the rest of the team at the count?"

Aiden looked irritated by Simon's question. It took an obvious effort for him to control himself. "He'll be along afterward. Like an aftershow party. That's always where the real party is."

Aiden Marx was done answering questions.

"Right. I'm off. You'll hear the commotion outside when the stuff arrives. You won't have to muck in, though. They can take care of everything. Just don't you two get up to anything I wouldn't do."

He limped out of the door.

Michelle and Simon stayed in the living room, staring at the TV. Neither spoke. Whatever reality show they were nominally watching kept going. Michelle pulled at the long sleeves of her top, keeping them down over her wrists. It was a habit she did a lot, Simon had noticed.

He'd overheard her and Aiden in bed a couple of nights ago. He hadn't meant to, but she had been talking so loudly he couldn't help it.

"Why's this boy here? What's he doing?" Michelle's voice was muffled but clear enough to make out the words.

Aiden's reply wasn't so clear, so she'd repeated her question.

"Work," Aiden had said.

"But he's not doing anything," said Michelle. "He just hangs around all day. And I have to cook for him."

Simon hadn't heard the reply, only anger in Aiden's voice.

Silence, then: "He's still got his phone. You took mine away from me."

"He's got no one to call. He can keep it."

"But he—"

The slap was unmistakable. Then Michelle's cry of pain. Then more, until Simon couldn't tell if he was hitting her or if they were having sex. Simon smothered his head with the pillow and tried to pretend he was anywhere but there.

Michelle pulled at her sleeves again. He caught a glimpse of darker skin beneath the cotton. Was that just a habit? Or was she hiding something?

Any further thought on the subject disappeared as Michelle spoke to him. Simon jumped, he was so surprised. "Want to see something?" Smiling as she spoke.

"What?"

She stood up. "Come on. You'll like it."

He reluctantly allowed himself to be led along the corridor, even though he knew he shouldn't be doing it. He knew it led to Aiden Marx's private study, and Simon wasn't allowed in there. His heart pounding hard, he was wishing once again that he'd never agreed to come here.

"Come on," she said, "what you afraid of?"

Everything, he thought.

She opened the door to Marx's study.

"He leaves it unlocked. Doesn't think I dare to come in." She smiled. "He's wrong, though. He thinks I'm not clever. I'm cleverer than he thinks."

She stepped inside, and Simon followed.

A desk at the far end, a cupboard behind the desk. A computer on the desk. Flags on the wall. Heritage Party literature in boxes on the floor.

Michelle crossed to the desk, tried to open one of the desk drawers.

"What you doing?" he asked.

"Looking for something," she said, as if explaining something very complicated to someone very simple.

"What?"

"A key, if you must know."

"For where?"

She straightened up and looked at him, clearly irritated. "Just a key. I want to show you something." She bent over the desk again.

Simon began looking around the room. He picked up one of the Arthur King leaflets. The candidate's wide smile looked fake. Like every other politician. Why hadn't Simon noticed that before? And the slogans on the flyer were all so empty. There was nothing real behind them. A feeling of depression sunk inside him.

"I'm going back to the living room," he said.

Michelle replied angrily, "You're staying where you are. Till I find the key."

Simon should have responded in kind. Or walked away. But instead he just stood there. He remembered the toad by the stream at the back of the safe house. How he'd picked it up, held it tight. Squeezed it. Felt like a god, the power of life and death over another creature. But then he'd let it go.

He knew how that toad felt. Ever since that day, people had been holding Simon, squeezing the life out of him, not letting him go. Nor did anyone plan to let him go any time soon.

As Michelle continued her rummaging, Simon took in the rest of the room. An iMac computer. Nice. No point trying to use the internet, Marx probably had it password protected. There was a full-sized cupboard behind the desk. God knows what was in there.

Curiosity got to him. He opened one of the doors.

And stopped dead at the sight of a horse's skull wreathed in dried flowers. It had green jewels for eyes. A white shroud-like cloak hung down from it. Something dark and dried splattered along the hem and up the sides. A wooden pole kept the whole thing upright. A collar and lead hung from its neck.

Simon staggered back. He was no longer in the room. He was back in the Falmouth house on that terrible night.

The night his family was killed.

Memories hit like lightning flashes in his brain, connecting synapses. He saw it all.

The intruders. What they did. And one above all the others.

The Horse.

He remembered. He saw.

He knew.

He turned and bolted for the corridor.

Right into the arms of Aiden Marx.

58

"Going somewhere?"

Marx held his shoulders firm, stopping Simon from getting farther. His eyes blazed with an anger that, until now, Simon had only glimpsed. Through peripheral vision, he was aware of Michelle behind him.

"Stay where you are, Michelle," said Marx.

Michelle stopped moving.

Marx returned his gaze to Simon, squeezing tighter as he spoke. "What you doing in here?"

"It was all his idea," said Michelle. "Thought there might be something worth nicking. He's a fucking thief."

"Shut up." Boredom at the woman's words mixed with Marx's ever-present anger. "I'm sick of your whining voice."

She fell silent.

"I'll ask again. What are you doing in here?"

Simon struggled to make sense of what was happening, but all he saw while looking at Marx was the head of the ghost horse, looming, jaws clacking, moving menacingly toward him. Ready to hurt him.

Not again.

Simon brought his leg back and kicked Marx's damaged leg as hard as he could. Marx screamed, loosened his grip. Simon gave another kick, even harder this time, and Marx let go of him, losing his balance and crashing to one side.

Simon didn't wait. Out the door. Down the corridor. Into the living room. The outside door was open. Through that, he ran into the compound. The cold hit him, and it brought back other memories: jumping from his bedroom window, running through snow and slush to get help, desperate to survive.

He looked around. The gate was closed. Marx's car was parked in front of the house. He looked inside it. No keys. He gave a small scream, anger and frustration in equal measure.

Another look around. He had to decide on a course of action. Commit to it. Now.

The gate. Could he climb it? What about the hedge? There was reinforced fencing in the bushes, and he'd glimpsed something near the top. Razor wire? Not good.

The gate, it was. He ran toward it, checking all the time to see if Marx was after him. He wasn't. Not yet.

Constructed of metal panels bolted together, the gate was about three times Simon's height. Sticking out slightly, the bolts were set into frames of about one centimeter in thickness. They were the only things he had to grip, to help scale the gate. He grasped one of the frames, fingers clawing to grab hold of the cold hard metal and pull himself up.

His fingers couldn't hold. He dropped to the ground.

Another quick look around. There was noise behind him. He had to try again.

Holding as tightly as he could, he managed to get a tentative grip. Simon hauled himself up from there. He gasped as his legs bent. It was the most exercise he had done in ages. He had become so unfit. If he ever got out of this, he would never do that again. Never allow himself to—

His left foot made it onto the first border. He pulled his right foot up, then reached above him, hands desperate for purchase. Made it.

He tried to move his left leg to the next panel and—

There was a blur before his eyes, something against his face, something around his neck.

He was being pulled backward and down.

His grip gave way, arms windmilling and grasping.

His feet loosened, pedaled in thin air.

He hit the ground roughly, the air knocked from his lungs. Gasping for breath.

He looked up.

The fat old man, Robert, who looked after the dogs stared down at him. He was holding the end of a wooden stick with a leather noose on it. The noose was wrapped around Simon's neck. A flirt stick, he remembered it being called.

Still staring upward from where he lay on the ground, Simon saw Marx appear. Then Michelle behind him, smiling.

Marx seemed to be in pain, which only increased his anger. "Clever fucker, aren't you? Or you think you are."

Simon managed enough breath to speak. "I know who you are . . ."

"Good for you."

Emboldened, Simon continued, "I know what you did to my family. You murdering, fucking . . ." He started to lash out with his legs, trying to kick anyone within range.

Robert, not as old or powerless as he looked, kicked Simon in the side, connecting with his kidneys, sending another whiplash of pain around his body. He curled up, didn't kick anymore.

"You fucker!"

"Let it all out," said Marx. "That's the way."

"So what are you going to do now? Kill me? Like you killed the rest of my family?" There were tears in his eyes as he shouted. He was unaware he had been crying.

Another smile from Marx, lacking any humor or warmth. He leaned down next to Simon, wincing, the effort costing him pain in his leg. "Remember I said I had a plan for you? Well, it's starting now."

He stood up.

"Put him where he can't do any damage. You know where I mean."

The leather noose around Simon's throat was tightened and he was dragged across the compound, toward the far corner. He was being taken to the cabin with the mad dog.

59

Tom was back on his feet. His body healing, his mind reassembled. He had started running again, after a fashion, along the clifftop path. Short bursts, just grateful to be able to move again. Pearl seemed happy with him again and he with her. Their relationship was growing tentatively. Respectfully. Taking into account the other's feelings and needs.

It was the night before the election but Tom was trying hard not to be interested in the outcome. It was only local; it didn't matter nationally, despite what Tarpley had said. That was just opportunist hyperbole. Wannabe fascist bullshit. He felt bad for letting Simon down, blamed himself even though he knew there was nothing more he could have done. Simon would be another ghost of failure to haunt him.

Lila was staying the night at Anju's. Although she hadn't come out and said it, Tom reckoned she had wanted to give him and Pearl time together alone. And given the opportunity, the reunited lovers had made the most of it.

He lay in bed on his back, one arm behind his head, a sheen of sweat covering both their bodies, Pearl's head on his shoulder, "So you're staying around, then?"

"Keep doing that for me and I will . . ." Pearl's voice was muffled by his body, smoky curlicues of sleep drifting up from the edges of her words.

Part of him wanted more than that, certainties, clear answers now. No, she wouldn't be leaving, wouldn't try to track her parents down. Yes, her future was with him. The depth of feeling he had developed for her had surprised him.

He didn't want to disturb the calm of the room, so he said nothing. Lay there, listening while Pearl's breathing deepened, turning wakefulness to sleep. That she was there with him would have to be answer enough for now.

He closed his eyes, tried to join her.

And his phone rang.

Pearl's body jolted as if struck by lightning. Tom also jumped. She looked at him, surprised. He reached over, took it, checked the number. Recognized the name.

Simon West.

Answered it.

"Hello?"

Heavy breathing, like the speaker's mouth was covering the mic. Then a voice, hushed, tense. Whispered yet made loud by the proximity to the mouthpiece.

"Is that Tom? Tom? Killgannon?"

"Yeah, it's me. Simon? Is that you?"

"Yeah, yeah . . ."

"What's up?"

"I need—" A gasp, as if he was looking around quickly. "Help. I need help. You've got to come and get me."

"What—" Tom sat upright. Pearl stared at him, puzzled and scared by his reaction. "Where are you? What's happened?"

"I'm in . . ." His voice lower, the words blurred. "Aiden Marx. He's got this place in the country, this compound thing. I'm . . .

He's keeping me prisoner. Tom, you've got to help me. He . . . he killed my dad. It was him. I've seen it. I've seen the Horse."

"What d'you mean, you've seen the Horse?" Tom glanced at Pearl, who looked equally confused.

"He . . . look, he honestly doesn't know I'm calling. He must have forgot I've still got my phone. I'm nearly out of battery. Please you've got to help me—"

The line went dead. Whether from lack of battery or something worse, Tom couldn't know. He looked at Pearl.

Her eyes asked a question. One he didn't know if he could, or even wanted to, answer.

6∅

"How do i look?"

He was wearing his new clothes and waiting for her approval. Shelagh barely glanced at him. "Fine." She no longer cared. Just wanted to get this over with, and then she'd never have to see this idiot again.

It was Election Day in Falmouth—a small ripple there, virtually ignored by the rest of the country. If Arthur King and Ben Tarpley were to be believed, however, it was the start of a new era in British politics. The first wave before the Heritage Party tsunami crashed into Westminster and washed the old order away. Shelagh didn't care about politics. She focused only on the task that Jack Ketch was assisting her with. After that, it would be sunlit uplands for her. And no downside.

"You haven't even looked at me."

Shelagh sighed, put her phone down. That desperate, puppy-like look in his eyes—wanting to please, wanting approbation—was tiresome. A puppy. More like a feral dog. And she had the bruises to show for it.

When she had embarked on this course of action, she knew she'd have to make sacrifices. And she knew she would have to enlist allies. She had made mistakes with Tom Killgannon and Pearl Ellacott. A shame because Shelagh really had intended to start a new life in that village, selling her pictures, living happily ever after. But those bridges were burned. Now she had Jack Ketch. On paper, he seemed like a better choice for the job, but now she couldn't stand the sight of him.

Sacrifices. She had expected to trade whatever she could for help. It was necessary: the goal was worth it. Her body had worked in the past, and sometimes she'd enjoyed the trade. But not always, as her scars attested. She had thought this one would be happy with money, grateful for the attention from her. But she'd misjudged him and had paid for it. Now she just wanted to finish the job. No plan where to go next. It didn't matter, as long as she got what she wanted and got out.

"I said, you haven't even looked at me."

"I'm looking at you now. Happy?" Calm down, she told herself. You still need him. She forced a smile. "Sorry. Tense."

He smiled, relieved he hadn't upset her. Jesus, she thought. She could really have fun with this one if she wanted to. But she wasn't going to hang around to find out.

"You comfortable in those clothes? Not too tight? You can move all right?"

"Yeah," he said.

"You've got enough space in that jacket for what needs to be there?"

He pulled the knife out of his pocket. Posed with it. Smiled. Like a kid playing dress-up.

"Good. Stop waving it around. Put it back."

He did, with another smile. "If my brother could see me now."

"Don't worry," Shelagh said. "He will."

61

THE FIRST THING SIMON NOTICED on being thrown into the cabin was the smell. The place stank, worse than the dog pens.

The cabin was brick-built. Its interior walls were covered with heavy dark smears. Shuttered windows stopped natural light from entering. A dim overhead bulb threw out faint, depressing illumination. A bed was shoved against one wall with an old mattress on it and filthy sheets bunched on top. A TV set was in another corner, reception fuzzy. A seatless toilet was fitted to the far wall opposite the bed. It was the bleakest prison cell he could imagine.

On the floor in the center of the room, sat a person. The person heard the commotion as Simon was tossed in, slowly turning their head away from the TV, focusing on Simon. One look, and Simon drew himself back against the door. The figure stood, came slowly toward him.

Male. Big. Young, probably. There was something wrong with him, like he was wired wrong. There was power in his walk. But sickness too.

He stood right before Simon, who recoiled from the stench of his foul breath.

This was the mad dog.

The mad dog smiled. He threw back his head, emitting a high-pitched, ear-bracing scream.

Exactly like a horse's panicked neighing.

62

ELECTION DAY EVENING. The night after Tom had received Simon's phone call. He had phoned Penrose as soon as the line went dead. And that, Tom had thought, would be that. Penrose had assured him the police would arrive at this compound, gain entry, find Simon, arrest Marx for kidnapping and murder, and that would be that. And Tom had been content.

But upon phoning Penrose the next day for an update, the police officer had been evasive. Tom had asked him to come around as soon as he could.

Now Penrose sat in Tom's kitchen facing Tom, Pearl, and Lila, trying to explain himself.

"So is Simon safe?" The first question Tom had asked.

Penrose had insisted on sitting down before answering. That didn't bode well.

Pearl leaned forward. "Simon said on the phone he was at the compound."

"Well, yes."

"What d'you mean, well, yes?" said Tom. "Surely you've got him out by now."

Penrose looked apologetic. "I referred your call on, and I was told it's not that simple. Simon's over sixteen. He ran away from his foster home. Or at least left it voluntarily. Technically, legally, he can do what he likes."

"But he said he was being kept against his will," said Lila. "That's kidnapping."

"Again, not clear-cut. Aiden Marx is a tricky customer. Believe me, there's nothing the force would like better than to grab him for something. But we must tread carefully."

"Why?" asked Tom.

"Aiden Marx is a bastard. As nasty as they come. On the verge of the big time in the criminal world before he went inside. Drugs, extortion, prostitution, human trafficking, all of that. And vicious with it. He did time over the years, in and out, leaving a string of broken people behind him. But eventually, he was caught. Burglary, of all things. Why he'd decided to do it himself when he had people to do it for him we'll never know. Red-handed, no two ways. This time no witnesses recanted at the last minute. This bad guy was going down for a long time."

"There's a *but* here, isn't there?" asked Pearl.

"There is," said Penrose. "My colleagues on the force were a bit overzealous in the arrest, shall we say."

"Not crossing the t's and dotting the i's, you mean?" said Tom.

"More like acting as a '70s tribute act when they got him in custody."

Lila frowned. "What?"

"They beat him up in cells," said Tom. "That what you mean?"

Penrose nodded. "Which they shouldn't have done, obviously, especially with everything they had on him. He got put away, but not for long. Or not long enough. His lawyer brought a case against the police force. Asked for a lot of money. Got it."

"Jesus. How much?"

"Over a million. His attorney said he could never work again and must be kept in a manner to which he had become accustomed. Force had no choice but to swallow it. He had them bang to rights on it. No way around it. *Daily Mail* had a field day. Villains have too many human rights, the whole lot."

"So what?" asked Tom. "So now no policeman will move on Marx for fear he'll sue them again?"

"We want him put away for life, but we also have to make damned sure we don't mess it up this time. Marx has reinvented himself as a patron of the arts. A respectable, wealthy philanthropist. Real posh, all of that, but then there's talk of illegal dogfights on his grounds. So he's not *that* reformed. Normally that would be enough to arrest him, but the powers that be are letting things like that slide so they can get him on something bigger."

"Like kidnapping?" said Lila. "And murder?"

"I never said we weren't going to make a move on him," said Penrose. "Only that we weren't going to do it straightaway."

Lila started to complain, but Penrose held up a hand to stop her.

"I've passed this up the line. All the names and registration numbers from outside the Fear Machine. And the fact that I followed our friend Punch to Marx's compound." It was Tom's turn to try and interrupt, but Penrose stopped him. "It's all connected in some way. And Marx is planning a big get-together tonight. That's why they were dismantling the fighting cage. They were moving it there. Probably be dogfights as well. A jolly event to celebrate Arthur King's presumed victory in the election."

"So the place'll be packed full of far-right villains," said

Tom. "Dogfighting, illegal bare-knuckle boxing, the lot. Why don't you move in on that? It's perfect."

"Because it's a private party, for one thing. And we want to arrest Aiden Marx on a charge more serious than dogfighting or fairground fighting."

"And of course, he might sue you again," said Pearl, sarcasm dripping from her voice.

"Well, yes, actually. My bosses' plan is to wait until after tonight's event—likely tomorrow. We will have built a credible case in order to get a warrant to search his premises. Then Simon gets out."

Silence.

Broken by Lila. "So we just leave him there?"

Penrose looked pained. "Temporarily, yes."

Another silence, broken by Tom this time.

"We could do it," Tom said, risking a glance in Pearl's direction. Her look wasn't favorable. "Well, why not? All we have to do is turn up to the party, get in, and leave with Simon. Say we're his relations or something."

Pearl couldn't sit still any longer. "And you think this bastard Marx will just hand him over? The person who's responsible for the death of Simon's family? The person who, for all we know, might also be responsible for putting you in bed for three days. Talk sense, Tom."

"*Might* be responsible," said Tom.

"Whatever. This is best left to the proper authorities."

"Tom's got a point, though, Pearl," said Lila.

Pearl stared at her sharply, like she'd been betrayed.

"Sorry. It's a good idea," she said. "Gets Simon out of the way before the police arrive properly. Makes sure he's safe. Tom said he was terrified in that call. We can't leave him there any longer. God knows what they'll do to him."

Pearl stared between Lila and Tom. Eventually, she shook her head. "I can't believe I'm hearing this. Maybe from him, but not from you, Lila. I thought you wanted a quiet life. Put all that pain and everything behind you."

"I do," said Lila. "But this isn't about that. I feel responsible for Simon. If I hadn't persuaded Tom to take him in, none of this would have happened."

"*Might* not have happened," said Pearl. "Or at least it wouldn't have happened to us."

"You wanted to help him as well, Pearl." Lila wasn't giving in. "Tom was the only one who didn't. And now he's the one talking about going to get him."

"Which should be left to—"

"Yeah, the proper authorities." Lila stared at her friend. Unblinking, unwavering. "So what are we going to do? Just sit here and let the boy suffer?"

Pearl tried to stare back. "You didn't even like him," she said, head down, mumbling.

"That's not the point, is it? I don't think Tom liked me much when he first helped me out. Especially because I'd stolen from him."

"What makes you think I like you now?" Tom smiled as he spoke.

Despite herself, Lila smiled in return. "You know what I mean. You don't just have a good deed done for you, then pull the ladder up afterward. You help."

Tom gazed at her with admiration. Lila noticed.

"Fuck off," she said, reddening.

They waited. Eventually, Pearl spoke to Tom.

"You said you wouldn't do this again. Go running toward trouble."

"I'm not running toward trouble," he said. "I'm just

doing the right thing. What if something happened to Simon before the police get there? I don't think I could live if I knew I'd had the chance to do something about it and didn't. And I don't think you could either."

After a thoughtful pause, Pearl asked, "What did you have in mind?"

The relief in the room was palpable.

"We just rock up, try to get into Marx's bash," said Tom. "Get Simon, get away."

"Break in, you mean?" asked Pearl.

"I don't think we'll need to. I've got an idea. And Chris'll help. Won't you, Chris?"

Penrose shifted in his chair.

"I'll take that as a yes, then. Right. Let's go get us an invite."

63

THE ELECTION RESULTS hadn't been counted yet, but the partying had already started at the Fear Machine. For one night only, on the grounds of Aiden Marx's country retreat.

There was a carnival atmosphere in the compound. The cage had been set up in one of the hangars, with plenty of space for bettors to watch, pillars of scaffolding rigged up the walls and across the walkways in the rafters holding man-operated spotlights trained on the action below. The other hangar was kitted out for the dogfights. Competitors had their caged dogs kept off to the side, the noise and smell rising. In the center of the compound, an open-air stage had been erected for Arthur King to make a speech celebrating his victory. Caterers manned the benches, offering beer and pizza, chips and burgers. Cars were turning up, one after the other, making their way past the black-shirted Morris men manning the gate.

Storm clouds had scudded across the sky all day, gathering and deepening once night began to set in.

"Fucking typical," said Marx, standing at the bottom of the house steps, looking upward. "Bet the rain starts when King makes his speech. Bloody charming, that's going to be."

"It'll be fine," said Punch next to him. He was dressed in his working clothes, holding his belled cap in his hand. He laughed. "Wonder what your artsy crowd would make of this."

Marx didn't laugh. "If they were honest with themselves, some of them would love it."

Punch kept smiling. "So is this who you really are, then?"

Marx turned toward him, eyes aflame. "Just do your job and make sure everything tonight goes according to plan."

"Judy'll be here soon, I hope, then we can . . ." But Marx wasn't listening. He had turned away, limped off, leaning heavily on his stick as he went.

"Wanker," said Punch under his breath, then looked around once more, hoping no one had heard him bad-mouthing the boss.

Michelle was standing by the house's front door. Jesus Christ, he thought. She was dressed like she was the lady of the manor, like some reality TV queen. Poor kid. But there was still something attractive about her. She looked damaged and that made her an easy lay. He smiled. When Marx got bored with her, Punch might have himself a go.

He watched as she smoothed down the front of her dress, checked her hair was right. Stepped out of the doorway, smiling, and into the field.

Just then, it started to rain.

FOR THE LAST TWENTY-FOUR HOURS, Simon had been locked up with a huge and terrifying presence. All the scarier because he could barely speak, just grunt. Violence emanated off him in waves.

After he'd first roared at Simon, Simon backed away. He acknowledged this was not his territory, that he was only an intruder, an unwilling and reluctant one at that. After that the boy—and he was a boy, just a huge one—had gone back to staring at the TV.

Simon, not knowing what else to do, had tried to engage him in conversation. "What's your name? I'm Simon."

The boy grunted in reply. But it seemed to Simon more than just a grunt. Like there were words wrapped up in there somewhere. Like he could speak, but it had been so long since anyone had talked with him that he'd forgotten how.

Simon had stood up, moved forward. The boy responded with a speed surprising Simon. Turning on him, he threw his head back once more and roared. He looked about to charge, his hands balling into massive, shovellike fists. Simon stayed where he was. The boy backed down again.

Simon's terror eventually subsided, replaced by uneasy boredom. Food had been pushed through a slot in the door, and they had both eaten. Simon had even managed to use the toilet, which was an experience he wasn't in a hurry to repeat. They had fallen into silence, Simon unsure whether the other boy was even aware he was still there.

Night fell, and the boy climbed onto the bed. Simon lay on the floor. He thought about his phone call to Tom Killgannon. Hoped he was doing something to get him out.

The more he thought about what had happened to him, what he'd been through, the more Simon thought that this was the end of the line for him. No one was coming to save him. No cavalry. No SWAT team. There would be just him and this boy, stuck in this dreary, reeking cabin.

Forever.

Simon was too tired to cry.

64

SHELAGH FELT UNSAFE with Jack Ketch. She tried to bury that feeling. Do what needed to be done, get rid of him, get out, get away.

He insisted Shelagh stop at a storage lock-up on a housing estate in Truro before heading out to Aiden Marx's compound. "Just one last thing." The smile seemed to run over his face like a delicious shiver.

She parked the car and locked the doors, waiting there while he retrieved whatever it was he wanted. The lock-up was one of a row of battered, rusting garages behind the kind of grim housing estate Channel Five documentaries were filmed at. Jack pulled the storage unit's door open.

As they got into the car earlier that morning, Jack had noticed her canvasses in the trunk.

"Hey, what's them?"

He made to pull out her artwork, but she put a restraining hand on his wrist. "Leave them, please."

"They paintings? What of?" He kept pulling, ignoring her grip.

"Just leave them . . ."

He managed to get one of them half out. Looked at it. "That's the Horse."

"I know."

He straightened up, frowning. "Why've you painted the Horse?"

Because I know what Marx has done to him. Because it was my only way of reaching for him. Her features hardened, as did her voice. "Please, just put it back where you found it. And be careful with it."

"But—"

"Put it back."

Reluctantly, head spinning with questions, he had done so.

"Now have you got what you wanted?" she asked after Jack shut up the storage and jumped back in the car.

He held up an old rucksack. Smiled. "Yeah. Nice surprise here for Aiden Marx. And anyone else who's around. Bit of a hobby of mine. Had to do this for someone else recently. But they asked for it." His smile was dreamy now, almost sexual. "Let's give him a good send-off. All of them. Be free of the past, eh? Make a new future."

Shelagh was unnerved. She had an idea what he was talking about. "Just make sure you do this after I've got what I want, and I'm well away from the place."

"Oh, yeah," he said, still dreamy.

She caught herself. Thank goodness he hadn't picked up on the fact that she'd just told him she was leaving without him.

It was dark and raining by the time they reached the compound. Shelagh pulled up to a huge metal gate, which slid back. There stood an unhappy-looking, soaked, bowler-hatted Morris man under an umbrella.

"Password?" he shouted.

"Camelot," said Shelagh.

He motioned to let them in. They drove through.

"Good job you got that text," she said.

"My *brother* wouldn't let me down." His voice twisting with unpleasantness as he spoke.

Part of the field had been cordoned off for parking. The black-shirted Morris men directed cars and vans to available spaces.

"Very organized." Shelagh parked where instructed, turned off the engine.

Jack looked at her. "You still haven't told me what it is you want from here."

"None of your business."

Jack looked hurt. "That's not fair. I've helped you. I got you in like you wanted, and if you want me to help you anymore, I need to know what I've got to do. So we can get out and away together."

Shelagh sighed, looked at him. The most dangerous, unpredictable puppy she had ever seen. "I'm looking for my son, Adam. He's here."

Jack frowned. "Your son? I don't understand."

"My son's here. And I'm going to take him away from here."

His frown deepened. "I don't know if I want a son. Just the two of us would be nicer."

"There isn't going to be a two of us. Not anymore."

Jack looked horrified. "Why not?"

Shelagh gave a crash laugh. "You really have to ask? After what you've done?"

Jack struggled to understand.

"Yes, I did want you to help me," said Shelagh. "Yes, we might have gone away together. But not now. You've got me in here. You've done your part. From now on, you're on your own. I'm getting my son, and I'm leaving. You can do what you like."

She got out of the car, indicating he do the same. He grabbed his rucksack, stood there staring at her.

"Bye, Jack. It was anything but pleasant."

She walked away.

65

THE CROWD WAS SO INTENT on enjoying themselves that Tom hoped no one would recognize him from the Fear Machine. Still, he pulled the collar of his jacket up and put his head down against the rain, hunching his shoulders. It gave him no protection against the weather but helped to deflect stray glances. It had been dark the night of his beating so he couldn't pick out any faces he recognized. He was sure the men from that night would be here, though. And it was mostly men that were there. White men.

The rain combined with the invading masses turned the grass to mud. Some people were slipping and sliding, their instability aided by their drug of choice. Lights were strung around the compound, making it look like a depressing funfair. He walked toward the first large hangar, entered.

And wished he hadn't. A dogfight was in progress. Two pit bulls in a wooden pit were tearing each other apart. Evenly matched, their teeth dug into the other, neither giving ground. The concrete floor was covered with bloodied sawdust. The dogs were bleeding openly. The crowd bellowed. The more blood and violence they witnessed, the more they screamed. The spectacle was repulsive, but Tom found it hard to tear himself away from it. The atmosphere in the hangar—the smell of sawdust, dog shit, and blood mingled with human sweat—spoke to something primal that went unacknowledged in most people most of the time. This place reveled in that acknowledgment. Some exploited it: at the edges of the crowd, money changed hands as bets were taken.

He scanned the faces, didn't see Simon or anyone he recognized. Tom went back outside.

Penrose was working the crowd on the other side of the field, Lila out on her own. Tom's plan to gain entry had worked perfectly. Penrose had put on his police uniform and stopped a car on the way in, a mile down the road. He threatened the driver with arrest unless he told them the password. He did so, willingly.

The policeman now looked across the expanse at Tom, giving him a small shake of his head. No Simon.

Tom nodded in response.

"No sign of Simon anywhere," said Lila, appearing at his side. They had tried to stop her, but she had insisted on coming. Forcefully.

"Where've you looked?"

"Everywhere." She shivered from more than the cold, looking around at the crowd. "It's like they put out a call for all the most horrible, sleazy, disgusting, thick people imaginable, isn't it?"

"You feel unsafe?"

"I'm not going back to the Land Rover if that's what you're thinking."

"OK. Just keep looking."

She drifted into the crowd once more.

A stage was set up in the center of the field. It looked sad, neglected even. Balloons tied to the screen at the back were being buffeted and thrashed by gusts of wind. A microphone stand stood alone at the front of the stage. A small lighting rig was at either side, thick cables snaking toward the house.

What Tom assumed was living quarters or a kind of house in the center of the compound seemed quiet. Would Simon be in there? Kept in his room away from everyone else? That sounded plausible.

A cheer went up from the dogfight hangar. With a sinking feeling, he knew what that meant. He hurried over to the house. Hoping everyone's attention was elsewhere.

66

After lila slipped away from the crowds, she found the boundary hedge and worked her way along it. She noticed it was reinforced with steel fencing and topped with razor wire. The front gate was the only way in and out.

Away from the others, the sounds faded, the lights dimmed. Her eyes became accustomed to the darkness, and she moved stealthily across the property. At the end of the field, she saw something dark against the darkness. Eyes squinting, she tried to make it out. A brick cabin with a heavy door and drawn shutters.

Her heart flickered, skipped. This looked promising. If Marx was keeping someone prisoner, she thought, this was just the kind of building you'd put them in.

Glancing around to check that she hadn't been seen, she slowly walked toward it.

Simon heard the clamor from Marx's big election night party outside in the distance. That was the last place he would have wanted to be—apart from where he was.

The other boy had calmed down. After eating, he had sat

on the toilet, loudly and noxiously voided his bowels. Simon had put his face up against the bottom of the door to try and breathe fresh air.

This boy was kept in worse conditions than the dogs, thought Simon, and that was saying something. It was inhuman. No wonder he was the way he was. Now the boy stared at the TV, trying to make out figures through the fuzz. Simon just stared at the set without taking anything in. Trying not to think what could happen to him next.

He saw something under the covers on the boy's bed. Books.

"Can I have a look at your books?"

The boy grunted.

Simon crossed over to the bed, picked up the books. They were ancient, well-thumbed, and filthy. Picture books, like a child of single digits might have read to them. The odd thing was that they were all on a similar theme: horses. A sense of dread ran through Simon as he flicked through the books.

"You like horses, eh?" The boy looked at him. Simon showed him the pictures. "Horses. You like them."

The boy nodded. Smiled almost.

"Right."

The boy drew himself away from the TV, shuffled over to Simon, sat down next to him. Pointed at the books, then at Simon.

It took Simon a few seconds to work out what he meant. "You want me to read to you?"

The boy's face was transformed when he smiled. Like a massive empty grapefruit half being pushed together.

"OK then, here we go . . ." Simon started reading.

LILA PUT HER EAR TO THE DOOR, listened. A voice came from

inside: faint, competing with the sound of a TV. She tried to block out the racket of the rain and wind, the clamor of the distant celebration. It sounded like someone was reading a children's story. Was that Simon's voice?

She tried to remember it. He hadn't spoken much when he'd stayed with them. She cupped her hand over her ear, tried to hear. As she did so, out of the corner of her eye she caught a figure coming her way. She quickly rushed to the hedge behind the cabin, hoping she hadn't been seen.

The figure approached the cabin, stood before the door, waiting.

Lila held her breath.

He was a slight man walking with a cane. Lila couldn't see his full face for the hood of his parka. The lights from the celebration lit the bottom half of the hooded face, keeping the top in shadow. He reminded her of the Emperor in the *Star Wars* films, except he was nowhere near as old. But he had the same malevolent presence. Lila guessed who he was.

She didn't dare move, barely breathed. Aiden Marx produced a key, gave a final look around, opened the cabin door, and stepped inside.

Lila stayed where she was, watching.

"'OH NO,' SAID THE HORSE, 'that means that the tractor will have to—'"

Simon stopped reading the book when he heard the door to the cabin open. He thought of making a run for it, but it quickly closed again. No chance.

Aiden Marx pushed the wet hood of his parka back. Took in the scene before him. "You've been getting acquainted. How sweet."

Simon stood. Behind him the boy groaned, unhappy at having his story time interrupted.

Marx eyed the door, then Simon. He smiled. "Thinking to have a go, are you? Feeling brave with all the noise outside? Come on, then. Give it your best shot."

Simon stared at him.

"Not sure? Really? You can take me, can't you? Old bloke like me, cripple . . . Yeah. All that stands between you and freedom." He held his arms out, away from his body. Showing there was nothing in his hands, inviting Simon. "Come on, then."

Simon, his body rather than his mind doing the thinking, launched himself at Marx.

Marx absorbed the blow, falling back against the closed door, laughing as he went.

This made Simon even angrier. He allowed his rage to bubble up to the surface and directed it at Marx, pummeling away at him with his fists.

"Not the face, not the face . . ." Marx was laughing as he said it, throwing his head side to side, easily moving his face out Simon's reach.

Simon hit even harder, trying to knock Aiden off his feet, get to the door and freedom.

Marx stumbled, fell sideways, grabbing for his cane, his smile momentarily gone. Simon pushed on, reached for the door handle—

And felt the air being squeezed from his lungs.

His hand dropped the handle, went instead to his chest. The boy's two huge, meaty arms encircled him. He squeezed harder. Simon tried to scream. With no breath behind it, it came out as a strangled wheeze.

"That's my boy," said Marx, laughing once more. He had

regained his cane. Simon felt his ribs about to shatter. "You can put him down now."

The boy dropped Simon to the floor. He rolled onto his back, gasping.

Marx stared down at him. The boy looked at Marx, seeking approbation. "You tried to escape," said Marx, shrugging. "You tried to hurt me. Horsey boy here doesn't like either of those things."

He closed his eyes. "Why . . . why are you doing this to me? What have I done to you?"

"You? Nothing." Marx put his hand into his parka pocket, drew out Simon's iPhone "Your father, on the other hand . . ."

67

"Can I help you?"

Tom turned, about to enter the house. A young woman stood behind him, dressed like a 1950s housewife. Odd. "Just seeing if Aiden's in."

"He's not," she said. "Who wants him?"

Tom smiled. "Not to worry." He took his hand off the door handle, turned, made to walk away. He didn't know who she was, but she was somehow connected to Marx. He could guess what was going through her mind. Was he a burglar? An enemy of Marx's? Or was he a genuine friend?

She looked conflicted, clearly at a loss for what to do.

"Wait. What's your name? I'll go and look for him," she said. "I'll tell Aiden you're looking for him."

Tom smiled again. "Not to worry. I'm sure I'll bump into him." He stepped away from the door, turned, and walked away.

He waited around the side of the house until he was sure the young woman had gone. She stood there a while, seemingly thinking, then stepped off, back into the crowd. He then slipped around to the front once more. The encounter with the weird woman had told him one thing: Marx wasn't inside the house. Good.

As expected, the door was locked, which did not mean it was impossible to open. Tom knew how to pick a lock. And judging by the quality, he reckoned it would probably take about thirty seconds. But there were people all around. Kneeling before it might attract too much attention. So he decided on another approach. The door didn't look too sturdy or strong, an indication that the man who lived here thought that he was unreachable. Tom gave another glance around, checked no one was watching, and leaned on the door. Hard.

It took a couple of attempts but it gave, and he was in.

68

SIMON STARED AT THE PHONE in Marx's hand like it had special powers. "What's my phone got to do with anything?"

Marx smiled. "When I sent my associates out to your daddy's house, they couldn't find anything incriminating about me. And they looked, believe me. But your father admitted to them, under much duress, that he had given what I wanted to you. So I set about getting it back."

Simon felt like the boy was holding him there while Marx punched him repeatedly. One piece of information to the gut, another, then another . . . leaving him reeling.

"But . . . why? What?"

Marx stepped closer to Simon. Smiled. "Let me tell you a story. You see, Raymond Bain wasn't the only shifty client your dear old dad worked for. And who he kept plenty of, shall we say, sensitive information on. There was me as well."

"What are you talking about?"

"We go way back, me and your dad. Worked together for years. The only difference between us is that I moved down here by choice. He had to hide in Falmouth, and bring you all with him. But your dad, small-time embezzler that he was, couldn't let it go at that. He found out where I was. Came to see me. Told me he had plenty of incriminating stuff on me too. Stuff that would make the police start looking at me again, getting into my accounts, even consider taking their money back. And putting me inside again for a long time. Throw-away-the-key kind of long time. All intimated, of course. Your dad said nothing so blatant. And when I asked him why he needed more cash so badly, he said, because I'm broke."

"He wasn't, though," said Simon. "We had that big house and everything."

"That house was rented. And that money-grabbing gold digger of a new wife was bleeding him dry. He couldn't access his secret offshore accounts in the Caymans because the police still had their eye on him. There was money unaccounted for after Bain's trial, and everyone assumed Bain had hidden it. Because that's what your dad led them to believe."

Simon said nothing. The giant boy had picked him up once more, gripped him firm.

"Lot to take in, isn't it? Finding out your dear old dad isn't the hero you thought he was."

Simon said nothing.

"So. Blackmail some funds from his old pal Aiden or go to the police with everything he had on me. It turns out every crooked deal I'd ever gotten away with, every penny of money your pop had laundered for me, he'd kept records and receipts." Marx shrugged. "What could I do? My hand was forced, obviously."

"So you killed him."

"Not me personally, Simon—never me personally. I learned a long time ago to always get someone else to do that deed for me. And do it in such a way so it would never be linked back to me."

"So the Horse isn't you."

"Haven't you guessed yet?"

Simon felt the boy grip him tighter.

"Oh God."

"Loves his storybooks, loves his horses. But most of all, he loves getting dressed up and acting like one. Can't tell the difference between what's real and what's not, bless him. To be honest, I don't think he cares. His idea of fun."

Simon felt sick to his stomach.

Marx continued, "Yeah, those four psychopaths took care of your family. But you got away. Which is why I sent Turnip Head after you."

"Turnip Head?"

"Not his real name, although it may as well have been. But he fucked up. And he was taken care of. But then Arthur King came on the scene, and off you went."

"But I came across him by accident . . ."

"I'm sure you think you did. But if we hadn't got you that day, there'd have been another. And then I saw you staring at your phone all the time, and you told me it had been a present from your dad. That's when I knew where my stuff was."

"And was it?"

Marx laughed. "Oh yes. All on there. I took it when you were asleep." He pocketed the phone. "I'll just hang on to it, if you don't mind. You don't need it. I mean, it's not like you're going anywhere, is it?"

"So why didn't you just take the phone off me when you met me? Why do all this to me?"

"Call me paranoid, but I had to see whether you were a plant, didn't I? Whether the coppers were using you and stuck you in here to get dirt on me. Turns out they weren't. Who knew? But *nah*, they couldn't care less about you."

Simon felt totally, utterly broken.

"Still haven't decided what I'm going to do with you," Aiden said with a sadistic grin. "Whatever it is, it doesn't involve leaving this cabin." He gestured to the big boy, the one who liked playing horsey. "Leave him here, we've got stuff to do."

The boy threw Simon onto the floor, stepped over him. They left, locking the door behind them.

Simon didn't move. He had nothing to move for.

69

"Jesus, is that you? Christ, you look . . . different."

Jack heard the astonishment in Punch's voice. And something else. Envy? Jealousy? Maybe he was imagining it. Maybe that's just what he wanted to hear.

He had just finished securing the last of his devices in the main hangar. There were four of them, one at each corner by a structural support. It was just like he'd done with Sullivan's caravan and car, though this required more force. It would be much bigger. Much more spectacular. A perfect symbolic way to say goodbye to one life and hello to the next.

Making his way through the crowds on the field and in the hangar, he had glimpsed numerous familiar faces, men he'd known for years. And none of them had recognized him in his new guise. They walked right past him. The anonymity this new persona gave him was powerful. He was different, stronger.

But Punch recognized him. He was standing at the back of the hall, away from everyone else. Looking for any person or thing that might disturb the evening's events. Doing his job like a good little soldier.

Jack stood up. Squared off to his brother.

"Judy, what are you—"

"Jack."

"What?"

"Judy's dead. It's Jack, now. Jack Ketch."

Punch stepped back, mouth slack. He looked, to Jack, like a magician who had lost his magic touch, a powerless hypnotist. Jack enjoyed the sight.

Punch quickly recovered, found a smile. Put himself back in control. "Judy— What you talking about?" He stepped back, looking at him askance. Jack knew his brother wouldn't compliment him on his new appearance. "Where'd you get all this stuff?"

"A friend."

Punch's smile turned into a leer. "A lady friend?"

Jack reddened, turned away.

Punch laughed, trying to regain the upper hand. "Yes, I was right . . . You got a woman to buy you all this?" Punch's voice dropped. Low. Lascivious. "What did you have to do for her in return?"

That was too much. Jack launched himself at Punch, the force of his body knocking his brother off his feet. He jumped on top of him, fists driving, releasing years of pent-up rage and frustration.

Jack's punches were too much, too strong, too quick. Punch couldn't get any kind of reply in, couldn't fight back. Jack's eyes closed. Muffled, inarticulate screams came from him.

Jack kept pounding, oblivious, but Punch became aware of people drifting over to watch this free fight. There were a few experimental whoops and roars of encouragement, the last thing Punch wanted. He managed to grab Jack's swinging fists, pin them down by his sides.

Jack kept struggling and wriggling like he had been hit with an electric charge.

"We're attracting a crowd, you fucking moron," said Punch.

The words did the trick. Jack stopped. Slowly, he got to his feet and looked down at his new clothes, now mud-streaked and battered. Shamefaced.

Punch turned to the gathering audience. "Nothing to see here. We've all had a drink." He laughed, hoping that would be that.

The crowd, sensing no further spectacle, turned away.

Punch looked back at Jack. "You fucking idiot. What d'you do that for?"

Jack stared at him, eyes like lasers. "Because you deserved it. For everything, for all those years . . . for . . ." He couldn't speak.

Punch shook his head. "Come on," he said, tone consoling. "We got work to do. Get your proper clothes on." He stepped toward him, placed his hand on his shoulder.

Jack gave a violent shrug, like he had been touched by something disgusting.

Punch stared. Jack tried to stare back, couldn't keep his gaze.

"So this is it, then?" asked Punch. "That what you're saying? Punch and Judy: RIP?"

Jack did not reply, kept his head bowed. Seemingly scared to look up, like he might be hypnotized again.

"Right. Well, if that's what you want . . ."

Jack relaxed.

Just as his brother turned and landed an almighty smack to the side of his head.

70

Tom closed the front door behind him as quietly as possible in case there was someone inside the house besides Simon. The outside noise immediately fell away, and he focused his senses on what was before him.

From the outside lights coming through the windows, he made out a living room, indifferently furnished apart from expensive-looking art on the walls. He could see a kitchen beyond, as well as a corridor. He took his phone out, flicked on the flashlight. Walked slowly down the corridor.

The first door he came to led to what looked to be the master bedroom. It contained enough domestic detritus to show it was shared by a couple. Boring decor again, almost utilitarian: a bed, a wardrobe, a mismatched dressing table, seemingly begrudgingly installed. He guessed this was the bedroom of Aiden Marx and that woman.

He continued down the corridor, past a bathroom and another bedroom. He looked inside. Recognized the holdall on the floor as Simon's.

After another quick, furtive glance behind, Tom stepped inside. He swung the flashlight around. Someone had done a bad job of tidying up. Simon's things had been carelessly stuffed into his holdall—like he'd been getting ready to make a run for it. Or maybe someone else wanted to remove all traces of him. Tom knelt, went through the contents of the bag. Among all the dirty clothes and trainers, he found a photograph. It showed a happy family, sitting around a wooden pub table, food and drink in front of them, umbrella above them. All smiling for the camera. There was Simon, younger, grinning in a way Tom had never seen him grin. Confident, relaxed, totally at ease with who he was and where he was. Like nothing could touch him. Next to him was an older woman, his mother. Opposite them was his father, whom Tom recognized from pictures, and Simon's sister. Computer-printed, it looked like the kind of photo TV news broadcasts show when a family had been killed. After going into Witness Protection, there was no trace allowed of Simon's previous life. His phone would have been wiped. Simon must have managed to print this before anyone checked. Judging from its crumpled appearance, he'd treasured it. Tom put it back where he had found it. Straightened up.

Back in the corridor, there was one door left. He walked toward the end of the hallway.

Marx's office wasn't locked, and Tom pushed open the door. Even though he hadn't yet found Simon, he thought that anything incriminating in Aiden's possession would likely be found here so he decided to have a quick look around. He checked the computer. Password protected, as he'd assumed. He checked the desk drawers, found nothing out of the ordinary. No smoking gun, literal or otherwise. He swung the cupboard doors wide open. And stopped dead.

The Horse's dark-green jeweled eyes stared back at him.

He heard angry voices.

The front door opened, closed.

"What's . . . What the fuck? Who's done this? Who's broken this lock?"

In response came a guttural groan.

Tom looked around the room for another exit, a hiding place. He crossed to the window. Too small to get through, locked. Back to the door. Footsteps were coming down the hall, quick but uneven, like one leg was being dragged. There was the tapping of a cane.

Tom's heartbeat doubled. He was breathing rapidly, eyes darting everywhere, sizing up every corner and shadow, gauging it for concealment. The cupboard was too small, too slim to hide in. He had nowhere to go.

He stood his ground in the center of the room, waiting for the door to open. Fists balled, adrenaline kicking in, fight-or-flight engaged.

The door opened and a man supporting himself on a cane entered. Tom knew this was Aiden Marx. He looked at Tom, the same mixture of surprise and anger that had been in his voice at the front door now in his eyes. Tom didn't let him get any farther. He launched himself at him, fists swinging. Connecting.

His first move was a roundhouse from his left, connecting with the side of the man's head. He crumpled. Tom kicked the cane away, so nothing was holding him up. He didn't need a follow-up punch; the man hit the floor, screaming and shouting.

Without waiting, Tom pulled open the door, ready to run down the corridor.

And found himself forcefully pushed back into the room. He stumbled over the man's prone body, lost his footing, falling backward. He tried to pull himself up, but his assailant was too quick.

"Get the fucker . . ." said Marx, still on the floor.

The other one picked Tom up, grabbing him in a choking

bear hug. Tom tried to wriggle out, but every move reignited pain in his ribs. He stopped struggling.

Marx got slowly and painfully to his feet.

"Right you fucker, let's get a look at you . . ." Marx came to stand in front of Tom. Smiled. "Oh. It's you. Can't take a warning, can you?"

"You know who I am? We've never met."

"I've seen you from a distance. In a cage. You probably don't remember."

"I'm not here on my own this time," said Tom. "I'm with the police."

Marx laughed once more. "Police have been here for some time. Have you looked outside? Spotted how many off-duty ones there are?"

"The ones I'm with aren't off duty." Tom squirmed against his captor, who then squeezed even harder.

"So what you here for?" asked Marx.

"Simon West."

"Not here."

"His bag's here."

"But he's not." Marx looked nodded to his henchman. "Keep him right there."

The boy grunted.

Marx looked from the boy to Tom. "I've got an idea. You won't be walking out of the ring this time . . ."

The boy roared.

71

SHELAGH SAW ADAM everywhere she looked. She hadn't seen him for years but she was certain she would recognize him. And he was here right now in Aiden's compound. No doubt.

She was starting to question whether she should have let Jack go. Obviously, she would do that eventually, when he was no further use to her, but he could have still had his uses in the compound. But she had something that weighed the chances in her favor. A gun in her purse. It had taken a lot of patience, perseverance, and money to obtain, and that along with all the years she had spent planning would be enough. It had to be.

She froze. At the other side of the rain-sodden crowd, past the stage and in front of the central house, she saw a limping man supporting himself on a cane. Even from that distance, she recognized Aiden Marx. And beside him walked a huge, hulking brute of a boy.

Was that . . . ?

"Oh God, oh no . . . What has he done to you?"

Thankful for the gun in her purse, she followed.

72

"Simon? simon?"

Lila had waited in the cover of the hedge until Aiden Marx departed from the cabin with an extremely large teenager. She counted to five hundred and, when no one else appeared, crossed slowly over to the cabin once more, ear against the door, listening.

"Simon?"

But there was no reply when she called.

She tried again, trying not to raise her voice too much, finding the right balance between being heard and being stealthy.

Louder this time. "Simon!"

There was movement behind the cabin door. Lila, heart skipping faster, knocked on the door. "Simon? Are you there? It's Lila. Simon?"

"What you doing?"

Lila jumped. She turned around. A young woman stood before her, dressed like someone from her mother's old Pentecostal church. An old before-her-time dress, a sensible coat, a faded umbrella held over her head. Shoes that would have been as sensible as the coat on anything other than this mud. It was like a child's idea of what a respectable woman looked like.

"I heard noises from in here," said Lila.

The woman stared at her. "So what?"

"I just thought someone— "

"You're not supposed to be back here. Why are you back here?"

The young woman looked scared, Lila decided. She was trying to sound authoritative, but her words came across as desperate.

"I was just having a wander. My boyfriend's busy with . . ." She gestured behind her. ". . . his own stuff. I got bored."

"I don't believe you, *Lila*." The woman uttered her name with a sneer. Thrilled she had picked it up when Lila had said it.

"You have me at a disadvantage, madame," Lila said, voice mock Austen. Trying to sound brave, ignoring the angry, mad flame dancing behind the woman's eyes.

"I'm Michelle. I'm Aiden's"—she thought for a second—"girlfriend." Pride in her voice as she spoke.

"Really?" Lila couldn't keep the surprise out of her voice. She looked about thirty years younger than him, at least.

"Lila?" Simon's voice was heard from behind the cabin door.

"I'm here to get you out," Lila said. "Tom and Chris Penrose are with me. You OK?"

"Yeah." His muffled voice sounded unsure.

Lila tried the handle once more.

"You're not allowed to go in there." Panic etched Michelle's face.

"Yeah, well," said Lila, "I'm going in. Problem with that?"

Michelle looked momentarily confused, as if actually trying to determine if indeed there was a problem with that. Not the sharpest tool in the box, thought Lila. She grabbed the handle again.

"Leave that door alone. I'm going to tell Aiden."

Lila turned. She didn't want this confrontation to become physical but she would fight if she had to. She hoped they would be able to talk, the woman would see she was beaten, and Simon would be released.

"I'm with the police. We know Simon's being held against his will. If you've got anything to do with it, then it's kidnapping. If you don't release him now, you're probably looking at jail time." She hoped she sounded convincing.

It didn't work. The woman smirked. "You're not police. There's loads of them here off duty. I know what they all look like. And you're not one of them. You're a liar."

"I didn't say I was police. I said I'm here *with* the police. And they're not off duty, they're looking for Simon West. Now, like I just said, help me get him out and we'll say no more about it. But if you don't—"

Lila didn't see it coming. Her umbrella thrown to one side, the woman launched herself at Lila, roaring all the while.

Lila fell back against the cabin door, arms up in the air, taken completely off guard. The woman screamed at Lila as she pressed her body backward.

"You can't have him, you can't have him! You can't make everything go away, it's not fair! It's not fair!" She pounded her fists against Lila's chest as she ranted.

Lila, thoroughly confused as to what the woman was screaming about, tried to push her away but she couldn't.

"I'll get Aiden, I'll tell Aiden!" She was screaming in Lila's face. "He won't leave me behind, he won't . . . He's my chance to get out . . ."

Lila had no choice. She cupped both her hands, drew them

out to the sides of the woman's head, and brought them onto her ears as hard and as fast as she could.

The woman screamed, her body crumpled. Lila shoved her away. She fell to the ground, writhing in pain in the mud, her screams reduced to whimpers, holding her ears as blood trickled through her fingers.

"You can kill someone like that you know."

Lila looked toward the source of the sound: it was Penrose.

"About bloody time," she said.

73

"RIGHT. OUT YOU GO."

Two blackshirts held Tom in Marx's office. The huge boy silently looked on, like a dormant automaton. Aiden Marx pulled the horse costume from the cupboard. On seeing it, the boy's face lit up.

"You want this, yeah?" said Marx, holding it out to him, then pulling it away when he made to grab for it. "This? You want this? Yeah? Yeah?"

The boy was still smiling but that smile, Tom noticed, was starting to curdle. Marx knew when to call a halt. "You can wear this in a while. Don't worry. And you'll be in the cage when you do it." He pointed at Tom. "And this is a bad man. Bad man." Like he was talking to a dog. "He wants to be the Horse. But you're not going to let him, are you?"

The boy shook his head violently from side to side.

"Are you?"

More violent head shaking.

"Good lad." Marx smiled. "We'll get over there now. Remember what you've got to do."

The blackshirts pushed Tom through the doorway and

out of the office.

Marx turned to the boy. "Right. Now I've just got to go and see how Bully fights. You know Bully?"

The boy nodded.

"Good. Well, I've got to see him fight and then win, and then I'll be there to see you, OK?"

The boy greedily grabbed the horse costume, not caring if Marx was there or not.

"*Ow. what did you do that for?*"

Jack rubbed his face, pain rising like a huge bruise under his skin. Even his jawbone was sore. He sat sprawled on the concrete floor of the hangar, looking up at Punch. He hurt from more than just the physical attack.

"To make you come to your senses," said Punch, looking down at his brother. "Get up, idiot. And stop talking bollocks. We've got work to do."

Punch turned his back on him, began walking away, muttering to himself. He stopped when he realized Judy wasn't with him.

"Come on, I said we've—"

Jack Ketch held a knife in front of him.

Judy had pulled some dick moves before, thought Punch, but he'd never pulled a knife on his own brother. It looked like one of Sullivan's hunting knives, big and mean-looking.

They stood in the gloom of a secluded area of the hangar. No one was too close, saw the weapon, or paid them any attention. They probably appeared like just a couple of drunks arguing. The real fighting would be viewed at the building's other end, soon enough.

"Come on, Judy." Punch used his consoling voice, the tone he always used to talk Judy out of one of his moods—periods, Punch laughingly called them. "Put that away before you—"

"My name's not Judy. It's Jack. *Jack*."

Punch attempted a smile, holding out his hands in what he imagined was a friendly gesture. "Whatever you say, *Jack*." Making a point of overpronouncing the name.

Jack just stared at him.

"Still, good name, Jack Ketch. Keeping it in the family. Mum and Dad would be proud of you, choosing that."

"Fuck Mum and Dad." Jack's face was almost crimson with anger.

In that moment, Punch recognized there had been a profound change within his brother. This wasn't like any of the times before, and it called for a fresh approach.

"Jesus, Ju—Jack. Bit harsh, isn't it?"

"You don't get it, do you?" Jack moved toward him, knife unwavering. "I'm not coming back. I've met someone, and she's shown me a new life. With shopping. And coffee. Coffee shops. And I'm taking it. With her. I'm saying goodbye."

"To me?"

"To you, to all this." He waved the knife around the hangar as he spoke. Punch watched the arc the blade made.

"OK, if you want to. Go."

Jack frowned. "What?"

"Go. I won't stop you."

"Really?" Jack couldn't keep the surprise out of his voice. "That's it? You won't fight me?"

Punch moved closer to Jack. "What for?" he asked. "What's the point? You've obviously made your mind up." Edging nearer to him.

Jack still held the knife, but let it fall by his side. Almost smiled with relief. "I didn't think you'd say yes so easy. I had all these things planned that I was going to do to make you—"

Punch sprang onto his brother, hand grabbing for the knife. Jack realized what he was doing at the last second and just managed to pull the weapon away from his brother's grasp. He pushed it into his brother's stomach. Felt it puncture skin, then organs. Slid it in.

It was hard to tell who was the most surprised. They held each other in what looked like a lovers' clinch, staring at each other, unmoving.

"Wow," said Punch. "Wow. You did it."

"Yeah," said Jack, barely able to believe it either, "I did."

Punch's grip on Jack slackened, his eyes became unfocused.

"It should have been you and me against the world, like it always was," said Punch. "Punch and Judy. We're a team, you and me, even if you didn't want to be Judy anymore. We're a team, aren't we?"

Jack didn't answer. He felt tears well in his eyes.

"Aren't we?" Desperation crept into Punch's voice as his grip weakened even more.

Jack saw that even now, after what he'd just done, he wanted his brother back. Needed him. "Come on . . . You and me against the world. Yeah? Yeah?"

"Yeah, Punch, yeah."

Punch slid down Jack's body. Jack stared, helpless, as Punch's eyes rolled back into his head and he lay still.

Jack felt like he was just an observer, watching something unfold that he wasn't part of, that he didn't understand. Like he had stepped outside real life for a second and he was waiting for everything to click back into place once more, pick up from where it had left off.

Blood pooled beneath Punch's unmoving body.

Not knowing what to do, where to go, Jack turned and ran out of the hangar.

74

"SO WHERE'VE YOU BEEN, THEN?" Lila was still buzzing, the adrenaline from the fight speeding around her body.

Penrose raised his arms in apology. "Sorry. There's quite a few of the force here. I was trying not to bump into them."

"Might have done your career some good if you had."

Penrose looked appalled at the suggestion. He looked down at the woman writhing on the ground at Lila's feet. "Who's this, then?" he asked.

"Michelle, apparently. Aiden Marx's girlfriend. Simon's in there, and she tried to stop me getting to him."

Penrose looked stern. "You could have done her serious damage, you know. People have died from getting their ears boxed."

Lila became defensive. "I didn't have a lot of time to think, did I? And she wasn't in a mood to talk."

"We'll get her bandaged up. Sort her out."

Lila's hyped-up voice rose. "*After* we get Simon out. She's one of the bad guys, Chris."

He nodded. "Suppose you're right." He crossed to the door. "Simon? You in there?"

"Who's that?" came the muffled answer.

Penrose and Lila exchanged relieved glances. Penrose spoke again. "Police Constable Penrose, Simon. Lila's here with me. Is there any way you can open the door?"

"It's locked," he called.

"Don't suppose her down there's got a key," said Lila.

The woman on the ground groaned.

"Guess not. You any good with locks, Chris?"

Penrose studied the lock, tested the handle a few times. He stepped back. "This usually works best." He raised his booted foot, slammed it down on the door as hard as he could. Lila jumped back in surprise. It didn't open but he'd clearly done some damage. He raised his boot, did it again and again until the door gave, smashing back on its hinges.

"Chris Penrose, secret badass . . ."

Penrose smiled at Lila. "After you, miss," he said like a gentleman.

When Lila entered, Simon was flattened against the far wall, staring at her in disbelief. The place stank, and she gagged.

"Jesus Christ . . ."

Simon crossed the floor. Confused, like he didn't know what to do next.

"Come on," she said, "let's get you out of here." She put her hand on his arm.

He grabbed her, flung his arms around her crying, then sobbing so hard it seemed he would never stop.

75

AIDEN MARX MADE IT to the dog hangar just in time to see Bully.

In the short time he'd owned and trained the dog, he had come to regard him as something special. The Romanian he'd bought him from had been right. Watching him in the ring, not just ripping apart his opponents but doing it with such aggression, focused rage, and determination, was a joy for Marx. Probably the biggest joy in his life right now.

Out of the ring after another victory, getting his wounds treated, the dog was still raring to go. Marx was like a proud father, especially after the way the dog looked at him after a fight: eye to eye as if to say, I did well, didn't I? That was for you. Yeah, he was proud.

A new fight was about to start. Bully was being announced. The crowd cheered as Robert held him with the flirt pole, Bully straining against it, the scent of blood in his nostrils, muscles quivering with anticipation. Eyes wild, snarling. Going to be a good one, Marx thought. Only an idiot would bet against Bully.

His dog's opponent was a similar size and weight but

different with black coloring, which explained the name Satan. His dark coat made his eyes look all the more menacing, his teeth that much whiter. Like Bully, Satan was ready for the fight to begin.

Marx had seen Satan in action before, even tried to buy him a couple of times. But the dog had been slapped with a Not For Sale notice. Marx understood why. He was *that* good, just about as good a fighter as Bully. That was why he'd chosen him for tonight, to give the bettors a show for their money. Satan's owner stood behind his pitman, just as Marx was. They nodded to each other. Respect. Camaraderie. What the game was all about.

Marx felt most alive when he was watching his dog pitted against another. His heart hammered, pulse raced. The thrill, the adrenaline. And all around him, everyone else was experiencing the same emotions. All individuals, but together they were part of something bigger. This was when Aiden Marx knew who he was, and it had nothing to do with art or ecology or any of his other business deals. This was pure.

The dogs were released to a roar from the crowd. The power of that crowd surged through Marx. A direct current right into his soul. His body was electric. And he was singing his heart out.

Bully, jaws open, went straight for Satan's throat. Satan dodged, not letting him get purchase on his flesh. Going in turn for the top of Bully's head. Clamping down hard.

Bully growled, tried to shake him off. Pushed him toward the edge of the ring.

Satan gave no ground.

Bully kept pushing.

Satan bit down harder. Blood ran from the wound, over Bully's eyes.

The crowd cheered at the sight of first blood being drawn.

The metallic scent of iron enraged the dogs further. Bully swung his head around, tried to unseat Satan's jaws. Then back, then forth, the wound deepening each time, Bully forcing Satan to slip so he would gain an advantage.

Satan, being pushed backward, slipped.

Bully got in there. Aiming for the other dog's neck once more, he found Satan's cheek, dug in. Satan growled. Bully bit harder.

This fueled Satan. He flung his head around, trying to get rid of Bully, blood and spittle flying, growling all the while, jaws chomping on air, trying to clamp down on anything. Bully kept biting.

Satan twisted his head, managed to get his jaws beside Bully's thick neck. Made an incision. Bully tried pulling away.

And that was when it happened. Pure chance. Or mis-chance.

Satan's teeth clamped down on Bully's main artery. Blood arced out of the ring, hitting the first few bettors.

The crowd went ballistic. This was what they came for. This was what they paid to see.

Marx stared, not believing what he was seeing.

Bully's eyes were crazed. He let go of Satan's skin, tried to spin around, see what had happened to him. Satan held on, jaws clamped harder now, tossing him this way and that like a stuffed toy.

The crowd screamed. Some for Satan, some for Bully.

Satan sensed triumph. Bully went limp in his jaws. The pitmen entered the ring.

Satan's handler forced the leather noose of the flirt pole over Satan's head, managed to prize him off Bully. Robert, Marx's handler, picked up Bully's dying body, carrying him from the ring.

Marx rushed to the ringside.

Robert laid Bully down by the side of the ring. Looked at him. Sadness in his eyes. "You want to take him?"

Marx knelt beside Bully. The dog was pumping blood, eyes emptying of life. Not understanding what was happening, looking desperately at Marx for an explanation, reassurance. Wanting confirmation that he would be able to fight on.

Marx just stared, open-mouthed.

Behind him, Robert was clearing the hangar of bettors. They understood, giving Marx the space he needed to be alone with his dog. He held Bully tight, ignoring the blood seeping into his clothes. He felt Bully's diminishing heartbeat against his chest.

Slower. Slower.

Bully died in his arms.

They were the only two in the hangar now, Robert had seen to that. Everything else receded into blackness. Only Bully and he mattered. And in that private space he had created, Marx cried for his loss.

Eventually, the wave of grief crashed over him. Left him cold, bereft. Unmoving.

Then a voice interrupted his sorrow.

"Hey there. Remember me?"

He looked up.

There stood Shelagh.

76

"THERE'S TOM!" LILA SHOUTED and pointed him out to Penrose and Simon. Tom was being marched by blackshirts toward the bigger hangar, and someone dressed as a horse was beside him. She made to run, but Penrose restrained her.

"Don't," he said.

She turned to him, ready to argue, ready to break his grip. "Get off me, I've got to—"

"No," said Penrose with conviction. So much so that Lila stopped arguing, stopped pulling. "Look at what's happening. Where he's going. You're not going to get him out of there or away from those blokes, are you?"

"And you are?"

He stared at her. "Yeah, I am."

In that moment, she believed him.

"Oh fuck," said Simon.

They both turned to look at him.

"That's him. The Horse. Who killed my family. The big boy who I was locked up with . . ."

Penrose looked at Lila. "Get him to the Land Rover." He handed her the keys. "I'll get Tom."

Lila put her arm around the distressed boy, maneuvered him toward the field where their car was parked.

Penrose followed the blackshirts into the hangar.

77

Aiden Marx looked up, blood-covered, cradling the still-warm corpse of his dog.

Shelagh had planned this moment for years. Schemed over it, sacrificing her life for this moment. She'd spent nights lying awake and days lost rehearsing the speech she'd make. Imagining every possible permutation of events that would lead her here. Also imagining Marx's response. Her ex-husband's response. But whatever she had imagined, nothing had prepared her for the actual moment.

He squinted up at her, frowning. Like a memory he was having difficulty remembering.

"It's Shelagh, Aiden. Your ex-wife. The mother of our son." Her voice wavered as she spoke. She fought, kept it controlled. "Remember now?"

Aiden Marx looked at her, then down at the dead dog, seemingly trying to reconcile the two things existing at once.

"Bully's dead," he said.

"What a shame." No emotion at all behind her words.

"He shouldn't have died. He wasn't meant to. He was a champion; he was my boy . . ."

Staring at this pitiful man who had been responsible for so much hurt in her life, Shelagh felt no compassion, no remorse within her.

"Are you upset about that? Then good."

He focused. His memory was returning now. "Shelagh."

She smiled. "Yes. Never thought I'd actually find you, did you? Thought you'd hidden from me too well."

"What are you doing here?"

"I've come for what's mine. I've come for my son."

He stared at her once more, not comprehending. "Your son?"

"Put the fucking dog down, Aiden, and listen. I'm here for Adam. I'm not leaving without him. And you can't stop me."

The gears of his mind slipped back into alignment. He gently placed the carcass of the dog on the floor of the hangar and stood up to face her. His previous vulnerability was dissipating, the more characteristic cruelty returning to his eyes.

"Shelagh, my darling ex-wife. You don't look a day over thirty years older than you should be."

This was more like the welcome she had expected. The person she had rehearsed dealing with. "Still the same pathetic cripple you always were," she responded. "Except before your deformity was just inside. Now it's outside as well. Suits you. Bet that leg hurts too. Good."

"What d'you want?"

"Adam, my son."

He laughed. Eyes brightening. "You think you can just waltz in here and take him, do you?"

"Why do you care? The only things you ever cared about were your dogs. And even they're dying on you." She kicked the corpse of Bully.

Aiden grabbed her shoulder. Hard, his fingers digging in. Eyes glaring.

She stared right into his eyes. "Oh, it's the rough stuff again, is it? The only way you know how to respond to a woman, yeah? Makes you feel like a big man. I know all about that. I've got years of scars to show for it. And you know what? I'm proud of them."

"Bet you are. Fucking tart."

"You know why I'm proud of them? Because every single one reminds me that you're no longer in my life. Every single day I wake up and rejoice because of it."

He laughed again. She continued.

"Not sure how to answer? Not surprised. Here's the big man, sitting in a pathetic little heap crying over a dead dog. The big man. You're a piece of shit."

His fingers gripped even harder, but Shelagh's gaze did not flinch.

"No clever little comeback?" she said. "Course not. Never were one for using your words, were you? Not that bright upstairs. And squeeze me all you want. Try and hit me even. Go on, try. See what it gets you. You won't like it. Because I'm not scared of you anymore."

He blinked. Unsure of himself for the first time in his life with her. This wasn't the woman he used to know. She was harder, even angrier, surer of herself, physically and mentally.

"Scared of me, are you, Aiden? You should be. Because I gave my life up for you. My career. Art school. All because some flash little gangster got me knocked up and thought he was doing the honorable thing by marrying me. And then seeing that our child was . . . the way he was . . . hating me for it, blaming me."

"The way he was. He was a fucking retard, Shelagh."

Tears formed in the corners of her eyes. Angry, she wouldn't let them. "No. Adam just needed specialized care, that's all."

Marx laughed. "He's had that, all right."

"You had your chance to get away, Aiden. Why did you take him? You didn't want him."

"No, but you did. And I knew it would hurt you more if I did that."

She flinched at his words.

"So where is he? Here? At some special school? He should be out of there by now."

Marx laughed. "He's over in the other hangar. Should be ready to fight in the cage about now." He started laughing. Couldn't stop.

Shelagh stared at him. Of all the answers she had expected, this wasn't one of them.

Marx's eyes blazed with a cruel fire. "I had no interest in that fucking thing, that son of yours. I brought him up like one of my dogs. No, not like one of the dogs. Worse than that. All he was good for was his anger. He's a very angry boy. And I made sure I used that."

His words chilled her. "What d'you mean?"

"He used to love dressing up as the horse at Christmas, remember? The 'Obby 'Oss? When he was little?"

Shelagh thought of the paintings she had done of him from memory. "I know."

"Well, he still does. Go next door and see."

She had to do something. All the years of pain—memories of her life that he'd ruined, everything he had made her do—coalesced inside her mind.

"Aiden. Look." He followed her gaze down to her hand. She had taken the gun from her purse, was aiming it at him. "I came prepared."

He looked momentarily surprised, then an ugly grin spread across his face. "You're not going to use that. You wouldn't dare."

Shelagh didn't blink, didn't take her eyes off his face. "Which knee is it? The left one?"

The gun firing wasn't as loud as she had thought it would be, but it was loud enough. Marx had a few seconds to stare at her in shock before his leg gave way and he collapsed on his side on the ground.

"*Oops*," she said.

Marx stared at the remains of his leg, now attached to the rest of him by just a few bloody tendons. Blood was pumping out. He had landed right beside the dead dog at his feet.

Still unblinking, Shelagh fired again, this time taking out his other kneecap.

Marx screamed.

"Haven't got a leg to stand on, have you? *Ha ha.* You'd better get those seen to. You're losing a lot of blood. You might die."

"Fucking bitch."

Shelagh smiled. "Oh, Aiden, couldn't you have come up with something more original to say?"

She pointed the gun at him again, this time in his left upper arm. He tried to protest, tried to shift out of the way but it was to no avail. She fired. His arm exploded. She quickly moved the gun to his other arm. Fired again. He lay still, curled around the dead dog in a bloodied heap.

Shelagh didn't know if he was breathing or not. Didn't care.

She turned, left the empty hangar, and went to find her son.

78

WHEN THE CAGE DOOR SLAMMED behind Tom, he looked out at the crowd. They were, literally, baying for his blood.

He gave his full attention to the cage. The big boy wore the full Horse costume now: the skull and some kind of decorated shroud. Tom wondered how he could see out of it or move in it. But he would not underestimate him. He'd already felt the power in his arms.

"It's the 'Oss!" shouted the blackshirt ringmaster.

The crowd cheered.

"Against this fucking specimen!"

The crowd bayed once more. It was clear who their favorite was.

Tom tried to block everything out and concentrate on his opponent. He ignored any residual pain in his joints, muscles, or ribs. He tamped down memories of his last turn in this ring. This time it was one-to-one. This time he had a chance.

The ringmaster stepped outside, closed the gate behind him, locked it. The crowd counted aloud down from five to one. A bell rang.

It was on.

The Horse charged at Tom, arms outstretched. Tom jumped out of the way, felt his ribs creak. The Horse stopped, turned. Took a swing at his face. Tom just managed to duck, feeling the force of muscle and bone as it whizzed past him. There was power in that kid's arm. If it had connected, Tom would have been in trouble.

Tom's first impulse in a situation like this was to fight back but he was trying to think defensively. This was still a kid, a mentally incapacitated teenager, exploited by someone who should be caring for him.

Tom didn't have time to think of a strategy. The Horse was coming for him again.

Tom acted on impulse, feigning with his right fist, causing the Horse to curl his left arm to block. Tom threw his left straight into the Horse's stomach. The Horse staggered, winded. Tom threw another punch, connecting in the same place. Tom hated himself for doing it. But didn't know what else he could have done.

The crowd booed.

The Horse threw back his skull head and howled.

The crowd cheered.

The Horse pawed the ground, ready for the next assault. Tom braced himself. The Horse ran at him. Tom stretched as high as he could, feeling things along his ribs tear as he did so, and grabbed the cage above him, pulling his body up and out of the way.

The Horse crashed into the cage wall.

Tom tried to turn around and climb up the cage.

He was too slow. His body screamed in rebellion at what he was trying to make it do, and it cut off his supply of needed strength. Arms unable to hold him anymore, he dropped to the ground.

The Horse came for him again. Tom was too tired to move, had no choice but to confront the boy under the hood and hope that he could at least stop him from doing any more damage.

When the Horse was near enough, Tom threw a punch. The Horse anticipated his action and grabbed his arm. Tried to bend it backward.

The pain was excruciating. Tom was pulled into the Horse's body by the action. He tried to use his other arm to get in some quick rabbit punches, but he couldn't get the angle right.

But he inadvertently did something else.

He dislodged the Horse's skull.

The Horse dropped Tom's arm, both arms going to his head to push the skull back in place. Tom jumped backward, as far away from the Horse as he could, pushing himself up against the metal of the cage once more.

Tom quickly came to a conclusion. The Horse was only the Horse when he had the skull on. Lose the skull, lose the fight.

Or that's all he could hope for.

While the Horse attempted to put the skull back into place, Tom ran at him.

The Horse looked up, saw him, speedily put his skull back in place, and floored him with a fist.

Tom hit the ground painfully, the wind knocked out of him.

The Horse stomped Tom's leg.

He screamed from the pain.

The crowd cheered, whooped.

The Horse pulled his foot up to do the same with the other leg.

Tom, anticipating the move, rolled out of the way and, with as much strength as he could muster, scrambled to his feet. While the Horse was still off balance, Tom grabbed the skull off his head.

Surprised, the Horse wasn't quick enough to respond. The boy underneath bellowed in what sounded like pain.

Tom didn't stop to think. He threw the skull against the cage, hearing the sound reverberate around the makeshift arena.

The crowd booed once more.

Tom let the skull fall to the floor then brought his booted foot down on it as hard as he could. And again. And again. As hard, as forceful, and as fast as he could, until there was nothing left but bone shards and shattered green glass.

The Horse roared. But this time he didn't launch himself at Tom. He fell to his knees, scurried along the floor of the cage, grabbing as many bone shards as he could, trying desperately to put them back together, willing them to re-form into a skull.

Even more booing came from the frenzied crowd.

Tom, breathing heavily and holding his ribs, looked down at the boy. He should finish him off. That's what one part of his brain was telling him, the trained part. Neutralize the threat. No matter what or who it is. Cry about it afterward.

But he could not move.

Tom became aware of a commotion in the crowd. Then a noise at his side, like someone in the audience had thrown themselves at the cage wall. Or been thrown.

A woman's voice was heard through the din.

"Adam . . . Adam . . . Adam . . . It's me, Adam, me, your mother . . ."

The crowd quieted, puzzled, wondering whether this new person was part of the show.

"Adam . . . Adam . . . please, look at me. Down here, please . . ."

The Horse stopped what he was doing. Looked to see where the voice was coming from.

"Oh my God," the woman said, "what's he done to you?"

Something was making its way through the pain in Tom's body. A memory. He recognized that voice, couldn't place it. But didn't think it belonged here.

"Adam . . . Adam . . ."

Tom knew this was the best chance he would get.

With the Horse distracted, Tom began slowly making this way around the cage wall, one arm cradling his ribs.

The Horse stepped forward, peering into the crowd.

The Horse stood completely still, mesmerized, by the woman's voice. And then Tom realized who it was: Shelagh.

Tom made a final run for the door in the cage. "Open it!" he yelled at the ringmaster who, shocked that events had gone so differently than expected, did so.

Standing behind the ringmaster was Officer Chris Penrose.

"Had enough?" he asked, eyebrows arched.

79

JACK KETCH WALKED TOWARD the compound's open gate, tears streaking his face, openly sobbing. The reality of what he had just done had finally hit home.

The black-shirted Morris man had long since departed. Jack turned and looked back at the party. His old life. He was, literally, walking away from his old life. And he was doing it alone. Because he had just realized something: Shelagh had strung him along, just to get what she wanted. They were not leaving together. And he had been too thick to see it. In a way, that hurt more than what his brother had done. And what he had done to his brother.

His thoughts flew and fizzed in his mind like cartoon demons released from a witch's cauldron, soaring and biting and not allowing him to focus. He tried to think straight through his tears, his grief, but couldn't.

He put his fists to his head, screamed, trying to make it all stop. It didn't.

He shoved his hands in his pockets, found something else there apart from the knife. His phone. He took it out.

Make it stop, make it stop . . .

All he had to do was press one button on his phone. And the whole place would go up like Christmas.

Just one button.

Make it stop, make it stop . . .

He pressed the button.

PART FIVE
MORE THAN ONE
ROAD TO HELL

8∅

"QUITE A NIGHT, wasn't it?"

Tom looked across the table in the café at Falmouth University at Professor Ben Tarpley. He looked immaculate in an expensively understated suit and tie, hair perfect, teeth dazzling, tan standing out too much for winter in Falmouth. He sipped delicately from the rim of his coffee cup. Replaced it in the saucer, waited for Tom's response.

"Your candidate won."

"Indeed. Rather fortuitous he chose not to attend that aftershow party laid in his honor, wasn't it?"

"Almost as if his boorish foot soldiers had served their purpose getting him elected, and he never had any intention of going near the place."

Tarpley smiled. "Your words, not mine."

It had been quite a night, and sense was still being made of it. The firebombs had sent everyone screaming. And not everyone had survived. Luckily, Penrose had managed to get Tom out of the hangar to where Lila was waiting with Simon in the Land Rover. They had just reached the gate when the bombs went off.

Penrose wanted to turn back, but Tom and Lila overruled

him. Simon said nothing, but it was clear he never wanted to set foot in that place again.

Arson was the official explanation. Blame was laid on a disgruntled business associate of Marx's. Marx himself wouldn't be able to throw any light on the matter because his body was found, severely wounded, next to that of his dog. With both arms and legs amputated, he was now in a persistent vegetative state in a local hospital bed and was not expected to recover.

It was difficult to tell how many or who was unaccounted for, as it was an illegal gathering and no one used their real names. The police had months of fun ahead of them.

Tom had scanned the news and asked Penrose what had happened to Shelagh and her son, but nothing was known. He had to assume they had managed to escape the mayhem of the fire. He felt only pity for her and hoped she found peace. Her son as well.

Simon was again staying with him and Lila. For how long, they didn't know. But Tom wasn't in a hurry to throw him out, and Simon was in no hurry to leave.

And then there was Pearl.

She had cried when she saw an injured Tom being helped into the cottage by Penrose and Lila, dragged painfully upstairs, and laid out on the bed.

"We got Simon," Tom told her between labored gasps, "We got him out. They're all gone now. All gone."

She let him sleep. For as long as he wanted.

When he woke up, she was still there.

"Thought you'd be gone," he said.

She didn't answer. It seemed like she had too many words in her head and couldn't decide which ones should come first.

"Never again," he said. "Definitely. Promise."

"You said that last time."

Tom's turn not to reply.

"I understand why you had to do it," she said. "But I really couldn't go through this again. And neither could you. I love you, Tom, but I hate seeing you like this."

She left the room.

Now TOM WAS UP AND AROUND, walking with the aid of a stick and tying up some loose ends. That was why he'd revisited Ben Tarpley. Same place as last time, Tarpley looking like he had never moved from the spot. Same supercilious smirk.

"So who was Aiden Marx, then? What's his importance to you?"

"To me? No importance. He had money, though. Lots. And he was a believer. Ready to fund the cause. Beyond that, nothing."

"He kidnapped his disabled son and tortured him, leaving him locked up in a cabin and turning him feral."

Tarpley sipped his coffee. "How shocking." His tone said he could not care less.

"Doesn't it bother you that those are the kinds of people you recruit for your cause?"

"Recruit for my cause? Mr. Killgannon, I don't recruit anyone. I'm an academic. I write books and give public lectures. Appear on TV. I'm not in the habit of recruiting anyone to any causes. Should people share my worldview, then all well and good. And I'm grateful for that."

Trouble slid off the man like oil from a hot pan.

"You were behind all of this. Not noticeably, of course, but there, in the background, putting a word in here and there. Setting up a club where white working-class men could get rid of their rage while reconnecting with their mythical past. Telling Marx the best way to get rid of his problems, how he could keep it on-brand with your weaponized nostalgia, dressing up psychopaths as folk legends. And stepping back when it looked like you were going to be linked with any of this. And then Arthur King. Your biggest experiment yet. Congratulations."

Tarpley raised his coffee cup in acknowledgment.

"I saw you, you know," said Tom. "In the Fear Machine. Up on a gantry. Giving the order for them to pull me into the cage, beat me up."

"Did you? It was very dark in there, I should imagine. Difficult to make anything out, I should think."

Tom stared at him. "It won't last, you know."

"I seem to be doing just fine for now."

"But it won't last. You can't fool all of the people all of the time, as the old adage goes."

"But I don't need to, Mr. Killgannon. Not everyone agrees with me, and that's fine. But those who do . . . they're never going to stop."

Tom laughed mirthlessly. "'Course, the irony is, this land fit for heroes you're selling them, this harking back to the golden age of our country, this blood and soil, if all your followers actually lived back then, they'd have had truly horrendous lives. Most of them would be peasants blindly following their feudal lord, dead by their mid-thirties."

Tarpley's turn to laugh. "Was it ever thus?"

Tom sighed. He felt tired. From more than just his physical aches. He stood up.

"Going so soon?" said Tarpley. "I was enjoying our talk so much, and we were just getting started." He was gloating, it seemed.

Tom stared at him. "You been watching the news, Tarpley?

Something's coming. Something big. In China at the moment. Some killer virus. And it's going to spread. Over here, I should think. And all of the plans you've got are going to be wiped out because of it."

Tarpley's smile froze on his face.

"I don't think the gravedigger will be singing his song just yet, Mr. Killgannon. But call in anytime. Always a pleasure."

81

After offering the bottle around, Tom poured himself a glass of wine. "Cheers." The rest of the table replied. Tom replaced his glass. Smiled.

Faisal, Karima, Anju, Lila, Pearl, Tom, and Simon were crowded around Tom's old kitchen table. He had made a massive lasagna for dinner. The food might be not as good as the Mirzas', but at least his wine was better.

It was nearly a month since the events at Aiden Marx's compound and everyone was hoping to move on. Simon had settled in well back within Tom's household, and Tom had made him more than welcome, telling him he never had to move again, if he didn't want to. It seemed like Simon was happy where he was. Or as happy as he could be, given all that had happened to him. He was also planning to resume therapy with Faisal.

Pearl and Tom were stronger than they had been in a long time, perhaps ever. As were Anju and Lila. Faisal and Karima had shown some initial hesitation in accepting the invite, but Tom had assured them everything was definitely in the past now.

It was a good evening. Friends. Lovers. Family. And a toast from Tom, "New beginnings, new chapters."

They all toasted in agreement.

LATER, WHEN EVERYONE ELSE HAD GONE or gone to bed, Tom and Pearl sat curled together on the sofa. Pearl still had wine, Tom a whisky.

"Good night," she said.

He nodded. Lost in his own thoughts.

"What?"

He looked up at her. "It was all for nothing, wasn't it? All that running around, that nearly losing you, all of it."

"You got Simon back. That's what you set out to do. Look at him now. Happiest he's been for ages."

"I cleared up the mess I was responsible for, you mean. We should have looked after him better in the first place."

"Come on. We did the best we could. It wasn't our fault what happened. But you got him back." She squeezed his arm harder. "And I am proud of you for doing that. Especially when I see what you went through."

They sat in silence for a while.

"But the bad guys still won," said Tom, eventually. "Overall."

"The bad guys always win," said Pearl. "All we can do is keep our own little corner of the universe clean."

More silence.

"I've been thinking." Tom felt Pearl stiffen beside him. "Nothing to worry about. Just something somebody said. I'm good at this. Finding people. I've got skills I can use, and I don't need to get hurt using them. Or get everyone else around me hurt. I could go into business."

"As what? A person finder?" Pearl smiled, surprised at his words and her reaction. "A private detective?"

"Well, that's a bit embarrassing to say out loud. Especially in Cornwall. Let's say *inquiry agent*. Or what you said, people finder. An agency for missing persons."

"Wouldn't that be dangerous?"

"No more than working behind a bar come closing time on a Friday night. It's using my skills, keeping my mind employed. I don't want to go back to how I used to be, that's not who I am now. But Lila's right. I can't just go bird-watching. This sounds like, I don't know. A way to use what I'm good at? Whatever. I think it's something that just might work."

Pearl took his words in. "How would you afford to do that?"

He stared at his drink. "I've got a bit of money put by for a rainy day. I could dip into it. Get set up." He laughed. "Give Lila a job in the office if she wants it."

Pearl smiled. "She wouldn't be happy in an office. She'd want to be out on cases with you."

"True."

Pearl frowned. "But what about the other thing? Witness Protection? Isn't it a bit dangerous? Putting your name out there?"

"The old guy's gone. Forever. But Tom Killgannon? Maybe this is what he does. Who he is. This is how I find the new man and get rid of the old one. What d'you think?"

She hugged him harder. "I think we should go to bed."